THE CAT
DID NOT DIE

OTHER CARAVEL MYSTERY BOOKS BY INGER FRIMANSSON

Good Night, My Darling

Shadow in the Water

The Island of the Naked Women

THE CAT
DID NOT DIE

Inger Frimansson

Translated by
Laura A. Wideburg

A Caravel Mystery
from Pleasure Boat Studio
New York

The Cat Did Not Die
by Inger Frimansson

Translation from Swedish by Laura Wideburg

ISBN 978-1-929355-89-1
Library of Congress Control Number: 2012948384
First U.S. Printing
Original publication in Swedish in 2000 by Norstedts

Design by Susan Ramundo
Cover by Laura Tolkow
Cover photo and Author photo by Jan Frimansson

A Caravel Mystery
an imprint of Pleasure Boat Studio: A Literary Press
PBS books are available through the following:
SPD (Small Press Distribution) Fax 510-524-0852
Partners/West Fax 425-204-2448
Baker & Taylor Fax 800-775-7480
Ingram Fax 615-287-5429
Amazon.com and bn.com

and through
PLEASURE BOAT STUDIO: A LITERARY PRESS
www.pleasureboatstudio.com
201 West 89th Street
New York, NY 10024

Contact Jack Estes at pleasboat@nyc.rr.com

The Cat
Did Not Die

SHE WAS AN AVERAGE GRAY CAT, THE KIND THAT PEOPLE CALLED A COUNTRY CAT. She lifted her nose and meowed, as she'd already done many times before, day after day. But the noises from the humans had disappeared. The house was closed up and locked. She hissed at her kittens, who'd grown up. Autumn was here, and her teats had dried up. She scratched at the ground, clawing the surface, digging deeper. She found a ragged piece of cloth with a greasy, strange taste.

For the second time in her life, the cat was afraid.

A woman came to that place. She saw paw prints and the marks of digging claws. From a wound in the earth, she saw something stick out.

The woman froze, stifled a scream, tried to breathe.

She'd seen a part of a human arm.

The arm was wearing a watch. She did not want to look, but she had to. Although it was muddy and damaged, she still recognized the brown leather wristband. She'd once helped him fix it—she'd brought the watch to her room and, while sewing, managed to poke her fingers a number of times with her needle.

She'd already started to miss him.

She bent back and screamed straight up at the bleak, frozen sky.

The Man

1

DUST ON THE ROAD. Fine powder from pulverized gravel. He did not like the dust. It got into his pores and into his nostrils, and it stuck in his throat to dry it out. He did his best to avoid roads, but there were places where he had to walk along them. In the ditches, he could see wild strawberries, and their ripe red flesh was covered by the gray poison. He saw this as a betrayal. He could eat these wild strawberries, but they would make him sick. A clump would find a place to grow in his insides and kill him.

Nature had not intended this. Nature had made the berries and fruit so that humankind could eat and be healthy.

He heard the sound of a motor in the distance, an angry roar increasing in strength. He found himself forced to step into the ditch, and the brushwood irritated his wrists. He thought the car was Japanese, but these days he couldn't tell the different brands apart. Once he'd finished doing his license plate game, finding the numbers from 001 to 999 in chronological order, he'd lost interest in cars. Back then he still used to go into the villages, and he'd wander through the parking lots or creep close to the highway exchanges and sit there for hours with his notebook and his pens: blue for odd and red for even numbers. All in all, it had taken him five years to find them.

After that, he decided to keep to the forest.

He stood for a while, looking up and down the road in both directions. He listened so that he could find the perfect time after the car had passed and before the next car appeared. Of course, he couldn't know exactly when the next car would come. It was just a feeling he had, as if a scale had come to a perfect balance with two weights—complete harmony. He held his breath for a moment, and then crossed the oiled gravel road in eight long strides.

The sun's heat burned through the branches of the pine trees. It bit into his skin and forced water from his hair, making his forehead glow and throb. A picture of his mother came to him. He smelled the scent of potatoes in her apron as he pressed his face into its stripes, remembering her hand on the back of his head: its heaviness, its ladle shape.

No, don't think now.

He had to search for Cat and her kittens. He'd made a bed for them in one of his dresser drawers, but it hadn't helped. She was gone in the morning. Three kittens were left behind, lying on the rags, but they were dead. The other two had disappeared with her. She'd taken them one by one in her mouth.

2

THE TINY KITTENS GREW QUICKLY. Things were easier when they were tiny. His life was his own, then, as they mostly slept and nursed.

Now they ran around with small, silly four-footed jumps. He liked watching them and using an old piece of string for them to chase. They had warm, see-through claws. Whenever he held them, they would bite him with their pink gums, making little marks of hair and milk.

One of them resembled Cat. She had the same fur, a light, striped gray. The other was larger and fluffier, but a bit more on the shy side. He'd given them names, but he'd already forgotten what they were. Cat was restless, however, and every day she would take the kittens and disappear with them. Every day he had to go search for them. This made him nervous.

Cat became his cat one evening four years ago. Those days, he would do odd jobs for Holger. He'd help out with cutting the lumber in the forest. They'd kept at it, using power saws, the entire day, and the buzzing noise still echoed in his head.

That was his last day. His palms were cracked and tender. His skin was itchy from the pine tar. Holger was parking the tractor, and then took out an envelope with the money.

"Oh, there's one more thing," Holger said, his eyes narrow and sharp.

Foreboding came over him, creeping up his back and taking the air from his lungs, but he did not ask what it was about. He just waited.

Holger went into the shed and came out with his shotgun. He called up to the house, and Kaarina came out, as if she'd been keeping watch. She was holding a shoebox in her arms. She carried it carefully and tenderly, and her face was streaming with tears.

"You get back inside now!" Holger shouted.

Kaarina set the shoebox down on the ground, turned and ran back inside the house. She was a large, ungainly woman, and the man could never figure out how she could run so quickly on her swollen, spidery-lined legs.

Holger handed the shotgun to the man.

"You can take care of this, can't you? You've been hunting before."

The man nodded, while feeling his testicles itch.

"I'm going to have to go inside, now," Holger said. "You just leave everything right here when you're done. I'll take care of it later."

Yes. Four summers ago. He would mark the day on his calendar. He would fill in the box with his pen with indelible ink. The entire white box with the number. It had been number eight in June.

On that number eight in June, he had opened the lid of the shoebox just a little and heard tiny mewing sounds. No, no more. He did not want to see them. He did not want to hear them. He put the lid back on right away, but one of the little creatures had slipped out over the edge.

He'd been afraid that Holger had seen it, but there was no movement at the window. Instead, he heard muffled screaming. He also heard Holger yelling and the noise of a chair being thrown over.

The kitten sat on the ground. She had white paws, with claws out. Her tiny, flat face looked up into his. Then she took a little jump into his pants leg. He felt her claws like tacks dig into his calf. He stood without making a sound. From the house he could hear Kaarina shriek again.

Then he pointed the barrel of the shotgun at the box and fired.

He left the farm at once with the kitten clinging to his leg. It seemed that the kitten was growing from his leg like a bunch of grapes. He'd seen grapes in a picture once, bunches and bunches of grapes which were grown in a greenhouse. This greenhouse was on a slope near Lake Vättern.

He did not dare bend down and lift his pants leg until he had reached the forest.

The kitten was light gray. She was scared to death. Warm. She was the one. She was Cat. Cat made his home into her own.

3

When cat gained weight and her body began to swell, the man understood that she was going to give birth. And one day she was ready.

He'd made a cage of chicken wire and strips of wood. He'd taken the chicken wire from Holger's place. He put Cat and the kittens into the cage. Cat raised her hackles and hissed—it seemed as if her body was electrified. When he stuck his finger inside, she bit it. He screamed from dismay.

While he was inside looking for a bandage, Cat took advantage, knocking over the cage and disappearing, leaving her kittens behind. The man sat on his front steps and blood seeped through his bandage. He thought about his mother and how she would take his hand toward her mouth, stick the tip of his finger into the large space between her jaws and suck all the evil away.

His mother used to pull him in a little wagon. He didn't remember this himself, but she would tell him about it later and even showed him the wagon. It was painted green and had horizontal bars. A memory flickered around slats as wide as the depth of a little palm.

"You didn't walk right away." He heard her voice in his head, as if she were close by. "Of course, I couldn't carry you everywhere, so I bought this old wagon from Klut-Karlsson."

That's right. The old wagon.

The jerk in the roll of the wheels. Over sand and over roots.

"And I knew where I had you. You couldn't get out of it. You sat inside and were my little dumpling. Your happy red cheeks."

He saw that picture. He had golden locks to make a crown of gold around his head.

Klut-Karlsson had the store down in the village. He had a receded hairline and his forehead had waves and bulges. It was like you could see all the experiments and ideas inside his head. He'd gotten his nickname *Klut* from the bark strips wrapped in cloth that he'd decided to sell as a cure for toothache. You were supposed to place the clump into brandy and then press it against the painful tooth. The strips of bark were imported from Africa. He said they came from the acacia tree and contained *gummi arabicum*. This was what was said to help the pain.

"Good to see you, my boy," he'd say. "Want a hug?" He'd stretch out his long, lumpy arms.

When he didn't hear an answer, he'd say, "How's your mother doing? Tell her I'll come by this evening for a bit. That is, if she has time to see me."

"You must be nice to Klut-Karlsson and you must like him, too," his mother exhorted him. "We have him to thank for so much."

When the knock at the door came, he had to go into the bedroom. He slept in there with his mother. They had a sofa bed. Klut-Karlsson would always bring something with him, a comic book or a bag of roasted almonds.

"Please be good and stay inside the bedroom for a little while," his mother said. Her lips were different, redder, and her movements were quick and clumsy.

He would lie in bed not moving a muscle. He would listen but not hear a word. Not even a whisper. Sometimes, he thought that they had left the house, but he didn't dare leave the room to see. He didn't dare leave the bedroom until his mother entered it again. She'd often gotten ready for bed.

"Aren't you asleep?" she'd ask with the same amount of surprise every time, and he saw her dark hair was hanging down her back. It was all messed up.

He shook his head, but was on his guard.

"Why not?"

"You have to sleep next to me."

"So you say, you little rascal."

"Has Klut-Karlsson left?"

"Oh, he left a long time ago. He was just here for a little while. And now it's time to go to sleep, both you and me, because tomorrow is a new day."

However, the nights that Knut-Karlsson came to visit meant that neither of them could go to sleep. He would lie on his back and notice every lump in the mattress. He heard his mother toss and turn, and sigh. He would reach out his hand for hers, and she would finally take it.

He was filled with so many words and thoughts. Nothing could be allowed to leave his lips, however. She would finally fall asleep, and her hand would fall out of his. He would listen to her breathing. It was irregular and filled with sounds. He experienced an emptiness and sense of despair. He had to take short breaths as if he'd run very fast, and his breathlessness would turn to tears. His mother slept, shifted a bit, coughed.

He would turn over on his side and go to sleep.

4

THE MAN FOUND KAARINA WITH THE HENS. He smelled the eggs and the old bird shit.

"You scared me!" she said, but her voice was mild, not tense. She never screamed at him.

"Where's Holger?" he asked.

She pointed toward the house.

"What are you doing?"

"Getting the eggs."

He followed her into the barn. The air was thick. Chaff swirled in the light streaming through the cracks.

"I'm getting the eggs, I told you," she giggled.

"I know."

He felt the heaviness of her breast which he held and weighed in his hand. Kaarina against the wall of the barn. Her hands. Her heat rose past his ears. The light cloth of her dress. How he explored, how he searched, how he pulled. Her small words and groans. When he thought the word *Holger* and imagined the sound of Holger's clogs, when he thought as hard as he could: Holger's sunburned face looking at them, falling over them like a shadow, everything turning cold and all sound suffocated – it stiffened, it searched, it dove in, into her burning hot hidden place.

He took the path through the cemetery. The sun was hot on his neck.

"One day I am going to be gone. One day you will be all by yourself."

Now it had come true. Now he was all by himself.

He hadn't wanted to listen to his mother since she said it so often. Her words lost their power.

He knew that she was down there under the stone with her name. She had taken care of everything in advance. For example, the dove. A dove made of alabaster was resting on the edge of the grave. Its head was under its wing. It was at peace.

"Then you can imagine that it's me. Since otherwise it might be hard for you to understand."

The young priest, the one who came from Stockholm, said that it was forbidden to have such silliness in a Swedish cemetery. The notification was for all the cemeteries in all of Sweden. A command from the civil office. Augustsson, the rector, gave him an earful.

"What a bunch of crap! You can get a dispensation! If a member of the parish really wants an alabaster dove, she's going to get an alabaster dove! I am sure that Our Lord has nothing against that!"

The dove had started to change color a bit. Almost looked dirty. He understood that this was because of air pollution. It came from far away. The coal districts of Germany. He kept a nail brush in his pocket and every time he visited the grave, he wetted the brush and polished the alabaster surface until his knuckles ached.

5

There was a house lived in only during the summertime, where he sometimes went. He would keep to the forest like a moose. A man and a woman. He watched them on their porch. The glowing ends of their cigarettes. He would stand there and watch them and they didn't know a thing.

He liked going out at night. He was like Cat in that respect. He was so light-footed that no person could hear him, which was necessary to remain unseen.

He wanted to be the one to decide when he would be seen.

In school, they had tried to force him to be the kind of person he was not. In school he had a name and responsibilities. That was a long time ago. He was his own person now, and he could do what he wanted.

One day he was out in the bog and he happened upon two moose calves being born. The first one was slipping out right as he came by. There was a gap, and he saw her. The moose cow was standing with her back bent and so busy with giving birth that she did not notice him. He had come downwind, so he was able to change his direction and drop down into the sedge. A short time later, the second calf was born. The two newborns were giving off steam. It was the time before the trees leafed out, so he kept squatting and quiet behind the tufts of grass. He was so close that he could make out the moose cow's tongue and the wind brought a raw smell of blood.

He wished his own mother were still alive. He would have liked to talk to her about this birth. Later, he told Kaarina, but as she was listening, her face turned loose and flabby, as if she didn't want to take his tale to heart.

This evening he was watching the couple who had come to the house the same way he watched the moose. Their car was parked near the shed. Number five-five-seven. And nearby there was the ax stuck in the wood of the chopping block. During the first days after they'd arrived, the man had been busy there. Splinters whirled around him. He'd sworn and carried on, and he'd often take a break to smoke. The chopped wood was still lying on the grass as no one had bothered to bring it in.

He'd watched them many times before and they had no idea he was there. The woman. She washed her hair outside and he watched the water drip from her brown nipples. Once he watched them have sex. They were behind the food cellar, and they were naked and totally quiet. He'd just been walking by in the forest. He liked seeing that and he'd come back many times in order to see it again, but it never happened. Just that one time.

He told Kaarina what he'd seen them do. Kaarina became frightened.

"Keep away from them. They could get angry."

Kaarina was such a scaredy-cat.

He didn't like the way the woman looked. She had blonde hair, like down, and her lips were pursed and she never looked happy. The man, on the other hand, looked like someone he wouldn't mind showing himself to. The man's black eyebrows would rise, and the man would say something calm and dignified.

No, he could not take that risk.

That one time she had been on all fours like an animal and he'd watched the man's hard, white buttocks.

Afterwards he'd gone right back into the forest and he wished that Kaarina would come. He wished very hard that she would come. But Kaarina was not the one who came to him later, and he did not want to go to their farm all that often. Holger would find out and then he'd get a strange look on his face, as he did when he got angry.

It was midnight. A woodcock passed by with a sparse, clipped sound in the darkness. The man and the woman were not going to sleep. They were talking loudly on their porch, but he could not figure out their words. The woman yelled something and her voice was high-pitched. She started to run in the slippery grass. The man ran after her. He was wearing wide pants.

He stood in the forest and watched how the woman ran and the man caught up to her. He had such long legs and the woman was tiny and thin. She had no hair down there like Kaarina did, but she had full, bulging breasts.

"Let's go inside!" was what he heard, and then the door closed behind them.

At that moment, he felt something soft at his ankle. Cat. He saw the kittens sitting not far away.

Just as he thought. They'd come here.

6

SOMETIMES HE REMEMBERED THE MOVEMENT. That is to say, his body remembered how his legs braced against the bottom of the wagon and the knottiness of its wood. And his mother, half-turned away. Her knuckles, her large hand on the pole. The sound as she pulled. The squeaking from the wheels.

Now that he was grown, he imagined he sat in the wagon and leaned forward with his arms out as if he were rowing without oars. Swiftly crossing the meadow. Grown up. Big.

He had no idea what had happened to the wagon. He could have used it for the kittens. He would pull them and silence their longing.

It was due to him that they even existed.

7

HE APPROACHED THE HOUSE DURING THE DAYTIME. Their car was gone again. They often left the house, and he wondered what they were looking for all the time.

The house had always been there. His mother had talked respectfully about the people who lived there before. In her day. She also talked about the animals which used to be there, too.

There was a heifer that would go on the attack whenever anyone approached its pasture.

"We tried to trick her," his mother would say. "I was just a young girl in those days and I could run as fast as the wind. But that heifer caught up to me and ran next to me for a bit, and she would've knocked me over, because she was such an angry thing, but she'd forget to stop and just keep running. She hardly had her horns yet and she was brown. I'd dive down and roll under the fence and out of the way. Oh my Lord, you can imagine how my heart was beating!"

The master was good to his animals. They knew it and they were calm. All of them except that heifer. She must have had a screw loose in her brain. Things were all right until the heifer grew up and her horns were dangerous. The master decided to sell her to the slaughterhouse.

"The master had such a kind heart and he was so gentle. He could not stand it when they came to take his animals to the slaughterhouse. He'd had them since they were babies. You've seen how

21

tiny piglets can be, how they are a naked little bundle, how tightly they press against their mothers and look for the teats, as all young mammals do. In fact, you did that, too, although you don't remember. You would search with your lips and then suck. I would hold you, just like this I'd hold you, wrapped in a blanket with tight fringe . . . and one time when I put you down, you began to suck on that fringe. You got a lot of fuzz on your gums, and you screamed and flailed. I didn't understand that sucking on a blanket could be dangerous. I was such a beginner, you understand. I knew nothing about small babies."

He'd heard this not once, but many, many times. He never said anything. Maybe his mother knew that. Maybe she knew how much he liked to listen to how things were before he was big enough to notice things for himself.

"The people living in that house had a daughter, just one, no other children. The girl was named Susanne. She was younger than I was, but we walked to school together anyway. All us girls envied her because of her name. No person had a name like that. At least not anyone we knew. Susanne. Sometimes I would come home with her. Her mother would heat milk for us. She'd put spoons with honey into the mugs. I remember that she had trouble with her back, so she always used a cane."

8

H E THOUGHT ABOUT HIS MOTHER.
       He thought: I'll head over to Holger's place.
He thought: Kaarina. If she's there.

When he arrived, Holger was standing behind the house and the hens were clustered by the fence. He'd covered the way in with a board. Now Holger bent over and grabbed at the feathered flock. The one he grabbed was yellow and delicate and it flapped its wings wildly.

The ax was ready at the chopping block.

He walked around the house without being seen. Kaarina was on this side. She was bending over a basket of laundry. Her sweater, its elbows gray and full of holes, was tucked in.

He thought he should call to her in his low voice and make her happy.

Maybe she wouldn't be happy. Maybe she would scream from surprise and fear. But she saw him before he'd decided what to do. She dropped a piece of clothing back into the basket. It was slippery and wet.

She made a gesture which said: I know you're here.

He slowly walked toward her. If he could make her start to giggle then her soft side would show, and her skin.

"Little Kaarina, giggly-girl, come into the forest and play."

She shook out the laundry and did not reply.

He had made his way to the lilac bushes, where he stopped and watched her continue to hang up the laundry. His body was heavy with desire, and his hands went to its root.

A slamming door. Holger came out onto the porch. His shirt was speckled with blood. Holger's open mouth and the hole where his words came out. His blue-eyed gaze. Kaarina's hands lifting the laundry.

He walked away with his desire still burning.

9

HE WAS A TALL, STRONG MAN WITH LARGE HANDS, WHICH WERE SURPRISINGLY NOT ROUGH. He had trouble finding clothes that fit. He either didn't realize or didn't care that the legs of his pants did not reach his ankles, which were left bare. As he strode through the bog the picture of his mother faded away.

Evening was falling, although there was still light. The air was warm. In the evenings, the bugs and mosquitoes came out. The swallows were ready for them, flying out with their beaks wide open. He hadn't been hungry for a while. That morning he'd eaten some eggs with Kaarina. She'd boiled them in water. He'd filled his stomach with them, but now his stomach was empty.

His mother was most worried about how he was going to feed himself later. She'd said that she ought to teach him and that he could also look at her cookbooks and ask her questions, but that hadn't happened and now it was too late.

That morning he had touched her. He had pinched her ear lobe, first softly and then harder. Deep inside, he already knew the truth anyway. Her arms were bent with her hands in fists as if she was trying to defend herself against a threat. Those days he was grown and slept in the attic. She still slept on the pull-out sofa. He often wished he could still sleep next to her, but no grown son slept next to his mother. They could not be naked in the same bed.

So it had happened, and it happened at night, and now there was nothing that he could do about it. She kept still in her twisted position. He kept pinching her ear lobe.

"Mamma!" he said. In fact, he was screaming.

But her eyes had film over them and her jaw hung slack. He remembered that she once told him that if it happened, he was to "close my eyes and tie up my jaw so I don't just lie there staring." So he tried to do that. He drew his hand over her eyes, and it seemed her eyelids were closing, but then they sprang open again. Then he found a handkerchief, which he folded into a triangle and tried to fasten it underneath her chin, but her chin resisted his efforts. He tied a knot at the top of her head, which did not turn out so well, as the ends looked like rabbit ears, hanging sadly from her head. He couldn't do anything about it, so he left her like that.

"Go to the pastor's wife," she had told him. "She will take care of me and put everything in order, and go do that before anyone else shows up. Certainly before the pastor and pallbearers show up."

So while dawn was still breaking, he hurried to the pastor's wife without any breakfast. He wasn't crying because he could not really understand what had happened.

The young pastor's wife was named Ingelise. Later on, she moved away to Skara or Hjo. He couldn't remember where. That morning she appeared on the porch steps wearing a blood-red bathrobe, and, as soon as she saw him, she knew what the matter was.

"Just give me two minutes," she said. "Just two minutes."

Then they both ran. She ran ahead, and he ran behind her. They knew that there really wasn't any hurry any longer, but they ran anyway, as if they needed some kind of confirmation. The pastor's wife was wearing tiny, black boots. He saw the boots sink in the mud and her steps become heavier. He couldn't do anything to make things easier for her.

Still, she was quick and strong and didn't mind the mud. She placed her boots on the floor in the entryway and hung up her coat. She was wearing jeans and a dark blue sweater.

She poured water into a basin and began to wash his mother's twisted body without removing her nightgown. The arms of the dead woman were still in the air with the fingers of her hands turned inward. The pastor's wife did not say anything while she worked. Her mouth was tightly closed, but he saw that the tip of her tongue poked out.

Afterwards, Ingelise went to the kitchen to get the vase of flowers standing there. She brought it back to the room and placed it close to where his mother was lying.

He thought it looked nice.

"Your mother is not suffering any longer," she said as she dried off her hands. "You have to think of that when you realize that she is not here any longer and you feel all alone."

He had not realized that at all. That his mother was suffering. He thought about this for weeks afterwards, and even now, years later.

The pastor's wife was wearing a cross on a necklace. The cross swung as she leaned toward him.

"I think you should come home with me," she said. "I bet that you haven't had breakfast."

They walked back much more slowly. The pastor's wife had someone helping her in the kitchen, as they were supposed to be preparing for the pastor's fortieth birthday. The woman was named Ragnhild, and she began to brew coffee. She prepared a sandwich for him on a kind of bread that he'd never tasted before. Later he thought of that bread as Death Bread.

The pastor's wife started to take care of practical matters. She called Dr. Dahl, who went over to write out the death certificate. She found men who could carry his mother's body out of the house, and there was another woman, Dora Granberg, who would clean death out of the house. That's what they called it there. The smell of death would be cleansed away by soap and water.

"You're a good boy," The pastor's wife said. "You could probably do this all by yourself. But I promised your mother that I would get Dora Granberg when the time came. That's how your mother wanted it."

He felt betrayed. The pastor's wife seemed to know more about his mother and her thoughts than he did.

He stayed the entire day at the pastor's manse. The pastor's wife asked whether he wanted to stay the night, but although his house was empty, he wanted to go home.

The old pastor, not the young one, came the next day. He talked a great deal about the man's mother, and praised her diligence and hard work.

"And if that young priest gives you a hard time about her dove, you just come to me," he said.

He didn't remember much about the actual funeral. The pastor's wife helped him find black clothes. He felt he looked good and that people looked at him with a bit more respect. The pastor's wife also took care of arranging the coffee and cake, not to mention the tiny glasses of sherry.

The night after the funeral, he lay in bed and thought about Ingelise, the pastor's wife.

10

THE MAN WAS STANDING AT THEIR GATE, AND SAW THAT THEIR CAR WAS NOT IN THE DRIVEWAY. He squatted and tried to call Cat. He'd seen Cat as he approached, and he saw the kittens near the fruit trees, too. Cat was trying to teach them how to climb trees.

She was gone.

Those shining, empty windows. He'd watched the woman clean them. She'd been wearing flowery shorts and a bra, but no shirt. He watched her strong, browned arms as they scrubbed and rubbed. Sometimes she took a cigarette break. When she started the second floor, she used a ladder. Once, she stumbled and almost fell. She was carrying a bucket and was more worried about it than herself.

A long, long time ago, his mother had come to this house to play with that girl Susanne. It was hard to imagine that his mother had once been younger than he was now.

One day when his mother was still alive, they'd gone to the wild raspberry patch, and they'd spent the entire day there. The next morning she'd made juice with the berries and jam. The seeds of the jam stuck in their teeth. While they were standing in the thicket picking berries, his mother began to tell him a story.

Susanne had had a tiny horse all her own. It was brown and friendly and she enjoyed feeding it tufts of grass. It was too tiny to be ridden. Susanne's father was so kind to her to buy her a useless little horse which could only eat and drop manure. When the tiny horse was let out with the other horses, it was the one who was in charge. It would show its teeth and flick its ears back, and then the other horses would leave it alone.

He approached the house, keeping his ears attuned to any noise. He had his hands up as if he needed to protect himself.

He remembered that his mother had played in that great room, and it seemed as if he almost saw them inside, those girls, and he thought it was strange that they'd grown up and now they weren't living any more. It was the same thing with humans and with animals. They started little, they grew, they got old, they died.

A wave of melancholy came over him. An overwhelming sense of loneliness. His mother had once stood on this lawn with her little girl feet. She would tap the window so Susanne would look up. A smile. Easy, relieved. She was sitting with her homework and it was boring her. She relaxed her shoulders and stood up. Susanne's mother would be in the kitchen. Where else would a mother be? Susanne the little schoolgirl put her books and papers away. "I'm going outside to play with Ebba," and it was a strong voice, not a meek question. The door slammed shut behind her.

He saw both girls as if they were right in front of him, looking the way they had in an old photo his mother had once shown him. They resembled each other. They both wore hair bands on their short hair. They had on skirts and wore black shoes. Their little, tiny bodies. How they would run down the stone stairs and into the forest to play hide-and-seek between the tree trunks.

He closed his eyes and could smell that smell, the one of stinking wolf fur. There were wolves in the forest in those days, and his mother had seen one earlier. From that day on, no one was allowed to go into the forest to play. A man with a hunting rifle would have to be there.

He felt sweat dampen his palms and a shot of fear and excitement. He no longer knew where he was, but he had to get inside. He felt something brush against his knuckles. No, just a shadow of gray, hunting, the glistening of a predator's teeth. He shook the door handle, which was locked. They had secured the house tightly. All the windows were locked, too, and the back door. He felt his way across the lawn, wild and frightened:

The kittens! Cat! Were they in trouble?

He wanted to call them to him, but his lips were frozen. He could not say a word nor form a sound. Hurry to the shed! This was easier to break into as the catch was not locked.

Inside. He closed the creaking door and held it, listening for any sound. His mother had told him about the howling of a wolf. The howling had come from the edge of the forest and terrified her. Her fear had made her ill and she spent the rest of the night shivering, and every time she closed her eyes, she saw the yellow eyes and the hunting nose turned toward the sky.

He pressed his eye to the gap in the doorframe and tried to see out. It was still light and the swallows searched and the grasshoppers buzzed. He saw no fur. Yes, there was a paw trying to get under the door. He yelled out loud and stomped his heel on the ground. He held both hands against the door for dear life. It scratched and hissed out there and his eye saw how the frightened girls ran toward the outhouse and he wanted to scream: faster, faster! He heard their high-pitched screaming. He did not see the wolf, but the scent of wolf was there, which made him shake, the way his mother shook from what the people called "wolf fever."

After that time, she had been sick in bed. She would scream and scream. The doctor said that she had met a group of hunters. None of them had seen any signs of a wolf. Maybe she had been sick that day.

His mother looked out the window as she told him the story. She straightened her back with righteous anger.

"They never believed me. Of course, in the beginning they might have. Then later they said I'd been seeing things. But not before they'd searched the forest for days, looking for the wolf. It was right during harvest time, and the rain came a few days later and they lost part of the harvest. They blamed me for it."

He slid down but did not let go of the door. Outside things were quiet. The scratching had stopped. He looked at his white, chafed hands. He could see them in the dark, and they were sore.

Instead he began to hear rhythmic chewing and a vision of what had once been the barn appeared to him. He saw the brown backs of the horses and went over to them. They were standing in their stalls, head to head, so that when he'd pushed through to the closest one, he could also pet the one across the aisle. Straw and manure. He squatted with his back against the wall and the big horse head reached down to him. A quiet, shimmering eye, a muzzle which puffed, wrinkled, and searched for a lump of sugar. He let the horse inhale his scent, and the air from the horse's nostrils was warm and sweet. Calm filled him, and he felt how it moved through his body to his head and made him sleepy, so that his brain slowed.

He thought that he wanted to go home. He would sneak back out the door and run and run and run. The grass underneath his feet would be dry so he wouldn't slip and hurt himself. He would run the entire way to his own house without stopping once and although it was a long way, he would not slow down, and once he was home, Cat would be there. Cat would be at the gate with her kittens nursing next to her, butting their heads against her stomach, and she would be purring and licking them.

Come inside, he would pant, because he was so tired after running. Cat would get up and follow him into the house and the kittens would follow her. All four of them would lie down on the sofa. He would lie on his back with a pillow under his head and the kittens would find a cozy spot next to him. Any time at all, he could reach out and touch them and feel that they were alive.

11

H E HEARD THEIR CAR RETURN. He was standing next to the window covered by spider webs and watched them drive up. The man and the woman. This was all wrong. Not now. He shook his head and his bangs flew back and then forward again. He held a nail pounded into the wall, which made his thumb throb and he could smell rust and blood.

The woman was wearing a colorful dress. Her shoulders were hunched and naked. Her body was doing something different. It looked like it had shrunk. Her straight hair covered her eyes.

Both of them walked into the house. He thought he could have been still inside when they'd gotten home. That would not have been good. Especially if he had broken a window. He'd done that once. It was not hard. If he had thought that Cat was inside, he would have done it.

Once he'd found her in the bedroom of that house. On the second floor. He took two pillows with him when he left. He'd put them in his own bed, thinking they would keep Cat at his place. But she would always leave anyway.

Now here he was in the barn.

There was dust and sunlight on the walls and the rotting harnesses, but no more sounds. The horses had stopped chewing. They were no longer standing in their stalls with their weight distributed on three legs while the fourth was raised to rest. Only the marks of their teeth were left on the stall door wood. Old chips on the floor. No straw. No sign of horse hair.

He crawled forward on his hands and knees. The woman was sitting on the porch with her knees drawn up. The man was behind her, but turned away, saying nothing. The woman was talking. He watched her mouth move. The man gestured with his hands and went inside the house.

He stood next to the door and the woman came into focus. He saw her heavy mouth and the wrinkles on her nose. Her face never did have a calming effect. Now she sat with her legs wide apart so that he could see her knees and her thighs. He noticed she was wearing white panties. No, her face was not calming and neither was her body. He found a strange desire rise in him, but it was not what he usually felt with Kaarina; it was an angry desire, almost an un-desire. Now and again he had imagined her in his room at night. She would laugh in his face and all her teeth would show. He imagined she would bend over him so that her breasts touched his throat, and he would bite at them and pull her toward him. Then she would writhe and fight and he would be forced to hold her still. She would be sinewy and strong, but he was stronger. She would spit out harsh words and he would cover her mouth with his hand, and he thought of Holger and Kaarina. That's what Holger would do. Once she calmed down and was still on his sheets, then he would start to take off her clothes.

He wondered what her name was. He'd heard that man call her name. It was a short, odd name that he'd never heard before, so he could never remember it. No one he knew had ever had a name like that.

She was still sitting on the porch and the man came back outside and they had glasses of something in their hands and they were drinking, yes, drinking.

Then he caught sight of Cat at the edge of the stairs. She appeared tiny and gray in the grass. He went to the door and opened it slightly. Cat would see him there and she would come over to him, bringing her kittens with her.

12

Everything went quickly after that moment. He never had the time to realize what was going on.

He reached toward the soft white skin, had to press down, had to cut off air.

But it was much too late.

He had been caught by surprise.

He could see the glimmer of iron – he felt oncoming pulsing darkness.

That was all.

Beth I

1

When they turned into the driveway by the yard, they felt that something had changed during the few hours they'd been away. It was just something they sensed, nothing they could see with their eyes, but it was threatening, nonetheless. Beth rubbed her nails over her thighs, which were covered with sweat.

"Ulf . . .," she said, as if he, being a man and two years older, would have an idea what it was that was off and could do something about it.

He didn't answer. She saw that the corners of his mouth had turned up, but that did not mean that he was smiling. His mouth never revealed the true state of his feelings. He was made that way. His mouth turned up no matter what was going on in his brain. In the beginning, as they were getting to know each other, she'd been deceived by that mouth, but now she knew better.

"Ulf, something's wrong. Do you know what it is? I'm scared."

The man sitting next to her turned off the engine and they both stared at the house. It stood surrounded by greenery, painted red, the idyllic picture of summer Sweden. Everything looked normal. The door was properly closed, just as they'd left it, and the curtains, which had been ironed, were still as they should be. Beth had put together a bouquet from grass, since the meadow flowers had withered during the heat. Up on the hill, there were a few scraggly bluebells and tough yarrow.

Grass was abundant and it was pretty.

Ulf cleared his throat and drew his fingers through his hair.

"I think you're imagining things."

His voice lacked confidence.

Earlier that afternoon, they'd decided to go on an excursion to Tidaholm. They'd already been to all the shops and knew what they sold, but they decided to have another go at finding something. Beth found a turquoise green summer dress in the boutique by the town square. All of the clothes were on sale, except for a rack near the back with a handwritten sign: *New for Fall.* The dress was thirty percent off.

It had been an extremely hot summer. Harsh odors of plants burned by the sun. Farther away there had been forest fires, but not in this area. Other areas of Småland, near Kalmar and Växjö. Beth was always wearing shorts and he would laugh at her, not in a harsh way, but in a way filled with love. *You look like a girl in those, a teeny-tiny girl!*

Well, that's the way she decided to interpret his words.

That they were meant in love.

She thought the grass was, for all intents and purposes, dead. On the rounded food cellar it was rough and brown. Earlier in the day, they'd pulled themselves up and walked around in the tufts of grass. They'd held onto the twigs of overhanging cherry branches. Those small black cherries; some of them were shrunken and they had a flat flavor. Her stomach had turned after eating them, and they gave her gas.

She slid off the cellar on her ass and then looked at her shorts.

"You've gotten them all stained," he said, and although his voice had a touch of irritability, she didn't want to hear it or let it get to her.

She walked over to the barn for no real reason, the edges of the grass sharp on her feet. She needed to move. She couldn't bear to be close.

Close to him, that is. Just that person.

The cat ran over to her. She was like a tiny gray-and-white lioness. She meowed demandingly. Every day the cat came to their

40

place. Every morning when they stepped out on the porch, she came running over the dewy lawn. It was a funny sight as the cat shook its paws to shake off the water. Beth decided to give her a name: Lioness. "*Lioness!*" Ulf was amused. "This is nothing but an average farm cat. Can't you see that this cat has another name, a totally normal name, like Stina or Maja, if it even has a name at all? In the country, people have plain kinds of names and traditions. No person in his right mind would call a cat Lioness!"

As if he knew what he was talking about!

She could tell that this was not a wild cat. She probably lived on a nearby farm, but seemed to like their place better. Beth had trouble understanding why. They never let the cat come inside the house. Now the cat wound itself around her legs and Beth felt the fur soothe her smooth cool skin, which still itched after being shaved two days ago.

"You know I can't pet you," she said. "I wish I could, because I really want to. I want to pick you up and smooth that matted coat, and you could lie on my lap and be soft and your little motor would start. I'd listen to your purring and be as calm and strong as you."

As usual Beth felt her face begin to swell and her nose start to run. She was allergic to cats.

"Lioness," Beth whispered. The cat looked at her. The cat was completely still with her yellow eyes like glass with black slits.

They would watch her come from the forest. She would have a mouse or a vole. The catch was always dead. At least, they were always spared the distressing sharp-clawed play. The cat would sneak into the barn with her prey. Sometimes, when Beth went to get firewood, she could hear the crunching and chewing inside.

One early morning in the beginning of the summer, Lioness brought something else which she set down carefully on the stone paving beneath the stairs. It moved and squeaked. They realized that the cat's shape had changed: her stomach no longer bulged out and her coat was lifeless and without shine.

During the night, the cat had given birth to two kittens.

2

THE HOUSE WAS NAMED SKOGSLYCKAN AND WAS FROM THE TURN OF THE LAST CENTURY. It was a typical country place, painted red with white window frames. A long time ago, Beth's maternal grandparents had lived here. In fact, her mother had been born on the large table in the roomy kitchen.

When Beth and her sister Juni were little, they were fascinated by the thought that their mother had been born on the very wooden surface where their plates were set. It was sometimes so hard to swallow their food that it formed globs in their mouths which they had to secretly spit out and hide in their napkins.

How could anyone ever give birth lying on a table?

Beth had given birth to twins in a hospital delivery room at Karolinska in Stockholm. Her twins would have been seven in October.

"What are we going to do today, Ulf?" she called up while he was on the cellar roof. "How about we go somewhere after lunch? Drive somewhere?"

Her scalp itched. She rubbed it with her knuckles to avoid scratching open the skin. She really ought to wash her hair, but things were so primitive here, especially since the hot water tank had broken and never been fixed. So she would have to heat some water on the stove, fill the buckets and carry them to the porch. Flies would always circle around when she stood on the lawn with her head bent down and her hair all wet. She wouldn't be able to see them, but she could feel their feet creeping over her body, their noses on her skin.

"Sure," he said as if he wasn't really paying attention. "We can go out for a drive."

Practically every day they would get in the car and drive to one of the small villages in the vicinity to buy the newspaper, or cigarettes, or wine. The silence in the house would get to be too much. They were not used to silence. They were not used to their own sounds and voices freed from ceaseless background noise. They would feel a nagging restlessness as each day wore on, so they would go out and buy a number of things which later on they found completely useless. Such as the electric grill. Neither of them was good at grilling, and whenever they tried, the result was almost inedible. Chewy meat covered with black – or its opposite, so bloody it looked raw.

Really not much more than dead matter, Beth often thought.

She knew that the process of decay in a body began shortly after death. After a few short hours, the rank smell of 'corpse' would begin. Why did slaughtered animals not have that smell? Why did meat not start to decay at once? Was it treated so that the process was slowed? She had never asked anyone about it because she feared that people would think she was strange.

And now here they were, back at the house again.

They sat still in the car for a while. Beth broke the silence. "I'm scared, Ulf. There's something not quite right. I'm scared." His body seemed so large and so close to her. *I love you*, she thought. *You can never leave me. Not ever.*

"Come on," he shrugged. "Let's go inside."

A swallow swooped down, almost touching the hood of the car. Swallows could be aggressive at times, especially when their young were leaving the nest. One morning a swallow had pecked at Beth's hair, but when she told Ulf about it, he didn't believe her.

"Come on," he said again.

They climbed out of the car, but left its doors ajar. Disquiet crept along Beth's body from the hollow in the palm of her hand, along her arms and through her stomach and spine. She had to dig under the appointment book in her purse to find the keys. She handed them to him.

"You open it." she said.

3

As soon as they walked into the living room, they knew their foreboding had not been just imagination. Someone had been there. The window facing the forest was wide open, although it was neither damaged nor broken open. Only ajar and the hook in place.

Ulf had barely stepped past the threshold and now he held onto the door jamb as if there'd been an earthquake.

"You washed the windows the other day," he whispered. "Maybe you forgot to close this one all the way."

"No, I didn't," she said, an automatic response.

"But someone opened it. Did he climb in through it?"

She shook her head.

Then they both saw that the drawers to the chiffonier had been pulled out. Beth's mouth went dry. The drawers held nothing but handkerchiefs, matchboxes, and old board games which had been Beth and Juni's when they were young. Someone had been rummaging and jumbled things. A clean and pressed kitchen towel had been flung on the floor. But it seemed nothing had been taken. There was nothing valuable in the house to take. They always took their money and credit cards whenever they went out. Beth folded the towel back into the drawer and shut all the drawers with both her hands.

Ulf hadn't moved.

"You shouldn't touch anything. Fingerprints."

Beth whirled around. "Do you really think that the police have time for this? A simple break-in where nothing was taken? They have enough on their plates with next to no resources. Remember when Anki was raped, and nobody cared to do anything at all, even when she saw the man later passing by on the street? She recognized him and ran to a store nearby to call the police. Do you think they bothered to show up then? No. An hour later and then it was much too late! So who can count on the police these days?"

"Beth," he said calmly.

She ran into the kitchen and grabbed a log. She was furious now, and she ran up the stairs. At first everything seemed normal on the second floor. Just as they'd left it. The cover was on the bed, Ulf's dark blue sweater was draped over a chair, the desk was untouched, the ancient television was on its same little table and its cord was still unplugged. Unplugging was the only way to turn it off.

Then she saw that the pillows were gone. Small, decorative pillows which had their astrological signs cross-stitched on the front. Her mother had made them when she was still happy doing craft projects as surprises for others. Sagittarius and Virgo. Her mother had seen the patterns in a magazine and mailed away for them. Just two stuffed decorative pillows. Beth usually put them at the head of the bed after she finished making it, and she knew she'd done the exact same thing that very morning. Now they were gone.

Ulf had followed her up the stairs and the two of them stood in the middle of the room. The heat was intense. A wasp kept hitting the window.

"Somebody has been here," she said, as her shoulders sank. She could smell her own sweat and fear.

Ulf stared at her.

"You can see it for yourself," she said. "The pillows are gone. Someone has come here and made off with them."

"Pillows? What the hell are you talking about?"

"The pillows Mamma gave us. You know, the ones with the astrological signs on them."

"Oh, those. Maybe you put them somewhere else. I mean, who would break into a house to steal a few old pillows?"

46

"I have no idea," she whispered. "I really don't know."

They did not find any other signs that someone had been in the house. Beth took out the vacuum and cleaned every room thoroughly, as if she could erase the uncomfortable feeling of invasion: someone alien had been there.

They only had one more week of vacation. After that, Juni and her husband would be moving in. Beth and Juni were co-owners of the house since the days when their parents had gotten too old for upkeep of a summer house.

Her mother had begun to show signs of the slow, oncoming changes in her brain. She would break into a sudden rage over nothing. Not too often at first, which always surprised and confused everyone, but as the months went by, they realized something serious was going on. Finally, the doctor informed them that she was suffering from dementia. It was incurable.

For a while, their father had taken care of their mother at home, but inevitably the burden was becoming too much. Every time Beth came to visit, she was surprised how much he'd changed, himself. He'd gotten more silent and all his energy went to keeping their mother clean and proper and to defend himself whenever she went into her rages.

They'd both turned seventy-eight. Beth's father had been vice president for Svärd's Furniture. He'd worked at the company from its beginning, and it was still flourishing. Her mother had owned a hair salon. Beth had felt proud about her parents, especially her mother, because what she'd done was easier to understand. Her mother worked magic with her customers and changed heads of unwashed hair to shiny, scented locks. At times Beth was allowed to watch when the young women were getting their hair done for their weddings. Then Beth could stand on the upholstered stool and hand her mother combs and hair pins.

"When your wedding day comes, I'm going to make you look just as wonderful!" her mother usually said, while her face turned dreamy and her eyes looked into the distance. "My Beth, you will be the most beautiful bride of them all!"

"What about Juni?" asked Beth.

"Juni, too, of course. Both of you are my daughters!"

Her mother never had the chance to dress them for their weddings. Beth never married. Juni met her husband on a Caribbean cruise and the captain married them on the ship.

Their parents now lived in a tiny apartment in the city of Falköping.

"I believe that she feels at home here," Beth's father had said. He would repeat this over and over as if to convince himself that he'd done the right thing by finding this apartment. Nevertheless, Beth knew that he'd lost the will to live. He had nothing more to look forward to, and day after day he had to fight with his ever-more-confused wife, the woman he'd once had taken as his beautiful young bride.

Beth would sometimes bring all this up to her sister, but Juni was more down to earth.

"That's life," she said. "That's what will happen to all of us, so make sure that you really live while you can. One of these days, it will all go to hell."

Beth's sister was named Juni because she was born in the morning on Midsummer's Day. Juni was now forty and the same age as Ulf. Juni'd actually introduced Ulf to Beth. They were both journalists and worked in the newsroom. Beth had just turned thirty and her friends had planned a party. Juni was invited, and she came, thinner than ever, with spiked hair. Juni was high on some kind of drug, and a heavy, sweet scent surrounded her.

"I got you a present, Sis," she whispered as they hugged in greeting. "I brought a guy. And you know what? It's like he was made for you. He's just perfect!"

Ulf was standing right behind them. He looked well-groomed – that was Beth's first impression. Proper in a gray blazer. However, she could feel his erection when he danced with her.

They never got married. It just didn't happen. They decided to pledge their troth, which seemed more honest, more pure. They exchanged rings of white gold. Beth's ring also had a tiny red ruby. Sometimes when she looked at it, she couldn't help but think of blood. She felt their love circulated with their blood: my beloved man and friend.

4

B ETH WASN'T HUNGRY. She peeled potatoes and put them in the pot. She lit a cigarette and then remembered that they'd agreed not to smoke in the house. She went out onto the porch and stood in that clear, light silence. The sun beat down on the tufts of grass although it was now starting to set behind the pine trees. Full darkness would not come until just before midnight, but even then the sun would barely be gone. It would be a foggy twilight, and nothing could hide.

The previous night, she'd woken up and decided to walk around barefoot in the grass. She'd seen a moose in the birch grove. It moved slightly and made some sounds. A moose was a tall, well-known shadow. She was just thinking of going inside to wake up Ulf, but a gust of wind made her nightdress blow and that was enough. The sound of branches breaking and the moose was gone.

Now she drew a drag and let the smoke fill her mouth before she blew it back out. She saw a wagtail in the raspberry patch. There was a nest underneath the roof and she'd seen a chick with a gaping beak in it. She was a bit afraid that Lioness would try to catch it.

"Ulf," she called. She heard him walking around on the second floor.

Ulf opened an upstairs window and looked down. "What's up?"

"Well . . . , I was just wondering where you were."

Ulf pulled his head back inside and she heard him coming down the stairs. He opened the door and came outside.

"You making some food?"

"Just some potatoes."

"I'm not hungry."

"Neither am I."

"What time is it?"

Beth shrugged her shoulders.

"You know, we could just go home," he suggested.

"Home to Hässelby?"

He nodded.

"Why? We have a whole week left."

"But we've been here for such a long time."

He walked down onto the stone paving. It suddenly came to her that he looked thin, hollow, on his way into old age. She realized that one day she was going to be alone. Women lived longer than men. She'd be stumbling along with her walker on the nursing home's well-scrubbed floors while he, Ulf, would be long dead. The hardest thing would be the lack of sympathy, she thought. People would say, "That's the way life goes," in a useless attempt at comfort, because she would just be one of many, another clone of an old, white-haired lady without history and identity.

"We agreed to be here for another week!" she called after him.

He turned and his gaze was fixed vaguely somewhere behind her.

"Forget it, I take it back."

"And we're supposed to visit Mamma and Pappa tomorrow," she continued. "Don't you remember the plans we made? We promised to be there on Thursday. You remember that?"

He'd already reached the gate. "I don't hear you!" he called back to her.

"We're supposed to go to Falköping tomorrow," Beth said, but quietly, so it would not reach him. She put her cigarette out on the stairs, rubbing it until there was nothing left and the loose tobacco in the butt fell out onto her fingertips.

She went into the kitchen and took down two wine glasses. She poured the wine her sister had left behind, tasted it. It was a deep red. She watched Ulf pace outside, small, jagged steps, and there was something strange about him which made her impatient but also fearful. So she had to open the door and call him back to her.

He came against his will.

"Let me just look at you!" she said, but didn't like how her voice sounded.

She held out a wine glass to him and they stood silently in the kitchen, drinking.

"Ulf," she whispered and crept next to him. Ulf's body became stiff and resistant. "Tell me how much you love me."

Ulf pushed her aside, and set his wine glass on the table with a quick, powerful movement.

5

It was late at night as they walked toward the clear-cut. Beth tripped over twigs and roots. Ulf was walking next to her and sometimes steadied her, but with anonymous hands, not the hands of a lover.

And what about her!

Nothing but a plain woman!

She saw a silver gleam in the blueberry bushes and she had to go and see. It was a fish, recently dead, a perch, flat on the ground, and pine needles covered its eye.

She was drunk now; in fact, both she and Ulf were extremely drunk.

"Look!" she whispered. "That's strange! There's no water around here, so how can a fish be on dry land?"

Ulf went up to it and poked it. His fingernails were short and clean.

"Yes, this is really strange."

"As if it fell from the sky."

Ulf flipped it with his foot. Its gills were open and red. A fly circled around it.

"Where would this have come from?"

"I don't know," she whispered back, but as yet did not feel afraid.

Ulf struggled out of his backpack. He took out a sticky bottle and two paper cups. Madiera, which they had made themselves from apples. They kept it in the food cellar, but they didn't drink it very often because it was syrupy and much too sweet. Ulf placed the bottle between his knees and pulled out the cork.

"*Skål då!*"

"*Skål* . . . . You know, I can't get that fish out of my mind."

"Stop gabbing about that!" he hissed at her. "We'll never know what that was all about, so it's just as well to forget about it!"

"What's going on with you, Ulf?"

He whirled toward her. She saw, suddenly, that his lips were pale and chapped.

"There's nothing going on with me!"

"There must be something. I know that much. Tell me, even though part of me doesn't want to hear. You always tell me I'm a person who hides her head in the sand. I'm a coward. But Ulf, I want you to tell me. I won't run away even if it's horrible or dangerous and will change my whole life. . . . . Still I'm going to dare to listen. . . . . It's better if we're totally honest, right?"

Beth laughed but her lips were stiff.

Ulf lifted the paper cup to his lips, and Beth watched his Adam's apple move. Ulf grimaced.

"You're right," he said finally, with some hostility. "Something is going on. Maybe it would have gone away on its own. But here you are, insisting that it all comes out and so now we have to talk and talk."

His speech was slurred and thick. He stopped himself, as if he were giving Beth the chance to put her hands over her ears, throw herself at his feet and beg him to be quiet. She'd done that before.

She didn't do it now.

So he told her.

"Ylva and I have been talking quite a bit lately, and we've somehow gotten closer to each other again. You know how it is, if you have a child with someone, you're always . . . close."

"Close?"

"That's what I said. Close."

She felt as if her body had gotten strangely light, as if her feet had lifted from the moss and she was swaying above the ground, right over the trunks of the trees. The vague thought that he was getting pine sap on his pants went through her mind, but it no longer would concern her, since Ylva, Ulf's ex-wife, would now take care of everything having to do with him: his clothes, his thoughts, his son.

"Does Albin know?"

They'd gone to bed now, but for her the room was spinning in the darkness.

"What are you talking about?"

"Does he know that you and Ylva are meeting again?"

"We'd never stopped."

"You know . . . as you said . . . getting close again."

"Albin is not going to suffer because his parents are no longer fighting."

Beth threw the sheet off. It was holding her down, making it hard to breathe.

"How did this happen?" she whispered. "How did this *closeness* come back? Tell me. I want to know."

Ulf sat up onto the edge of the bed, straight-necked.

"I don't really know. Her guy, Robban, had moved out. Then we . . . I really don't know how . . . we . . . these are the kinds of things that just happen . . . where there are no answers."

Beth was crying softly now, her thoughts incoherent.

He was turned away from her, and his voice was cold and sharp.

"Beth, you forced me to tell you."

"And what exactly does *close* mean?" she screamed back. "Huh?"

"You said that when you have a child with someone, you stay close. You said that up at the forest clear-cut."

"*Close* was the wrong expression maybe. Do you always have to keep track of every word I say? A child binds people together, and that's a fact you can't get away from."

Beth turned the light on. Ulf looked ill. The hair on his arms was up, as if it was cold on the second floor, as if it were fall already, November.

"Of course you mean a living child," she said.

"Oh, for the love of God, don't start up with that again."

"Why shouldn't a dead child bind people together? Bind them even closer? Or maybe two . . . our two tiny twins . . . they lived one day before they died."

"Get control of yourself. You're losing it."

"And what if you had been a support to me then? If you hadn't turned away and left me to deal with things all by myself? What if instead we had grieved together? If you hadn't been so selfish. You were scaring me. Juni would call and ask whether I was all by myself and told me I shouldn't be on my own, so she would come over with paté and purple grapes and tell me that I had to eat and get strong again!"

"That was a hit below the belt . . . and I've heard it a hundred times. I've heard it too often. It doesn't make an impression any more. There's no reason to go on talking. It's not working. I can never reach you; I never have been able to get through to you, not with this."

Beth could not stop: "Juni would ask, *Where's Ulf? Why isn't he here?* What was I supposed to answer her? 'He's at work. They were short-handed so he had to go in.' . . . ? If I had told the truth . . . it would have reflected on me, too. I couldn't keep my man at home. My man, the father of my dead children. She would have been furious with you and I wasn't up to dealing with her anger and the risk . . . if by telling her, I would lose you, too, and I needed you so very much! Yes, I needed you to *be close*, if you'll pardon my saying so!" She laughed out loud.

Ulf bowed his head.

"I was grieving, too," he said, roughly. "And you know that pretty damn well. But in my own way. Not everyone grieves like you. If only you could realize that somehow! I couldn't write at all. My words tumbled together and turned to slop. I couldn't cry, either. Not like you. You were able to get things out of your system by crying. And in that way, you stole my grief from me!"

"Oh, no!" she screamed back. "You can't say that! There's always enough sorrow for everyone!"

Ulf kept silent.

"Albin wasn't able to have his little half-sisters," she continued, and she knew she was going too far, but wasn't able to stop herself.

"I knew he was sad about that. The entire time that I carried them, we talked, Albin and me, every single day. About children and how they begin their lives in the womb. And then . . . he knew he'd gotten two sisters but that they were never going to come home and he was never going to get to see them or touch their small, warm heads. I explained about the fontanelles, because he was old enough to understand. A big boy, five years old, your son Albin, and mature in spite of everything he'd gone through."

Ulf stood up, searched through his clothes for his cigarettes, and then his heels thundered down the stairs. She followed him dressed only in her translucent nightgown.

Nylon, she thought. No, this one is normal cotton.

If!

If she only could!

Let the glowing end touch and she would burst into flame!

They stood on the porch and smoked. Outside it was cool and humid. The color of the bushes had deepened. She felt the soles of her feet burning, so she dipped them into the dew on the grass and shivered. Out by the trees, something light was moving. Was it the cat? The cat on the prowl for voles?

"You know, these days, they let you take photographs of your dead children," she murmured. "You can even take the babies home for a few hours if you want, so that you can have them in your own home. Maybe even keep them overnight. It's a way to start the grieving process. The psychologist that I see these days told me about it."

"That's really sick," he said, as if pressured. "Take corpses home!"

"They're your own children!"

"But still!"

"You can wash your dead little child and put on diapers and the clothes that you would like them to have, and then you could light some candles and make a proper deathbed. So that they don't just disappear, like ours did. They just disappeared into the basement morgue, into the freezer. Those tiny bodies that I kept warm with my own blood for seven months taken to a freezer!"

"Well, I saw them," he grumbled. "I saw them when they were born. But not for long. The nurses rushed out with them right away.

And of course, I saw them in the incubator. I looked at their tiny, bent legs. If only you had been up to seeing them before they . . . but you were so tired and . . . you said you didn't. . . . "

"You should have talked me into it. You must have understood how I was! After all that horrible. . . . I was in shock. Didn't you get it? How I could not handle anyone but myself, and barely that! I had to heal and recuperate, but afterwards, if I had only known. . . ."

She'd stayed in bed for thirty hours. The pain had been overwhelming, had blotted out her longing for the babies, even the ability to think. The next day they brought her by wheelchair, but it was too late. The two baby girls lay side by side, facing each other, wrapped in yellow blankets. One girl's upper lip had risen slightly and Beth could glimpse white gums.

She turned to look at the doctor, but she could not meet her eyes. She had an unexpected burst of sympathy for what the woman would be forced to say. She heard the breaking voice from far above her.

"Well . . . it's so hard sometimes. Sometimes in this profession, you feel totally powerless. And two such sweet little girls. I understand what you must be going through."

No, the doctor could not understand. Not any more than she, herself, could understand what had happened. She, the mother, who had carried them close to her heart, who had waited for them with her whole being, with terrible longing.

They planned a real funeral service, which was held at Hässelby Villastad Church. The hill leading to the church was covered with wet leaves. She remembered that she'd slipped and almost fallen. She saw her father's face and it was the first time that she had ever seen him cry. His shoulders were shaking and his hair was thin. And her mother.

"You'll get over this! You'll get over it and, after you rest for a while, you can try for another baby."

The funeral director was a woman named Margit Gustavsson. She did not suggest that Ulf or Beth be at the preparations. It was a relief. Margit's hands were flat and wide. These hands had taken care of the children, put them in the same casket with their faces turned toward each other. Beth had chosen the hymns and insisted on a spring hymn even though it was the middle of fall. That psalm gave her hope that life would continue. She wasn't a religious person, but she found comfort in thumbing through the hymnal and, during the service, she sang the spring hymn by heart with a high, driving voice.

Afterwards, they had all gone to Hägerstalund's Restaurant to have lunch with relatives and friends. As they drove there, she saw the school where she worked. She was on maternity leave. She was supposed to be home with her children for one and a half years.

6

ULF CARRIED HER UP THE STAIRS. At times he could be both strong and gentle. He placed her on the bed without any irritability whatsoever. In fact, he laid her down carefully and gently. The walls were still whirling around her and she still had weak buzzing in her ears. He lay down beside her, his feet small and cold against her skin. He slid off her nightgown, and his rough hands were on her. She struggled to find some sexual excitement, tried to writhe and moan in the attempt. Now he was pushing her legs apart to find his way in, but she was all closed up tight in that place between her legs.

This made him stop.

"Sweetheart, I really want to," she said, but her voice was tired as she put her hand on him, as if milking him, but he rolled over and, before long, just went to sleep.

She closed her eyes and tears squeezed out from underneath her eyelashes. Not because of him, but because alcohol made her fragile and depressed. It was always like this, always.

A noise!

She thought that Ulf was up or that the radio was on, broadcasting church bells calling the faithful to high mass. Then she realized that Ulf was there beside her, and she was afraid. The nearest church was miles away.

Suddenly the memory of the freshly caught fish in the middle of the dry pine needles came to her. She lay deep in the middle of the mattress. The room was light. It must be morning.

Thirst made her tongue feel like a dried-up slug.

"Ulf," she whimpered, "can you wake up? I heard something."

He was on his side and his eyes were open, looking straight at her. She stretched out her finger and gently touched his forehead.

"You're alive, aren't you?"

A quick movement quirked his mouth.

"Did you hear it?"

He shook his head.

"There was something. Listen! You must have heard it. It sounded like church bells."

As she watched him sit up, she realized how sweaty she was. Her nightgown was completely damp. She felt chilled as she sat up.

"No," he said gruffly. "I don't hear anything."

"Well, it's gone now, but it was there. It seemed close by, as if a bell tower was right outside our bedroom door and someone was there pulling the ropes."

"Sorry," he said. "I didn't hear a thing."

"Then you must have still been asleep."

"I've been lying here dozing and thinking."

The phrase 'and thinking' made her uneasy. The previous night came back and she remembered everything.

"What time is it?" she mumbled.

"Almost seven."

"Seven. As much as I want to keep sleeping, and I need it, I don't think I can fall asleep again."

Ulf turned to lie on his stomach and placed one of his arms over her legs.

He was crying.

She moved carefully and snuggled close to his side with her head under his shoulder.

"Everything went so wrong yesterday," he said and his voice was gravelly. "Sometimes the words just come out so wrong . . . so ugly. Not the way a person wants."

She stroked his hair, and her lips brushed the inside of his neck.

"Why did this happen to us, Beth?" he asked. "How did things get so wrong between us? Do you have any idea?"

"That's just the way it is sometimes. Let's forget all about it."

"You mean, just repress it?"

She moaned slightly. Her face was turned into the pillow case and there was a smell on it, the smell of her own unwashed hair.

"My head hurts so much, Ulf. Don't you have a headache? It feels like my entire brain is just one big hurt!"

"It's the Madeira . . . or maybe the different kind of drinks we had."

"Maybe not."

She took his hand and pulled it toward her, down beneath her stomach.

"I really have a bad headache, too," he whispered.

"Lie on your back and I'll give you a massage," she said.

He lay with his head against her thighs. She felt slow and leaden. Her fingertips turned shiny as they massaged his forehead, went toward his nostrils, and then circled through his thick, curly hair. She realized that his eyebrows had changed. The hairs were longer and rougher. Her paternal grandfather had eyebrows like that. They stood straight out like screens shading a porch. She saw that Ulf's ears now had hair growing inside. She'd help him trim the hair away later. People couldn't do that by themselves.

"Is it nice?" she asked. "You like what I'm doing?"

The head between her thighs nodded. "You were always good with your hands."

She smiled slightly. She suddenly wanted an ice-cold soda.

"I'm going to take a shower at my parents' place."

"Damn! When were we supposed to get there?"

"Today."

"No."

"Really. We talked about it yesterday."

"I forgot."

"We have to go."

"Come on, do we have to?"

"Really, we do."

"Can't we just call them and say we can't make it?"

"You forgot to bring your cell phone, remember?"

"Well, we can drive until we find a phone booth."

"We'd have to call them right away, though. Old people get so confused when you change their plans."

Ulf didn't say anything.

"All right, if you get up and get dressed and drive to the nearest phone booth right away, then all right! But you have to do it."

"If that's the case, I guess we ought to go. But you have to drive."

"You're nuts."

"I can't drive. I'm still slightly drunk."

"As if I'm not."

"Well then, we can't go because neither of us can drive."

"Ulf, we can't do that. You know Pappa's been looking forward to our visit so much and he'd be so disappointed, what with Mamma's condition. . . . He has a living hell there."

Ulf shrugged his shoulders and wrenched his head away. She leaned forward and caught him, holding him tight.

"Come inside me, come inside me."

He laughed but with confusion.

"I mean it! I want you! Do it! Do it!"

He heaved himself up over her as his member stiffened, but he kept his eyes closed and when he came, he called out with a short, unfriendly sound.

7

ONCE THEY'D GOTTEN UP AND HAD COFFEE, THINGS FELT BETTER.
Beth had taken two pills for her headache but still felt as if she
were coming down with a cold. She was standing in the still-cool
kitchen, wearing her new sundress.

"How do I look?" she asked.

He peered at her and his eyes were shining.

"It's fine."

"Maybe it's not really the right color for me. Maybe I shouldn't
have bought it."

"No, no, it looks good."

They walked together into the garden. No birds, no sound except the rustling of the dried leaves as they were shed from the trees.
More than usual. The air was already hot. Ulf walked around the
entire house and checked the windows to make sure everything was
properly locked shut.

He looks so worn out, Beth thought. She threw out her arms and
fervently wished for rain. *Come, rain, please come, please come!*

Beth could not see the cat. Beth was always afraid that the cat or
one of its kittens would be hiding underneath the car and that either
she or Ulf would not notice as they drove away. She knelt down to
look, and the pain in her head slid forward.

"Green light," she called. "No cats."

He handed her the car keys.

"You still better drive."

Her parents' apartment was in a two-story building built in the thirties. Beth parked in the spot for visitors. This late, they should have brought something like a bouquet of flowers or a box of chocolates. Beth had had to drive fairly slowly and let people pass her. Nevertheless, she kept feeling faint and worried that she'd drive into the ditch. Ulf sat next to her with his eyes closed, and she felt irritated about that. Weren't they both just as tired?

Beth peered up at the windows of her parents' apartment. They had green curtains with large geometric figures, an ugly remnant of the seventies, from her parents' old house. The window panes were streaked with bird dirt. There were no plants on the windowsills, but there was a spiral mobile hanging from one of the curtain rods.

It reminded her of a swarm of flies.

Ulf was already out of the car and he slammed the door before walking around to her side. She saw that someone had raked a pattern in the rough gravel. A plantain stuck up from the ground. Her calves were so tired they felt tender and shaky.

"Well, let's go inside." Was it really her voice speaking? Was it really her own feet in those brown sandals?

"No way out of it now." His words came to her from far away as if they were tiny buzzing insects. She lifted one foot and fell over.

Gravel stabbed into her left knee.

She felt no pain.

His hand pulled her up and she found herself shaking her head. *No pain. I just fell, that's all.*

She didn't know if she'd managed to say it aloud.

The outside door was wide open. No soothing cool darkness. A piece of rug over the entry hall floor. Her hand on the handrail. Then her entire arm. Step by step she pulled herself up.

Ulf was close behind her.

"Your knee is bleeding, Beth."

"I'm okay."

"We'll have to clean that scrape out properly. You'll probably get it clean when you shower, though."

Her head was truly spinning now. She had to stop.

Beth had an old, white scar on that same left knee. That time she was still a child and she'd been biking around a curve when she fell. Just before that, she'd gone into a church and stolen some postcards. It was totally unusual behavior for her, plus she didn't really want the cards. One was a picture of Jesus with a halo and the other one was a black-and-white photograph of the church itself. Even though she didn't want them, she still took them.

As she got up in dusty silence, a sudden light, white and blinding, appeared over the ridge. She leaped up onto her bike, still pressing the postcards to her chest. They hadn't fallen from her hands even during her tumble.

A man in a flatbed truck had pulled up.

"Let me drive you home."

She didn't want that so she pressed her lips together and kept silent.

"You must be in shock if you can't talk. Don't worry, it's only temporary. It'll pass away."

The man spoke in short sentences. He had a rattling voice.

"Let me take you to the emergency room. I don't know where you live. And you're not saying a word."

He had a long, narrow face and a shaggy beard. He lifted the bicycle into the flatbed of the truck and then picked her up and placed her in the front seat. She saw a great deal of trash on the floor. Colorful candy wrappers. She still couldn't say anything. Still, he talked to her and he was kind.

"My name is Arne, what's your name?" he said. "I don't think that you've broken any bones. The best thing would be if we could contact your mother and she'd take over from here. But right now we don't know where she is, so we'll solve this problem another way. My fiancée works at the emergency room and I'll take you there. I found you, so, in a way, I have to be responsible for you."

She sat straight up in the seat and her one thought centered on the postcards. People would find out that she was a thief. She'd even stolen from God and the church. Her punishment would be awful.

It turned out that Arne's fiancée had gone to lunch, so Arne began to lose interest. She wished that she could start crying as a nurse led her into the examination room and lifted her up onto the examination table. No sound left her, not even a sniffle, and she made no attempt to get up and run away. Maybe this was part of her punishment, and if she got through this, maybe she would be forgiven just a little. The postcards were still in her hand.

"I have to wash you off just a bit." Hands that pried and turned so that she had to let go of the postcards. Once she saw the postcards lying on the floor, her words returned to her, and, with them, the ability to cry. She could hear her own voice as her pant leg was pulled up over her knee. They called Arne in, and he had to help hold her down. She cried and cried and felt afraid more from her own crying than from the actual pain.

They put in four stitches. She was able to tell them where she lived. Duvgatan 3.

"I'll drive her home," said Arne.

She walked with one leg straight. A tight bandage kept it warm.

"You've got a touch of shock," said Arne. He sat close to her and his hand held her to make sure she stayed in the truck.

"You better leave off the bicycling for a while."

He'd brought the postcards along, and after he helped her get down from the truck, he gave them to her.

She said that they weren't hers.

"Take them anyway."

She took them.

"Do you need me to come inside with you?"

"You don't have to."

"All right, if that's what you want."

Arne took down the bike and leaned it against the wall.

"It looks like the handlebars got pretty bent," he said a bit worriedly.

"Pappa can fix it," she said shortly. She wanted him to leave. She needed to be alone.

"Well, goodbye, then. Take care of yourself." He offered his hand and she noticed hair growing on his fingers, but she took his hand and shook it because she didn't know how to do anything else.

Pus showed up in the wound a few days later. She was wearing a small bandage by then, and it was barely attached anymore as the glue no longer stuck. She looked at the cold, sticky mess on her knee. Her class teacher noticed her picking at her wound, pulling threads of pus out. He gave her a pat on the head.

"Doesn't anyone take care of you at home?" he asked. Stern wrinkles formed around his nose. "Don't pick at that sore. It's disgusting."

The school nurse tended to her wound. As the nurse cleaned it and put on a hot compress, the pain made Beth start to cry.

Was the pain the real reason she was crying?

Each and every time she had to go to the nurse's office, Beth's throat would get thick and tears would well up, and she'd start crying again.

"This can't be hurting that much anymore," the nurse said with irritation as she touched Beth with clinically clean hands.

"It's not that. It's just that I have a stomach ache," she said before she could stop herself.

"So you have a stomach ache."

"Yes, I do."

"Does this stomach ache appear often? Like once a month perhaps?"

She nodded.

"How old are you now?"

"My birthday is in September."

"Let me take a look here. Born 1961. So you're going to be turning nine?"

She nodded.

The nurse's eyes were kind as she took a brochure from a cubicle on her desk.

"Read this when you get home. Having a stomach ache once a month is something entirely normal. There's nothing to worry about. You're just a little early compared to the other girls, but you're entirely normal."

8

HER FATHER STOOD IN THE APARTMENT DOORWAY. With the door open behind him, his hair was a white halo.

"I was watching through the window to see when you got here," he said. "Do you mind if I run out and do some shopping?"

"Right now?" Beth asked, as she stepped inside. Her father gestured as if he wanted to hug her, but he stopped himself and started pacing on the hallway rug.

"You see, we don't have anything in the house to eat.. I can't leave her home alone for even a minute."

"Are things really so bad? You can't leave her alone at all?"

"Well, sometimes when she's asleep. But these days you never know what she'll try next. And for a week, really, she hasn't slept much. Because of the heat, I guess. Do you know there's been no rain since May twenty-seventh?"

A vein in his eye had burst, leaving a red spot. Beth had trouble looking at it.

"Should I come with you?" she asked.

"Not necessary. Go see your mother instead and try to get her moving."

The apartment had three rooms and a large, square kitchen. Beth and Ulf went into the kitchen after Beth's father had gone. They could hear his footsteps on the gravel below. There was a coffee cup standing on the kitchen table. It had no saucer underneath. Some milk had spilled on the glossy tablecloth. Glasses and plates were piled up in the sink.

"He can't keep up with the work," Beth whispered. "He was always well-organized, but now . . . he just can't keep up with it all."

Ulf sat down by the window and opened up the newspaper, *Falköpings Tidning,* and then he began to read.

Beth found a glass in the cupboard and filled it with water. She drank.

Her mother was propped up on the high bed, which was heaped with pillows. She'd been trying to put on lipstick. There was lipstick on the sheets and her clothes. The lipstick had broken in half. Her wrinkled eyelids were covered in gold glitter, and her eyes moved stiffly below them. She was wearing a flowery nightgown and a fur boa was draped around her shoulders. It appeared to be a thin, slinky tail.

Beth moved up to the bed.

Her mother's room smelled of powder and lemon. It seemed as if her mother had not noticed Beth at first. Her mother picked up a hand mirror and began to look at her teeth. She began to poke at the spaces in her upper gum.

Beth sat down carefully on the bed. Her mother turned her head and gave Beth an apathetic, veiled look. Nothing in her face resembled the woman and mother that she'd once been.

Beth cleared her throat.

"Hi, Mamma," she said. "We're here. We've come to visit you."

The woman in the bed did not answer, but raised the mirror closer to her face and pulled at a hair growing from her chin. She jerked it out. She giggled.

"Mamma, it's me. It's Beth."

Her mother's pupils were turbid, her mouth a red slash.

"Are you the detective?"

"Mamma, what are you talking about?"

"Why didn't you get here sooner? I've asked for help, but you kept taking your time, just taking your sweet time. And before you know it, I won't have anything left."

Beth grabbed her wrist, which jangled from all the gold. Her mother's skin was cool and soft as silk.

"Mamma, it's me, Beth, your daughter. Don't you recognize me?"

Her mother continued as if Beth hadn't said anything.

"All the rings." Her mother's voice was deeper, more gravelly, more like a man's. "I've been looking and looking for them. Now I know that there are cameras everywhere and whenever I fall asleep, they come. The agents come and take my rings and my jewelry."

"Look, Mamma, you're wearing them. Your watch and your rings."

"Those agents, they come whenever I'm asleep. Don't try to fool me. I know what's going on. You see, I'm not stupid, no matter what you think!"

"Please, Mamma. What agents? What are you talking about?"

Ulf appeared in the doorway.

"How are you doing, Susanne?" he asked.

Her mother's eyes brightened. Her hands quieted.

"Why Ulf, my boy, have you come to visit an old lady?"

Beth stood up and waved Ulf in. At the same time, her mother whipped off the bedclothes and swung her legs over the side with unexpected agility.

"Come on, then, no time to waste!"

Beth's father returned with grilled chicken halves and potato salad. He'd also bought beer and juice. They sat down while he set the table. They'd already each had a cigarette on the balcony. Beth's mother was fully dressed. As they were about to start eating, Beth's mother leaned over to Ulf and whispered: "What kind of a person is this that you brought here?"

"But Mamma!" Beth exclaimed.

"Don't pay any attention to her," said her father. "And don't let it get to you. She's not the person she used to be."

Beth took her napkin and was about to wipe some lipstick from her mother's chin. A fork glistened and missed stabbing Beth's hand by a fraction of an inch. Her mother lost her balance and would have fallen if her father hadn't steadied her.

The woman who had once been Beth's mother looked at Beth with a cool glare.

"I've seen through you," she said. She lowered her voice. "I've seen what lies inside you, and it's not a pretty sight. It's a stinking, infected pustule."

"Mamma, stop it, you're making me unhappy."

"Let's eat!" Beth's father half-shouted in an almost angry voice. He used to sound like that after he'd come home from a hard day's work to find Beth and Juni fighting at the dinner table.

"Ejnar," Beth's mother said. "Ejnar, is this supposed to be the detective? Can you trust a woman like that?"

After dinner, once they started to drink some coffee, Beth's mother appeared to return to normal. However, her face was thinner and the bones around her eye sockets were sharp like the edges of a crater. Her hair was long but had thinned out so that in places the scalp was visible. This made her seem somehow vulnerable and defenseless.

"I know all of this is so hard on your father," she said. Tears ran down the furrows in her cheeks. "Your father is a real gentleman. A real and true gentleman."

"I know," Beth said as she stroked the back of her mother's hand. "I know what you mean."

They began a normal conversation, slowly at first, but then it moved right along. Beth's father asked how they were doing at the house and how long they intended to stay. He asked when Juni and her husband were planning to come. He already knew the answers, but he wanted to keep the conversation flowing.

"Juni looked so thin the last time I saw her," Beth's father said. "You don't think she might have some kind of serious illness, do you? You should know, Beth, if anyone does."

"I think she's just not eating the way she should," Beth replied.

"And how's Werner? What's he doing?" Werner was Juni's husband.

"We hardly ever see them these days. They're always working. They've got too much going on."

"I can understand if Werner is busy. Those people at the bank are always busy. But what's Juni doing to keep her so occupied? What's she up to?"

"She's a freelancer, Pappa. That means that she's always writing articles for all kinds of newspapers. There's one called *Metro* that she often has articles in. I don't think you've seen it, but it's a newspaper that they hand out for free in the city subway."

Her father turned toward Ulf. "For free? How can they do that?"

"The ads pay for it," said Ulf.

"That's strange."

"They have one in Gothenburg, too. And these kinds of papers are showing up abroad, as well."

"But I don't understand. You don't pay for it? So it has nothing but ads?"

"No, no, no, the ads just pay for it. They have real articles. In fact, there's been some fairly decent reporting in them. Sometimes I've managed to earn a few bucks selling an article to them, myself."

"Still, it has to cost something to put it out and pay the journalists and the printing costs and all."

"Well, they don't have any distribution costs. People pick them up in the subway."

"That is really strange."

Beth looked at her father. She noticed his long, beautiful fingers. He certainly could never have imagined this life in his old age. They should have taken trips together, played bridge, eaten well, enjoyed life. Beth had the desire to take her father in her arms and hug him for a long time. But they weren't really huggers in her family. They had little physical contact. He might become embarrassed or even angry.

Her mother suddenly got up from the table and went to the sofa, lifted the sofa cushions and peered underneath them. She began to mutter inaudibly to herself. Her voice increased in strength.

Beth's father looked tired. "She's started to search again."

"What's going on?"

"First and foremost, she usually looks for her jewelry. It's this searching which really is exhausting. She moves the furniture around and moves stuff so that in the end you can't find anything."

Beth took hold of her mother's skirt.

"Mamma, are you looking for your rings? See, you're wearing them! And you're wearing your watch, too. Can't you see that?"

The old woman's eyes shifted away and then jerked back.

"Are you trying to stop me?"

Beth looked at her father. Ulf got up from the table and walked over to the window.

"Don't pay any attention to her," Beth's father whispered. "You can't get through to her when she's like this."

Her father walked over to the sofa and took his wife by the shoulders.

"Susanne," he murmured, "are you tired? Why don't you take a bit of a rest?"

She fell into him with her cheek on his shoulder. A lock of white hair fell against her lips.

He spoke slowly, "Though I don't know if it's a good thing to let her sleep during the day, because then she can really get going at night. And then there are times when I really have to . . ."

"Pappa, do you think you can get her into a home?"

Her father fell silent, disapproving.

"But, Pappa, you must see . . . you can't keep going like this. You're not all that young yourself. If you find her a place, then you'll be more free. You can come and visit us in Hässelby. We can go to the Science Museum and do things that you enjoy. Maybe go to a concert or the theater."

"We'll have to see, Beth, we'll just have to wait and see. Take it one day at a time. And you see, I don't want to force things if I don't have to."

Her father helped her old mother lie down on the sofa. He lifted her legs up, and straightened out her stockings. Then he went to get a sheet and covered her carefully. Beth's mother lay there like a little girl.

"Should we have another cup of coffee?" he asked them.

"I don't know. We probably should get going," said Ulf.

"Yes, yes, of course, and by the way, I should warn you . . . I've read in the newspaper that some criminals escaped from Tidaholm prison. It said that they were very dangerous. So be careful out there."

"Yes, I saw that, too," said Ulf.

Beth got ready to go, but a chill went down her spine.

"How can a person just be careful? I mean, what should we be careful about? If they've escaped, what are we supposed to do . . . just say a prayer they don't break into our house?" She felt really upset.

Ulf stared at her and said, "The paper says they're armed and dangerous. How did they get weapons? You'd think they couldn't get any in prison, right? Let's just hope they're caught before they hurt anyone."

"Let me look at the paper," said Beth.

"See for yourself."

Her father picked up the paper and unfolded it. The headline screamed from the first page:

Dangerous prisoners on the run: Escaped from Tidaholm.

A thought of the kittens crossed Beth's mind, and she became uneasy.

"Let's get going."

9

TWO GIRLS WERE SITTING ON THE STAIRS AS THEY WALKED DOWN. They were so absorbed in their game. They only looked up when Ulf asked them to move. They each had their own toy horse with long, shiny manes.

"What are your names?" he asked, but they just stared shyly at him and didn't answer.

Once they were back in the car, Beth began to cry. Ulf didn't ask why but started the car and backed out of the parking space.

After a while, he said, "It's just too bad what's happened to Susanne. She's really gone downhill."

Beth sniffed.

"I feel sorry for Pappa."

"I feel sorry for both of them."

"True. But she probably doesn't know what's happening. Maybe she's happy and strong in her own little world."

"Maybe. It's a good thing none of us knows what the future holds."

Beth lit a cigarette.

"What if it's genetic?" Beth asked quietly. "What if I become just as crazy and confused as she is?"

"Don't worry. I'll just put you in a home," he laughed.

"You wouldn't dare. I know how to get back at you. No, I'm kidding. But let me tell you, sometimes she makes me afraid. That other person, that strange and frightening Susanne, must have been there the whole time. Deep inside, the whole time, that is, when we were small, Juni and me, and back when she met Pappa. But no one suspected a thing. That's what I find so horrible."

She thought back to the horrible incident earlier while Beth had helped her father do the dishes. Her mother had come into the kitchen, taken a package of milk from the refrigerator, and no one was able to stop her from emptying out the milk into the toilet, and then opening the box so she could pee into it. When her father tried to take it away from her, she hit him in the face with her fist. Beth saw tears spring up in her father's eyes.

As they drove, Beth said, "Maybe she doesn't have enough to think about. If only we could have given her grandchildren. Either Juni or me. It doesn't matter which one of us. That might have slowed down this process. Sometimes I really believe that."

She swallowed, then added, "At least I tried."

"*We* tried," Ulf corrected her.

"Yes, we tried. But Juni and Werner don't even want kids."

"What do you know about it? Maybe they did, but couldn't, and so they didn't want to talk about it."

"Juni doesn't like kids. She's told me many times that she doesn't understand them. But maybe she was just saying that to protect herself."

"Everybody wants kids!" he exclaimed.

Beth started crying again because she remembered that last day in the classroom. It had been hard coming home afterwards because the day had been so difficult. Even the air in the classroom had been stuffy. This gave her a headache. And then the kids were acting up and not paying attention, so that she finally whacked the pointer on the desk so hard it broke in half. One of the girls then began to shake and hyperventilate as if she were going into an epileptic fit. Beth was not able to calm her down.

It was a freshman class, and she hadn't known them all that long, but from the first day, the atmosphere in the classroom was defensive and even hostile. They were supposed to have had a different teacher, but she'd quit at the last minute. Beth should not have been placed as their homeroom teacher since she was about to go on maternity leave. Neither she nor the class deserved this, but there was no other choice.

Beth had left the classroom and gone to the principal. Her eyes were aching.

"I have to go home," she said. She placed her fingers on her forehead.

The principal, Carin Lagman, was sitting at her computer. Beth still remembered the blouse Carin was wearing that day. It had a pattern of horseshoes and stirrups.

"Oh my goodness, have you started labor?" Carin asked, worried.

"No, it can't be that. But I really don't feel well, and I have to go home."

"Should I ask someone to go with you?"

"No thanks. It's just that I have a really bad headache, that's all."

It had been a sunny, blustery day. The rowan trees had already lost their leaves, but the leaves on the birch trees were still green. Bus 119 had come fairly quickly, and she took it to Markviksvägen. Then she just had a quick walk up the hill. She felt tired as she opened the door. She remembered how the dust swirled in the rays of sunlight as she walked into her apartment. She felt heavy and leaden. The first contraction came as she was hanging up her jacket. It was much too early. She had just gone into the seventh month. She'd had some Braxton-Hicks contractions before, but this was something else. She realized that this was the real thing. She waited a moment and tried to breathe calmly and slowly. Then a second contraction came with such force and squeezed her spine so hard that she had to yell.

She called Ulf immediately. He was off reporting some event and no one knew when he was going to get back to the office.

"What's his assignment?" she asked, sniffling.

"He's at the Swedish Academy, waiting for the announcement of the winner of the Nobel Prize in Literature."

"But I've gone into labor!" she exclaimed.

They promised to send him home the minute he returned. Besides that, they couldn't help her. No one could help her. She would have to get through this on her own. She'd felt strong and happy before, waiting for this moment.

She had never imagined that it would be so painful.

She called for a taxi. The driver was a large, calm man who had red hairs poking out of his nostrils.

"We're gonna get you to the hospital on time, honey," he said to comfort her. "But if not, we'll get through this, because right here you got all the expertise you need! I'll just pull over and if the babies come out before the ambulance gets here, I'll catch 'em! I've done it before and it went just fine."

"What was it, a boy or a girl?" she panted.

"A little guy. A boy. But that wasn't here, that was in Köping. The paper came and took a picture of us. I still got that picture in my wallet. I'll show you if you wanna see it. It's the Mom, the little guy, and me. It looked like I was the proud papa! She said she was gonna name the boy after me, but I don't know if she really did. But it's a nice thought, and I really appreciated it."

Beth imagined that he was expecting her to ask him what his name was, but a new contraction forced her backwards and made her press her teeth against her lower lip.

She remembered the entrance to the maternity ward. A patient was inside, wearing a thin, knitted sweater. She was holding her back and had a glassy expression. Beth tried to catch her eye, but it seemed as if a veil was drawn over the woman's face. She was entirely occupied with what was happening to her and her unwieldy body.

Ulf must have appeared around that time.

Ulf, her beloved husband and friend. He must have arrived by then and he stayed with her the entire time. First the rest of that day, then the entire night, and then the following day until midnight. She remembered that he didn't even try to take a nap. Once he ate a banana, and she remembered the smell, which made her nauseous. She was also nauseated by the banana mush in his mouth when he said something. Just the sound made her irritated and mean.

The twins were born at ten that second night. Her labor had lasted more than thirty hours. The babies were tiny and incomplete.

They both were marred by large, ugly birthmarks. One had the birthmark on its left chin and the other had it on the throat.

It was as if they'd been stamped: Unacceptable!

Then all the questions started coming to her. Why did this have to happen to her and to Ulf of all people? Two babies that were not meant to live. So unjust, so cruel. And why? Maybe there was something wrong with their baby hearts. Maybe it was just that their hearts were too small and unfit. Things must have started to go wrong already at the embryo stage. Her inner being was shaken. There must be something wrong with her. She was not good enough. She'd given birth to animals, not people. Animals with beaks and gills.

She was never pregnant again. No one was able to explain to her why. Maybe something closed her down. Maybe her fear was like a big, insurmountable wall. Her fear that this same trauma could happen again.

Immediately after the birth, Beth started to mentally separate herself from the babies. She was wiped out and sick. She'd seen in the faces of the people around her that something had gone terribly wrong. She'd watched the midwife tense up and turn away, busying herself with putting away the medical supplies.

Beth didn't ask any questions, which seemed to make things easier for everyone.

Much later, she'd regretted that, but of course it was too late.

She wished that she'd been able to hold them, to look closely at them and let her fingertips examine the contours of their bodies, and not be afraid of their birthmarks.

She'd wanted to name the girls while they were still in her body. Nice, modern names like Alexandra and Frida. Maybe they would have lived if they'd been given their names, she thought.

Ulf didn't think so. She and Ulf were different in so many ways. That became clearer and clearer to her in the following months.

10

ULF DROVE THE CAR ONTO THE ROAD THROUGH THE FOREST. It was really not a true road but rather a path which had been driven on, bumpy roots and all. Beth surveyed the blueberry bushes. There wouldn't be many berries this summer, and the ones she could see were already shrunken and dried out.

Then she caught sight of a moving shadow, something gray, and she gripped Ulf. Her voice was strained and hoarse. Ulf stopped the car.

"What did you see?" Ulf asked.

Beth shivered in the heat.

"I don't know . . . maybe it was an animal . . . maybe it was the cat, Lioness."

"Well, what the hell do you think it was? Did I run over it?"

"No, no."

Ulf turned off the engine and started to get out of the car. This terrified her.

"Drive!" she yelled. "Just drive! Let's just get back home! I'm tired, that's all, just tired deep into my bones."

They each poured a glass of whisky. Beth sat on the stairs. The sun was on the other side of the house, but the evening was still hot. She felt her muscles beginning to relax.

"*Well, that's that,*" she said, and let the edges of her mouth turn up to make a smile.

She thought that Ulf was standing behind her, but when she turned, she saw she was alone.

She hummed a bit, but the tone was hoarse and false.

"Lioness!" she called. "Here, Lioness! Here, kittens! Kitty-kitty-kitty! Where are you, kitties?"

She heard the sound of a crow from far up in the woods. Many crows lived in the forest, and always had. You could sometimes see their silhouettes against the sky. Crows lived in life-long relationships. He and she, *Corvus corax*. In the stairwell leading to the second floor, there was an engraving of a crow. Her mother had found the picture in a magazine and put it into a frame.

"Crows feed on offal and carcasses and they caw about strife and death," her mother had told her.

Beth thought about her mother, who had grown up here. When her mother had been a child, the fruit trees in the yard had just been planted. Now the trunks were covered with lichen and moss. No one took care of them any more through pruning the dead branches or removing the spider nests. It was melancholy to think about, but not much anyone could do about it. Many old houses were just left to fall apart. At least this house could come alive a few months every year.

The silence began to disturb her. She took a mouthful of whisky and shivered.

"Ulf!" she called. "Where are you, Ulf? What are you up to?"

He came around from the other side of the house, his lips, a thin, firm line. He looked strange. Beth stood up, holding her breath.

Ulf put a finger to his lips. She stared at him, her heart beating. "What's wrong?"

He was now right next to her, but he did not turn to embrace her and he kept totally silent. At that moment, she saw what he must have seen. Something was by the storage shed. Movement. A figure. Beth grabbed Ulf's arm so tightly that the whisky spilled from her glass.

11

NSANE WRATH, ANCIENT AND POWERFUL, COULD BREAK OUT FROM
DEEP WITHIN HER.

It came upon her now.

She marched across the lawn. A pillar of strength had formed
inside her, and her anger and rage wrapped around that pillar. She
said nothing, but a growl began in her throat, and it gained in power
with every step she took.

A stranger had dared to come onto her land. A dangerous, evil
criminal who had escaped from prison and who had already broken
into her house once before. The thought that he might be armed
did not even enter her mind. Her brain was no longer rational and
controlled. Only one thought boiled within it:

Attack and defend!

Ulf was a man, and this was usually a man's role, but she had become
the strong one now and he followed her, perhaps in order to hold her
back. That made her even angrier.

As she passed the woodshed, she pulled the axe from the stump
with one jerk. It hung heavy and secure in her hand as she neared the
storage shed. She heard everything with the utmost clarity.

Just let anyone try and stop her!

Just let him dare!

Her rage rose to boiling, and although she was stepping on net-tles with her bare feet, she felt no pain. She pushed the door open with her hip and went in.

Inside.

Yes.

There he was.

Just as she knew he was. He had a large, swaying body. He took a step toward her as if to stop her. Or maybe to hurt her. His hands gripped her, held her throat, throttled her. A brief moment of feel-ing faint.

"You devil!" Her voice rose to a roar. Was it her or was it him? He was gripping her hard now, and he writhed before her eyes, and she screamed and screamed, but not from fear. Her right knee jammed his balls. He flinched but did not let go. Then he fell back-wards, breathing hard, and she was free.

Maybe she could have stopped then. If only she had done so, stopped at that moment and been content. If only Ulf hadn't fol-lowed her, maybe she would have stopped right there.

From the corner of her eye, she saw the stranger pull himself together. He was getting ready to attack and he was angry. She was still standing there and so he had every intention . . .

Air rushed into her lungs and she lifted the arm holding the ax and she turned the ax so the edge was ready to come down and then the edge came down right into his forehead.

The noise was a dull thud.

This was not real.

12

S O THERE IT WAS.
  Silence. Not even a fly, an insect, a sparrow.
Not even the trace of a breeze through the tree tops.
Beth stood there, the ax in her hand. Her lip had split.
He was in my territory. He had evil intentions.
Ulf appeared. Poor Ulf. She realized with sorrow that Ulf was
to be truly pitied.
Look at me. The thought went through her.
Ulf's mouth was agape, twisted and swollen and he pulled at his
eyebrows with fluttering fingers.
Ulf said nothing. He asked no questions. He stared at the floor
and slowly began to shake.
The stranger had collapsed at her feet. There was blood on Beth's
knees and blood splattered on the wall. She looked at his forehead
and the two tiny pieces of bone which had fallen out and which had
mixed into the mess on the floor. She noticed the colors: red and
gray.
This was not real.
The stranger was lying on the floor with one arm askew. He was
wearing a plaid shirt.
Details began to sink in. Brown pants. No socks poking out from
his sneakers. Red, sticky hair. No, not red, his hair was blond. He

was on his back staring straight up. Not seeing. His eyes were like a doll's. Then red flowed over them.

She saw that fluid was coming out of his mouth. Many times his arms jerked. Spasms. His thumbs bent inwards. There was no heaving from his chest. No sigh, no last words. Just slippery blood and steam.

Beth had to pee, but her legs were like stone. She closed her eyes and let the urine run hot though her underwear. She began to breathe more normally. Then the shaking started. Her legs shook so hard they knocked together. She wanted to say something, but words were meaningless. A vision of a chain of swallows set high in the wide, light blue sky. Ulf looked like a cardboard figure.

Earlier whisky had made her head spin, but it wasn't spinning now. Nor was she calm. She had to let her brain have time. Her brain needed time so that it could begin to form words again. She turned with difficulty toward the door. Ulf was still standing in the entryway, looking like a sick, elderly man.

"Who is he? He's dead, isn't he?" Ulf's voice. She heard his voice and realized that he had been talking for some time. Or maybe he was just thinking out loud.

She had no idea.

Her voice was broken and splintered: "He . . . killed me."

Ulf stumbled toward her and went down on his knees next to the stranger and began to pull at the stranger's clothes.

"Help me! He has to get air! Then run and call for help!"

She fell to her knees next to Ulf. She felt dizzy. She felt her nails pull at the plaid shirt. Ulf bent forward with his ear to the man's chest. He yelled at her. "Shut up! I can't hear! Shut the fuck up so I can listen!"

I wasn't saying anything, was I? She thought. She was shaking so hard that she put her hands between her knees to keep them still.

"Damn it all, I don't hear anything!" Beth watched him lean over the man's mouth and saw their mouths meet. The man's legs jerked. He stretched his legs and his toes in his worn-out shoes pointed downward.

He's still alive! Beth began to laugh hysterically. Her laugh bayed and screeched.

Ulf stopped what he was doing. Blood covered his hair and there was blood around his nose. He looked at her and her laughter turned to tears. The man was totally still now. He was not breathing. She noticed that he was wearing a watch. She watched Ulf's fingers slide under the leather band and search for the man's pulse. Beth slithered backwards quickly.

"Beth . . . ," he whispered. He was shaking and shivering so that he could hardly speak. "You've got to run inside and call . . ."

She heard him but only noticed the rhythm of his words: *run inside, run inside, run inside*. She sat on her hands and did not move.

They lifted their feet as they stepped over the threshold. Outside, the ants crawled past in long, brown lines. Ulf shut the door behind them. He looked around as if trying to find something to lock the door, but found nothing. Instead, he slammed against the door with his shoulder.

Beth fell forward among the nettles and vomited over the dried-up, brown plants. She noticed chunks of chicken and tomato, with a liquid of whiskey and beer.

Her entire head was ringing.

Ulf did nothing to help her as she crawled on all fours among the nettles. She hyperventilated, and when Ulf began to walk toward the house, she could only crawl after. He sat down on the stairs, and she rolled over, screaming and howling, beating her fists on the ground.

Ulf stared right into her eyes. He leaned over to touch her. She fell silent.

His hands grabbed her and shook her.

"He . . . kill . . . killed . . . me."

"No, Beth, no he didn't."

"He strangled me. I'm strangled."

Ulf slid down next to her in the grass and hid his head behind his arms. He curled inward, into a fetal position as she wailed.

"He just stood there and he strangled me! He did! He did!"

"What are we going to do, Beth? What are we going to do?"

She could only repeat the same sentence, her defense: He killed me. He was the one.

Finally, she pulled herself together a little and began to crawl again. She reached the stairs and pulled herself up. The whisky bottle was still there, as well as her glass. She undid the cork and wanted to pour herself a drink, but her hands were shaking too much. She lifted the bottle directly to her lips and took a large swallow. When she put the bottle down again, it was covered in blood.

Sharp, still, calm.

She wanted Ulf to be near her, but she did not want to go back that way. Her voice was tiny, like that of an animal, as she called to him. He came and she gave him the bottle and heard the glass clink against his teeth.

Twilight had come. Again Beth heard the cawing of the crows, but she refused to look at the sky. Her throat hurt as if she had been screaming loud and long. That man had touched her and certainly left marks on her neck.

"What time is it?" she asked. Her words were tense, but the tone had returned to normal.

Ulf did not answer.

"We have to go to the police, Ulf. It's our duty to go to the police."

She watched him turn his head toward her. She had a glimpse of his face and his hair covered with spider webs. She wanted to reach up and pluck them away, but her arm was too heavy to move. Her weight pulled her to the earth – down, down to the grass and the earth.

As soon as she came to, she remembered everything.

"You fainted," said Ulf.

"Everything turned black. But I remember everything."

Ulf did not ask if she had hurt herself.

"We've been drinking. We can't drive," she said.

"No, we can't," he said.

"There was supposed to be two of them."

"Two of what?"

"Prisoners."

"What are you talking about?"

"What the hell!" she exclaimed. "Have you suddenly gotten stupid?"

"Those prisoners wouldn't have stuck together. They would have split by now."

"How would you know?"

"I really think the other one's long gone."

"Where would he be, then?"

"No idea. Probably went straight to hell."

"Well, what should we do, then?"

"Don't ask me."

"Who else am I *supposed* to ask?"

Ulf sat still but scraped his fingernail against the stone stairs. Some kind of yellow lichen had started to grow on them. Neither one of them looked toward the shed. Beth felt a mosquito land on her hand and start to suck. She let it be as she watched its body grow larger and darker from her blood.

"What time is it?" she asked again.

"Twenty to ten."

"We have to sober up. If we show up at the police station like this, they'll arrest us for drunk driving."

"All right, let's sober up, then."

They climbed inside the house. Ulf walked through again, making sure everything was locked.

The cat was outside and they could see her white face in the twilight. She was looking at them and meowing loudly.

"Go home!" Beth yelled. "Go home! We don't want you around any longer! Get out of here, stupid cat!"

It took them a long time to wash under the faucet. They stuck the bloody clothes into the Swedish tile oven and burned them. Then they fell onto the sofa, one at each corner.

Beth was wearing nothing but underwear, and she felt cold. She wrapped the blanket around herself, and didn't mind that it was scratchy and made her itch. Her legs were still damp from the urine, and it chilled her. She began to have goose bumps, and then she began to shiver.

"Ulf, I think I'm going to throw up."

Ulf was staring at the rug.

"Are you listening to me? I think I'm going to throw up!"

Ulf did not move a muscle.

"Ulf, let's go tomorrow," she whispered. "As soon as we wake up, let's leave this place as soon as possible. Go talk to the police. Only be here long enough to have a cup of coffee and then we're out of here."

The word *coffee* brought a wave of nausea, and Beth had to run for the kitchen and lean over the sink. Afterwards, she drank some water and washed her hands thoroughly. She kicked off her underwear.

There was a mirror in the kitchen. She leaned toward it to take a good look at her neck. She expected to find marks of fingers, but there was nothing. The kitchen was dark, so she turned on the light to have a better look.

Nothing there. Smooth skin without a wound.

She grabbed her own neck and pressed as hard as she could, ripping her skin with her fingernails.

"He strangled me," she said, and she was much calmer now. Much calmer.

13

THE MORNING WAS COOL, BUT THE DAY WAS SUPPOSED TO BE JUST AS HOT AS ALL THE OTHER DAYS. Neither Beth nor Ulf had slept. They sat in their corners on the sofa the whole night through. Every once in a while, Beth would lean her head back until it hit the wall, and she would doze. But each time she shut her eyes, the man's ear was there, just the ear with blood and brains oozing out. Finally, she had to get up and turn on the lights, even though dawn had come. She brought something to drink, and they drank in silence.

They sat on the sofa and smoked and did not care that they were smoking inside. The ashtray was filled to the brim with stubs.

She would turn her head toward Ulf and whenever he shut his eyes, she asked him quickly if he was asleep. She did not want him to fall asleep and leave her feeling totally alone.

Ulf finally answered. "No, Beth. I'm not sleeping."

Beth felt as if she had slept enough for the rest of her life. She felt overcome by sorrow.

"Do you still love me?"

It was the wrong question at the wrong time, and she knew it. Ulf closed his eyes again. Beth turned her head toward the window, thinking she had seen something. A twig scraped against the glass.

Beth shuddered and thought that she would throw up again. Her stomach was empty. What if the man was breaking into the house now? What if he had come to? What if he had gotten up and staggered toward the house? She would open the door to invite him inside. She would run her hands through his hair. *Take me, do what you want with me*, she'd say. *Underneath this dress I am completely naked.* He would look her over, and the wound in his forehead would not be deep. Just a little scrape, that's all. *I can wash away the blood if you want me to. Why don't you just have a seat. Lean on me. I am good at taking care of people. Just ask Ulf. Ulf has known me for years and can vouch for me . . . . I really didn't mean to harm you . . . really, I didn't . . . you must realize this.* Then he would come right up to her and she would be able to smell his sour breath. '*So you know how to take care of people,*' he would say. He took her by the neck and bent her like a bow. His head right next to her mouth and her ear. Beth struggled for breath and started to scream.

The day was going to be hot, but Beth decided to wear jeans and a sweater with fringe on the long arm sleeves. Ulf was in the bathroom, and Beth could make out low rumbling sounds as if he were crying.

Beth started to brew some coffee and kept walking over to the window again and again. The shed appeared normal. A sparrow was on the roof, shaking its tail and taking tiny prancing hops.

Beth leaned against the wall and blew on her cup of coffee.

Ulf entered the kitchen.

"I made some coffee," Beth said, thinly.

Ulf did not reply, but did pour himself a cup from the machine.

Beth forced herself to breathe.

"We have to go to the police, now," she said. "They ought to be grateful that we've taken care of one of their prisoners. Risking our lives. He was going to kill me. He probably felt threatened when I appeared."

"You came at him with an axe, Beth."

"The axe was right there. I needed it for self-defense."

Ulf nodded mechanically.

"Yes. You took it for self-defense."

"I'm freezing," she said. "I think fall is coming early."

Ulf snorted. Scorn was in his eyes.

"In fact, we've done society a favor," she said, swiftly. "An awfully big favor! That's what we've done! Risking our own lives. In fact, we should sue the police department! Sue the entire prison system! They can't keep their lousy prisoners . . . so that we normal, honest people . . ."

Ulf drank the last drops of coffee.

"Come on, let's go and get this shit over with."

Ulf was going to drive. He floored it while the engine was in neutral, and a large stream of black smoke came out of the muffler and covered the grass. The car lurched. Beth hissed at him: "*What the hell are you doing?*"

"Why don't you drive, then?"

Once they got on the road, the motor ran more smoothly, but every once in a while, it coughed as if it were about to go on strike. She wanted to say something, but realized she had no words. She wanted no thoughts, nothing in her brain. She turned on the radio. She noticed Ulf grimaced, but he did not ask her to turn it off, even though his Adam's apple moved up and down.

The music was some kind of dance band music, and it beat against her temples.

Will she ever enjoy music again? Would she ever be able to put a nice Mozart CD into the player and relax as the music streamed over her? Would she ever be able to enjoy anything that had been part of her life ever again?

Her life! Rage began to bubble up inside her. She closed her eyes and pushed her thumbs over her lids.

"What should we say when we arrive at the station?" she said after some time has passed.

"That's entirely up to you."

She reacted as if she'd been punched.

Numbly, she asked, "Can you turn on the heat?"

"Have you lost your mind? It's already one hundred degrees in here!"

"Please. I'm freezing."

He did as she asked.

She lit a cigarette.

"They're going to ask us a ton of questions," he said with anger in his voice. "Don't you get it? They're going to ask each of us separately."

"Well, so what if they do?"

"So what if they do," he mimicked.

"We're going to say the same thing."

"You think?"

"Well, what are you going to tell them, Ulf? How do you plan to tell them what happened?"

"I'm going to say . . . damn it, give me a cigarette, too."

She dug a crooked one from the pack and looked for the lighter, which he'd once given her. Her initials were engraved in the silver: B. S. for Beth Svärd. She'd received it three years ago on her thirty-fifth birthday.

"All right," Ulf said. "We saw that someone had snuck into our shed. We'd already had someone break into the house, and we'd heard about the two prisoners who'd escaped from jail."

"No! We can't say that!" Beth exclaimed. "If we say anything about the prisoners, those guys had weapons! And then we wouldn't have gone out to the shed, we'd have locked ourselves in the house!"

"Indeed," Ulf said, stiffly.

"Please, Ulf," she whined.

"That's what we should have done! They'll ask why we didn't. They might even bring up something like *excessive force*."

"He attacked me!" Beth screamed. "That fucking idiot jumped me the minute I entered the shed! He tried to choke me to death! Let's say I was in the yard chopping some wood, or maybe I went into the yard intending to chop some wood . . . and then I saw something behind the shed door and when I carefully entered, he attacked me and tried to strangle me . . . but I managed to lift the axe and . . . you came . . . and you saw how he fell . . . how he let go of me and fell to the ground."

Beth stopped talking and instead began to sniff and then began to cry. She let her hands fall to her lap. She wanted to light another cigarette. Her hands began to shake, so that she had to use both of them to steady her fire.

Ulf hit her on the leg without even looking away from the road. "Calm down, damn it!"

"It feels as if you're not on my side. As if you're not covering my back!"

"I'm on your side."

"Really?"

Ulf nodded.

"Are you sure?"

"I'm on your side. So, you went out to the yard to chop some wood. But why would you want to chop wood when it's so damn hot?"

"The water heater is broken and we needed some hot water. People always need hot water."

"Well, if they come out, and they are going to come out, they'd see that we had a large wood pile already."

"All right, let's say something near the truth. We share the house with my sister, and we share the chores, and we need wood for when the weather turns colder. That's not hard to understand."

"That makes sense."

"And now it was your turn," Ulf continued. "We're a modern couple and a modern woman can chop wood as well as a man. We'll use that, and that will get them on our side. And there you are, with the axe in your hand, ready to chop wood when you see something in the shed. It looks like a person . . . so you go over there to ask what he wants, and you don't think it's dangerous. You just happen to have the axe in your hand as you walk over there."

Beth nodded. "And when I get there, he leaps out at me and grabs me by the throat . . . you can still see the marks . . . and they can send me to their fucking technicians if they have to."

"I wouldn't swear if I were you. It gives a bad impression. Be calm and collected. Well, not collected, because they wouldn't expect you to be . . . but just don't swear."

"Sorry."

They'd come up behind a truck. Ulf prepared to pass. As he swung back into their lane, the news came on the radio.

"The Tidaholm police department reports the capture of the escaped prisoners from Tidaholm prison. The capture went off without a hitch. Both men were hungry and exhausted after hiding in the forest for four days, so they turned themselves in. They surrendered their weapons, two Sig-Sauer pistols, to the police. The men have now been returned to jail."

14

At Tidaholm city limits, Ulf stopped at a gas station and they could see the headlines revealing what they'd just heard on the news:

Escapees Caught!

They bought copies of every newspaper and sat in the car reading them. Beth felt as empty, as if someone had peeled her insides with a potato knife to cut her inner organs clean away. She had the taste of iron in her mouth.

Ulf placed the newspapers aside and leaned his head on the steering wheel with his arms dangling loose.

"Now the hounds of hell are after us," he whispered.

Beth could hear her own heartbeat's regular, dull strength. She wanted to open all the car doors and start screaming. Beth touched Ulf with her ice-cold fingertips. She petted his hair and his shoulder. He jerked up straight.

"If it's not one of those prisoners, who the hell is lying dead in our shed?" Ulf asked numbly.

Beth yawned, but not from being tired. She needed oxygen, warmth, life.

Ulf raised his voice.

"Beth! You've killed a total stranger! An innocent fellow human being! Beth, you're now a murderer . . . a murderer!"

At that, Beth opened the car door, jumped out, and began to run. She'd left her shoes on the floor of the car, so she ran with the soles of her feet crunching the stones of the pavement. She kept running. Bits of gravel dug into her heels. In spite of the pain, she kept running.

She noticed that people were stopping to stare at her. Someone called out. It seemed to her as if they were a wall around her. She was running a marathon, and although they didn't yet know it, they soon would grab her with their pure, small-town hands and their faces would screw up as they pulled out chunks of her hair.

"You killed him! He was one of ours and you murdered him! Murderer! Murderer! Murderer!"

She kept running until she could run no more. A wooden fence hit her in the stomach. The creek, smooth as glass, was down the slope beyond and she watched it placidly flow past stones and through clumps of grass.

The car slid up behind her and then the door was opened.

"Jump in!"

Ulf was angry now. It was rare to see him so passionate. She was going to shake her head no, but she thought better of it, and, with bowed shoulders, she got into the car.

Ulf was angry all right.

"What the hell?"

She brushed off her feet and noticed how white and ripped up her nails were.

Ulf growled: "What the hell is the matter with you?"

She adjusted the passenger seat until it was completely flat. She lay down and closed her eyes.

"Just drive," she said with a mouth that seemed made of broken leather shreds.

His voice was thick and strange, too, as if his palate were misshapen. As if his tongue were covered by blisters and fungus. As if it were almost too difficult to speak.

"Where would you like me to drive?"

"East of the sun and west of the moon."

Ulf turned the car around.

A memory shot back, clear as if it were yesterday, but splintered like a kaleidoscope. She was twenty years old. She'd decided to make herself appear child-like, her hair in braids, even her eyebrows dyed brown. Of course, this tactic did not work. She'd imagined he'd feel sorry for such a sweet young thing, more a girl than a woman, but she realized her mistake right away. It gave the inspector even more of an upper hand. He could not be influenced. He stared at her through his silver-framed glasses and gave her orders while hissing at her. He scared her. She was afraid, and so she lost her concentration.

Ulf and Beth drove back to the house. Neither one of them could think of anything else to do. Halfway home, they stopped at the side of the road, as they both had to pee. As she squatted in the dry grass, she noticed that he was watching her. She kept squatting and let it all run out. It was a great relief.

"I'm not feeling so well," said Ulf, and his normal tone of voice had returned. "Could you please drive the rest of the way back?"

Ulf went to lie down in the passenger seat just as she had done. She sat down in the driver's seat next to him.

"Ulf," she said, pleadingly.

He opened his eyes.

"I do love you, Ulf."

"I know."

"Let's not let anything come between us. Let nothing . . ."

"Yes."

"Not even all this."

"Just shut the fuck up and drive already."

The cat lay on her side, with her nursing kittens, on the front porch. They noticed her as they turned into the driveway. The cat and her kittens stood up and arched their backs.

Beth went around to the back door. She lifted a pitcher of water directly to her mouth and let the cool liquid cascade out over her gums and teeth. Water ran down her neck and over her sweater.

Through the window, she saw Ulf heading toward the shed. Goose bumps sprang up on her arms. She slowly walked up the stairs and took off her damp sweater. She stood on the rug for a moment, rubbing her eyes. She heard Ulf coming back into the kitchen. Then the sound of vomiting.

She pulled on a T-shirt and sat down on the bed, too numb to react. Did he call for her or not? Did he call her name? Her neck burned like hot metal.

Ulf came upstairs at last. He was old. She was old. Their limbs ached. They were slow and heavy, and they could no longer run up the stairs quickly. Their hair had thinned, and their skin was dry and wrinkled. She didn't need a mirror to know this. She touched her cheek and felt her tough, tight skin.

He sat down on the edge of the bed and let himself fall backwards. He was still sniffling roughly and brokenly, but eventually he could find words.

"He's still out there. The body is right where we left it. Lots of blood, too. There's a dead man in our shed and it's not some nightmare. It's all too true. We have to do something and we have to do it now. Either we drive back into town . . . or . . . if we don't . . . we must . . . before someone discovers it . . . we don't have a great deal of time left. We don't have any time at all."

She was lying on the bed and she nodded toward the ceiling.

"Who is he?" Ulf wondered. "His people are going to start looking for him soon."

"Be quiet!" Beth hissed. "I don't want to think about his having a family!"

"Somebody will be missing him sooner or later."

"We'll figure out something by then."

Ulf was extremely pale, and sweat dripped from his nose.

His weakness made her feel strong.

"Ulf, we're going to take care of this. We'll get rid of him and then we'll get out of here. We will never, ever have to return to this place."

"Of course we'll return. If we don't, people will start to wonder why. And then they'll jump to conclusions, and you know how gossip gets around."

"We don't have any neighbors."

"There are other houses around here. There are farmers and other summer visitors. People who come here just like we do."

"All right, all right. We'll think about that later. First we have to get rid of . . . what's out there. I mean, the body. No one will ever have to know. Let's think about this rationally and practically. Why should we go to the police and report something that really never should have happened? It will ruin our lives and we'll end up . . . in prison. You, too, for aiding and abetting."

"Oh, Lord," said Ulf.

"People disappear all the time. How many thousands of people vanish and never reappear? That man out there . . . he can become one of them."

Ulf gave her a confused look.

"You and I are the only ones who know, Ulf," she pleaded.

"*If* no one saw us," he said numbly. "Or maybe someone did and wants to blackmail us."

"Not very likely. There's not a soul around here. I'm one hundred percent sure of that." She was completely strong now. "All we have to do is get rid of all the traces and of course the . . . body."

"How?"

"Well, we can burn it up."

"No," he said. "There's a burn ban for the whole area. The fire department and the police would be on us. . . . ." His voice turned sarcastic, "Yes, fantastic idea, to burn up the body and bring everyone around. Try and think for a change."

"Hmm, how about bringing him to the chalk pit? Just leave him there? Or maybe say that we found the body there when we were out hiking?"

"What the fuck! No! They'd trace it to us in no time. And he's too heavy for us to carry out there, so we'd have to drag him and that would leave traces. Make a drag mark. The police technicians would figure us out in no time. Not to mention that anyone could see us at any time! All sorts of people take walks in the forest."

"What are we supposed to do, then?" she yelled. "Do you have any bright ideas?"

Ulf sat up in the bed and sighed.

"We'll just have to bury him right here. A deep fucking grave that we can stuff him into."

15

THEY FOUND A USABLE SPOT JUST BEYOND THEIR PROPERTY LINE. It was partially hidden by bushes and a few tall birch trees. The ground was tightly covered by meadow foxtail growing in tangled strands. Twigs and branches, partially rotten, had fallen there. They broke apart when touched.

They'd each gotten a shovel from the garden tools in the shed, but left the door firmly shut. They'd wedged a doorstop in front of it, and Beth wished there was a lock and key.

The minute Beth stuck her shovel into the earth, she knew she was in for a difficult job. It seemed impossible to dig. The soil was as hard as cement. She could not get the shovel more than one centimeter deep. She'd put on boots for this task and now she stood leaning on the handle and felt as if the heat was suffocating her. She watched Ulf, who was a few feet away. He hacked at the ground. The blade bent from the strain.

"This isn't going to work," Beth whispered. "This will take weeks and weeks."

Ulf bent down and brushed away a branch.

"Don't be so damned negative," he said.

Beth lifted the shovel and forced it down with all her strength. The tough grass shielded the ground like a rug. Beth's hands were already forming blisters. She went to get a pair of gloves.

If I just count to fifty, she thought. *After I count to fifty, maybe I'll have gotten somewhere.*

Ulf was already piling up a heap of soil and clay which was so dry it started to fall apart right away. Ulf went to find a poker and a scuttle.

A forceful jab with the poker, then a scoop with the scuttle.

Beth noticed stones and roots. *This patch of earth had never been disturbed, or, rather, hardly disturbed,* she thought, as she picked up a flattened beer can and scraped it so that the gold-like metal glittered. She threw the can behind her. Ulf handed her the scuttle along with a cruel glance as he said, "You're certainly good at using tools."

She closed her ears to his comment as she scraped away the dirt, leaving white scratch marks on the stones. She jabbed the poker into the ground and turned it as tears welled up in her eyes from sheer exhaustion. She hacked, hacked, hacked, slowly deeper and deeper, as the afternoon turned into evening.

It seemed an eternity for the hard clay earth to break into smaller, sharp-edged pieces. Eventually there was a smell of kerosene and moisture. Beth could sit on the edge of the hole while she hacked, resting her knees.

Ulf went to get some water. Beth drank it and felt the ache in her wrists and the soreness in her buttocks and even her ankles. There were blisters all over her hands, both on her palms and in the spaces between her thumbs and her fingers. This earth was stubborn, resisting as if it did not want any extra burden. Beth noticed a round grub, which rolled up when she touched it. There was a single earthworm, pale and thin, which did not move as she cast it on the pile. This useless soil was good for just one thing.

Twilight came. They ought to have eaten something, and Beth was tortured by visions of food: hamburgers, pea soup, crisping bacon in the pan. These visions made her weak and dizzy, but she did not feel hungry. Instead, waves of nausea swept over her and she had to hurry and think of something else.

But with the twilight came a cooling breeze. Everything became easier to do. Although they were tired, they had renewed energy, and by midnight the grave had been dug and was large enough to contain a human being.

Beth had been longing for this moment, but at the same time, she had been dreading it, because she knew that a worse task was yet to come: Opening the door to the shed and going inside.

16

HIS BODY WAS JUST INSIDE THE DOOR. Beth forced herself to look at it. The buzzing of many flies made her wave her arms, but she said nothing.

The smell.

Ulf had his hand in front of his nose.

"It's been too hot," he said. "Decomposition goes much faster."

Beth turned and ran back to the house. She returned with safety pins and handkerchiefs.

Don't think, don't think, don't think.

They helped each other pin the handkerchiefs over their mouths and noses.

Beth glanced quickly over the top of her handkerchief at the man at her feet. His plaid shirt had slid up so that she had a view of his stomach. In spite of the darkness, she could tell that the skin had changed color and had a greenish tinge.

She forced herself to stop looking. She did not want to remember any more details, any more images. That man would remain a stranger she could forget forever and ever after.

They managed to lift him onto the wheelbarrow. They were both wearing gardening gloves, which made their movements clumsy, but at least they did not have to touch the dead man directly. He was heavy and his body was stiff. He looked like an awkward mannequin poking out of the wheelbarrow. He had dark, tufty hair. Beth had imagined blonde hair. In the minimal light, Beth could see his eyes staring accusingly right into her brain. She hissed at him that it was his fault. Like a mantra: *It was your fault. You did it. You did it. It was your fault.*

Ulf pushed the wheelbarrow. His back was bent as he almost jogged over the bumpy ground. Beth wanted to call out to him and ask him to wait for her. *Let me help you!* It was too late. He was almost there. When she caught up to him, they stopped the wheelbarrow along the long edge of the grave, and, using all their strength, they tipped it over. The corpse fell directly into the hole.

Ulf reached for the shovel.

"Wait," Beth said. She felt she had to step away and gather some meadow flowers, dried up as they were. She crept along the ground like an animal, and when she returned to the grave site, her cheeks were wet. She cast the flowers into the hole and they fell onto the dead man's chin and chest.

"Stop that fucking nonsense," Ulf said, but his words seemed to cry behind locked jaws.

Beth pretended not to hear him.

She made the sign of the cross as she had seen it done in the movies. She placed a finger in front of her mouth and whispered: "Rest in peace and forgive us our trespasses, as we know not what we do."

After that, they both hastily filled in the hole.

17

D AWN ARRIVED.
A blackbird at the top of a pine tree was singing. Beth could see its black shadow shape. She had always loved the sound of a blackbird's song, and realized that it had been a number of weeks since she'd last heard it. The songs usually would stop by the middle of July as the first sign that summer was nearing its end.

They had cleaned up the grave site as best they could. They'd stomped the ground flat and spread out a layer of branches, twigs, and grass. They'd scattered the dirt which was left over. Finally they'd returned the wheelbarrow to its place and hung up the poker and scuttle.

Beth had boiled some water, which they used to clean the axe, the shovels, and the floor of the shed. They scrubbed away the worst of the stains from the wall.

"They'll fade over time," Ulf said. "And it's not like people are going to come to inspect. No one will have any reason for suspicion."

"What about my sister Juni?" Beth whispered.

"Juni's not the type who's that active, is she?"

"What about Werner?"

Ulf gave her a sly look. "You can say that your period came on suddenly and was a real gusher . . . . That happens to women sometimes, doesn't it?"

Her blood for the dead man's? As if they would bleed into each other on the same floor?

She could not breathe for an instant.

Thoughts of the man's possible family forced themselves into her mind. She didn't want to think of that, but she hadn't noticed a ring. If he wasn't married, maybe he lived with someone. Maybe he had children. Maybe they were already starting to look for him.

If his family came to her door, she would say, *No, we hardly have visitors here. He hasn't been here. Sorry. I have no idea where he could be.*

Where did he come from? It was such a long way to the nearest neighbors that they'd never bothered to get in touch. She knew nothing about them. Nothing about the kind of people they were. Not even their names. She and Ulf liked solitude, which was why they came here. They enjoyed having no contact with other people.

Beth boiled some more water and they stood behind the house and washed their entire bodies. Dried black dirt was lodged under their fingernails. Beth took a nail brush to them. When she dried herself off, she felt the pain of her tender and chapped hands. She searched for some hand cream, but she didn't find any.

"I'm old now," she thought. "It's all over for me. It's all over for us."

Ulf had gone to bed. She wished she could go to sleep. She needed the sleep. It was another day now, and they'd been up all night. She had never worked so hard before in her life. Still, she had to keep watch. She did not want to let go, fall asleep, become defenseless. Wrapped in a bath towel, she sat on the porch. The sun was already hot. The day would be merciless.

The cat appeared. Beth had not seen her since yesterday when they had gotten out of the car. The cat lay down a few feet away. The golden eyes shone.

"Where are your kittens?" Beth asked.

The cat stood up suddenly and wrinkled her nose like a dog. Then she began to shake from fear.

"Get out of here!" Beth yelled. "Go home, stupid cat! Don't you ever come back here again! Go back where you came from! Maybe your family misses you!"

18

A SOUND CAME TO BETH IN HER SLEEP. The sound of a car. Beth was inside, stretched out on the sofa naked, with the bath towel spread over her body. She had fallen asleep like that.

She was uncomfortably thirsty, her muscles ached, and her skin was tender. She did not move.

Yes, it was a car. She heard a door slam and she heard a woman's voice call out.

Beth leapt up and rushed toward the stairs. Ulf was already coming down, and his eyes were red around the edges. He'd managed to pull on a pair of shorts.

"Someone's coming!" she said as she ran up the stairs in four giant leaps, pushing Ulf away. She ran into the bedroom and locked the door behind her.

From below she could hear footsteps and then voices. She heard someone say Ulf's name. A few sentences of small talk. She pulled on a skirt and a sweater and sneaked to the window. A red sports car was parked next to theirs. Who owned a car like that?

A woman's voice.

"No, Kaiser! Heel!"

The sound of a dog barking.

I have to go downstairs, she thought.

It was her sister, Juni. Juni was extremely thin and smelled like perfume. A brown-and-white dog leapt around her.

"Sit, Kaiser!" said Juni. She wore a great deal of make-up and her hair, as always, was a bird's nest of blonde tangles.

"Hi, Juni! So you decided to visit us!"

"Yes, here we are. How are things with you?"

"We haven't been . . . feeling well . . . the past few days," Beth said.

Juni observed her for a minute. "So I see," Juni said in a friendly voice.

Werner came inside carrying a large bag with the logo of a bucking horse on it. Beth noticed the logo. Werner dropped the bag on the ground, walked up to Beth, and gave her a hug. Beth thought that Werner had gotten fairly bald, and she noticed small rivers of sweat on his sunburned brow. Werner used his index finger to scratch his mustache.

"When unexpected guests drop by, it's time to put on the coffee pot!"

Werner's voice was unusually high for a man of his size and Beth had never found it to fit Werner's corpulent bulk.

Juni cleared her throat. "They've been sick lately, poor things," she said, as she lay her arm around Beth's shoulders.

"Look at you! You've really lost weight! As thin as a scarecrow!"

Werner quoted: "'In Småland the farmers are thin as rails and there's no grass growing in the pasture.' Do you know who said that?"

No one answered him.

"You need to get something more in your stomach," said Juni. "Listen to your big sister!"

"You're a fine one to talk about eating . . . you're so . . ."

"Come now, Betty dear, and calm down! You know I only want what's best for you. By the way, we're just staying one night. If that's all right with you, of course. I know that we weren't supposed to arrive until next week, but we decided that we weren't going to stay here this summer at all. We thought we'd just drop by and let you know. On the other hand, it would be nice if you answered your cell phone now and then!"

"We forgot our cell phones in Hässelby," said Ulf.

"Doesn't anyone really know who said 'In Småland . . .'?" Werner continued stubbornly.

"Sweetheart, how you do go on and on," Juni said. "Well, it probably doesn't matter so much about your cell phones since the reception out here isn't good. But it would have been nice if we could have contacted you. But as it is, we just take the long view. We just wanted you to know you might as well close up the place for winter when you go. We won't be back here. We'll be out of vacation days, anyway."

Werner said, "May I inform you that it was Albert Engström who said 'In Småland the farmers are thin as rails.' Just so you know."

"That's nice," said Ulf. "Now we know. So, just that I get it straight, you two aren't going to stay here at all this year?"

"We've found a place by the sea," said Juni dreamily. "It's a huge place . . . . We're renting from a friend of ours. You know, Ulf, I've always wanted to spend some time by the seaside."

The dog slowly came near Beth until its nose touched her leg. Beth jumped.

"Is that a new dog?" she asked.

"Yep! We call him Kaiser. He's a real sweetie, aren't you, Kaiser? He sleeps on our bed at night. You're my sweetie-sweet, aren't you, Kaiser?" Juni had bent down to scratch Kaiser behind the ears. The dog sneezed and shook itself.

"Where did you get him?" asked Beth.

"One of my colleagues," said Werner. "They really didn't have any time for him. They were thinking of putting him down."

"Putting him down?" Beth repeated.

Her brother-in-law snapped his fingers. "Like this. One prick of the needle and off they go into that Happy Hunting Ground in the Sky."

Juni grabbed Beth's arm.

"Oh, rats, I forgot! You're allergic to animals, aren't you? How are you feeling? Are you having any trouble? I can take him outside."

"I'm fine," Beth said. "I'm not feeling anything right now."

"Well, we'll be gone soon enough. We're leaving tomorrow morning ."

Ulf sank down into the sofa and Beth gave him a shy look. Ulf's face was gray and the skin underneath his chin seemed bloated.

"Actually, we were thinking of going home today," Ulf said.

"Really? So soon?"

"I have things to catch up on."

"But now you have to stay another day! We've brought food! Crayfish, real Swedish crayfish! Not to mention the schnapps to go with them! Don't worry about a thing. We'll prepare all the food and you can just relax."

They all took a long walk together along the road. The dog was eager to run and jumped into and out of the blueberry bushes.

"Kaiser doesn't like taking long car rides," Juni said, laughing. "Look at his energy!"

"I wonder if there's a leash law around here," said Ulf.

Werner burst out laughing.

"I didn't know my brother-in-law was so righteous!"

"Well . . . the wild animals have their young to protect at this time of year . . ."

"Nah! Out in the countryside there's no such thing as leash laws! Correct me if I'm wrong!"

Beth pressed her fingers to her forehead. Her fingertips felt cold. She warmed them.

"Let's cross over to the other side of the road," she suggested. "Let's see if any chanterelles have appeared. They usually grow there."

Juni hugged Beth's shoulders.

"Don't you think it's been much too dry? Chanterelles need rain. It looks like it hasn't rained in ages here. We didn't get any rain in Stockholm either this summer."

"It's been the hottest and driest summer in ages," said Werner. "There've been wildfires in Småland and on Gotland, too. They say it's been sheer hell trying to put those fires out."

"It would be really great to get some rain," Beth said. She turned and tried to see where the dog had gone. It had been right behind them, and now it had disappeared.

"Kaiser!" Beth called, and tried to purse her lips to whistle.

"It's no big deal," said Juni. "He's around here somewhere. He doesn't run away."

"I was afraid . . . maybe he's not used to being in woods."

"He'll be able to smell his way back. He'll find us."

"How long have you had him?" Beth asked.

"Since March thirteenth. Kaiser is a Jack Russell terrier. He's very attached to Werner and me. We're his pack. It's really very sweet."

"I never thought you were all that fond of dogs."

"Neither did I. Actually, I was afraid of them when I was little."

"I remember that."

"And do you remember when we lived on Dalgatan and the Hanssons had this pit bull type of dog? White with an ugly nose and demon eyes. I think he hated kids."

"We used to tease him," Beth mumbled.

"We didn't know better in those days. What was the name of that beast again? Tjong? Tjang?"

"Tjack," said Beth.

Juni bubbled over in laughter.

"What a crazy name for a dog!"

Werner and Ulf were walking ahead of them, identical figures with their hands in the front pockets of their shorts.

Juni pushed Beth playfully.

"Aren't our guys two real cuties?" she giggled.

"Sure, they are."

"How much I long for the sea! You have no idea how busy we've been! We've even had to work evenings lately. I think the two of us are totally burned out."

"So I guess your freelancing job's working out for you."

"Really well, in fact. So it's really mostly Werner who's getting burned out. Sometimes I'm afraid that something's going to happen to him. That he'll just fall apart some day. He's at a dangerous age for men. And there's a lot of conflict in the banking world right now, as you've probably heard."

"Right . . . ." Beth looked around again and then put her hands to her mouth and called for the dog.

"Can't you just take it easy?" said Juni irritably. "He's somewhere around here."

"There's a cat around who's just had kittens. We have to keep an eye on him so that he . . ."

"Cats can take care of themselves."

At that moment Kaiser came running toward them out of the woods just ahead of them. His muzzle was covered with small, hard seeds. Beth's throat was tight. Her muscles ached, and black spots appeared before her eyes. All around them, the smell of pine needles and dry heat covered them like a tight, shimmering wave.

"Hey, Ulf!" Juni yelled. "What do you think of our new car? You haven't said a word about it! I imagine that's because you're green with envy!"

"It's nice," said Ulf in a low voice.

"Nice? Is that it?"

Ulf laughed stiffly and then asked whether they had enough storage space in the trunk.

"We don't need a lot of stuff on vacation," said Juni. "And if we find we're missing something, we'll just buy it."

"It sounds like you guys are really doing well these days," said Beth, working hard to sound as normal as she could.

"Well, we only have to worry about ourselves. So why not have some R & R?"

"Of course. You should have some fun."

"What about you two?" Juni lowered her voice.

"Well, you know, in our professions we don't earn so much."

"Of course. And Ulf's not exactly going anywhere, either."

"What do you mean by that?"

Juni continued quickly: "Well, I'm certainly not a superstar in my career but at least I've managed to get some notice. Have you seen that new political magazine?"

"No, I don't think I have."

"Well, I've gotten a couple of good gigs—do 'gigs' only refer to the entertainment field?—from them. I brought along a few copies, so you can look through them if you want. They keep to a small circle of freelancers, so it looks like I'm in their good graces." Juni wore an ironic grin.

Beth was listening with only half an ear. She floated through the stream of Juni's words.

"And, you know what? I did an interview with that American publisher, Sammy Blankett, the guy who is standing up to all those conglomerates . . . . He's got a fantastic tiny company, and he's pretty fantastic, himself, at least in the looks department. You've probably seen him on television. They had an interview with him a while back."

"Maybe . . ."

"Maybe! Come on, Beth, you have to admit . . ."

"It's not really my field."

"Knowing who Sammy Blankett is should be part of your general education!"

Werner had stopped and was waiting for them. "Is she going on and on about Sammy Blankett again? I'm warning you, Juni, I'll strangle you in your sleep if you keep on blabbing about that sex machine!"

Juni sighed. "You think everything is about sex! You don't believe men have other attractive qualities!"

Werner snorted. "I know more than you think! But ever since you met that American dreamboat, all you can do is rave about him and you never shut up! Enough already!"

"Yeah, yeah. All I was doing was telling Beth about my freelance work. Nothing for you to get so worked up about, my honey-bunch."

Juni threw her arms around Werner's waist and gave him a long and passionate kiss. The dog took two hops toward them and tried to squeeze itself between them. Beth gave Ulf a sideways glance. Ulf's face was a pale yellow. Beth tried to smile at him, but wasn't able to get his attention.

"Time to head back!" exclaimed Werner. "I'm pretty damn thirsty by now! Not to mention hungry as a horse!"

They decided to set the table in the garden. Juni had thought of everything: napkins, bread, beer, cheese, and even a large table cloth with a crayfish pattern.

The dog had had a large drink of water from an empty ice cream container and was now sleeping underneath the table. Every once in a while, its body jerked and its breathing quickened.

"He's dreaming," Juni explained. "Can you imagine that animals dream like we do? I wonder what he's dreaming about."

"Oh, I bet it's nothing more than a big juicy bone waiting just for him," said Werner. Werner's legs were thin and white below his khaki shorts. He was bringing two bottles of schnapps from the refrigerator. He winked at Beth.

"This is the real good stuff!" he exclaimed.

"Where are the party hats? For crayfish parties, you need the hats!"

"I have no idea. I thought you packed them."

"They've got to be in here somewhere!" Juni dug around in a large bag until she finally pulled out a plastic bag holding shiny paper party hats.

"I am sure as hell not going to wear one of those," Ulf said, a sudden hardness in his voice. Juni stared at him.

"What's wrong with you, Ulf?"

The entire table fell silent.

Juni continued: "I know we probably shouldn't have just shown up and surprised you . . . but I thought it would turn out okay anyway, especially with tasty crayfish . . . and . . . I mean, we're sisters, Beth and me! It's not like we're all total strangers!"

"He didn't mean it for you, Juni," Beth said. "It's just that . . . we're not completely well again yet . . . forgive us. It really wasn't meant to be a criticism of you."

Juni unwrapped the hats and put one on her head. She snapped the rubber band against her chin a few times. "So what have you been down with, then?"

"Some kind of flu, I think. High fever. Pain in our muscles. Right now I'm still feeling pretty miserable."

Juni leaned over and petted her cheek. "Just sit right here, hon. You, too, Ulf. Let us take care of everything."

Juni disappeared into the house and came out with a plate of steaming crayfish. Werner carried out bread and beer.

"Oh wow, look at those!" Beth couldn't help herself. She felt dizzy and was freezing and sweating at the same time.

"Perfect, aren't they! It helps to have friends . . . one of mine has a cabin by a lake!" Juni clapped her hands and told everyone to dig in. Beth put on a party hat in spite of herself. It was vomit green and had a dice pattern on it. She knew that the rubber band would start hurting her chin before too long.

Play along, she thought. *Just play along. Be normal.*

Once Beth had had a few glasses of schnapps, she began to feel a sense of calm spread through her body. She began to sing a schnapps song:

"I was a little parakeet
My owners were so cheap, so cheap!"

She cracked open a crayfish claw and sucked out the salty juice.

*"They give me herring every day
But all I want is rum and coke!"*

Juni gave Beth a relieved look.

"Skål på dig!" Juni toasted Beth. Juni's party hat had fallen back into her tangled hair. She blew Beth a kiss.

Beth raised her glass. Across the table, Ulf was obsessively buttering a piece of *pain riche,* moving the knife back and forth as if he had gotten stuck and forgotten how to finish. Beth heard her voice call his name.

"Skål!"

Ulf put down his knife and raised his glass. Drank.

"Let's have some music," Juni said. She walked over to her car and came back with a CD player and a heap of CDs. She was wearing tight-fitting cement-colored leggings and a light blue silk blouse. The skin over her breasts appeared to have aged.

"Here we have all the hits of summer! What do you want to hear? Swedish rock? Schlagers?"

"Don't you have any jazz?" whined Werner.

"Nope!"

"Well, then, put on whatever you want."

Mats Rolander's album *Kött och blod* poured out of the CD player.

Beth pulled at her collar with sticky fingers. Sweat flowed from every pore. *Water,* she thought. *I need water. Black, clean ocean water to take my body and chill it down. Make my brain clear again.*

"Beth, do you remember when we were kids?" Juni exclaimed out of the blue. "Do you remember that summer when we played with that kid . . . what's his name . . . Markus?"

"Yes, what about him?"

"He just came to mind. I saw him in the newspaper the other day. He'd just gotten a position as Vice President for some big company. I don't remember which one. Markus Fagervik. He's really come up in the world."

Werner began to warble a song about childhood.

"He was the child of one of Mamma's friends. I think his parents were going through a tough time. Maybe getting divorced. So Markus came to stay with us for a while one summer. Do you remember that, Beth?"

Beth nodded. They had all slept in the same room. Markus would lie in bed crying himself to sleep. He had an indescribably dirty teddy bear with him. They would hide his teddy bear and force him to search for it in the craziest places.

Juni cut a bit of cheese and popped it into her mouth.

"We weren't so nice all the time," she said while chewing. "I mean, he was probably really sad and unhappy because of his parents divorcing. That's the kind of stuff kids don't understand. Sometimes I can hardly bear to think about it."

"Well, don't then!" Ulf said.

Juni pretended not to hear him.

"One day we took him out to the shed," Juni said. "Remember that? We pretended that we were nurses that were going to operate on him. You, Beth . . . you went to get a knife from the woodshed and said you were going to cut him open."

Beth's forehead burned. She remembered the incident very well. The body of the boy on the milk table. His thin limbs, so pale. They'd forced him to take off his pants. Keep still, little Markus, breathe easily and it will all be over in a minute. But Markus did not keep still. He writhed and kicked and howled. One of his knees got

Beth in the mouth. It stung. The hand holding the knife. A grip on her arm. A slap on her face so her teeth rattled.

Juni had done it. Her eyes were wide open.

"Good Lord! You were going to stab him! For real!"

Markus barefoot. Standing on the floor. Snotty and swollen around his eyes. Juni helped him put on his clothes properly.

"When I get my allowance on Saturday, I'm going to buy you some candy, I promise! Your favorite candy! But don't tell anyone about this! Ever! Or we will never play with you again. And it will be worse for you if you tell."

The boy nodded and said nothing.

But that wasn't it.

She never would have really stabbed him.

Beth and Juni fought about it for a long time afterwards. *If you don't give me all your bookmarks . . . if you don't give me half your allowance . . . all your watercolors . . . then I'll tell!*

"But I didn't do anything!"

"I saw you! If I wasn't there, you'd have cut his thingy off!"

Beth drew in a deep breath. "That's not true and you know it."

Juni's typical mild smile.

"As true as I stand here, and that's more than you can say!"

Back then, evenings passed, evenings when she lay in bed and wondered if it were true. If she really would have used the knife . . . can a boy survive . . . without that? Emasculated. It was a long word and it stuck in her head.

No, she wouldn't have done it.

The pain had almost made her throw up when his knee hit her lips. The sound of her teeth. She had a swollen lip for a long time afterwards.

But she would never have . . .

Juni would lie awake and watch her. Juni's head on her pillow, Juni's cold, blue eyes.

"What are you staring at?"

No answer.

"Turn off the light, then, if you're not reading!"

Beth threw her book across the room. It fell on its spine and fluttered open.

Later that night, in the silence . . .

"I'm thinking about last summer. About Markus. And you, Beth."

Beth turned toward the wall. Her pillow began to get wet.

The floor groaned and creaked. Juni was coming toward her. A sour smell from Juni's nightgown.

"Don't cry, Betty. I promise, I won't ever tell on you."

"Promise? Cross your heart?"

"Cross my heart and hope to die."

So, in the end, she had confessed.

19

THE NO-SEE-UMS ATTACKED AT TWILIGHT. They'd survived even the long hot drought, and they flew right into everyone's eyes. Everyone began to itch.

"These bugs are driving me crazy," said Beth. "We're going to have to go inside." Beth got up and took her plate. The others followed her. They decided to sit in the living room. Neither crayfish nor beer had been finished yet.

Juni yawned and stretched her arms to the ceiling. "We should get together more often. We are sisters, after all."

"There's just not enough time these days," said Beth.

"You're right. What a strange life we lead. I mean, the lives of modern humans in general. Just think about everyone who used to live in this house in the olden days. Grandma and Grandpa and the ones before them. I wonder if they ever complained that they never had enough time. Of course, they were hard workers in a different sort of way."

Juni swept her eyes over the room. "Just think what happened here during the decades. Think about all the words spoken. People having sex, people fighting, people giving each other the silent treatment . . . all within these walls. I bet that someone even kicked the bucket here. It's really fantastic to imagine, don't you think?"

Ulf had gotten up so fast that the chair behind him fell over. Ulf's steps were wobbly.

"What's up?" Beth whispered, but he didn't answer. She watched him walk toward the door.

"Are you going outside to have a smoke?" she asked quickly.

She thought he nodded. She looked at her sister.

"We're just going out to smoke for a second."

Juni was leaning backwards with her legs stretched out under the table. She'd pushed two crayfish claws onto her canine teeth and a dill flower in her hair. It was grotesque. Crayfish juice had drizzled down the light blue silk.

"You two have been smoking like chimneys all evening," Juni complained. "But, all right, don't let me stop you."

Ulf was standing on the porch blowing out smoke. He spat onto the lawn. Beth laid a hand on his arm, but he jerked away.

"How are you feeling?" she asked. "You're so quiet."

Ulf scraped his foot against the top step.

"Tomorrow we're going to go home," Beth said. "Back to our own place. Tomorrow at this time, we'll be home. Try to think about that."

When he did not answer, she continued:

"Werner and Juni are really quite harmless. I know they can be a pain, especially when they outstay their welcome. But it's just one night . . . then they'll be on their way and we'll be heading home. And it will all be over."

Her voice seemed strange even to her. It appeared to come from somewhere outside of her body and echoed between her temples.

Ulf turned toward her. He stayed silent. Beth blew out some smoke.

"Ulf . . . no matter what, we have each other. Once we get into the car tomorrow, we can erase all this from our memories. It didn't happen."

Beth was about to say something more when the door behind them burst open. Juni embraced them both.

"Here are the lovebirds!" Juni's voice was drunken. "If you want some more crayfish, you better hurry. Werner's going to eat the last of them."

Beth felt something soft touch her leg. The dog stood for a minute with its nose in the air, and then ran over the lawn to lift its leg against a bush.

"Good boy, Kaiser! What a good boy!" Juni praised. "Go on and water that bush! Everything else around here is dying of thirst!"

The dog looked back at them and barked. Then it lifted its nose in the air. It stiffened, then shook itself, then pointed its nose and sniffed.

"Oh, he caught the scent of a hare!" Juni said. "Go get him, boy! Go get him!"

The dog scratched its hind legs in the grass a few times and then ran off. Juni clapped her hands.

"He's such a sweet little dog! You know, Ulf and Beth, Kaiser's really changed our lives.. It may sound silly, but . . . it's like a kind of richness . . . life is richer with him."

Beth put out her cigarette in the ashtray. Worry wormed its way into her stomach. A bird squawked from the wild rosebush. An aggressive noise. Above them, the blinking lights of an airplane in the night sky. No sound of a motor. It was much too high.

"Call him in," Beth said. "Call him in right now, and let's go to bed."

"What is wrong with you, Beth? Let the dog run for a while. It's good for him. You don't have to worry. I've told you so a thousand times. And in any case, Kaiser is our responsibility and not yours."

"I want him to stay on our property. If he won't, you're going to have to put him on a leash."

"Cut it out. He has a psychological leash. He won't go far."

"That's bullshit."

Ulf had jumped down the stairs and was striding quickly across the lawn. Beth found herself following him. She moved through the grass but her feet were like lead. Fear was growing within her and she wanted to run, but she had to force herself to keep calm. Dizziness darkened her eyes.

"Where the hell are you guys going? What is the matter with you people?" Beth heard Juni's voice falling away behind her. "Wait up!"

Ulf stood, arms at his side, watching the dog. It was sniffing the newly flattened earth. It was already scratching away the twigs and branches.

"Get him out of there," said Beth tonelessly.

Ulf did not move. The dog made a gurgling sound and stuck its nose deep into the earth.

"Kaiser!" Beth said. "Go away!"

The terrier did not react. Rage surged within her and her chest began to burn. She ran at the dog, grabbed it around the stomach, and threw it roughly to one side.

"Leave it!" she commanded. Her voice seemed to rip open a wound in her throat. The dog snarled, curling back its upper lip to show a row of small, pointed teeth. A growl throbbed through its body. Beth lifted her foot and kicked the dog away.

Right at that moment, Juni found them.

20

B ETH AND JUNI WERE IN THE KITCHEN DOING THE DISHES. Juni was washing and Beth was waiting with a kitchen towel to dry.

"You don't have to dry them. They'll dry on their own in the rack," Juni said. Juni's mascara had run over her cheeks, and she stood ram-rod straight.

"I'll dry them anyway," said Beth.

Kaiser was underneath the kitchen table. Sand and dirt were all over the floor.

They had yelled at each other as if they were children again. In the woods, Juni had run up to Beth and had begun to hit her and scratch her. Beth stood there without fighting back. A few moments later, Juni started crying and picked up her dog. She carried him back into the house. She slammed the door so hard the tiles on the roof clanked. She began to clear the table and to heat water for doing the dishes. Her movements were jerky.

Werner had left the house.

Ulf was nowhere to be found.

"Juni," Beth said as she followed inside.

Juni was standing over the sink with her tears falling directly into the water.

"I'm so sorry. I really am sorry about Kaiser. You've got to learn that dogs have to do as they are told. Otherwise you have no control over them."

Beth surprised herself by the strength in her own voice.

"I told Kaiser to go back to the house, but he refused to listen to me. He'd understood what I commanded, I could tell."

"He's not your dog!" Juni put a bowl into the dishwater and began to scrub it vigorously with the dish brush.

"He was growling at me. I had to show him his place."

"You could have just let him be."

"We have responsibilities living here. The dog has to stay within our property line. I don't want people to start complaining about dogs running around loose. There is a leash law until the end of August."

"I'm amazed how much you know about the laws around here." Juni lifted the bowl out of the water, but it slipped out of her hands with a splash that covered the counter.

"Whoops!" said Beth.

She was feeling strong. Her words were coming like a laugh directly from her stomach.

She went into the living room and turned on the CD player. She put in Eva Dahlgren and began to sing along.

She returned to the kitchen and shook the damp dish towel a few times in the air.

"I do know a thing or two," she said. "We learned that in school. There's a leash law all summer because of children out on summer vacation. Some kids are deathly afraid of dogs. That has to be respected."

Juni pulled the plug from the sink drain. The water thrashed and gurgled down the pipe.

"We should go over the plumbing sometime," Beth said in a friendly way.

Juni wiped her nose with her arm, leaving a long string of snot on the scant hairs. She took a paper towel and blew her nose. Then she opened a beer and drank directly from the can.

"There's not a single soul anywhere around," Juni said with hostility. "And no one could feel threatened by such a cute little dog."

"All right, maybe I should have done things differently," Beth said. "But still . . ."

Beth's words suddenly died away. Weakness overcame her soul and she forced herself to take deep breaths. *Be gone! Be gone!* She pressed her lips together and ran her tongue over her teeth.

Juni's wide open eyes, as she paused in lifting the beer can to her lips.

Beth felt a wave of sorrow wash over her. *We've changed so much, Juni, my sister; we're no longer the little girls who played and dreamed. We've changed . . . your sweet little child face with your cute little cupid mouth . . . we've changed and become misshapen because . . . flesh turns to grass . . . no one will ever escape that reality.*

Beth swallowed, smacking her lips.

"You kicked him," Juni said. "You gave him a real kick."

"I was just pushing him away. And it's not like I was wearing steel-toed boots or anything . . . just these sandals."

"You want to know something, Beth? I really don't get you at all. There are times when I am really . . . almost afraid of you."

Beth took a step toward Juni, but Kaiser lifted his head and bared his teeth.

"Don't worry, Kaiser," Juni said as if she were far away. "Don't worry, boy."

Juni drank a few more swallows of beer. She licked her lips.

"It tastes salty," she said. "Must be from the crayfish."

Beth II

1

<hr>

THE FIRST THING BETH NOTICED WHEN THEY GOT HOME WAS THE DANGLING THREADS OF A SPIDER WEB IN THE HALL. She felt super-sensitive as if her powers of observation had sharpened. Even her sense of hearing had changed during the summer. She was easily bothered by the most trivial of noises.

"I'm going to have to do a thorough cleaning," she said while she and Ulf were still unloading the car. "I ought to scrub down the entire house so it will be fresh and clean after being locked up all summer."

Unoccupied houses take on a strange smell. The windows have a thin gray layer with traces of fly footprints. Their house was like that now.

Beth and Ulf had bought this house after only six months of living together. Beth's parents had stood as guarantors for the loan, although her father had gruffly warned her: "It's much too soon for you two to take on this responsibility; you hardly know each other. Look at your mother and me. We had been married for twenty years before we bought our house." When Beth first saw the house, it was twelve years old and had been painted a sky blue color. Beth had never seen a house that color before, and it seemed a bit too shiny, too. The owners were a couple in their thirties who had an infant. The husband was a childhood friend of Ulf's who had to move to Karlskrona for business reasons. He was eager to make a quick sale.

Ulf had said: "We might as well go and take a look at it."

At that time, they each had their own one-room apartment. They'd started to talk about moving in together, but hadn't done anything about it. So they decided to go look at the blue house.

Something about the way the light fell into the living room pleased Beth. There was also an old chestnut tree in the yard which had somehow been spared the bulldozer.

The Chestnut House, thought Beth. *This place is big enough to hold our entire future.*

The chestnut tree bloomed in springtime with large white flowers, while in October, it covered the ground beneath with its shiny chestnuts. Beth would collect them in her pockets because she liked the way they felt. Once she'd seen someone's curtain made with chestnuts on strings, which would rustle whenever anyone walked past.

It was a one-story, three-bedroom house and the asking price was reasonable.

"It'll increase in value over the years," Ulf said.

They quickly agreed to the deal.

Beth carried a large bag of books inside. She'd thought she would relax during her vacation with lots of reading, but that hadn't happened.

"Is there anything to eat?" Ulf asked.

Beth went to the kitchen. The refrigerator was empty except for a bottle of catsup, a jar of pickles, and some mustard. Even the fridge had a musty smell.

Ulf said, "I'll go to the store and get something. What do you want?"

"No idea. I'm not all that hungry."

"Neither am I, but we have to have something."

"Well, milk, then, and some yoghurt."

Beth listened to the car leave.

Then she walked around her house barefoot. She noticed the potted plants had survived, though Beth was surprised at how indifferent she was to them. One of their neighbors, Birgitta Santesson, had looked in once in a while to make sure the house was in order. Birgitta Santesson was a widow of about sixty.

Beth walked into the bathroom. She'd had a headache the entire morning. At first, she thought it was because she was hung over, but this pain was different. It seemed to come from her jawbones.

I'll unpack and throw the dirty clothes into the laundry, she thought.

She felt slow and unable to decide what to do. The soles of her feet were warmed by the bathroom floor. Her heels were rough and she could peel white, leathery strips of skin from them. She looked at herself in the bathroom mirror. She'd combed her hair straight back and she could see the wrinkles in her forehead. When she lifted her eyebrows, the wrinkles deepened and others appeared. Her nose was peeling, as if she'd been tanning, but in reality she had tried to avoid the sun. She had large, dark red lips, and on the corner of her chin, she could see a pimple developing. The spot was shiny and tender. She leaned closer to the mirror. She stared at her blue eyes, her pale eyelashes, the bags under her eyes, the lilac shadows.

"What the fuck, Beth, what the fuck."

She found she was saying this out loud and watched her lips move: *whatthefuckBethwhatthefuck.*

She opened the window and bent over the windowsill. She hung there even though it hurt her midsection, and the farther she leaned, the more her jaws ached. In spite of the drought, it appeared that the lawn had been mowed recently. It was probably the widow, Birgitta, who had dragged the electric lawn mower over the grass. Birgitta was careful in her work, and it appeared she'd raked up every stray blade of grass.

"I always put the grass in the compost," she had told Beth, "and you ought to do that, too. Renew it in the circle of life. We must do these things so that life on our planet will continue. By the way, your lawn has moss. I was at the garden shop to see how you should get rid of it. They advised to cut the lawn often and to cut it short. Then the moss doesn't have a chance."

Birgitta was going to be by any minute. *Maybe I shouldn't open the door. That won't work. Birgitta has the keys.*

"Hello! Yoo-hoo! Anybody home?"

Speak of the devil.

Beth drew herself back inside from the window and went out into the hall. Birgitta was standing in the doorway, holding a basket of apples and grapes.

"This is for you. Welcome home! I assume you don't have anything in the cupboard right now."

Beth walked over to her. "Thank you so much. You are a dear. We should be giving you a present for all you've done for us . . . and we will, as soon as we're settled in again. Anything happen while we were gone?"

Birgitta's dark hair was pulled back into a bun. She'd recently begun using lipstick. Once she'd been widowed, Birgitta had come into her own. Her husband had been delicate and rather sickly, and Beth and Ulf had heard him complain constantly even through Birgitta's closed windows. Her husband had never let her out of his sight.

In those days, they'd had little to do with Birgitta. She kept to herself and was constantly in a hurry. They talked about it between themselves and decided that Birgitta probably wasn't doing well, herself.

Once her husband had died, everything changed. Birgitta drew her curtains back and her windowsills were covered with hibiscus and oleander. Her husband had been allergic to all fragrant flowers. They thought he was allergic to life itself.

"So nice that you're back home again. Though I thought that you were going to be gone a little while longer."

"We were homesick."

"Homesick in that wonderful place? A little slice of paradise on earth! I remember the photos that you've shown me. It seems to be absolutely fantastic there."

"It is," Beth said, wanting to change the subject.

"I see. So you're going back to work?"

"On the seventeenth."

"And you want a little time to yourself first."

"Yes, I need to recharge my batteries and make sure I'm ready to go."

Birgitta laughed. Then she firmed her mouth so that a number of tiny wrinkles appeared above her upper lip.

"There's something I have to tell you," she said, carefully gauging Beth's reaction. "Things haven't been completely quiet around here."

"What happened?"

"Lots of things, although not as bad as it could have been. Someone tried to break into your house."

"What?"

"At the beginning of last week. It was late in the evening and I was in my living room watching TV. I had a creepy feeling that something wasn't right."

Beth's molars ached and she put a hand to her cheek.

Birgitta closed the outer door.

"Let's go inside and sit down for a minute. I know I shouldn't be inviting myself in like this, but you know, I've been working in the yard all day and I just can't keep on my feet any longer."

"Oh, pardon me, I should have asked you in right away," Beth said. "Excuse the house, but we just got back."

Birgitta set the basket of fruit on the coffee table. She walked over to the French doors and opened them.

"If you don't mind," Birgitta said.

"Go ahead. It's stuffy in here."

"I opened up the doors at least every day to air the place out," Birgitta said defensively.

"Do you want to sit down outside?"

"No, no, I'm all right. I've been outside all day."

They sat down on separate sofas. Birgitta took off her sandals. Her feet were small and well manicured. Birgitta took a grape from the bunch and ate it slowly, as if stalling for time. She was wearing black silk shorts. Beth couldn't resist taking a look at her legs. They were surprisingly slim and trim.

"So," Beth said. "Tell me what happened."

"I don't know if I'd heard a noise, but I knew that something was wrong. So I crept to the window and when I looked out, I saw this guy fiddling with the locks on your French doors."

Beth was surprised to feel extremely uncomfortable.

"I see," she said.

"I wasn't able to make him out all that clearly, of course, but he was a big man, tall, blond; otherwise I would have thought, well, you know, all these refugees they've settled in Hässelby Strand these days . . . ."

"What did he do then?"

"Well, you see, he was working on the lock, and if you look closely, you'll see the marks. I was really frightened. I didn't know what to do, since I was all alone . . . not that Allan would have been much help, but you know what I mean. I thought I ought to call the police, but I knew that he'd get in before they ever got here and he'd make off with something. And Beth, I got so angry! I was totally enraged . . . God help me! . . . and I walked right over through your garden and yelled at that guy to get out of here!"

"Did he?"

"Can you believe it? He took off like a shot! Only afterwards . . . later that evening . . . my heart started to pound so that I thought I was going to have a heart attack right then and there. I thought, Birgitta, you've done all you can in this life."

"You were so brave!"

"Well, what's the point of having a neighborhood watch otherwise? That's what I thought. What's the point of putting up all those signs? Just a few signs around are no good at all! I mean, you might as well put your money where your mouth is."

"That's right."

"Still, I have to say the whole thing's made me uncomfortable. I did call the police afterwards, but they weren't too helpful."

"There are probably lots of break-ins during the summer. Someone broke into our summer place, too." Beth was surprised that she'd even brought that up. It felt more natural than not saying anything.

"Did he get away with anything there?" asked Birgitta, as she began to massage one of her sun-tanned calves.

"A few small things. Nothing to worry about."

"But just the thought that someone has been inside your home. Some person going through your stuff."

A car was pulling into the driveway. Ulf had returned. As he came into the living room carrying two full plastic grocery bags, Birgitta stood up.

"Welcome home, Ulf." Birgitta walked up to him and held his lower arms for a moment, peering up at him. "Now, forgive me in advance, but you two don't look as if you were ever on vacation at all. You both look exhausted and worn out. Was life really that terrible over in Västergötland?"

A soft thud by the French doors. Beth jumped.

"What the . . . !"

A cat had jumped inside. The cat stared at them. Its tail was stuck up and its fur had puffed up. Birgitta was nonplussed.

"Go on outside, kitty," she coaxed. She went over and shooed the cat outside onto the lawn. "I'll be over in a few minutes. But Beth, the lady who lives here, is allergic to animals, you see, so she doesn't like small kitty-cats."

Beth was freezing and held her arms close to her sides, shivering.

"I thought . . . ," she whispered. "There was a cat who looked just like that out in the countryside . . . ."

"This kitty just appeared one day," Birgitta said. "From nowhere. I know that you can't tolerate animals, so I made sure this cat never got inside your house. But I've started to feed it some milk and cat food. It's a young female, and I've decided to call her Missy. If no one claims her, I think I'll keep her."

2

During the night, it finally began to rain. Beth sat up in bed, leaning against the wall. She'd fallen asleep right away, but she was awakened a few hours later by pain in her mouth. One of her molars was aching and she could feel the nerve pulsing. She closed her eyes and tried to concentrate on something else, but the pain moved from the upper to the lower molar and back again. It was relentless and pounding. When she changed position, her nostrils flared to get more oxygen, and her breathing was shallow and quick, her whole body tense. Finally, she had to release a groan.

Ulf was lying awake. She knew he was awake, pretending he was asleep. Once he heard her, he turned on the light and stared at the ceiling, not at her.

"What's wrong with you?" he said irritably.

"I have a toothache."

"Well, call the dentist tomorrow."

Beth said nothing. He knew how afraid she was of dentists. He used to tease her about it, but not in a mean way, rather as a way to show his affection.

"Well," she said at last, "I guess I'll have to do that."

A moment later, hesitating: "Did I wake you up?"

Ulf turned off the light. "Yes," he said. "Yes, you did."

His voice was expressionless. She reached over and tried to touch him with her fingertips, but he was too far away. She did not want to move from her own position leaning against the wall.

That same moment, the room was illuminated by lightning, and a few seconds later came the roll of thunder. The tiles of the roof began to shake and clack. Immediately afterwards, the first large drops of rain beat on the window. Ulf got up to close it.

He stood in the room like a shadow. His rounded shoulders. His body.

"I love you," she said quietly, and she knew that he had heard her.

She forced herself to get up and go to the bathroom. She found some pain pills and swallowed them with a drink of water. She'd been sleeping without a nightgown, and now it felt as if she were exposed. She wrapped herself in her robe and went back to the bedroom.

"Please don't stand by the window," she requested.

Ulf did not move.

"It's dangerous. You could be hit by lightning."

"Bullshit."

"Come lie down. Let's try to get some sleep."

He stood awhile longer, but he finally came to bed. He lay turned away from her, and pulled the sheet and blanket over himself.

She repeated: "Ulf, I love you."

"I heard you, Beth."

"What are you thinking?"

"Nothing."

"Are you thinking about . . . what happened?"

He jerked and whirled around and hissed right in her face: "Did we or did we not decide never to talk about that again! Pretend it never happened! Did we or didn't we?"

"I'm sorry," she whispered.

"Then shut the fuck up. Use your brain, damn it, and don't be so stupid."

The pain pills weren't helping. She tossed and turned and kept pulling on the sheets. Ulf got up at last and walked with thudding steps to the guestroom.

"I've got to get some sleep," he mumbled, but he didn't sound angry any longer, just tired and sad.

Beth stayed in bed and listened to the rain. When it's been so dry for so long, rain seems to pour down powerfully. She heard the rain

146

sing as it hit the road outside. She thought about their place in the countryside. Was it raining there as well?

Against her will, images crept into her mind: the hard-packed clay earth starting to soften; the water seeping through the dry, thirsty soil; the man in his grave and how his clothes would start to get wet, how the soil and water would begin to fill his nostrils and ears and his wide-open eyes, unless they'd closed them. Did they shut his eyes? Otherwise, the gravel would have pounded down on the delicate membrane covering the iris. She thought of the pupil as nothing more than an opening. His body covered in openings, as is hers, as is all bodies. His body in the mud and unless they'd dug a sufficiently deep grave, the earth would wash away because of the rain, leaving the body open to inquisitive wild animals. Foxes and crows would come and sniff and dig, but they would not consume it as completely as carrion eaters would in the desert . . . they would leave enough behind so that . . . without difficulty . . . anyone who was walking past . . . a thief, a neighbor, his relatives . . . and since he was buried so close to their property, the discovery of the corpse, the Discovery . . . and forensic medicine could easily ascertain when the death occurred and how . . . they would see his skull, the broken forehead . . . they'd find the axe and compare its peen . . . or was "peen" the word for hammers?

Her mouth ached and ached. Once she'd had a nice old dentist. He'd been able to calm her fears. He'd been retired for some time and was now deceased. He'd said that she should go to the dentist taking over his business and that he'd tell the new dentist all about her fears and he'd set up an appointment for her usual time. Something must have gotten mixed up, though, because no one had called her in for an appointment during the past two years, and she certainly was not the kind to call for an appointment on her own.

Well, if they didn't want her as a patient there, she was not going to force her way in, although Ulf said that she was stupider than the train, since the only one she hurt by her stubbornness was herself. Her teeth would start to rot and fall out. And believe you me, he'd said, I don't want to live with a toothless old woman. She would yell at him and throw a pillow, but it wasn't serious. She just wanted him to shut up about it.

So one of these afternoons, very soon perhaps, the doorbell would ring. Or someone would pound on the door. She would have just come home from work and would think: *Don't open the door.* They would know that she was home and they would bang even harder: *Open up! In the name of the law!* So she would be forced to open the door and there they'd be. There would be two of them, wearing trench coats and hats as if they belonged in a black-and-white gangster movie. They'd pull out their badges. *Good day, we are from the police and we are looking for Beth Svärd,* they'd say. *Are you Beth Svärd?* How could she deny it? *Yes, what do you want? Have you come to investigate the break-in?* They'd look at her with contempt. Outside, on the street, there'd be the police car. *Please get your coat and come with us.*

She imagined two scenarios. In the first one, she would go and get her light summer coat obediently. They would walk on each side and would lock her door with a key that they'd gotten from Birgitta and, as she got into the back seat of the black police car, she'd glimpse her neighbor watching from behind the curtains. One policeman drove while the other was in the back seat next to her. She would keep as far away from him as possible. She'd ask: *Where are you taking me?* They would stare at the scenery and say nothing. *Where are you taking me?* Maybe they'd make fun of her question. Maybe they wouldn't answer. She imagined them bringing her into a small, sparse interrogation room. *We've made a significant discovery at your property in Västergötland.*

No more of that now. The other scenario was much better. At least it had a better beginning. She was much less cooperative. As the policemen stood there, she would say: *Excuse me just a minute. I have to go get my purse.* Before they'd have a chance to react, she'd slam the door in their faces and run out the back. She'd run over the lawn. Like a deer, she'd leap over the short, whitewashed back fence. She'd run past Hässelby's sport hall, with its old-fashioned sign, and then past the daycare center, where she'd once imagined her children would attend, and into the tiny thick forest near Lövstavägen. She'd be strong, rested, well-dressed, and so when she reached the road, she'd stop a car with a driver she did not know, and say *I'm on the run from an abusive husband!* The female driver would open the door and she'd hop in and speed, pedal to the metal, and before the policemen ever realized they were gone, they'd have passed Ödeshög like a Swedish Thelma and Louise. Heroines.

3

B ETH'S TOOTHACHE SUBSIDED A FEW DAYS LATER. Or Beth was able to put up with it better. Sometimes it would surge, and then Beth would pop a number of painkillers until it went away again.

Beth cleaned the house from top to bottom. Then she weeded all the beds in the garden. That really wasn't even necessary, as Birgitta had kept the garden neat while Beth was away. Beth never put in much of a garden as it would be impossible to keep up since she also had the summer house to deal with, but she had a few rose bushes, a climbing hortensia and a clump of bright yellow lilies. Beth couldn't get too close to the lilies. Their brown pollen stained every item of clothing they touched and it was impossible to get the stains out.

When she was in the garden, the local cat had hopped up on the back fence and watched her. Something about the way the cat looked at her with its cold unblinking eyes made Beth feel ill at ease.

One morning Beth put out a bowl of milk for the cat. She had no idea why she'd done so, as she would rather be quit of the creature. She wished it would stay in Birgitta's yard or return to its original owner. The cat watched her as she bent down to place the bowl near the foundation of the house.

"Come and get it," she said. "It's for you."

The cat stood up, balancing with all four paws on the back fence. Then it jumped to the ground and stiffly walked over to the bowl of milk. It didn't drink anything, but sniffed around it.

"What's the matter?" Beth asked nervously. "Do you think I might have poisoned it?"

The cat did not move. It was so still, it might have been a taxidermist's specimen. She thought that it would attack her if she made the slightest movement. For a few seconds, they both stayed still and just stared at each other. Then Birgitta came outside onto her patio, and the cat whirled around and slipped through the fence and away.

Ulf had already gone back to work, even though his vacation had not yet ended. He told Beth that he felt restless and it would be good to have something to take his mind off things. Beth still had an entire week of vacation remaining.

She also felt an unrelenting restlessness. When she was at home, she wanted to be out; and when she was out and about, she was filled with exhaustion and wanted to be home. She was always tired but never could get enough sleep.

She walked past the school one day, and as she looked at the low buildings with their tiled roofs, she was filled with nagging unease. The day was rainy and the schoolyard was shining and empty. A few yellow leaves whirled down. *Fall is coming,* she thought.

Many of the empty school's windows were open, and she could hear the sound of a drill. There were always a number of things which had to be repaired before school started again. The wear-and-tear on the building was enormous.

Beth tried to remember her former pupils. They would now be starting high school. Strangely, she could not remember a single face, or even a name. The high school was in a building farther away. She would not run into those children again. Others would take their places. The stream of children never seemed to end. She thought that she was getting older, more tired, less capable. She did not like her old job. She was not a good teacher. She had never wanted to become a teacher.

Beth went past Riddarviksvägen and entered the long boulevard which led to Riddarviksgård. Earlier in the year, Beth and Ulf had gone to a restaurant there for dinner. They'd eaten outside with Lake Mälar right at their feet and the sun going down. They'd shared a bottle of wine and afterwards had walked home along the narrow footbridge which led to the hillside.

How long ago that seemed!

Her entire life seemed to be long, long ago.

She turned right after she'd passed Riddarviksgård and walked along another boulevard. She observed the barnyard zoo with its hens and ducks. She'd been here many times on field trips with the children from her school. A few frozen horses were standing on the other side of the pasture. She called to them, even though she had nothing to give them. One horse, a chestnut, took a few cautious steps toward her. It tossed its head, and it shook its thin, white-striped mane. She could smell the strong odor of horse and she was filled with an overwhelming sense of melancholy.

"Come here and let me pat you," she said as the horse came up to her until it was so close she could stroke its muzzle, but when she reached out her hand, it spooked and took off back to the other side of the pasture so fast its hooves tossed off clumps of mud. Its fear spooked the other horses, and with nostrils flaring, they began to gallop in circles, sometimes slipping and risking a fall from the wet ground.

Beth drew her rain cap over her hair. The sound of hooves continued to thunder. Soon the owner would come out to see what was going on. She began to walk away quickly and headed for the large trees by Tempeludden. On her right, she could see the large ruin of a garbage-burning station. Its windows were all broken. Next to the ruin was a transfer station, where the citizens of Hässelby dumped their surpluses. Some of it went to charity and the rest was ground up for a landfill somewhere.

We could have brought him here, she thought, and instead of brushing the image aside, she imagined the scene in detail. If they had the corpse here, they could stuff it in a cardboard box and tie the box with string. Of course, it would be heavy, but if they came here at night . . . if the place wasn't locked up . . . and if they just heaved the corpse into one of the containers, the one labeled *For burning,* well, why not . . . more things would be thrown in over it and no one would suspect a thing . . . if the smell didn't . . . and then the thought overwhelmed her. The stench of a decaying corpse . . . the cloud of flies hovering when they opened the door . . . Beth had to hold on to one of the giant trees. She hugged it, breathing against its gray trunk, her tongue against its bark, and then she had to vomit.

Afterwards, she turned her face to the rain. Drops fell from the leaves of the tree. She closed her eyes and felt the sting of her tears. She kept standing there until her neck was stiff. Her toothache returned. *I have to go home and lie down,* she thought.

When she arrived at the small pavilion which gave Tempeludden its name, she saw another woman walking in her direction. In spite of the rain, she realized right away it was one of her work colleagues, Görel. She could tell by Görel's posture and the way she was walking. Görel was wearing a dark blue raincoat and a sou'wester. Only Görel would be wearing a sou'wester these days.

"Hi, Beth!" Görel exclaimed. Water was running off the tip of her nose.

"Hello."

"So you're out and about in this fine weather!"

Beth tried to laugh.

"Did you have a good summer?"

"It was fine. Yours?"

"Well, my mother-in-law went and died on us on Midsummer's Eve, and that set the tone for the rest of the summer."

"Went and died?" Beth repeated.

"Literally. She was walking across the lawn and dropped dead. She was just going to go and get her glasses from the house and just keeled over like a Colossus. She was a big woman, you see, enormous, really. And she had extremely high blood pressure."

"Oh my, that must have been dreadful."

"You can say that again. We were all out on an island in the archipelago. Martin jumped on his bike and managed to find a guy who was a doctor . . . the man lived on the island during the summer, you see . . . and of course everyone had been drinking because of the holiday . . . and, well, it appeared that she'd died instantly. Martin felt guilty. He thinks he should have done this or done that. He's down on himself for not spending more time with his mother.

I was the one who remembered her birthday and whatnot. He was an only child and she, well, she was eating him up, so to speak, so he fled from her, at least mentally. You know how it is. So it wasn't much of a fun summer, all things considered."

Görel barely paused for breath.

"I've just been going crazy with all this. The old hag was always between us, and now that she's dead, it's like she can still put a wedge between Martin and me. Right now I can't even talk to him, he's . . ."

Görel stopped and shook her head.

"Sounds awful," Beth said.

"That's the truth. By the way . . . why don't you come over and have a cup of coffee?"

Beth couldn't find a reason to say no. So a few minutes later, they were walking up the well-raked gravel path leading to Görel's house on Vidholmsbackarna.

Görel brewed the coffee and put buns in the microwave. They sat down at the kitchen table. The rain was falling so hard it seemed as if there had never been sunshine.

"At least the rain is good for the mushrooms," Görel said, not without irony. "Do you go out mushroom hunting?"

"Not really," Beth said, as she brought the cup of coffee to her lips. When the hot liquid touched her teeth, it hurt like hell. She didn't dare take a bite of the bun.

"I have a toothache," she said.

"You poor thing. When are you going to see the dentist?"

"Well . . . you see . . ."

"You don't have a good dentist? We have one. His name is Freddy and I can give you his number if you want it."

"Sometimes it goes away . . . maybe it will disappear on its own."

Görel stared at her. She had large, clear eyes.

"Do you really think that?"

Beth shrugged.

"Here's his number. In fact, let's call him right now."

Before Beth could protest, Görel had picked up the phone and was dialing. It seemed that she knew the number by heart.

"Tomorrow? That'll be fine. Thank you so much! You should see her. She's really suffering. Yes, I'll tell her. Love you."

She put down the receiver.

"You have an appointment for tomorrow morning at nine forty-five. They don't have much room for emergencies, but I got you in, because they know me."

"You say 'love you' to your dentist?"

"Oh, it's just the way we talk to each other. We've known each other our entire lives. Grew up together. We said we'd get married one day. To each other, that is."

"Kids say the stupidest things."

"Frankly, I don't think Freddy is all that happy with his wife right now. That's the impression I've been getting."

"I see."

"Or maybe it's just a feeling. Anyway, here's the address."

Görel got up and walked into the living room. A few moments later, she returned holding a photograph.

"Check this out."

The photograph showed a huge woman standing in front of a gate.

"That's what she looked like, my mother-in-law. It's crazy to be that overweight. She ate everything in sight. She'd even eat the butter right out of the package. Just stick her finger in and lick it up. I've got to tell you, Beth, she's always disgusted me. And there are times, times when I realize again that she and Martin are flesh and blood relatives . . . well, I just don't know."

Beth was feeling ill.

"Do you have a mother-in-law?"

"Sure, though Ulf and I aren't married, of course."

"Doesn't matter. It's the same thing. How's your relationship with her?"

"We hardly ever see Ulf's parents. They live in London."

"London?"

"They don't like the winters here in Sweden. They like Britain's green winters. So for the most part, they stay in London."

"Imagine that. London!"

"So, we don't see them very much."

"Lucky you! Having relatives at a distance is very nice indeed. Now, finally, for me, the distance is as far as it gets."

4

ULF LEFT A MESSAGE ON THE MACHINE: "WORKING LATE. Don't wait up for me."

Short. No other greeting. Almost formal. At first, Beth was so angry she flushed. It was still raining heavily outside, so Beth walked around the house, turning on all the small lamps. She really ought to make herself some dinner, but she was not hungry. She still had the taste of coffee in her mouth. She thought about Görel. It was amazing how little one knew about one's friends and colleagues. You could only see what they showed you. Sometimes you could imagine the reality behind the façade, that they had other personalities.

I have to keep strong, Beth thought. *I have to keep cool, strong and in control. School is starting on Wednesday.*

She went to the clothes closet. She stared at the long rows of clothes. The house had no other closets, but the clothes closet was fairly large. Ulf's clothes hung toward the back and hers closer to the door.

She walked inside and shut the door behind her. She breathed in the scent of clothes which were hardly ever worn. Ulf's black suit. When was the last time he'd worn it? She lifted its sleeve and brushed away a piece of lint. Felt the pockets. She found a twenty crown bill. She held it for a moment, then folded it and replaced it.

She burst into tears without warning, wild and uncontrollable sobbing, and she leaned into the suit and wailed. In the middle of her flood of tears, the contours of a man's face took shape. It was that broken, gaping mouth, with bangs brushed back. The stain of blood on the floor. On her bare legs. Reflexively, she clenched her right hand and felt the weight of the axe again. She felt her shoulders flex as she raised her arm. That sound.

The sound of iron hitting bone.

This was the worst part and it could come back to her at any time. That dull crunch like a huge eggshell breaking. Then: how he fell at her feet, as his fingers tried to clutch anything at all. That must have been what made those marks in the wall. His fingers trying to clutch onto life as it ran out.

She thought in confusion: *You killed me.* She mumbled out loud: "*You killed me.* . . . He would have killed me if I hadn't . . . everything I did was in pure self defense. He had me by the throat, but I pushed him away and I defended myself just as any normal ablebodied person would have done!"

She had sunk down to her knees and her face was twisted from her sobs. Cramps shook her body. "Mamma, mamma," she wept, as if her mother could have helped her. "Mamma, why did you give birth to me and let me live?"

Her sobbing quieted down at last. She found herself sitting on the floor of the clothes closet. Her head was throbbing. All the crying had heated her body. Sweat clung to her ribs and back.

Stop! Don't think!

Still.

His name? He must have had a name. Maybe a wife. Or a fiancée. Maybe a kid. Maybe more than one. They might not miss him right away. Maybe he was the sort who came and went as he felt. A man in charge of his life and habits. Eventually there would be an empty space in the circle he called his family. His woman. Beth imagined her as a forest being with long hair and a secret smile. Her naked, white back. Children like cherubs, fat white flesh, clutching her wrists. Beth imagined them ugly with misshapen features.

Her limbs ached as she stood up. She walked toward the bathroom and took off her damp clothes. She took a long, hot shower.

She stood for a long time observing her body. Her hands. Her private parts with thick hair.

She put on a nightgown. Although it was only six in the evening, it was already getting dark outside. There were low clouds over the sports hall.

She opened a cupboard and found a bottle of Bristol Cream. She poured a shot and emptied it with one gulp. She lit a cigarette and stood underneath the kitchen fan and smoked. The pain in her tooth was increasing slowly again.

"Damn it all," she swore. "Damn it all to hell!"

The telephone rang.

Beth was suddenly afraid, although she did not know why.

Five rings. She found herself unable to pick up the phone. Finally, it stopped ringing. Beth rinsed the cigarette butt under the faucet and threw it in the garbage.

Ulf had not told her what kind of work was keeping him.

Beth was inspired to call Ulf's ex. Ylva picked up the phone right away.

"Hello, Beth, how are you?"

"How did you know it was me?"

"Female intuition."

"No, really."

"I have caller ID."

"You do?"

"Most new phones come with that. How are you doing, though? You sound all stuffed up. Do you have a cold?"

"Maybe. I just wanted to chat for a bit. Hear how things are going."

"We've had an absolutely wonderful summer! We have nothing to complain about."

"Great."

"I rented that cottage on Fårö for Albin and me. It was in that vacation village near Sudersand, you know the one. Albin made a number of friends. And I got more tanned than I've ever been before in my life! You know how it is. You can lie between the dunes days on end and never lift a finger."

"Right."

"Sometimes you just need to relax."

"True. And did you make any friends? Meet someone special?"

"Of course."

"So are you in love?"

"Beth! What kind of question is that!"

"What? I'm just wondering."

"I believe that you are only truly in love once in a lifetime."

"Still in love with Ulf?"

Ylva's laughter was hard as it hit Beth's ear.

"You haven't changed a bit, Beth! So, tell me, what's going on with you guys?"

"What do you mean?"

"Well, how was your vacation? By the way, I was chatting with Ulf yesterday. He said that you had a great summer."

"Sure, we had a good one. But now he's back at work. And I'll start back on Wednesday."

"Lucky you. I've already been back at work for weeks." Ylva sighed. "Now we have to wait a whole year to get some time off again. Well, there's Christmas, but that's such a stressful time. By the way, when is Christmas Eve this year? I'll bet it's on a Friday! But of course you teachers have a good long vacation then!"

Beth was used to jibes about teachers and their vacations. People never thought about how much time teachers worked outside class hours. Lesson plans, correcting homework, continuing education, not to mention the long hours devoted to talking with parents, who often seemed to call her late in the evening.

"I have another call coming in. Gotta run!" Ylva said. "Bye, now. Take care."

Beth went to the cupboard and poured another drink. She noticed a man was biking past outside in the rain, and she realized that anyone at all could just look in and see her. She walked through the house closing all the curtains.

The telephone rang again, but when she lifted the receiver, there was no voice on the other end. Just the sound of air. "Hello!" she yelled and when there was no answer, she raised her voice even further to scream: "Answer me! Stop terrorizing honest people!"

A suffocating feeling washed over her.

Someone knew.

Someone was calling to scare her. Someone wanted her to break down and turn herself in.

No.

Instead, she'd be strong.

If someone had really found something, it would be in the newspapers. It would be splashed over the front pages of *Falköpings Tidning* or *Västgötabladet*, and then the national papers and television would pick it up and run with it. A murder victim, a man, would be like a bone to a dog as far as the tabloid press was concerned. She could already see the headlines:

Who is the dead man buried in the woods?

She put down her glass and decided to phone her parents. It took a moment before her father picked up the phone.

"Hello, Beth, what's up?"

"I just . . . just wanted to know how you were doing."

"How should I be doing?" Her father seemed irritated. "Nothing's changed. You saw how it is here."

"Pappa," she pleaded, "can't you find a good nursing home for Mamma? It's too much for you."

"It's easy to say that. But you've forgotten . . . people have responsibilities. Your mother is my wife."

"*Was*, Pappa, *was*! She's changed. The woman that you are living with is not the same one you married. That's the way life is. We change."

"She's still the same deep inside, Beth."

"All right, have it your way." Beth took a breath. "What else is happening?"

"What else could be happening?"

"Anything special?"

"Nothing is going on here," he said. He was tired.

"Well . . . I heard that they caught those men who escaped from prison. You know, the ones we heard about while we were at your place. That we read about in the paper."

"I've forgotten all about that."

Beth suddenly heard noise in the background, rustling sounds. She realized that her mother was probably getting into something and her father probably had to take care of it. She ended the conversation.

Beth drank one last glass of Bristol Cream and then went to bed. The sweet taste did not leave her mouth, even after she brushed her teeth. She remembered that she had a dentist appointment, and set her alarm clock. A few minutes later, she was fast asleep.

She awoke to a noise.

Ulf, she thought, and opened her eyes. The clock radio's yellow numbers showed her the time: 23:15. She swallowed and licked her lips. Her tongue felt dry.

Ulf had probably gone to the kitchen.

Beth swung her legs over the edge of the bed and sat there in her nightgown for a moment. The entire house was silent.

She got up and noticed that her nightgown was wrinkled and damp.

"Ulf?" she called.

She'd closed the door to the bedroom when she went to bed, so now she opened it carefully and stepped into the living room. Maybe Ulf had gone directly to the guest room, or maybe he'd gone to the room that they called the library. Maybe he was finding it hard to wind down after a hard day's work, so maybe he was sitting there with a beer in order to relax.

She stood on the Persian rug which had been a gift from Ulf's parents. The pattern seemed to come alive. It swirled around her feet.

"Ulf, are you there?"

Behind her somewhere a long, drawn-out sigh. She gasped and whirled around.

Everything seemed normal.

Her entire body trembled. She crept to the wall and found the light switch. The chandelier gave a soft, yellowish glow. She looked for something to use as a weapon, but found nothing. She forced herself to breathe slowly and deeply.

"Everything's under control, Beth," she mumbled to herself. "Everything is in order just the way it should be."

She walked into the hallway and found an umbrella. Her hands were shaking and she found it hard to swallow. Holding the point in front of her, she walked through each room.

Nothing.

She was the only one home. No Ulf, and no one else either.

She was all alone.

She remembered that Ulf had his cell phone with him. She could call him and find out when he planned to come home. She was irritated that she could not recall the number and she had to find her address book.

"The number you have reached is not in service at this time. Please try again later."

Of course.

She sank down into the sofa and turned on the television. She surfed through the stations. She wasn't tipsy at all any longer, but she had a dull, thudding headache. Maybe something else. Something to do with her heart. A clenching pain shot through her chest and pressed against her diaphragm, making her lose her breath. She'd never felt anything like it.

A few moments later, the attack subsided, and she found herself lying on the sofa. Her paternal aunt had died of a heart attack. Her aunt had barely turned fifty. She remembered how upset her father had been. How intensely he mourned. Her happy, enthusiastic Aunt Eva, who had climbed mountains and done a number of other wild things women of her generation usually did not do. As she thought about her, tears started forming under her eyelids, she started to pant and she felt another attack coming on. Once it came, she began to throw her head wildly and bit her tongue before she lost consciousness.

5

THE ALARM WENT OFF. Beth leapt out of bed. She was used to moving quickly when she heard the bell. She could tell by the sound of the tires on the pavement outside that it was still raining.

Ulf was home. He'd been sleeping with his back to her.

She didn't remember a thing after the cramping pain in her heart the night before. She imagined she'd lost consciousness there on the sofa. Did she manage to get herself to bed somehow? She wished that Ulf had come home and found her there—*my beloved Beth*— and gotten worried. *Should we call an ambulance?* She would have declined.

"I feel better now, really. It was temporary, only due to stress."

Ulf was not stirring. So she went to the bathroom and took a shower. Then she put on jeans, a blouse, and a jacket. She put on some make-up. It had been a while since she'd used make-up. Summer was over and it was time to go back to being normal, everyday Beth, who was in control of her life, who went to work every morning and who was needed and desired.

She brewed some coffee, but she wasn't hungry. Her tooth ached slightly. As she was brushing her teeth, Ulf came into the bathroom.

"I'd like some privacy," he said.

She went into the living room and listened to him. He peed for a long time, then washed his hands carefully. She opened the bathroom door.

"Did you come home late last night?"

"I left a message on the machine."

"Right . . . yes."

Ulf went back into the bedroom and crept into bed.

"I've got to get some more sleep."

"What kind of extra work did you have to do?"

"Just some overtime. Why?"

"Just wondering."

"I was interviewing a woman who fled here from Chechnya. Irina was her name."

"Did she get here recently?"

"No, awhile ago."

"Where did you find her?"

"Come on, leave it. What's gotten into you?"

He said nothing about the night before. So she must have found her way back to bed on her own.

She left the room without saying goodbye. She felt like punishing him. She had no bus pass, so she decided to walk to the subway station.

As she stepped onto the sidewalk, she saw the cat in Birgitta's window. The cat followed her movements with its eyes.

The Green Line was late. All through the spring this had been happening, and she'd hoped they'd figured out what kept breaking down. Something was wrong with the signals. It didn't really bother her too much, as she hardly ever used the subway.

She picked up a free newspaper and began to read. Ten minutes later, an overly full train arrived. She managed to cram inside and found a place to stand. It was one of the new trains. She'd only ridden this kind once or twice before. Every car had its own name: Sofia, Ulla, Ted. She liked that.

Her tooth bothered her and she dreaded the thought that soon someone would be poking away at it with sharp dental tools.

She got off at Odenplan. The dentist's office was on Norrtullsgatan. She checked her watch. She would just make it on time.

Strangely she wasn't feeling much of her usual primitive fear when she had to visit the dentist.

The office was new and clean. She gave her name to the receptionist and was encouraged to take a seat and wait.

"And, please, put on a pair of shoe coverings, if you would be so kind," the woman added. "You'll find them in the yellow bucket by the door."

The woman was very young. Her language was stilted and formal.

Putting on the sloppy blue foot coverings made Beth feel strangely vulnerable. People only wore shoe coverings in places where they could not defend themselves, such as hospitals, where people poked and prodded you mentally and physically. She leaned against the wall as she slipped them on.

A nurse came into the waiting room. "Beth Svärd?"

The nurse was hardly more than a girl. She was wearing a ponytail, which bobbed up and down. As Beth walked into the treatment room, she felt the old familiar unease and dizziness. She'd often had cavities as a child, and one time they'd even had to pull out one of her molars. She remembered how she'd passed out in the dentist's chair, and when she woke up, the tooth was still there. They couldn't get it out. Finally, they decided to put her to sleep and take it out surgically.

Dentist Freddy was tall and tanned. She thought he looked familiar. Maybe she'd seen someone who looked like him in an ad for men's underwear. She was ashamed of her thoughts.

"So you're a friend of Görel's," he said to make a more personal connection.

Beth thought she should thank him for taking her on such short notice, but the words would not come out. Every once in a while she could be struck dumb, as if the words did not know how to form themselves in her mouth.

She sat down in the chair and the bright, warm light was turned right into her face.

"Where does it hurt?" asked the dentist.

She could only make a gesture. The dentist was wearing a mask so she could only see his blue eyes.

"I notice that you bite down fairly hard," he commented. "How are you sleeping? Do you use a mouth guard? Do you know whether or not you grind your teeth?"

He's careful in his questioning, Beth thought. He doesn't come right out and ask me if I have a companion in bed.

"No idea," she said.

Beth tried to think about his wife and what Görel had said about them not getting along. Then the cramp in her heart came. It pressed the air right out of her lungs and made her jerk so that the tray of instruments flew to the floor. Then she shut her eyes and was gone.

When she woke up, he was right next to her. His blond bangs hung in his face. She thought it was Him, the One they'd buried in the ground. For a second, she thought she was going to lose her mind for good. She was not able to flee. She lay where she lay and her arms and legs were heavy.

Gradually she saw that she was at the dentist's.

She tried to laugh, which made the dentist relax. He patted her on the cheek.

"You gave us a good scare, there, Beth," he said. "We've called an ambulance."

She could not move. The chair she lay in was covered in her sweat.

"Something with my heart, right?" she whispered, as the tears began to set in.

"Has something like this happened before?"

"Yes. Last night. But it stopped."

"They'll have to take a look at you at the hospital. I'm not a doctor. I'm only good at teeth. You'll have to give me a call later on and make another appointment."

It appeared that the dentist thought she was not about to die. She was going to survive this attack and be able to handle her toothache later on. It had been such a long time since someone had been that kind to her. Really, really kind.

How fragile I am, she thought. *Maybe I'm going to fall apart completely.*

They took her to Saint Göran's Hospital. There they questioned her and fastened electrodes to her chest. She wanted to get up and go to the bathroom, but they said she had to lie still on the cot and not move.

"Who is your closest relative?" a young nurse asked. She had glasses and down on her cheeks.

She's nothing but a kid, Beth thought. They're all so young. It's me who's getting old. My life is over.

Then Ulf was next to her in that little examination room.

"How are you?" he asked in a thin voice.

"Remember Aunt Eva?" she whispered.

"No."

"I've told you about her. She died of a heart attack."

Ulf shrugged and stared at the wall. There were steps in the hall-way outside. Beth wanted to ask someone to open the door so that she could see and hear people who were alive.

She searched for his hand.

"What if it's genetic, Ulf? What if I die now? What if it's all over?"

She began to cry violently and uncontrollably.

"Calm down, Beth, calm down."

"It happened last night, too. I was all by myself and it came over me. I was convinced I was going to die . . ."

"You're in good hands, now," he said with tension in his voice.

They found nothing wrong with her, so they sent her home.

"Your heart is as strong as an elephant's," the doctor said. The doctor was a woman with thin, red lips. Her eyes wandered from exhaustion.

"What can this be, then? How is this happening?"

"There are many possibilities. How is your digestion?"

"Digestion?"

"Yes, problems with digestion can cause these symptoms some-times. Or perhaps you have been under great stress lately?"

Beth stared at her.

"Anyway, there is nothing wrong with your heart. That must be a relief to hear, right?"

A pager in the doctor's pocket began to beep. A hunted look came over her as she got up and held out her hand. "As I said, at least you don't have to worry about your heart."

That evening, Beth pulled herself together enough to make dinner. She put some salmon in the oven and boiled some new potatoes. She made a tasty-looking salad. She found a damask tablecloth in the linen closet which she hadn't used for a number of years. She set a beautiful table in the dining room.

Ulf had driven her home and then gone back to work. He was part of a group of freelance journalists who rented office space in Söder, the gentrified area of Stockholm. Ulf said he would be home by seven.

"Please stay home with me," she pleaded. "Just today, please stay home with me."

His face twitched.

"I can't. I have to finish an article today. Just lie down and rest for a while. I'll be back later this evening."

Beth took a long hot shower and then searched through her wardrobe to find a dark green skirt and soft white sweater. She knew that he liked her in those clothes. She put on make-up and made her hair into a French knot.

She saw her frightened eyes in the mirror.

She poured a glass of port and forced herself to drink it slowly. She turned on the radio and raised the volume until it filled the entire house. She felt warm and tired.

"So, how was the dentist's?" Ulf asked.

They sat at the dining table. The countess and her servant. A horrible farce, Beth thought.

"Well, I told you that I passed out because of the pain in my heart."

"Right."

She drank some wine, and then dried her mouth carefully.

"Have you ever thought noticed that you say 'right' too much?" she teased. "You say it far too often, but it doesn't really sound like you and you should cut it out."

Ulf wrinkled his forehead, but said nothing.

For a while, they ate in silence. She noticed he took a fish bone from his mouth. He held it between his fingers and examined it.

"So, the fish wasn't cleaned properly?" she asked.

"It's just one bone. No big deal."

"Something awful happened," she said. "When I woke up at the dentist's, I didn't know where I was at first . . . I thought we were there . . . in the country . . . and He . . . you know . . . *He* was the one standing over me. The dentist looked like him. The same eyes . . . the same bangs . . . yes, I know we were not ever going to talk about this again . . . but I realized . . . ."

Ulf was breathing loudly through his nose.

Beth could not stop herself.

"Ulf . . . I can't get away from him. I see him the minute I close my eyes. I think that he is here in the house with me . . . that he is going to . . . I hear strange noises and I don't ever want you to leave me. I want you here at home with me."

Ulf lit a cigarette. They'd started to smoke inside the house. It really didn't matter much to them any longer.

Beth lit a cigarette, too.

"It's like being caught in a horror film and being the main character even though I haven't signed the contract," she exclaimed.

Ulf let the smoke escape through his lips.

"And the director," she continued, "is the Devil Himself, or maybe God."

"So what are you going to do about it?" he asked with no emotion in his voice.

"Do?"

"Go to the police? Tell them everything?"

Beth felt a burning sensation in her stomach.

"How could you say such a thing!"

He grimaced.

"I just thought . . . no, forget it. Just forget it."

"Ulf, don't say such things! We decided to forget the whole thing!"

"Do you think that forgetting is even possible?"

She took a deep drag of her cigarette.

"We have to stick together on this. We can never leave each other. I love you and I need you and you must never leave me, never ever! Do you understand?"

They slept together that night and he held her and came into her the way he used to when their love was new and intense.

"Let's make a little baby," she whispered. "We'll start over. It's not too late. We have our lives in front of us and I love you."

6

BETH BEGAN TO MISS HER STEPSON ALBIN. She hadn't seen him the entire summer. He was an intelligent boy, wise beyond his years, and at times she could see Ulf in him. When he was smaller, he would visit often and at times even sleep over. She found it easy to be around him. He had a good sense of humor and his vocabulary was above average, which often surprised her because of Ylva's lack of higher education. Once Ylva had dreamed of becoming a psychologist, but quit her studies a few months later and now worked in a photo shop.

Ylva and Albin lived in one of the buildings near Råcksta Crematorium. When Albin was younger, he was frightened by it. Even the word *crematorium* bothered him. It was a hard, uncompromising word, filled with destruction and annihilation.

"They're our nearest neighbors," he told Beth once. He was six years old at the time. She had no idea what he was talking about.

"They come at night and they look into our windows," he explained. "Although they're dead, at night they can move around like spirits."

"Spirits?"

"Right. But I have my sword, the one I got from Grandpa. So I'm not afraid. Not really."

The burial grounds by the Crematorium were flat and deserted. As a joke, she'd said to Ulf, "If you bury me there, I will haunt you until you dig me up and move me somewhere else. Like Hässelby Villastad's Cemetery."

She knew that Hässelby Villastad's Cemetery was already almost full, but she'd said that to Ulf just in case she would be the first to go and he'd have to arrange her burial. In those days, they could joke about things like that. Death was something far away from them.

In the forest behind the burial grounds was the Grimsta natural area. Beth had often gone on outings with Albin on those wide grounds. They'd looked for woodpeckers and used Albin's new compass, a birthday gift when he was eight, to do orienteering. He'd learned to use it fairly quickly.

Ylva was a plump woman, totally natural, and she never put on airs. Her relationship to Ulf had always surprised Beth. She thought that they did not fit well together. Their marriage only lasted a few years. Then came a period when Ylva kept away from Ulf and did not let Ulf see his son, as if it were Ulf's fault, and only Ulf's fault, that the marriage did not last.

"Our marriage had become one great triviality," Ulf told Beth shortly after they met. "One gray stretch of indifference. Whole days would pass by without a word between us. And I couldn't handle living in . . . that silence. So I packed my bags and left."

Ylva had matured since those days. Beth thought about what Ulf had said before, that he and Ylva were becoming closer again. She could taste metal in her mouth. It was ten in the morning. She lifted the receiver and punched Ylva's number. A deep adolescent voice answered.

"It's Beth Svärd," she said. "Did I dial the wrong number?"

"Hi there, Beth," the breaking voice said, and Beth was distressed to realize she hadn't recognized Albin.

An hour later, Albin threw his bike down in the yard and came in. He had really grown a great deal during the summer. His hair stood straight up like the bristles of a broom. Beth came to give him a hug and felt the tension in his body. He seemed defensive.

"Sit down," she said. "It's been a long time. What would you like? A glass of juice? You must be really thirsty after biking this distance."

He looked at her politely.

"No, thanks, I'm good. Maybe a glass of tap water."

"It's no trouble, really."

"I know. I'm good."

"All right. How's summer been for you and your mom?"

"Fine."

"I heard you were on Fårö."

"Yep, that's right."

She found something new and unusual in his manner of speaking. A distance that had nothing to do with the fact his voice was breaking. She did not know what she should say.

"You've grown, Albin," she finally said.

He grinned.

"I hardly recognized you," she continued.

"Really?"

"And I haven't heard from you all summer."

"Well, you guys were in the countryside."

"We've been back for a while now."

"Dad said . . . ," he broke off and his face and neck turned red.

Beth cleared her throat and lit a cigarette.

"Well, what did your dad say?"

"Oh, nothing."

"It was something." Her voice was louder. "Tell me, I want to know!"

The teenager swallowed and pulled at a cuticle on one of his thumbs.

"Oh, he said . . . he said you wanted to be left alone . . . that I shouldn't . . ."

Beth blew out smoke.

"I see," she said. "He meant that I didn't want you to stop by."

"Not exactly . . . he meant . . . you needed your rest."

"And why would I need my rest? Did your delightful and thoughtful father mention why?"

Albin leapt from the chair.

"The hell if I know!" he spit out. "I don't give a flying fuck about your relationship!"

"Sorry," she said quietly. "I didn't mean . . . sorry, Albin. There must have been some misunderstanding. It's true I haven't been feeling well. Yesterday I thought I was having a heart attack. That's probably what he was thinking about. Sorry, Albin, I didn't mean to start a fight."

Albin walked into the living room, flopped into the sofa and turned on the TV. He flipped between channels before settling on MTV. Beth followed him.

"Would you like some ice cream?" she asked. "I have pear flavor. And some chocolate syrup we could pour on it."

"Sure," he said. "Thanks."

He almost sounded like himself again.

While they ate the ice cream, Beth struggled to find the right words.

"Do you remember when we used to play Memory?" she asked. "You used to be so good at it. You always knew exactly which pieces to turn over."

"It's called having a photographic memory," he said. He had ice cream around his mouth and Beth had to resist the desire to take her finger and wipe it off.

"A memory like that must be very useful," she said. "Especially for studying. I bet you learn things fairly easily."

"Yeah."

"How does it feel to be back in school again?"

"Fine, but strange. Tobbe, my friend . . . you remember."

"Was Tobbe your best friend?"

"Not my best friend, but still. It feels so wrong, so unfair."

"What happened to him exactly?" She already knew what had happened, but she hoped that if he talked about it, he might feel better.

"It was supposed to be a normal operation. He was getting one of his knees fixed. He never woke up."

"Was he allergic to the anesthesia?"

"I don't think so."

"I think the doctors have to check that before an operation."

Albin frowned.

"The whole thing is very sad, Albin. It's really sad."

Albin jumped up from the sofa. She noticed how tall and thin he was.

"I wanted to go to the funeral! I wanted to go and say goodbye!" he exclaimed. "You know, it's like we left him in a lurch! We get to go on with our lives and enjoy our summers, while he . . . have you ever seen a dead person? Besides the twin babies I mean? Someone who was older?"

Her heart felt pricked as if by electric shocks. She forced herself to breathe calmly. She closed her eyes and shook her head.

"No," she said softly. "No . . . I haven't. They say that dead people look like they are sleeping. Especially if they've been ill and suffering for a long time. Then they look . . . released. But your friend Tobbe . . . he was young, and, you're right, all young people should live a long time. But I don't think that . . . death is something to be afraid of. It's part of life."

Finally Beth's school term began and she felt relieved. Finally something else could occupy her thoughts. Her work could exhaust her, both mentally and physically, and the exhaustion helped her relax.

She was given a fifth grade class and for the first few weeks she was strong and enthusiastic. She still had trouble sleeping, however. She went to the care center and asked a doctor for some sleeping pills.

"You're young and healthy," he said. "There are other ways to fall asleep besides pills. Do you exercise? You ought to get out in the fresh air and jog or run or just take long walks. All sleeping pills can create addictions."

She did not dare insist.

Every night the memories came back.

How she crossed the dry lawn and came to the door of the shed. How he was standing there and lunged at her. How he fumbled in the air and she stretched up with the heavy wooden handle in her hands. And then the sound. The sound.

She often thought about Albin's question. If she'd seen a dead person. She did not think of herself as someone who had killed someone else.

No. It was an accident. He provoked her. The victim. The dead man. If he had not entered their property. It was their property, the part that was protected! If he had not done that, he would be alive today. He would not be torturing her now.

She would sometimes doze off but would wake up with a jerk, breathing heavily. She would be in a fetal position, her hands clenched, the palms marked by her fingernails. She felt her hands and wondered at their form. A grown woman's hands. They could not be her own.

That fall she had difficulty remembering the names of her pupils. They all seemed the same to her. Even the names were similar. There were four girls named Fanny. Four boys named Jens. Two each with Jonatan, Marcus, and Maria.

She had taken over the class from a colleague who had gone on sick leave.

All the girls dressed alike. Their pants were tight at the hips, flaring out, made of a flimsy, shiny material, and their jackets had fake fur collars. They all wore their hair in buns with no bangs. The boys wore their hair shagged in all directions and their clothes smelled dirty.

She did her best to make each student an individual, but they kept flowing together. Up until now, she was still able to raise her voice above the dull drone of theirs, but for how long?

Her job was to teach them useful things. Their background, their history, their community and culture. Teach them about life.

As the weeks went by, she found it difficult to speak. She was often hit by dizziness, which increased every day until she found she had to run her hand along the wall to stay upright. This was not something she could hide forever.

One Friday afternoon, Görel was waiting for Beth after the last lesson of the day. It was a day with frost in the air. The wind was strong, and Beth was freezing, longing for a thicker sweater, even though the heat was on in the building. The children had been loud and noisy and she found herself pleading with them, which was the beginning of the end. But she could not help herself.

When the bell rang, Görel walked into the classroom and opened a window.

"It's amazing how a group of kids can suck out all the oxygen in a room," she said.

"Your head gets tired," Beth agreed.

"Are you in a hurry to get home, or do you have time for a walk?"

Beth felt a shiver of unease.

"A little bit of a hurry," she said.

Her colleague took Beth's arm. "I have to talk to you," she said. "It's important."

Görel had brought her car to work that morning. She usually did not, since she lived only a few minutes away.

"Get in," she said. "Let's drive to Lövsta and take a walk there. It's so pleasant when all the fall colors are out."

Beth buckled her seat belt. Her temples were beating.

Blood, she thought. *I hear my own blood circulation.*

"Are you feeling well?" Görel asked.

"I'm just tired. Really tired. It's been an intense week. Thank God it's Friday."

"That's the truth. Are you and Ulf doing anything special this weekend?"

"Not really. What about you?"

"I thought I'd work in the garden for a bit. Bring in the furniture and hammock. I don't think that we'll be eating outside again this year."

"Well, it's been a good summer." Beth used the cliché mechanically.

Görel turned onto Kyrkhamnsvägen which led toward Lövsta's park area. She parked next to the beach on Lake Mälar. During the heat of summer, the place would be filled with people splashing in the water and sunbathing. Today there was just a flock of ducks. They pressed close together like one gray clump.

"What did you need to talk to me about?" Beth asked. "Something going on between you and Martin?"

Görel laughed nervously.

"Between Martin and me? No, not at all. It's something else."

They started to walk along the gravel path. On a hill to their left, an old school stood. Gunnar Sträng had once been a student there in the early 1900's, but the building had been empty for a long time. Lately the building had been renovated and made useful just like the stone building by Kyrkhamn which was now used by artists.

Beth pulled up the hood of her jacket.

"It's really windy," she said.

"Well, Beth, what I wanted to say was . . . what is going on with you these days? We've all noticed something's wrong and we're really worried about you. Beth . . . we're your friends and we really want to help you. If there is the least thing we can do for you, let us know."

Beth stopped, and the wind formed tears in her eyes.

"It's really nothing," she said. "I'm just going through a rough patch."

Görel held Beth's arm. Beth wanted to wrest herself free, but forced herself to be still and to breathe.

"You drink too much, am I right? Many of us have seen you swaying in the hallways. We could just close our eyes and ignore it, as that would be the easiest thing to do, but we're your friends. So I decided to be the one to talk to you. We've known each other for a long time, haven't we? And we've shared our secrets before, right?"

"*I* drink too much?" Beth exclaimed, and felt lighter. "I don't drink more than anyone else. Some wine, and some whiskey now and then. I'm not going to hide that. But I'll be damned if I drink more than you people."

Görel's face came right up to Beth's. Beth could see her large, rough pores.

"It's typical to deny it," Görel said. She sounded sad. "Denying it is what they all do."

"So you think I'm an alcoholic?"

"Please don't take it like that. It's not meant as a put-down. You need help. Help to stop . . . well, to put everything back to normal. Saint Erik's Heath Care has experts, and you're not the only one . . ."

Beth bit her lower lip and then broke out into laughter. Görel stared at her with empty blue eyes.

"Görel, you say that you're my friend. Let me ask you directly. Have you ever seen me drunk? Have *you*, personally, seen me drunk? Heard me slur my words? Have I ever reeked of alcohol?"

"Many of us . . ."

"You? Personally? You can't imagine that there could be any other explanation? Sure, I've been out of balance lately, but there could be other reasons than liquor. Right?"

"Please, Beth, can you tell me what's wrong?"

Beth lowered her voice.

"All right, I'll tell you," she said. "It's my heart. You can even call my dentist and check up on me. When I was there, I collapsed and he had to call an ambulance. I was hoping to keep it a secret, because I didn't want to play the martyr. So that's why I didn't tell any of you about it. But you see . . . it's genetic. My aunt, my father's sister, well . . . she died of a heart attack . . . just forty-nine years old. I've started to see . . . what that means for me."

7

She broke down completely that Monday. Beth had not slept well during the night. She'd tossed and turned. In the dark of night, she got the idea that someone had discovered the grave with the dead man. She realized that she had to go back to Skogslyckan and check to make sure that everything was still safe. She wondered whether she could convince Ulf to come with her. She would not be able to manage by herself. She did not dare. The images came and went in her mind.

An hour before the alarm went off, she got up. Ulf was sleeping on his side, mouth open. He'd always had an easier time sleeping than she did. The house was totally quiet. She looked out the window to see a hare sitting in the middle of the lawn and was surprised that it was so large. It swiveled its ears and Beth thought it would be nice to pet it. *I want to hold something soft in my arms.* From further away, on Sandviksvägen, she could hear the sound of a bus. The hare leaped up and scooted away into the bushes.

Beth yearned for daylight. She could not bear the nights any more Though now she could hardly bear the days, either. Just thinking about heading to school made her head ache and her temples throb. She swallowed some pain pills with a glass of lukewarm water. She thought about her conversation with Görel and how her colleagues had been watching her, studying her, and drawing conclusions. They must have had a meeting about it and Görel was

185

the one who took it upon herself to tell Beth about her colleagues' concerns.

Problems with alcohol indeed!

Görel had seemed embarrassed when she realized she'd put her foot in her mouth, but she did not apologize.

"Please, Beth," Görel said as they walked back to the car. "You know that I've always liked you and you have to know that I'll always be your friend."

Beth nodded. She said, "It's good to have friends."

Beth had longed to be left alone. Görel insisted on driving her home and would probably have come inside if Beth hadn't said that she had things to do.

Once she was home by herself, she turned on the water for a hot, scented bubble bath. She felt frozen from the inside out, as if her body would never feel warm and soft again.

The weekend had gone by slowly. Restless, Beth cleaned all the windows in the house and then drove to Vällingby to look for new curtains. Ulf worked all weekend, as usual. She didn't bother to ask him what he'd meant by telling Albin that she needed her peace and quiet. She did not want to get into any arguments. She wanted no conflict around her.

At the department store, she found a piece of dark blue art glass that she decided to buy, but she did not find any curtains she liked. They'd changed the store around and nothing was where it used to be. Beth felt very tired all of a sudden. Since it was Saturday, the store was packed with customers, and she'd found it hard to find a parking place. She'd had to drive to the top floor of the ugly gray parking garage.

She decided to go to a café for a *café au lait*. Then she punched her father's number. Lately she'd been calling him every day. He was the only one who could safely tell her of the local news, including whether a body had been found or not. He always read the morning paper and he would know before the national news could report. He'd tell her: *They've found someone dead close to our summer house.* He would still say "our."

Her father seemed to have a cold. He was in a bad mood and did not have much to say. Beth found she was irrationally angry toward the woman who had been her mother. If only her father would agree to put her in a nursing home.

So finally it was Monday and she had the entire work week before her.

So this is your life, she told herself. *Be glad you have a job and that you're healthy. You have a husband and you're not starving.*

She laughed weakly and tapped her mouth with her fingers.

"Ulf, I'm leaving now," she called into the stuffy bedroom air. She heard him move under the sheets.

"Wha . . . where are you going?"

"School of course. It's Monday. When are you getting up?"

"Later."

"There's coffee in the thermos."

"Thanks," he mumbled.

Say something, she thought. *Tell me you love me.*

Ulf was already deep asleep again.

Beth put on her new winter coat and looked at herself in the mirror. She'd bought it last spring and put it aside and had been eager to wear it the following winter. Now she noticed it seemed to hang loosely and looked too large. She must have lost a lot of weight lately.

When she stepped onto the front steps, she saw the cat. It sat on the garden path and did not move as she walked toward it. She felt forced to step aside into the grass, and her shoes got wet.

"Go away!" she hissed. "Why don't you go back where you came from?"

The cat stared at her but did not move.

Beth walked along Loviselundsvägen and turned left at Blomod-larvägen. The air was sharp and clean. Some children passed her on their bikes, ringing their bells. Once they'd passed, one of the kids turned and yelled something at her. She must have heard wrong, but she thought it sounded like *bitch.* She was already starting to feel dizzy and the blood throbbed through her temples.

"Pull yourself together," Beth commanded herself. "It's just a couple of kids!"

To the left she saw a burnt-out, abandoned house. No one had lived there for many years. The owner was a strange old man who did not want to sell the property. She noticed the broken greenhouse, the twisted iron fence, and pipes. The frost had not yet withered the large clumps of goldenrod which grew everywhere and did its best to hide the ruins.

When would things start to grow on the grave? How long would it take for the corpse to turn to dust? Ten years? Twenty? She would have to wait that entire time.

Once the snow started falling, she would be able to breathe easier. A great deal of snow fell there, at that elevation, and it would last a long time. Snow and cold would be her best friends.

She hadn't thought that much about the wild animals before, but as she walked now, she realized a fox might be able to get a whiff of the body. There were foxes in the area. The population was growing after years when fox mange had decimated the packs. A flash of heat warmed her back, but her fingertips still felt ice cold. She stuffed her hands into her pockets and tried to walk faster.

At the crosswalk, once she reached Sandviksvägen, she found two girls from her class waiting for the light. Anna B and Anna S. Beth tried to be sociable, ask them how their weekend went, but she was not able to do it. Dizziness overcame her and made her reach into the air for support.

Both girls stared at her. They appeared frightened.

"Oops," Beth said. "I almost slipped on the ice."

They walked away from her with straight backs, their heads together.

She decided to assign the students an essay. But she was not able to speak because her headache hammered harder and harder. The classroom seemed to be a boiling pot of stuffy air and loud noises. The students were running around the desks. One girl was blowing bubble gum bubbles. The gum was pink and slimy. Another girl hit the first one so that the bubble broke and splattered over her face and the two of them laughed loudly.

"Let's quiet down, now!" Beth called, but her voice did not carry. Her voice was weak, hardly more than a whisper.

They're just little kids, she thought. *They're just little kids and you're a big, strong grown-up.* She called again:

"Let's be quiet and calm down!"

Finally they were all sitting in their places. By then, her whole body was shaking. Her mouth tasted sour. She swallowed and got ready to speak.

"Take out your composition books," she said. "Let's write an essay."

She heard giggling and whispering in the corner, but pretended she didn't hear. She said, "Write about your way to school. How you get here. Or you can use your imagination and invent a way to get to school which has nothing to do with walking or biking."

To her surprise, the children quieted down, opened their books, and began to write. She thought she'd conquered them, and she pulled out her chair to sit down.

Something was on the chair. She'd been standing at the podium and so hadn't seen it before. She'd hoped she would have a chance to sit down and catch her breath now that the children were busy. The dizziness would leave and she'd be normal again.

But there it was: something on the chair. A green, see-through bottle. Inside the bottle, something was moving. It appeared to be a snake. She saw its body curl around. She remained standing and slowly raised her eyes to see that all the children were looking at her. They'd put down their pens expectantly. Their eyes were light and scornful. A whistling sound began to rise in her ears, louder and louder until it reached a crescendo, ending in a roar.

She grabbed the book on the podium and threw it at the class, ran to the door, wrenched it open, and ran away.

8

At first, Beth received a few weeks of sick leave. At home, she thought she would cry, because her eyes were burning. She was in the bathroom, staring at herself in the mirror.

"You are so ugly!" she told her reflection out loud. "You are an ugly failure who never should have been born! You never should have been born!"

People still wouldn't leave her alone.

One of the first days Beth was home, Görel appeared at her front door, accompanied by one of the girls from Beth's class. Maybe Malin, maybe Anna C. Beth saw them coming and Görel must have seen her through the window, because she waved. They had a bouquet of flowers. Beth was forced to open the door and let them in.

Görel hugged her. Beth could smell the snow on her jacket.

"The flowers are from all of us at work. Each one of us bought a rose . . . we hope that you will get better and come back to us."

"Thanks," Beth said quietly.

Görel pushed the girl to the front. Beth looked right into her eyes, which were porcelain blue. *Like enamel,* Beth thought. *Enamal.*

The girl said, "Well, I'm here to offer an apology." Her voice was hard and metallic, but small. "We didn't mean to scare you. Emil is a tame garden snake. He's my pet. He's actually really nice."

Görel patted Beth's arm. "See? They really didn't mean any harm."

"It's just I didn't expect it," Beth said. "I was so surprised. That's why . . ."

191

The girl did not take her eyes off Beth.

"We just wanted to play a joke on you."

Görel stroked the girl's arm, her entire face smiling down.

"But you have to be careful with your poor old teachers."

Then she said, to Beth, "They really did not mean any harm. Please understand. But at times, we're all extra sensitive. I've been that way myself sometimes. At those times, surprises are things we can't handle properly. By the way," Görel turned to the girl, "don't snakes go into hibernation at this time of year?"

The girl shook her head.

"Not Emil. He's awake year round."

Beth did not ask them to come inside. She leaned against the wall. The roses lying on the hallway table shone a bright yellow.

"Well, then, I guess we'd better get going," Görel said at last. "Rest up, my dear, and as soon as you feel better, come back to us."

The girl held out her bony, small hand. She did not say a word.

Beth stopped leaving the house. She watched videos, hundreds of them which they had bought over the years. She wore sweatpants which bunched loosely around her legs.

Occasionally Görel called and Beth felt she had to take the call. Autumn moved toward its end, and one day the ground was covered by a thick layer of snow. Beth could see animal tracks, both those of small birds and those of the cat, in the yard. One morning she saw footprints, the marks of shoes, right beneath her bedroom window. Someone had been walking around the house at night. Maybe a peeping Tom. Neither she nor Ulf had noticed a thing, which made her feel afraid.

Now Ulf often worked overtime. Once a week he went to the grocery store and bought food, but he never asked Beth to come with him. He also did not request that she take a shower or get dressed in better clothes.

She rarely saw anyone besides Ulf. At times she could observe people walking by on the sidewalk while she was sitting next to the kitchen window. She started to feel as if they were acquaintances.

There was the woman in a yellow coat who walked her dog. The dog was black and shaggy, and Beth thought that she might like it. One time the dog did his business right next to their mailbox. Beth was going to run outside in a rage, but the woman in the yellow coat had immediately gotten out a plastic bag and picked up after her dog. The woman seemed pleasant. She was always talking to her dog.

Maybe I should get a pet, Beth thought. *A pet might help me forget.*

The neighborhood they lived in was quiet and pleasant. Beth felt she needed the peace and quiet, but she was also afraid of it. When the pictures came into her head, she turned up the volume on the television, lit a cigarette, and began to sing the old German Christmas carol "O Tannenbaum." Just the first verse, over and over. It was the only verse she knew, and for some reason, that Christmas carol was the only one which popped into her head. She sang at a high pitch and her voice would shake, until the pictures faded from her mind.

One evening at around six, the telephone rang. She didn't even care to answer, but it might be Ulf, so she did.

The voice came from far away. It was a woman's voice, which was weak and breathless, but still clear. "Are you Beth?"

"Yes," Beth replied in a whisper.

There was no answer. Beth said louder:

"Yes, I'm Beth Svärd."

It seemed that there was the sound of quiet crying on the other end.

"Hello?" said Beth. "Hello? Who is this?"

She heard nothing more and soon the line went dead.

Beth's hands began to shake. She paced around the house until she found her packet of cigarettes. She lit one and drew a deep drag. The door handle ratted and a moment later, Ulf came inside. Beth ran to him.

"I've been so scared!"

"What's going on with you?"

"Someone called here. It was a woman's voice . . . . She asked if I were Beth . . . then she said nothing more . . . . She seemed to be crying."

Ulf hung up his coat.

"So many crazies these days."

"Then she just hung up the phone . . . or maybe the line was cut!"

"Don't make such a big deal out of it."

"It is a big deal. Let's get a private number."

"That's not necessary. Certainly not because of one phone call. It was probably someone playing a prank."

"What if it keeps up?"

"Don't worry about it. Just rise above it. By the way, isn't it time to eat?"

That evening he was intimate with her again. They had shared a bottle of wine but they did not talk to each other. They had played classical music as they sat beside each other on the sofa. Then Ulf put his arm around her and gently pulled her to the thick, white rug on the floor. He pulled her off her pants and they made love to the sounds of the *Pathétique*.

She cried afterwards.

Ulf stroked her head and whispered that she had to try harder to get better.

"Be normal, Beth, just be normal. You can't keep going like this. On sick leave day after day. That can't be good for you. It's not good for us."

She was on her back, holding his face between her hands.

"Is there anything that could be good for us, Ulf? Anything at all?"

Ulf sat up and moved away from her. He lit a cigarette and started to smoke.

"There is," he said at last.

"What could it be?"

"Why don't you . . . tell someone about what happened?"

She got angry.

"*Tell* someone?"

"Yes, but not the police necessarily. How about a priest, Beth? Priests are bound to secrecy. I see how this whole thing is eating at you. You'll never get over it until you tell somebody and receive . . . some absolution."

"What about you, then?" she asked. "You're involved in all this, too. At least as much as I am."

"True," he said, tiredly.

A thought came to her.

"You haven't told anybody, have you?"

"Of course not. This is eating at me, too. It would be strange if it didn't. But when you get right down to it, I was not the one who swung the axe."

9

ULF LEFT EARLY THE NEXT MORNING. He was supposed to interview a Swedish artist living in Copenhagen whose provocative murals had irritated Danish authorities. Beth felt relief when he left. His words kept repeating in her mind: He was absolutely serious when he suggested she should go talk to someone.

About that awful thing.

Just touching on it, making it more visible, more real!

Her heart was icy as she imagined the situation. There would be a priest with drooping cheeks who would listen quietly until a bit of reservation would come into his eyes. Not only reservation but also a bit of anxiety.

"I can't tell you what to do," he would say. "I feel you should look into yourself to decide what would bring peace to your soul. You know what I mean, don't you, dear child?"

Beth felt completely on her own. It made her feel tortured, not strong. She paced the house, her body completely tense. She was breathlessly afraid of the anonymous woman on the phone who might call back at any time. Who was she? Did she know anything about what had happened? Maybe it was just a prank or some disturbed person who picked her name at random from the phone book. Maybe it was complete chance that the woman picked her.

The daily mail brought a letter from her father. When she saw his handwriting on the envelope, she realized it was uneven and shaky.

He'd become an old man. She sat down at the kitchen table and tears began to run down her cheeks.

She wished she were a little girl again. Her father would have taken care of her and protected her from all bad things. She would be able to start over. Everything would have been different.

She was nervous when she opened the letter since her father seldom wrote. She felt a growing tenderness for him due to all that he had had to endure. *I've disappointed him*, she thought.

Immediately, she chased away the thought.

It wasn't my fault! Not my fault!

She began to read:

Dear Beth,

I have thought a great deal about what you said regarding Mamma. I realize that you were right. We can't keep going like this. We just can't do it any longer. I have weighed your suggestion about a nursing home for Mamma. Of course, I've read a great deal about bad homes where the old people are not taken care of properly. That worries me greatly. But now I find I have no choice. I really have done everything I could, and I am not able to continue. What do you think, Beth, am I doing the right thing? I've talked to Juni, too, and she agrees with your suggestion. I've contacted a brand new nursing home. The director seems to know what she is doing. Her name is Marit Svedberg, and she has promised that Mamma can just try out the place at first. Maybe this week already. Best wishes from your Pappa.

She picked up the phone and called him right away and he answered immediately. He seemed stressed and unhappy.

"I'm going to drive over right away," she said. "I'm going to jump in the car and head over there now. I have some days off from work."

She could tell by his voice that he was happy to hear that.

When Beth drove off, it was raining, a cold and slushy rain that could change into snow at any time. Earlier, when she'd opened the paper, she'd been surprised to see it was a Tuesday and the end of October.

Driving was pleasant. It was wonderful to leave the house. She listened to the purr of the motor, and enjoyed the sound. She was happy to be out. Traffic increased as she neared Enköping. There were a number of trucks lined up in the right-hand lane. As she passed them, she felt exhilarated.

She'd left a message on Ulf's phone: "I'm going to my dad's for a few days. Call me there if you need me."

When she reached Västerås, she pulled into a shabby rest stop to have a cup of coffee. She drove the rest of the way without stopping. When she reached Fallköping, dusk had come. She decided to do some grocery shopping before heading to her parents. She was tired and felt it throughout her entire body as well as in her head.

She drove to her parents' house, parked, and got out. She was uneasy about meeting her mother, but when she entered the apartment, her father was alone. He was wearing his brown cardigan with leather patches on the elbows. He'd had that cardigan as long as she could remember. His face appeared thin and fallen and his eyes were clouded. She noticed he'd been crying.

"Pappa," she said softly. She hugged him. His body was fragile and small. She thought she ought not to hug him too tightly or he would break. His skeleton wouldn't bear the force.

"They've already come to take her away," he said quietly. A sour smell came from his breath. His fingers plucked at his sweater.

"Who came?"

"The woman director, Margit Svedberg, called and said they were ready to take her in. I didn't realize it could go so quickly. The director came here herself. She said she wanted to see how Suzanne usually lived, what kinds of things she had around and stuff like that."

"She seems to be a very thoughtful person, Pappa."

Her father stared blankly at the window.

"Pappa. It sounds like the director really cares."

"They came and took her and she went willingly without saying a word. I'm not sure she even understood what was going on. I'd been worrying about this moment for so long. I remember my own mother . . . your grandmother, of course . . . how she was as strong as a tiger when they came to get her. Your aunt Lisbet had been taking care of her for so long . . . but Lisbet had come to the end of her rope. She told me how your grandmother had clung to the doorjambs with such strength that they almost broke her hands trying to pry her loose."

He swallowed and leaned against the kitchen table.

"So Mamma went with them just like that?"

"Well, she was singing, too."

"Singing?"

"'Red sails in the sunset.'"

"She always liked that song." Beth realized she was talking as if her mother were already dead. She quickly said, "She likes that song."

Her father smiled slightly.

"Did you go with her?"

"Of course I did. She has a fine room. It doesn't look like a room in an institution. She has a wide bed that she can raise or lower, and there is furniture that is a bit older as well as modern furniture in the general living areas. She seemed to feel right at home immediately."

"That's good, Pappa."

"Yes." He sighed. Then he said: "Are you hungry? You've driven a long way."

"I bought some shrimp and a bottle of white wine on my way here. We can have that."

"You're such a sweet, thoughtful girl."

As her father walked, Beth noticed that he had a hunchback. *No, this is all wrong!* She wanted to shout. *I'm not a sweet and innocent little girl!*

For the first time, sincere words formed in her brain: "I, your daughter, Beth Svärd, have killed a human being."

Her brain practiced the words over and over, but she could not bring herself to say them. *Me, your little girl, Beth, I've killed a human being.* Strangely, she found the words did not affect her. She shrugged her shoulders. Out loud she said, "Why don't we set the table here in the kitchen?"

10

===

BETH FOUND A BOTTLE OF SLEEPING PILLS IN HER FATHER'S BATH-ROOM CABINET. She took one of the small white pills and, a short while later, she was deeply asleep. It was the first night in a long time that she'd slept so well. Her father had made up the sofa bed for her, and she was nestled in sheets that her mother had embroidered with a monogram. They had a closet smell to them, since they hadn't been used for a long time. At first she was freezing when she undressed, so she wrapped a blanket around herself as she crept into bed. The door to the hallway was open as it had always been when she and Juni were little girls and afraid of the dark. The movements and sounds of the adults had been comforting.

Her father was humming and talking to himself as he walked around the house. He'd called the nursing home the evening before to see if everything was still all right.

Ulf had called Beth, too. Beth could hear restaurant noise and voices in his background.

"How long are you planning to be there?" Ulf asked.

"Don't know yet. Maybe a few days."

"Your dad needs you."

"Yes, he does. We're going to visit my mother tomorrow."

"Sounds good. I've got to run. 'Bye, now."

Beth wanted him to stay on the line longer: *Wait, tell me that you love me and that you're longing for me and that you had been worried about my driving so far with the roads in this condition.*

Ulf said nothing of the sort.

"'Bye," she said.

So she'd slept and when she woke, the sun was streaming into the living room window. From the sofa bed, she could see a spider web on the ceiling. *I should help with the cleaning,* she thought. *He knows so little about cleaning. And we should pack her clothes. She's not going to come back now.*

The smell of coffee came from the kitchen. Beth swallowed, and she noticed she had a slight sore throat. Her father came to the living room, peeked in. He was already fully dressed.

"Are you awake, my dear girl?"

"What time is it?" she answered.

"Just after nine."

I've slept the whole night through, Beth thought.

On the low, long, mahogany bookcase, Beth saw the graduation portraits of herself and of Juni. Between them was her parents' wedding photo. They seemed so young. Her mother had childlike round cheeks and her father still had hair. The thick, dark shock of hair had shrunk to a thin white ring around a bald dome.

Beth got out of bed. The floor was hard and cold against her feet.

Her father had already set the table in the kitchen. There were two cups and a plate with crisp-bread, margarine, and cheese which had started to sweat from room temperature. She realized that he'd been sitting and waiting for her.

"Do you think I should call the home now, or wait for a while longer?" he asked.

"I'm sure you can call now."

Beth tasted the coffee as her father went to telephone. It was bitter and burnt. She listened as her father spoke to someone at the home. When he returned, his lips were pursed in surprise. He firmed his lips to speak.

"They said that everything is going just fine. I can hardly believe it."

"Oh, go ahead and believe it."

"That young woman, Merit, was the one I spoke to. I asked if my wife was asking for me. Merit said she had, but in a nice way, not hysterically. We are going to go and see her today, aren't we? I want to be with her as much as possible. You understand, don't you? I think it's a good idea, so she doesn't think I've given up on her."

When they'd gotten into the car, her father said he felt shaky.

"Look. My hands are trembling."

Beth took his thin, cold hands into hers and rubbed them.

"This is a major change for you," she said. She could tell how clichéd it sounded. "For both of you, of course."

Her father carefully drew his hands back.

"Life is full of changes," he said. "By the way, Beth, I forgot to tell you something, or did I already say? Anyway, Merit Svedberg, the young woman I was just talking to, and her husband are looking for a house in the countryside. They know about our place and have even driven past it."

"Skogslyckan? Our house?"

"That's right."

"Were they there . . . recently?"

"I have no idea. But she might make you an offer. I did tell her that neither you nor Juni were really all that interested in selling Skogslyckan. Since it is our old family place, and people just don't get rid of their inheritance that easily."

The nursing home was called Solhöjden and it was located a bit out of town. It was a one-story building, recently built, clean, and painted in pastels. Beth thought the name was typical for such an institution. Both nursing homes and day care centers often had the word "sun" in them, as if the name itself brought sunshine to a place that was worn down by lack of money and hardened, burned-out personnel.

Beth was afraid of Merit's interest in Skogslyckan. The thought that the woman might have gotten near it brought a burst of heartburn and the taste of burnt coffee to her throat.

Her father was giving her a strange look.

"What business is it of theirs to come by our place uninvited?" Her voice was filled of tension. "It's closed down for the winter."

"Well," her father said, "it was probably earlier in the year. And I think it was her mother who drove past, not Merit. Susanne knew her mother, if I remember right."

In the nursing home, Beth's mother was sitting at a table eating lunch. She looked up but then kept on eating with quick glances to each side. Beth's father hurried to her and reached out to stroke her hair, but she writhed away from him. Food started to dribble down her chin. She was sucking on a mouthful of mashed potatoes.

"Beth came to see you," her father said softly.

Beth's mother looked up briefly and then looked away with no sign of interest.

"Hi, Mamma," Beth said.

The old woman's jaws chewed away. Hair poked from her chin. She was far from the fastidious woman she'd once been. A sly sparkle appeared in her eyes and then she yawned long and loud, revealing saliva and food.

"How are you doing?" Beth's father asked. "Did you sleep well in your new bed?"

Beth's mother plucked with her fingers, which had become rough and gnarly.

Beth sat down in a chair beside her mother, but she felt restless and it seemed that everyone in the room was looking at her. Beth did not know where to look. A rather large woman, in a wheelchair but smartly dressed in a skirt and pink blouse, rolled over to them. She stopped right in front of Beth.

"So who are you?" the woman said in a hostile voice.

"My name's Beth."

"What did you say?"

"Beth!"

"Bett?"

Beth nodded.

"So, you're Bett. What kind of an odd name is that?"

"I don't know. It's just my name."

"You don't live here with us, do you?"

"I live in Stockholm," Beth said as clearly as she could.

"Stockholm where the king lives? And where Greta Garbo is buried? Finally buried in the Storkyrkogård, the big cemetery? Wasn't that an awful thing to do to a dead person? Move our beloved idols here and there?"

"You're right . . ."

"Well, what are you doing here anyway?" The woman stuck her face right into Beth's. Beth's back started to sweat. *I'm wondering the same thing,* she thought. Out loud she said, "I'm visiting my mother."

The woman grabbed Beth's arm. Her fingernails were long and discolored.

"Let me tell you something," she hissed. "You have no business running around here and being young. And I know who you are, by the way. You are not a nice person. You're false. Do you know who Mata Hari is? Well, do you?"

Beth twisted to get free, but couldn't. A nurse came to her rescue.

"My dear Gerda, what are you doing to one of our guests?" the nurse said by way of apology. "Come with me now, and I'll give you some raisins."

The old woman let go of Beth's arm and made a happy noise.

"Gerda wants raisins," she said in a high-pitched, little girl's voice.

The nurse smiled. "You're Susanne Svärd's daughter, aren't you?"

Beth nodded.

"Back in the old days my mother went to her for her haircuts."

"Oh, I see."

"That was a long time ago. My mother is gone now."

"Oh, I'm sorry."

"Our mothers used to socialize, too. There was a whole group of them who hung out together. One time they all went to your mom's old homestead. It was called Skogslyckan, wasn't it? My mom used to talk about how wonderful it was there. She wished she'd had a place in the country, but . . . well, that never happened."

The nurse held out her hand. "I'm sorry, I forgot to introduce myself. I'm Merit Svedberg and I'm the manager here at Solhöjden."

"Oh, right, Pappa mentioned you."

"By the way, do you still have that summer house or have you sold it? It would be too much for your father now, right?"

"My sister and I have already inherited it."

"I see. So you come up to visit around here sometimes, then?"

"Yes," Beth said shortly.

"You hadn't perhaps . . . thought of selling it, have you? I'm just asking. It's so beautiful in the forest. My husband and I have been talking about how nice it would be to move to the countryside."

Merit lowered her voice. "Ove, that's my husband, is actually planning to start a pig farm, can you believe it? Pigs, of all things! Organic, of course, and treated in a humane manner, you know, slaughtered at the farm so that they never feel any stress. That appeals to my guy. He's an animal lover and he comes from a long line of farmers. The guidance counselor told him to forget about farming, as there's no future in it. So now he works at a bank, but he's never been happy there. It's so closed in. He wants to start over, and I don't have anything against it, either. I can commute, since it's only a couple miles from your place, right? And we already have two cars."

A flush of heat crawled up Beth's chest, and she felt that she was beginning to smell like underarm sweat.

Merit was chatting on. "And so we could also have some horses. Icelandic ponies, maybe. When you're that far out in the country-side, you might as well."

Merit's smile was friendly, her eyes sparkling with enthusiasm.

"Well, we don't plan to sell," Beth said brusquely.

Beth felt that Merit watched her expectantly. But was there a bit of spiteful glee in her eyes? Merit had a thin, narrow face, and her lips were coated in a bright red color that had smeared off onto her teeth.

"All right," Merit soothed. "Don't be offended. Keep it in mind, though, please, just in case. You never know unless you ask."

The next morning, Beth dropped her father off at Solhöjden, but didn't bother to go inside herself. She went back to the apartment instead and began vigorously cleaning until noon. Her sore throat had gotten worse, and she'd already stopped by the drugstore on the way back to pick up some medicine for it. Still, she was feeling ill.

The entire time she was vacuuming, a thought had tumbled through her mind, a thought that frightened her and began to make her stomach hurt. She finally understood she would have no peace from it.

She had to go to Skogslyckan and see the grave with her own eyes to make sure that it hadn't been disturbed, that no one had discovered it.

She was obsessed now. She had to go to find peace.

During the night there had been snow. White, fluffy snow. The temperature was a few degrees below freezing.

Beth finished by washing all the windows. Then she went out to the corner store and bought two bottles of beer. She set them on the kitchen table. She wished she'd found some bottles of stronger stuff, but the store did not carry a wide assortment. The design on the label was cheerful, though, with dark blue flowers.

Blue is the color of hope and comfort, Beth thought. *We need that color in this house.*

By the time she was ready to go, it was already quarter past one.

She tried to call Ulf, but he had his voice mail on: "This is Ulf Nordin. I'm busy at the moment, so try back later or leave a message after the beep."

Beth waited for the beep, but then she couldn't find anything to say, so she hung up. Her mood worsened.

She walked outside and started her car. She drove around randomly at first, but then found herself on the road out of town. She suddenly recalled the saying on a plaque in the teacher's lounge:

If you're afraid, do it right away!

Yes, indeed, she thought.

In town the roads were slushy, but once out of the city, the snow was drier. She followed the big road with fields on both sides. The last time she'd been on this road, the sun had hung, burning hot, in the sky until the air was hard to breathe. She'd been exhausted and had a hangover . . . and the horrible thing had not yet happened.

Now it was late autumn. For all practical purposes it was winter.

Some cows were huddling together in the middle of a field. They lifted their heads and lowed as she drove past. Beth sat up straighter and pressed harder on the gas pedal. It seemed as if she had to hurry so that she wouldn't chicken out and turn around.

Eventually, the roads became more narrow and crooked. Beth had to reduce her speed. Sometimes the surface was covered in snow, and one time her car slid. Again she had the strange feeling that she was in a movie. A thriller. Maybe it should be called *The House that God Forgot*. Only in the movies do women take off like this. The music would be creepy and the audience would watch as she, Beth Svärd, drove up to the house, and the next moment there would be a zoom of the house, starting at the top and gliding down the side to the front door. And there, behind the curtain, was a movement. *Don't go inside, you stupid cow,* the audience would think. Everything would be exaggerated to produce the greatest moment of horror for the viewers.. Those who were more rational would see through the tricks and smile, while the fearful would be so scared that they wouldn't want to be alone.

The scenario calmed her.

She stopped the car at the forest road leading to Skogslyckan. She could still forget the whole thing and drive back. Things seemed surreal, as if she were at home in Hässelby dreaming a dream from which she could still awaken. A nightmare that this house lay in wait for her, threatening her.

Now here she was, awake, with the dream cold and real.

She had to go through with it. This would help. After this, she could go on with her life, be in control again. She'd be the same old Beth she'd been a half year ago. And she'd find the way back to Ulf.

The snow was heavy in the forest. She decided that her car could still make it through, though, since they'd put on winter tires. She felt small tremors twitch the skin of her face, still she shifted into first gear and turned into the hilly, narrow driveway to the house. The snow was pure white and she could see the typical tracks of hares. Her father had once taught her that a hare's tracks look like a Y. "See, just draw a line between them and you have a Y."

Dear, sweet Pappa, she thought, and was hit by a flood of tears.

At the halfway point, she had to stop. The well-known panic attack had come over her. She remained sitting with her head leaned backwards and she tried to breathe as she sought to convince herself that there was nothing wrong with her heart. Her doctor had said so. It was just stress, and thousands of people had the same kinds of symptoms.

A few moments later, the attack subsided. Beth had turned off the motor. She opened the window and let the raw air stream in. She listened to the wind in the trees.

When she wanted to start the car again, the engine would not turn over. This happened every once in a while, so she wasn't deeply upset. All she had to do was wait for fifteen minutes or so and it would turn right over. Beth put on her gloves, opened the door, and got out.

"So, Mr. Hitchcock, master filmmaker," she said out loud. "Of course the car won't start. All I need to do now is drop the keys and the Frankenstein monster will leap out at me from behind a bush and chase me all over creation."

Since there wasn't far to go, she thought she might as well leave the car and walk. She wasn't used to the forest at this time of year, and things looked strange. Snow covered the bushes and the trees had empty, gray branches. Beth wanted to light a cigarette, but realized she'd left the pack in the car. With determination, she stuck her hands into her pockets. The snow was deeper than she'd realized, and she wished she'd worn real boots. Her socks and shoes were getting wet from the melted snow. This would certainly make her cold worse. Underneath the snow was a slippery layer of ice. Her steps grew slow and she found she was puffing.

She saw the house, which seemed huge and unusual since it was not masked by the leaves of trees. It made her uneasy. Drifts of snow covered the roof and one of the clay tiles had loosened and slid down into the gutter. In this harsh light, she saw that the house needed to be repainted. Its red color had paled and a green tinge had begun to creep up the sides from the ground to make the house look ill-kempt. As she stared, she realized how tense she was. Her back was straight, her shoulders raised, her head stiff and at an angle, listening for any sound.

The gate was stuck. They'd have to oil it. Drop some sewing machine oil into its hinges. They'd do it this summer when they came back. They'd have to buy some Falu red paint and spend a number of days painting the entire house, but the work would go swiftly if they all helped. Then everything would be back to normal. They'd sit under the trees and read and in the evening they would make some good food and have a bottle or two of wine and everything would be back to normal as if nothing had ever happened, nothing at all.

Beth found herself standing on the garden path. Such an unusual silence. A few chirps, repeated, the clink-clink of frozen water drops falling off a branch, rustling of invisible beings in the bushes, birds, probably, the kind which ate larvae all year round. She saw nothing, noticed only the sounds.

She walked slowly up to the house. The reflection from the snow blinded her and hurt her eyes, causing them to tear up. She pulled off one of her gloves and wiped her nose with the back of her hand.

At that exact moment, she knew someone had been there. She saw the clear footprints. They marred the snow, leaving open spots where the yellow grass poked up. She stood still, her arms halfway lifted.

She listened.

No sound.

Nothing but the rustling of the birds.

The footprints led up to the window. Someone had stood there and peered inside.

Of course it could be nothing to worry about. People were curious about how other people lived. People could act like peeping Toms just to see how she and Ulf had arranged things inside. Not to mention real estate agents. Maybe it was even that Merit Svedberg and her husband who'd been by.

A wave of relief came over her. She shook herself like a dog shaking off water. She followed the footprints around the house. The soles of boots had trampled the snow underneath each window. But these traces were recent. It could not have been Merit Svedberg.

She pushed on the window frames, but they were secure. No one had broken them open to get inside. She put her hand in her pocket, and felt the spare keys for the house. She really did not need to go inside. There was no reason for it. Everything appeared normal. So did the shed. The footprints had gone there as well. *That man with his blonde, shaggy bangs . . . . No! Don't scare yourself!* As she hissed these words, saliva ran down her chin. The silence smothered her, covered her like a bell jar. She had to move, to shake her arms, jump and run around. Her lungs ached and she could not get air.

"Oh!" she yelled and it was a short sound without echo. She walked to the back fence, to the opening there which they used when they were too lazy to walk around to the gate. Ulf would say that they should put a real gate here, too, an iron gate.

When Beth bent over to go through, she heard a ripping sound and realized her jacket was torn.

"Damn it," she muttered. Her new jacket.

Now she was on the other side of the fence and she had to go on, go forward, go that short stretch to that place she'd seen whenever she closed her eyes, that place which scared her to death, that place she had to see with her own eyes, to see. . . that there was nothing to see.

But there was.

There was something there after all.

The footprints in the snow were coming back to her from the other direction.

She saw that the prints came from a pair of rubber boots.

She saw they had come from the place.

What she saw made her twist her hands together. Made her head swirl. Made her sink on her knees into the snow.

A number of shiny, brown pine cones had been placed on the grave and not by accident.

They had been arranged to form a narrow cross.

11

THAT NIGHT BETH RAN A HIGH FEVER. Earlier that evening, she'd felt worse and worse as she sat by her father to watch TV. She felt freezing. Her father got up and turned off the television.

"I've been watching you, Beth," he said, uncertainly. "Something is really bothering you. Am I right?"

Beth shrugged her shoulders. Her eyes were burning, but her fingers and toes felt frozen solid.

Her father came right up to her.

"Maybe you think you can't confide in your old father about your problems when I have plenty of my own. It's very thoughtful of you, Beth, but I want to say . . . that I'm here. If you need me."

Beth blew her nose.

"Would you like something to drink? I think there's still some cognac in the bottle."

"Yes, please."

Beth heard her father rummage in the kitchen, opening cupboard doors. Eventually he returned with the bottle of cognac and two glasses.

"I'll have some, too. Let's drown our sorrows in drink."

His laugh seemed ironic.

"It must be awfully empty and weird for you," Beth said. "Your whole life . . . and now this. You've had a really hard time since Mamma got sick. You're a bit too old to be playing nursemaid."

"Why don't we just taste this cognac? It's high quality. Damned if it won't go down like a dream."

Beth realized she'd never heard her father swear before.

They drank. Beth felt the cognac warm her throat. Her father still watched her from beneath his bushy eyebrows.

"Is it Ulf?" he asked.

"What?"

"Things are not working out between you two these days, am I right? Even an old dad can figure some things out."

"I just don't know. Really, I just don't know."

"Are you being gentle with one another? Are you being kind, Beth? When you were a girl, you could be hard to get along with sometimes when things did not go your way. I remember . . . well, you've always had a hot temper, my girl. Maybe you've calmed down over the years?"

Beth turned red.

"There were times when you would be a real fury and we'd never know why," her father continued. "Juni was never like that."

"People are different," she said evasively.

"Yes, that's true, even though you were raised the same way. Do you know what I think? I believe that you and Ulf are still sad that the two of you never had children. You've become fixated on that. You're putting all your energy into that old sorrow."

"We had children!" Beth exclaimed.

"Yes, but you know what I mean, Beth. Have the two of you ever thought about . . . adoption?"

Beth felt relieved that talking about children no longer seemed difficult.

"We haven't given up hope yet," she said.

"No. No. Of course not. But if you do want to adopt, you had better start considering it now, before it's too late. Let me think. How old are you, Beth? Thirty-six?"

"Thirty-eight. I just had my birthday."

"There you go. Happy Birthday, belated. September, right? The twentieth?"

"That's right."

"I remember that day so well. It was such a superb fall day. Later that year there were some horrible storms . . . . The woodshed roof blew off. I had to go out to the family house and help my father-in-law repair it. He had a fear of heights in his old age. Do you remember that?"

"No," Beth smiled weakly. "I only remember that he was beside himself with rage once when Juni had climbed the cherry tree. He got out a bicycle pump and was whacking her little butt with it. Hmm . . . maybe I got my red hot temper from him."

Her father sat quietly for a minute.

"Well, they're all gone now," he finally said. "So many of them and now all gone. Soon it's going to be my turn. In a way, now that Mamma . . ."

"Did the two of you have a good life together?" Beth interrupted.

"Yes, indeed, you could say we did. In fact, we had a very good life. We were people who could compromise and work things out. We grew more alike, Susanne and me. That makes it doubly hard now."

"You'll have to come to Stockholm and visit us," Beth said. "God, am I ever freezing. Do they ever turn up the darned heat in this building?"

"You think it's that cold here?"

"Absolutely. Don't you?"

"You haven't gotten sick, have you, Beth? Why don't you let me feel your forehead? . . . My dear child, you're burning up!"

Beth had called Ulf at least ten times but only got his voice mail. The same message over and over. She was tucked into the sofa bed. Her father had covered her with two thick blankets.

Now her father was asleep, and although the door to his bedroom was shut, she could hear the thunder of his snoring. She felt as if she were in a dream of her childhood, when she and Juni would visit their maternal grandparents.

At times then she would be awakened by some sound or another. Perhaps a creaking or groaning of the house itself, which frightened her so that she had to lie stock still in her bed. She would hear the sound of her grandparents' snoring coming from their room. It should have calmed her, but it made her feel abandoned, as she was the only person wide awake in that large, living house. She could hear the tick-tock of the pendulums, then the chime of the quarter hour, half hour, three-quarters hour (or is it the stroke of one o'clock, two o'clock and three o'clock.) One loud stroke and then its high-pitched echo. She'd tried to figure out how many hours were left until dawn and the secure sounds of morning.

Beth's grandmother had always been the first one up. She'd go to the bathroom and there'd be a great deal of huffing and puffing before she flushed. Wearing her worn-out bathrobe, she'd go to the kitchen and start clattering around preparing breakfast. Then Beth would hear the creaking of her grandparents' double bed as her grandfather stretched out to cover the entire mattress. He had a bad back. He'd moan and groan and let out large farts that would have made both Beth and Juni break out in laughter if they'd both been awake.

Juni slept like a log. Beth, wearing her nightgown, would sneak out of bed and down the stairs to her grandmother. Her grandmother would give her a long and heartfelt hug.

"Go back upstairs to bed, and I'll call you when breakfast is ready," her grandmother would say.

Grandmother liked her peace and quiet in the early morning hours.

So Beth would shuffle back to bed and creep into her still-warm sheets. Even if she were still tired, she did not want to fall asleep again, so she would stare at the brown stains on the ceiling.

She could hear Juni's breathing from the other side of the room. Now and then, Juni would murmur as if something hurt her. A great deal of love would fill Beth's heart. Her big sister. If she'd dared, she would have crept into Juni's bed and they could snuggle in the same warm depression and hold each other until dawn.

Now she was a grown woman. As soon as she closed her eyes, she would see the grave with its pine cone cross.

She had turned around and fled in panic. She'd felt as if there were someone right behind her. Someone with a stiff, sneering grin waiting for her. Still, there had been no one there. Just the trees, cold and bare, straggly in the raw air. She swallowed and the saliva got stuck in her throat. She began to cough as she ran down the hill toward the grave. That cross! She'd have to remove it! She took off her jacket and began to sweep all the pine cones into it. She wrapped them up in the jacket as if they were a present, and began to run again. Her heart was beating so hard that her ribs were starting to ache. She kept slipping because of her smooth soles, but she finally reached the car.

Just for a moment, she panicked that the car wouldn't be there. But it was. She dumped all the pine cones onto the snow. She found it hard to unbutton the snap on her jacket pocket and while she was struggling with that, she suddenly was terrified by the thought that she might have lost her car keys while she was running. But there they were in her pocket. Then she dropped them while trying to unlock the door. Finally, she was able to open it and climb inside. Her skin felt as if it were being pricked by thousands of tiny needles. Her face was wet from crying.

She had to sit for a moment with her hands underneath her legs to warm them up. At last, she was able to turn the ignition over and back ever so slowly down the driveway and onto the main road. As she reached the turn-off, she saw the cat. It was the same one that had come last summer. The cat was all alone now. It was thin and its fur was matted. There it was, sitting in the snow, and when she caught its eye, it leaped at the car. She yelped, and almost reflexively tromped the gas pedal to the floor. She shot right onto the main road without even looking to see if it was clear.

Her hands were shaking as she clutched the steering wheel. It seemed as if she had forgotten which way she was supposed to head. She made a U-turn right in the middle of the road and revved the engine, hurtling down the road, slipping and sliding and, as if in slow motion, she saw another car coming directly at her in the same lane. She screamed.

She must have instinctively hit the brakes and jerked the wheel to the left. Then all was quiet. She heard a car door slam and caught a glimpse of a man's face, white as a corpse. He was walking toward her. He was wearing a knitted stocking cap. He leaned forward and began to move his large lips.

Beth hit the gas and left the man in her rearview mirror. He stood on the icy road with his arms raised as if to appeal to heaven. His mouth was a large gaping hole.

It slowly became clear to her that it could have been a major accident. Her fault. She had been in the wrong lane. In her father's living room, lying in the sofa bed, a thought hit her: What if the other driver had taken down her license plate number? Would he call the police? What if she were discovered?

That other thing, would it be discovered, too?

Sleep refused to come to her. Finally, she went into the bathroom and took two of her father's sleeping pills. Then she fell so deeply into sleep she might as well have been in a coma.

12

BUZZ. Buzz. Buzz. Over and over a buzzing in her brain. Beth rolled her head back and forth a few times before she opened her eyes behind tiny, swollen slits. At first, she did not know where she was. The room was dark. A narrow stream of electric light came through a crack in the doorway. She heard her father get out of bed. His heels thudded. He knocked something over. Then the buzzing stopped.

Of course. The telephone.

It seemed there was a jolt beneath her eyelids as she woke. Was it still night? She took a look at her watch, but could see only the green glow of its hands, not the numbers.

Something with Mamma, she thought. *Maybe something with Ulf. No, Father would come to the door and hand me the receiver if it were Ulf. No, it must be Mamma. She's gotten worse, and they're asking him to come.*

Her father was not speaking, but he had not hung up the phone. She could hear him clear his throat as he listened. The old smell of fried potatoes came to her nose. Her father had made dinner the night before, but she hadn't been hungry.

Oh no, she thought. *It's that cross.* In sleep, she'd forgotten all about it. Now the cross of pine cones arranged on the grave came back to her. *Who put them there? Somebody must know. Somebody might have seen everything.*

The room was chilly and she put her hands between her thighs to warm them. Their coldness went right through her skin.

She heard her father raise his voice. He was trying to calm someone down.

Who was he speaking to?

She had to get up. No sense in staying put. Shivering, she wrapped a blanket around her body and opened the door to the hallway. Her father was leaning against the wall. He was in his light blue pajamas and his fly was not totally buttoned. She caught sight of his shrunken penis and quickly looked away.

"I'm still here," he said into the phone. "Take a deep breath."

Beth heard loud sounds of wailing and screaming.

Her father looked at her in confusion. His hair was mussed, on end, making a wreath.

Then he held out the receiver.

"Something awful has happened," he said. "Juni is on the line. Werner has died."

13

BETH DROVE BACK TO STOCKHOLM THE NEXT DAY. She'd promised her sister to be there as soon as she could, so Beth drove straight to Juni's apartment in the Östermalm district of Stockholm. She felt strong and eager to help. Now she was the one to help her big sister the same way her sister had helped her when the twins had died. That seemed like a hundred years ago.

Juni was standing at the window waiting for her, and she opened it and threw down her keys for the main door of the apartment building.

Once Beth was in the apartment, they held each other for a long time without saying a word.

She told Beth that it had been so quick. It had been evening. Werner had come home from work saying he was tired.

"And what was I to think? He'd been complaining he felt tired for a while. Everybody is always tired. I'm tired, too," Juni said. She was sitting on the sofa, curled up, with her dog Kaiser in her arms. Her fingernails had been bitten to the quick.

"Just go lie down for a little nap, sweetheart, I said, and he said that it was a good idea. And he went into the bedroom and I heard this gurgling sound and then thump! I knew right away something was wrong so I ran into the room and there he was on the floor. He was on his side and his breath rattled, and spit came out of his mouth, and I screamed 'Don't die! Werner, don't die!' and I picked up the

phone and called emergency but it seemed like forever until the ambulance arrived—I really ought to report it. They shouldn't take so
long when it's an emergency—and I yelled at them when they arrived, I said 'Why did you take so long, he's dying!' but they said that
they'd gotten there almost immediately, and I'd been sitting on the
floor doing mouth-to-mouth as best I could, and Kaiser was there, he
was right in the middle of everything, and Kaiser ran to the window
and began to howl—it sounded terrible, but he must have understood
what was happening—dogs are smarter than people when it comes to
things like this—they have some kind of sixth sense. And now, and
now . . . .he's never going to see his master again!"

Juni stopped speaking and burst into tears, wailing, the sound of
raw grief.

Beth sat still, not able to say a word.

After some time, Beth said, "Do you want anything? Should I
make you a cup of coffee?"

Juni shook her head. Her face was misshapen. The dog put his
paws on her chest and licked her cheeks. Juni sobbed for a while
longer before she began to quiet.

"They started right away with all their medical apparatus . . . but
. . . it was already too late, of course . . . his heart had stopped. My
wonderful, beloved Werner . . . and now he's lying in some cold
morgue somewhere. Beth, I loved him so much. You can't imagine
how much I loved him. That fucking job of his, it sucked his life
right out of him! People think you have such a great life if you have
some money, but they don't understand the price you pay, and he
paid for his money with his life!"

The funeral was held a few weeks later. It was a large, expensive
gathering. There were long eulogies in church. A young woman
sang a solo. Beth recognized the woman. She'd occasionally seen
her in Hässelby. The newspapers had written articles about her. Her
name was Waltraut Eng. She was with a hulking, lumbering man
who did not seem like her type.

Juni wore a black woolen dress, a hat with a veil to hide her
face—the portrait of heavy, old-fashioned grief. She looked coura-

222

geous as she went up to the coffin which was covered with a blanket of flowers. Juni recited a gripping, poetic speech that she'd written herself, and that she'd used in the obituary:

"Where you've gone there is no darkness and no light. Just quiet, a place of gentle waves where my words to you, my beloved, may come to you, stay with you, and never cease. My thoughts will wind around the love we shared, will always share. My tenderness will never fade. I shall live in the memories of the life we shared. Your bright dreams I will carry through time until that day when we meet in Eternity."

After the service, Juni served a buffet in her apartment.

"Werner would like this," she declared. "He would approve. He always likes having his friends and family in his home."

Beth noticed that Juni used the present tense about Werner, as if he were still among them as an invisible spirit.

The young singer had also been invited and Beth noticed that she had a thin engagement ring on her finger. She thought with dislike of the man she'd seen in Waltraut Eng's company.

"I think I recognize you," Beth said, weighing her words carefully. "You don't happen to live in Hässelby by chance?"

The woman nodded.

"So do I," Beth said. "I live on Markviksvägen, right near the Sport Hall, if you know where that is."

"Oh, yes, and I live right on the water near the center of town in one of those apartment buildings."

"I think I saw an article in the paper about you?"

"Oh, yes, they do write up something about me every now and then."

"Are you often called upon to sing . . . for these kinds of occasions?"

"Yes, as a matter of fact. Weddings, too. I like to sing whether it's in sorrow or in joy. It, like, intensifies the emotions. Like, it helps people to grow."

Beth found her choice of words an odd mix of formalities and slang. She wanted to keep talking to Waltraut, but Juni came over, laid her hand on Waltraut's shoulder and whispered into her ear.

"Of course." Waltraut stood up and walked over to a small table where Juni had set a porcelain-framed portrait of Werner between two tall, white candles. She sang a few songs based on Harry Martinsson's long story-poem "Aniara" to which she'd composed the music.

Beth found she was standing next to Ulf. She took his hand and held it ever so tightly.

We're still alive, no matter what, she thought. *And we have each other.*

She never told Ulf about her visit to Skogslyckan. She'd wanted to tell him as soon as she'd seen him, but the time hadn't been right. Now she didn't know if she'd tell him or not. No suitable moment had come. Maybe she would never need to say anything. Ulf might tell her to go for therapy again. That thought alone made her feel nauseous.

She tried to catch his eye, so that she could smile at him and show him that she loved him and never wanted to be apart from him, but he stood ramrod straight and did not look at her at all.

The evening after the funeral, Ulf broke the news to her about a new plan he had to travel overseas. He'd be gone for quite some time. He'd gotten a fantastic job from a magazine to report on the Maasai people living near the Serengeti in Tanzania.

"I've been talking to Juni," Ulf said. "Maybe she'll have the chance to come with me and do some articles for several other magazines, too."

"You've been talking to *Juni?*"

"Yes, this area of the world is the Cradle of Humanity . . . . Do you know they've found traces of our earliest human ancestors there? That's her angle. We came up with it yesterday, actually. It would be great to take her mind off the horrible stuff that's been going on."

"Juni? What about me?"

"You're stuck on sick leave. Juni and I are actually going to *work.* We're both journalists. We make our living by *reporting!*"

"You don't have to be so mean," she said.

"What do you think that the state insurance is going to say if you just took off overseas? Not to mention your colleagues? Or your boss, for that matter!"

"You just don't want me along, do you?"

"Damn it, Beth, that's not true."

"You and Juni cooked up this plan without me!"

"Don't be ridiculous! Why the hell would we do that?"

Beth began to cry, and slid down to the floor, banging on the parquet with her fists.

"You can't do this to me! Leave me here on my own! I won't be able to handle it! You've got to take me with you! I can't be on my own!"

Ulf was standing by the window smoking.

Beth felt a movement tickle her hand. She thought it was a dust bunny at first. Then she realized it was a flesh-colored spider with thread-like legs. She shuddered and sat up.

"I really won't be any trouble," she said in a stifled voice, her head turned away from him. "I'll help carry stuff. I could make sure nothing got lost. I could wash clothes and make food. I won't say a word when you need to write. I'll be quiet and take care of myself. But, please, please, please, don't leave me here on my own!"

"What about that bad tooth of yours? You shouldn't travel until you get that fixed."

"Oh, it won't be a problem. I'll make sure that it's taken care of before we leave."

"What about that *heart attack* you had?" he said. "We can't take sick people along. You know that."

"You know as well as I do that was a panic attack brought on by stress," she said. "I need to get away for a while, too! I won't ever get healthy unless I do. I'll never be able to go back to work . . . ."

"All right," he said. "But first call the state insurance and get their permission to leave the country. Everything's got to be in order before we leave. And you'd better remember one thing: We are going there to work. You're there only on our terms!"

Kaarina I

1

K AARINA HAD MISSED HIM. So she went to his house.
     She went there only when Holger had gone to town. Holger went every other Friday for a meeting with his fellow farmers. He usually was gone the entire day. He took the bus to town early in the morning, and, especially if the meeting went well, he'd sometimes stay overnight in a hotel. He would always smell of tobacco and soap when he came home, and he always brought a box of meringues.

When Holger was not at home, he wanted her to stick around the farm. He'd say that you could never tell what would happen if she left. People were not trustworthy.

But those Fridays, when he was freshly shaven, wearing his white cotton shirt and had his portfolio under his arm and heading off for the bus stop, those Fridays were her freedom days. Before she left, she put the kitchen in order. She washed the breakfast dishes, wiped off the dandelion-colored wax tablecloth, hung the kitchen towel on its hook to dry, and swept the floor clean of the breadcrumbs from the morning's toast. She'd never let him see a mess if he happened to pop back for some reason. He'd done that before. Either the stupid bus hadn't come, or he somehow decided that he didn't want to go after all because someone he couldn't stand was going to be at the meeting. If he came home for whatever reason, he could not complain if the house was in order.

She usually heard his voice before he even reached the door. "Kaarina! Where the hell are you, Kaarina!" he'd yell.

And she'd rip off her apron:

"What's wrong, Holger? Did you forget your meeting in town today?"

He'd give her a cold look. "Forget? What are you talking about, woman? I have things to do on the farm! Find my overalls and cap, why don't you!"

So today here she was.

She stood by the window and watched the sun rise through the tops of the birch trees. The sun's arc was lower in the sky today. She could tell the passing of the seasons by where it rose. She watched Holger walk down the hill. He walked vigorously with no signs of wanting to come back this day. She knew that he was going to get on the bus; and later, as the clock chimed eight and she heard the diesel engine of the bus roar, she knew he'd gone for sure.

Kaarina felt desire rising in her as she climbed the stairs to her room on the second floor. She changed into her wide skirt, because it was still summer and the heat made the sand soft and mild. She slipped into the bathroom and took a washcloth, wetted it and shyly cleaned herself down there. She took some hand cream and rubbed it into her hands and throat.

The hens watched her as she walked out of the house and into the yard. They ran toward her, their toes spread in the dirt.

"Go away!" she said impatiently. "I'm not here about you! Go away!"

The hens hopped at her, their eyes darting, their combs and blood-filled wattles flapping. They could sense her behavior was different today. She hadn't come to feed them or clean the hen house of its dirty straw. There were no handfuls of oats for their feeding trays, and her hands, the ones which usually slid out eggs, carefully, one by one, from beneath their breasts, had other things to do. She shook her skirt and they scooted away cackling.

"The fox is coming!" she hissed, narrowing her brows, and she snickered as they darted away, wings flapping.

She slid through the gate and closed it securely. She felt a sudden need to hurry, so she increased her pace to just under a run. Running was something she'd stopped doing years ago. She crunched through piles of dead, drought-burned leaves. The sound made summer feel like fall, even though there was still no chill in the morning air. She thought of those evenings when her bedroom had been so hot as to be suffocating, and she'd just wrapped herself in a sheet. The heat of the day would soak into the walls of the house. Around midnight she would get up and open the window slightly. She would hear that Holger was sleeping, tired after a hard day's work. She was beginning to have trouble sleeping, perhaps because of her age, when now she had stopped having the monthly visitor. She felt coarse and dry.

Sometimes her nighttime thoughts turned into tears. Of fear? Of sorrow? Wondering. Worrying.

For a long time she kept such thoughts to herself. She did not want to talk to Holger. He might get the wrong idea . . . and she also did not want him to know. But one day Holger himself brought up the subject of the man. They were sitting at the breakfast table and he looked up at her. She saw a bit of egg in his beard.

"I really could have used his help right now," Holger said, but he was not really displeased, just annoyed that the man he'd depended on to do various jobs had not been seen around for a while. They didn't talk about how long it had been. Just that he hadn't been there.

"Have you seen him around, Kaarina?" Holger's tiny brown eyes burned into hers. She shook her head no.

He drank the coffee that she'd brought from the stove. He put a cube of sugar between his teeth before he drank.

Again, Holger gave her a sly look.

"We were supposed to fix the fence over by Vrängen," Holger said, his thoughts as slow as his words. "I need help. If he's not here, you'll have to pitch in."

"He'll show up," she said and realized at that very moment how much she really missed the man. "Be patient. He'll be here before you know it."

Days passed, and still he did not appear. She missed his rounded, heavy shoulders, his shaggy bangs, and the quick shift in his blue eyes the moment he caught sight of her.

His breath as he stood between the stalls.

"Kaarina, may I touch your neck? It throbs as if there's a tiny animal inside. Do you really have a tiny animal inside of you?"

How he could make her laugh so that her entire body was ready to receive him and to keep him, holding him tight between her legs even though he was strong and had large thighs. "Kaarina, Kaarina," he protested as he tried to free himself. It was always a fun game between the two of them. Almost always.

So one day Holger decided to look for the man, had gotten on his bicycle and pedaled away. He returned that afternoon, his forehead rubbed raw from sweat and dirt. He spoke up right away about what he'd found, unlike his usual taciturnity.

"I went past his place and guess what? It's all locked up. Looks like no one's been around for ages. Do you know anything about this, Kaarina?"

"No," she replied, an empty sound in her voice.

"We should have heard something about all this," he muttered. He went to the faucet, turned the water on and took a long drink. "We really should have heard something by now."

Kaarina thought: *Maybe he's sick, who knows?* And she wanted to ask Holger if he'd actually knocked on the door or taken the time to carefully look through all the windows.

2

So Kaarina found herself walking through the heaps of sun-burnt leaves. The forest was silent. No birds anymore. They usually gathered together on the roof of the barn just before their long migration. She knew that the air could change overnight. First there would be the wave of chilly wind and then the rain would start and make the air damp. The water of Leksjön would turn black and opaque. The last aspen leaves would fall onto the lake's surface.

When she was young and Lena still lived with them on the farm, they all used to go to the lake to swim.

As Kaarina walked, she thought she should have taken Holger's bike. Her own bike had a hole in the inner tube. She'd asked Holger to fix it, but he had never gotten around to it. After a while, she'd stopped asking, which meant she'd stopped riding her bike altogether. Besides, her legs were not as limber as they used to be.

She took a short cut through the forest, which she could not have done if she'd had the bike anyway.

She remembered that when she was a child, the forest used to frighten her. Those tall, straight tree trunks and the sound the wind made as it murmured through them. How they played games with light and shadow.

Those early memories were nothing more than fragments.

She remembered that she'd been lifted up to some window. She could see a fire-red light in the distance and hear a boom like thunder.

Cold, quick touch of fingers from a woman that must have been her mother.

The train car. She was so tired but she had to keep looking out the window. *Go to sleep.* A hard, strange voice.

She was eating a slice of bread with *juustoa*. She could still remember the word for the slightly sour cheese spread on bread as dark as earth.

She was four years old. She remembered being helped down to the platform. The snow drifts were high above her head. Britt was waiting for her and Klas sat in the wagon. Britten and Klas would be her Swedish foster parents. She'd never been able to pet a horse before, and in the excitement of nearing a real horse, her pants became warm and wet.

Then she was eating oatmeal in the large kitchen. She felt the pulsing heat of the stove. Back then she never could have imagined that she'd eventually be the one who knew best where everything was kept in those tall kitchen cabinets.

Holger and Lena were older than she was, so she became their little sister.

She stayed, although that had never been the plan at the beginning. She was supposed to stay only as long as the war lasted.

But one day Britten took Kaarina in her arms. Kaarina had already been there awhile and had learned to understand what was said to her and how to reply.

"Do you remember your father, Kaarina?" There had always been something sad in Britten's face, in her lean cheeks. Sometimes at night, Kaarina had heard her weep, but she had thought nothing of it. Her own mother had cried at night, too. Kaarina thought crying at night was just something that grown women did.

"Do you remember your father?"

Kaarina heard the words but did not understand the question.

Britten stroked Kaarina's hand.

234

"Your father was a brave man who fought for Finland."

"Isäni!" she cried, because she suddenly remembered that the man in whose lap she'd sat, the man who wore the gray uniform, was the same man that in Swedish was called *father.*

Every once in a while, her Mamma Kerttu would send a letter, but Mamma Kerttu wasn't dependable. Her letters would be written in someone else's loopy handwriting following stilted dictation.

"Your mother does not know Swedish," Britten explained. "She's gotten someone to help her. She writes that they have not forgotten you. She says, *have a little patience.* Well, it's fine with us if you stay. When you came here, you were so underfed it looked like you'd stopped growing. And if there's still not enough food back there at home for you, you can just stay right here on the farm with us."

The letters stopped coming after a while. The last letter had been a card. Kaarina had just turned nine. She still had the card in a drawer. It had a cat on the front. The cat wore a pink rosette on its collar. Kaarina's mother had written:

Paljon onnea 9-vuotispäivänä. Äiti.

Britten said, "She must be wishing you a Happy Birthday."

3

SHE'D BEEN TO THE MAN'S HOUSE BEFORE, BUT SHE'D NEVER GONE INSIDE. The house was painted red and already it looked a bit fallen in, the roof so bad it might soon collapse.

He'd lived there with his mother.

"The Hill Cottage," Holger had called the place and grinned each time he said it.

The house's garden was at the foot of a hill. Hence the name.

Kaarina walked right up to the gate and immediately knew that he was not there. There was no one in the house and no one had been there for a long time.

She went to look through the windows anyway, even if it were useless.

Heavy, dark furniture. Two pillows, with horoscope patterns, on the sofa. High up on a cabinet, as if to protect it from mishaps, stood a dusty, worn-out globe.

She walked around the house. A ladder leaned up against one wall. Many rungs had broken off. What if he'd fallen down and gotten hurt? But then he'd be around here somewhere, and she'd see him.

The kitchen had been cleaned and the dishes put away. A bucket stood on the table as if he were going to go and get some water. This surprised her. She saw a faucet made of stainless steel. She also saw a washbasin with some clothes soaking in it. A layer of slime had formed on the surface of the water.

Something soft and cool brushed against her legs. She wasn't startled.

It was a gray cat with light stripes. It pawed at her and meowed. A bit farther away she saw two kittens playing.

"Here, kitty, kitty," Kaarina said quietly as she squatted to pet the cat's fur, feeling its tiny, hard skull.

Kaarina found two empty bowls near a pile of wooden boards. The cat ran ahead of her, crying the whole time.

Kaarina shook her head, feeling an uneasy premonition. The man was always careful with animals, something she'd known about him a long time. She'd seen his face when Holger brought out the cardboard box with the kittens. Kaarina had been furious. She'd cried and tried to take the kittens away, but Holger stuffed them in the box anyway.

"He's the one who'll take care of 'em," Holger had said as he went to get the shotgun. Kaarina was forced to say goodbye to the small, warm bodies. She'd stuck her hand into the box and felt their tongues. She was still crying as she brought the box to the porch. The man was standing there holding the shotgun. She saw the dread in his eyes and how he wanted to refuse but could not.

He'd been a quiet man.

He did what people told him.

The rest of that day, Holger had been especially sweet to her. His voice was thick as he said, "You know we can't keep all those cats. You understand, don't you, Kaarina. They just multiply. The best thing would have been to suffocate them the minute they were born. You made the mistake of becoming attached to them. You saw them as more than just animals. You didn't want to let them go."

The next day, Holger went into town and returned around lunch time with a video. It was a comedy called *Jönssonligan*. Holger managed to connect the TV to the video player without losing his temper.

"Why don't you make some coffee?" Holger said to her. "Cut a few slices of cake, too. Now it's time to see a movie!"

She frowned and did not touch her coffee, but the movie was funny, and her mood lightened in spite of herself. After the movie, as he let it rewind, Holger gently stroked her shoulder.

"Aren't I right?" he said. "We just can't have so many cats around."

The mother cat, Grållan, was still on the farm. She was already old, and that litter had been her last. Grållan's stomach dragged. Holger would watch her sometimes. Holger did care about animals in spite of what he'd said.

"Do you think she's missing them?" he asked once.

But never mentioned them again.

Kaarina was cold and wished she'd brought her cardigan. The wind had increased and the tree trunks had started to sway.

Kaarina began to walk away from the house. The cats followed her for a while, but finally the kittens were hungry and the mother cat stopped to let them nurse.

His cats.

He wasn't there.

Kaarina thought that the cats would turn feral, just as Holger predicted. The cats would multiply until they filled the entire world.

Still, the cats were not her most pressing concern right then.

4

KAARINA WALKED TO ANOTHER FARM, A FARM HE'D TOLD HER ABOUT. She saw that it had been closed up for the winter, so she dared to come onto the property. She did not know the owners. All she knew was they were from Stockholm. They'd inherited the place.

The rain had come at night for the past week, so the grass was starting to recover and grow after the summer's drought.

The curtains were closed, so Kaarina could not look inside. Perhaps she would not have dared, no matter what. This was trespassing, of course. Kaarina had the uneasy feeling that someone was watching her.

Kaarina had to pee. She walked behind the house and squatted near the food cellar. She saw a number of plastic bags filled with empty bottles. Four or five bottles were scattered around.

What kind of people are these? she thought.

On the left side of the shed, she saw an overgrown potato patch. In another spot, a few stubs of berry bushes stuck up from the ground. Obviously these people did not care about gardening.

Then she remembered what he'd said.

He'd talked about a man and a woman. He said he'd hide in the forest and watch them. Once he'd asked Kaarina to come with him, and she'd grabbed his wrist and yelled that this was not a nice thing to do. People should not spy on other people.

Of course, this was exactly what she was doing right now.

She'd held his arm and he'd broken free. She was furious as she remembered . . . that strange woman and her nakedness. And how he liked watching her.

He'd wrenched himself free and she'd hit him and scratched at him with her short fingernails.

Both laughing and crying.

Something had fallen by her feet.

His childlike voice: "My watch! You broke my watch!"

The leather band had broken, but he wasn't angry. He laughed.

Kaarina had taken his watch home and repaired the band. The leather was well-worn and soft, but she still got blisters on her fingertips from the work.

5

HOLGER ARRIVED HOME ON THE 7:20 BUS. He'd brought her a square package. He liked to give presents.

"Let's eat first," he said. He put on his black vest which was held together with a length of rope as a belt.

Kaarina set the bowls of potatoes and red beets on the table. She'd made a simple meal. Holger sat forward with his arms on the table peering at her. He had a quiet grin.

"So, how were things in town?" she asked.

"You can finally move around on the streets. The children are back in school. And the summer people have left."

Holger ate, chewing noisily.

"So what did you do all day long?" he asked, settling back and cracking the knuckles on his left hand.

She felt herself blush.

"The usual," she said, hoping to change the subject.

Holger was content and in a good mood.

"I looked in on Egon and we talked for a while," Holger said. "He says he's going to shut down. He's getting old, he says. The hell with that. He's as old as I am. His boy was out there, too, you know the one, the boy that became a policeman."

Kaarina nodded. "Yes, Lars-Göran. We were in the same class in school."

"Lars-Göran, is it? That's right, that's his name. He was the policeman who caught those criminals, you know, the ones that escaped from jail. He said that they were actually relieved they'd been caught. They didn't want to see another damn bug ever again. He said that they were so eaten up by mosquitoes that even their mothers wouldn't recognize them."

Kaarina thought of calves which died from too many bug bites.

"Those so-called bad guys weren't so dangerous anymore," Holger laughed. "Just two snotty boys who'd gotten what they deserved."

As Kaarina placed the coffee pot on the table, Holger lifted up the package.

"Take a look, Kaarina. See what I bought you."

She opened the box and saw a pair of shiny, new green boots. She lifted them to her nose and took a deep breath.

"Good quality!" Holger crowed. "I noticed you needed a new pair!"

He had noticed that her old boots leaked.

Kaarina went into the mudroom to get a pair of rag wool socks. She sat down at the kitchen table and pulled on the socks and the boots. Even though she had thick calves, the boots fit well. Holger got onto his knees and tested the fit with his finger.

This was as close as he'd ever allow himself to be.

6

KAARINA WALKED TO THE FIELD WITH HOLGER. She did not want to go. The work was hard and she was not as limber as she used to be. Holger had tried to find someone else to help with the job, but he just couldn't .

Neither of them said a word about the man who'd disappeared.

"Can you believe this country still has unemployment?" growled Holger as he told her to pick up some of the heavy poles for the new fence.

Then came days with unceasing rain.

One morning the old cat Grållan was dead. Kaarina found her in the kitchen. The cat's upper lip was drawn back in a grimace.

Kaarina decided to bury her using the boot box. The box was too short, so Kaarina took a knife to cut open one end.

Her foster sister, Lena, had bought the cat for fifty öre. Her cat must have been at least twenty years old! Lena bought the cat the same summer that they'd sadly understood that it would not be possible to keep Lena on the farm any longer.

Lena's behavior had reached a turning point.

She'd gotten strange around the time winter was turning into spring. She became sly and stubborn and barely answered when spoken to, although she talked more and more to herself behind her bedroom door.

By then, there were only the three of them left. Britten and Klas had found their resting places in the churchyard. They'd died only a few months apart. Lena had planned to move into town that fall because she'd gotten a job at the state liquor store as well as a rundown apartment with a view of the river.

But then something made her change.

"Kaarina, try to talk some sense into her," Holger had said. "You womenfolk have your own ways. She doesn't listen to me. Only God knows what's wrong with her."

Lena was ten years older than Kaarina, but they'd always behaved as if they were the same age. In the room underneath the gable, Lena pulled open a drawer and showed Kaarina what she'd been writing. Her movements were feverish and her voice metallic.

A command: "I'll read. You'll listen."

Kaarina sat on the edge of the bed. The words coming from Lena's mouth were strong but strange. Kaarina felt afraid.

"What is all this? Did you make it up yourself?" she asked.

Lena nodded. She picked at her hair until her bun loosened and her hair fell like a curtain in front of her face.

"I have so much . . . here inside," Lena said as she hit her forehead with her palm. "It hurts, you see, so I have to write until it comes out."

Afterwards, as they were going through Lena's things, they found reams of completely scribbled-on paper. The stacks of paper were everywhere: in the wardrobe, in Lena's dresser drawers, under the rug, and under the mattress as well.

Holger threw it all into a sack.

"What a bunch of crap. This stuff ruined her. I don't want it in my house."

Holger emptied it all into the burn barrel and set fire to it. It burned with black, spiraling smoke. Without Holger's noticing, Kaarina had managed to tuck a few sheets inside her skirt band. Later, she locked herself inside the bathroom to read them and the words seemed to seep into her, to make her mouth dry, her lips stern.

Your black claw, your gripping claw,
Against my brokenseashell nakedness,
How it flays me,
How it reveals my lungs
And you came
And you were the Good Shepherd
howIlaughhowIlaughhowIlaugh
or the Lord Man H
and I bent over and received you
I received you
And the Judgment Day Ore
Judgment Day
Ore
It sounded:
What I wanted.
You.

Brokenseashell? Lena wrote words which did not exist.

Kaarina kept those sheets of paper in her underwear drawer. She rarely took them out. They made her depressed and afraid, but she also didn't choose to throw them out. Someday maybe they would give her an answer. An answer about what had happened to Lena.

Holger had to call Lena's apartment building to let them know she would not be moving in. Initially, Holger thought that Lena could stay home, but she became violent and screamed all night, throwing her chair around and locking the door to barricade herself inside her bedroom.

One morning a gray, pungent smoke began to trickle out from underneath Lena's door. Holger used his shoulder to break down the door. The floor was burning. Lena had set fire to a heap of paper and stood in her nightgown howling like a bull.

Holger ripped the bed cover from Lena's bed and smothered the fire. Meanwhile, Lena crept to the corner of her room and screamed. Holger had to force her to stop.

Doctor Bergström made a house call. When he arrived, Lena was sitting quietly in her red skirt.

"I would like you to come with me, Lena," said Doctor Bergström.

Kaarina bit her lip so hard, she bit it almost in half, but Lena made no protest. Kaarina brought Lena her coat. It had been a chilly day with rain and wind.

"Take care of Grållan for me, Kaarina," Lena said. There was a strange eagerness in her movements as she put on her head scarf (wasn't she already wearing a coat?). "She's your cat now. Take good care of her until I come home."

Lena never came home.

They visited her in the hospital once. Lena did not recognize them. She was sitting in the day room. The sun shone on the polished floor, making sharp reflections.

They had brought a box of pralines. A nurse took the box from them and said that she would portion out the candy.

"Otherwise, she'll just eat them all at once," the nurse said by way of excuse. "Lena has a tendency to binge."

Lena had always been large. She'd taken after her father. She had the same broad shoulders and broad hands.

Now she was enormous.

They saw her from the back at first, but they didn't recognize her until she turned her head. She was wearing a patterned cotton dressing gown barely large enough to cover her. Her hair had been chopped off right above her ears. Her eyes appeared tiny and remote in her swollen face.

Holger stopped abruptly right in the middle of the floor. The smell of cooking food. The sound of cheerful accordion dance music from a speaker in the ceiling.

"Lena," Holger said, but so softly that only Kaarina heard him.

The nurse stood behind them.

"Lena," the nurse said. "You have visitors. Your brother and sister are here to see you."

The colorless lips formed a smile. The woman Lena had become lifted her hands and clapped them once so loudly that her cheeks shook. Kaarina had to force herself to walk toward the formless female shape.

"Hi, Lena," she said quietly.

Lena's lips continued to smile, but in her eyes there was no recognition.

"It's me, Kaarina. I thought I'd tell you about . . . Grållan." Kaarina tried to continue, but her voice had gotten thick and she had to turn away and close her eyes tightly, tightly.

"There are times when she goes inside herself," the nurse said. "It's part of her illness. And she's also been given some strong medicine. But I think that she feels fine here."

At that moment, Lena lifted her huge arm and held it straight up in the air. The arm was in an awkward and stiff position. Lena laughed, but her laugh was low and rumbling.

"Let's go!" said Holger. "There's a strange smell here and I can't stand it. Let's get out of here."

They walked into the hallway. Lena stayed still, her arm up in the air.

"I promise, she's doing fine here," the nurse said. "She's calm and follows orders. She's no longer plagued by her voices. That's the most important thing for us right now. We'll have to deal with the rest later."

"Fine, fine," said Holger. "But we've got to go. We don't want to miss the bus."

Holger was totally silent during the ride home.

That evening, he said that it was a shame that they'd cut off her hair.

"Her hair was so thick and brown. It was nice to watch her take care of it. But I imagine it was too hard for them to deal with, so that's why they had to cut it off."

Kaarina nodded.

She felt a throbbing emptiness inside her body.

That evening, Holger came to her bedroom. He was dressed in nothing more than a shirt and underpants. Kaarina felt shy, but a moment later, she lifted the quilt so he could climb in. His feet and legs were ice cold.

"Don't mind me, I just want to lie here for a while. Don't be afraid, I'm not going to do anything to you."

"I'm not afraid," said Kaarina in a whisper.

He lay there with his back to her, but placed her arm around his body. She noticed that he was shaking.

"It wouldn't have worked with Lena," Holger said. "She would have burned the whole house down around us."

"That's right," whispered Kaarina. She moved her fingers as if to pet him, but he held her hand still.

"Those nurses," he said. "They won't let her do any of that writing stuff . . . and all that other crap which just destroys her."

That October, they received word that Lena was dead. In spite of the closed doors and locks, Lena had managed to escape the ward. They noticed almost immediately and went to search for her, but it was too late.

She was found by one of the guards in the late afternoon. She was as far away as possible in the large park setting. She lay underneath the hawthorn bushes. She'd slit her throat with a razor.

7

THE GRAY CAT WAS BECOMING LESS SHY. One morning when Kaarina was feeding the hens, she heard a lost cry. The cat was sitting in a stall. It was thin and ragged, and there was a gaping wound on its left side.

Kaarina moved slowly and carefully. Back in the house she found a bowl in the kitchen and filled it with milk.

The cat looked completely starved.

She knew it was his cat. She recognized it. The cat resembled Grållan, but was smaller and its paws were completely white. Kaarina thought the cat had come because it felt empty inside.

Kaarina had buried Grållan behind the red currant bushes. She'd cried as she did so.

More than she'd cried for Lena.

The cat came to their house almost every day after that, and Kaarina gave it milk and leftovers from their previous night's supper. Holger saw her carry bowls outside, but he didn't say anything. If he had, she would have told him off.

She thought about the kittens that had been with the cat. They should be big by now, but not big enough to make it on their own.

Kaarina thought that she ought to look for them. Holger was out in the forest, but if he came home, she'd tell him that she was going to look for chanterelle mushrooms.

Holger always worried that something terrible would happen to her if she left the farm too long. Since Lena's death, his fears had gotten worse. It seemed like he was afraid he'd be left all alone.

Kaarina had never chosen to stay on the farm. It had just happened. One day flowed into the next and one year into another. She and Holger were like an old pair of siblings. While Lena was still alive, Holger had tried to get her to move off the farm.

He'd cleared his throat carefully, as if for an important occasion. "You will probably want to find a future for yourself. Find another line of work than being an unpaid house servant on an old, crumbling farm."

Holger had a tendency to exaggerate. The farm was far from crumbling.

"Maybe," she'd said. "But not right now. I'll stay for a little while longer. If you let me, that is."

The corners of Holger's mouth inched upwards, and he grimaced as if he'd bitten into a sour apple.

And so she stayed.

As Kaarina walked, she thought about the man who'd disappeared. She knew that sometimes he dreamed of being a longshoreman at faraway harbors.

"Maybe I'm meant to go to sea," he told her once. He told her in words and sweeping gestures of the dreams he'd had during the night. How he'd stand on the bow of a large, mighty vessel and how the wind blew through his hair.

"I saw its white hull," he told her." And its name was painted with large black letters: *Oceania*. Can you dream about things that don't exist? And when I woke up . . . I tasted salt on my tongue."

What if he had just decided to go to sea?

No, that really wasn't like him. He dreamed and longed for things that weren't there, but he was not the kind to change dreams to reality.

The path into the forest smelled of damp earth. All at once, the cat appeared. Kaarina bent down to pet it, but it hissed at her and ran to the side. The cat's wound had started to heal on its own.

"Kitty, where are your kittens?" Kaarina said. "You should find them and bring them to our house. It's going to be cold soon and you'll need a warm place to live."

The cat stopped and looked at her as if it understood what she'd said. The cat opened its pink mouth in a loud cry. It stared at her. Then it started to pad away and Kaarina decided to follow it. Every time she hesitated, doubting what she was doing, the cat ran a few steps back to her as if it were showing her the way. Kaarina thought that the cat was leading her to its kittens so she could take them home. Maybe even Holger would be happy with the arrangement.

They got near the farmhouse owned by that man and woman from Stockholm. Kaarina stiffened. *We shouldn't go here.* She felt uneasy and thought about how the man had been squatting behind bushes, spying on them. That was an ugly thing to do. Improper. Maybe even dangerous. She'd told him so. *What if they discover you? They'll get furious and call the police!*

He'd laughed and had asked her to come with him.

But now it was the cat and her kittens. Kaarina would find them soon. They'd come scooting out of their hiding place when they smelled their mother's scent. They'd be tiny and starving. She'd lift them in her arms and carry them and the mother cat would follow, not wanting to leave them.

Kaarina looked up from the shiny brown leaves on the path. She gently called for the kittens. At first she'd lost sight of the mother, but then saw her again right next to the fence. Her tail was thick and straight up in the air and her back curved up in an awkward manner.

She called to the cat. She jumped and disappeared in the grass.

Kaarina walked a few steps toward her and stopped short. A cramp knotted her stomach. She saw marks of paws and claws in the damp earth. And then that awful sight, sticking right up from the clay.

She did not want to look at it but she had to.

A part of a human arm.

A horrible dizziness came over her and she had to howl. She fell to her knees, leaning forward onto her knuckles. Yes, she'd seen correctly.

It was a male arm, partially chewed away but still with recognizable blonde hair. The arm wore a watch. Although the watch was dirty and crooked, she recognized it immediately.

She'd found him.

8

WITHOUT THOUGHT, SHE STARTED TO ACT.
Why did she do so? Why didn't she just run away when she'd stopped screaming? Why didn't she run to Holger and ask him to call the police?

She didn't really know.

Instead, she began to cover him again with more sand and dirt.

He had been partially exposed to the elements and the animals. That was a terrible insult.

When you are dead, you should be protected and safe.

Now wild animals had been at him: foxes and ravens.

She had to vomit when she thought about that.

She went back to the shed, found a spade behind it. It was bent and rusty, but was still useful for digging. She'd gone through the hole in the fence to get it. She dug up dirt from the abandoned potato plot, carried it back, mounded the earth into a suitable shape, and when she was finished, she took some leaves from the smaller rowan trees and made a design on the earth.

The cat had disappeared while she worked. However, a few hours later, as she headed home, the cat was at her heels.

That night, Kaarina lay stiff and straight in her bed.

So many thoughts.

So many sights.

He's been found, she thought, and sorrow filled her lungs so that she had to place her pillow over her mouth to keep her screams silent.

He's been found and he is dead. Somehow she'd known. Somehow she'd known he was not coming back.

But he could not have put himself into a grave!

Kaarina thought about the man and the woman, especially the woman. Fury forced her to get out of bed and pace the floor. Her thick socks kept her footsteps from Holger.

Holger had looked at her very intently that evening as they watched TV, but he hadn't asked her anything. He was too afraid that something would change her and she'd be like Lena. Women are such strange beings with their blood and hormones. They were different creatures from men.

Kaarina could not help returning to the grave. When the pattern of leaves blew away, she made a new one with twigs.

He was a man no one mourned.

She would mourn him.

Now she was no longer wept.

She hid his watch in one of the shoes inside her wardrobe. It was one of the black pumps she'd worn for her birthday once but hadn't worn since. She'd kept them in the wardrobe, but her feet had changed. The shoes no longer fit. Time made feet grow.

She had taken the watch from his arm, which was not hard for her to do. Once she was back home, she cleaned it with some cotton on a match. The hands stood still. Dirt and water had ruined the internal mechanism.

At times she would take it out and look at it and notice the thread with which she'd repaired the leather band.

"You are so good with your hands," he'd told her.

She longed for him, for his body. She'd never wanted him to know she'd longed so, but she was not reluctant when he pushed her against the wall and groped his hands under her skirt.

How he entered her and how she embraced the heat of him.

How her cheeks flamed and deep sounds which she'd tried to stifle would come from her throat.

Until everything was white and her mind was blank and she would fall down.

"Holger's coming," he'd whisper.

He'd say that so that he could laugh out loud at her sudden fear.

She often wished they'd had a place where they could be left alone.

He did have his small house.

But the thought never seemed to cross his mind to take her there.

And now the ever-after.

The strange woman and man. They did not leave her mind. Holger would certainly know their names and where they lived, but she could not dare ask him.

Kaarina would take care of his grave.

No one would be allowed to move it.

No one would disturb him ever again.

9

KAARINA NEARED THAT HOUSE AGAIN AND THE CAT FOLLOWED HER. The cat was still alone. Kaarina no longer thought about the kittens, but she wished that the cat would move into the house, into her kitchen. Once she'd tried to lift it, but it went crazy and bit her thumb so she had to drop it.

Kaarina opened the strangers' gate. She was no longer thinking about trespass. The windows were set low and the curtains were shut the way people do when they expect to be away for a long time. She put her face right up against the glass. Through the holes in the lace, she could see the furniture: a sofa and an old letter desk. The floor was covered by a white wool shag rug. Then she thought to look straight down. There was a tiny table right underneath the window which had a heap of magazines. And on one of the magazines was an address label.

She knew she had to get into that house.

Both outer doors were locked, as she'd expected. She would have to break one of the windows. She looked around and found some stones, round and sleek, meant to replace the ones on the gray stone porch. She bent down stiffly and hefted the top stone. There was a metallic sound by her feet. A key. Of course. People did this at all the farmhouses: hid a key which only a few people knew about.

The fact that she'd found the hiding place at once was a sign.

She held the key in her hand.

That man or that woman had been the last person to touch this key. They'd packed up their car and driven away, but before that, they'd hidden this house key underneath the stone.

The lock was stiff, and she had to shove with her hip to make the door give. She was not at all afraid. She entered the mudroom. They'd put all their garden furniture there for the winter. The chairs were stacked on the table. The striped cushions were packed in plastic bags.

Kaarina closed the outer door behind her and walked inside.

There was a weak aroma of tobacco left in the air. An ashtray was on a table and it had been cleaned, but there was one stub left. There were some clothes hanging on a hook. One shiny blue-green dress and a hat. She couldn't help smelling them. It was the scent of another human body, *her* body, that woman's.

That woman who'd run around without wearing clothes.

How the man told her about that woman and his lips parted and he grabbed Kaarina with hard hands.

That kind of woman!

And yet, the man had been drawn to her.

Kaarina stood still and listened. No. No sound. A throbbing headache began to appear behind her forehead.

Kaarina took a few steps into the big room she'd seen through the window. Now she realized that outside, the world was getting dark. Maybe snow would come tonight. Kaarina saw a brown sandal under the sofa. On the wall was a piece of embroidery with a flower motif. Kaarina walked slowly over to the window. The floor creaked and she thought that no one would be able to sneak inside this house if anyone was home because the floor would betray them instantly.

She saw the magazines. They were the same kind of magazines that she and Holger had at home. Yes, there was the address label on the corner of one of the magazines, just as she'd seen. Though she didn't have her glasses and couldn't read the name, it didn't matter. Her hands moved quickly to rip off the cover and fold it into a square.

This was all she needed.

Beth III

1

B ETH WOKE UP, STARTLED BY A SOUND. A large bang as if something had fallen over in the room.

At first she thought the wind had knocked something over. Then she realized the air conditioner sounded like a storm and waves crashing against a beach. She finally remembered where she was: in a bungalow with Ulf sleeping beside her in a wide bed.

Fear gripped her. Maybe it was a snake underneath the bed. Maybe the snake had crawled in during the day and now was coming out under the cover of darkness. Maybe the snake had knocked something over in the room and that was what had awakened her.

Beth had to pee, but she did not dare get out of bed. The lamp next to the bed was broken. They'd complained about it, but nothing had happened. She carefully lifted the sheet and waved air over her body. She did not want to wake Ulf directly because she'd promised not to make a nuisance of herself.

What would they be doing if she hadn't come along? Where would they have slept? Each of them in a double bed in their own room?

Beth had never seen her sister as a rival before. And maybe her sister really wasn't one. It had hardly been a month since Walter's death. Juni had loved her husband. There was no doubt about that.

But still. Would they have gotten two bungalows?

She heard a noise. A weak, creaking slither.

She couldn't take it any longer. She cried out.

The room was awash in electric light. Beth sat underneath the mosquito net and watched Ulf search the room, moving things around and swearing.

"We should have made sure our suitcases were shut," Beth complained. "Maybe something crawled into them to hide."

Beth thought of other things besides snakes. Creepy, crawly things. All sorts of creatures which lived in this country. She'd tried not to make a fuss about it, but her fear was too strong .

Ulf's face came right up to hers. His hair was curled and damp. He was starting to go gray. Beth had noticed it a few days ago in the harsh sunlight at the beach.

"What do you think Juni is doing?" Ulf said with an ironic grin. "She's not going to scream if she hears some kind of noise. Go back to sleep, for Christ's sake. And let me sleep. I'm here to work, you know."

It had been one week since they'd left Sweden, but it seemed like much longer. The trip had been exhausting and without the usual anticipation of a normal vacation. She felt as if she were on the run. Maybe all three of them were fleeing from their memories. The trip seemed a desperate attempt to forget.

They'd changed planes in Amsterdam, and the plane to Kilimanjaro Airport near Arusha had been delayed many hours. It really did not matter since they were not in a rush. Still, the long period of waiting made them irritable.

Just before midnight, the airplane cut into the tight, dark air of Africa. Beth could not doze on the plane. Her limbs ached and her legs and feet were swollen. She'd been sitting in the middle seat. Ulf, with his long legs, sat in the aisle seat. Juni sat by the window.

Juni had gone right to sleep. Later, Juni mentioned that she'd taken a sleeping pill. Beth wondered why Juni hadn't offered her one. She'd already used up the pills she'd taken from her father's place.

Oppressive heat was like a wall as they stepped out of the plane. Beth paused a moment on the top step. Everything seemed strange and different, even the air, which wrapped around her and set off a strong, primitive fear.

Insects were crowded clouds around the lights. Beth smelled a strong whiff of burning coal. Those few seconds of fear on the top stair made her regret coming with them. But what would have been the alternative? Stay at home in a big empty house? Lie alone in the bed and awaken in fear and horror?

Beth had actually found it easy to convince her boss that she should take the trip. She had feared there might be an argument. Now she realized that they all thought it would be nice if she left for a while. They felt awkward around her.

Her work had had responsibilities. They ought to have tried to bring her back, maybe even made the attempt to retrain her, but no one had taken the initiative. Beth found this a relief. Her boss had asked her to come to school to "discuss the situation." Beth had made an attempt, but as she approached the school and heard the playing children, the sound of their cries like the screams of birds, their feet hitting the pavement . . . she suddenly could not breathe and felt the pounding pain in her chest, that pain which now was so familiar. Fear made her ill and she turned around for home.

Her students had sent her drawings. The pictures had solid black lines.

"Welcome back!" one wrote in the accompanying letter, but the handwriting was that of a grown-up. The letter had made her so upset she'd ripped the drawing to pieces and burned it in the fireplace.

They followed the crowd off the plane to the arrival hall. The hall had a shiny wooden floor. Ulf walked in front of Beth, his camera equipment dangling from his shoulder.

"Well, here we are," Ulf said, turning to her. He looked happier than he'd been in ages. Beth took his hand and forced herself to speak.

"Just think . . . the Dark Continent. Who would have thought that we'd ever come to Africa?"

Everything went smoothly. Once they'd picked up their luggage and gone through customs, they found Mr. Graham holding a sign with their names just as they'd been told. Mr. Graham was Ulf's contact person. He appeared to be about thirty years old. His face was almost childlike in its roundness. He was wearing khaki pants and a large-patterned shirt. His hand was cool and well-manicured.

"*Karibu,*" he said and smiled at Beth.

Beth nodded, confused.

"*Karibu* means welcome in Swahili," Mr. Graham explained. "How was your trip?"

His jeep was parked outside on the street. He told them that they had to wait for a while.

"We have to drive in a convoy on the way to town."

Beth climbed into the jeep. Next to them on the sidewalk, a woman came walking past with two children. She was straight-backed and had a bundle balanced on her head. Her children stared at Beth with round, black eyes. The youngest child reached out a hand and moved his lips, looking straight at Beth. Beth felt uncomfortable.

"Should we give them something?" she asked.

"If you give money to beggars, you'll soon be a beggar yourself," Juni answered. Juni leaned back in the seat and lifted her arms in the air.

"A whiskey on the rocks and then to bed," she said. "How long do you think we have to sit and wait?"

Finally, the convoy, escorted by a number of police vehicles, started to move.

"Unfortunately, there have been a number of attacks lately," Mr. Graham explained. "You must be careful while you are here."

"But how? We're in cars, after all!" Juni exclaimed. "All we have to do is step on the gas, right?"

Mr. Graham gave her a worried glance.

"I'm afraid it's not that easy. They often block the roads with stones or other wrecks."

Beth tried to look out into the deep dark but saw nothing.

"There are people who are just so . . . evil," Mr. Graham said quietly. "Hostile. A shame on Tanzania. A shame!"

It got a little lighter near the town. The roads were still narrow and filled with potholes. Along the sides were low shacks with corrugated metal roofs. People sat talking in the doorways. They looked up as the cars came by, waved and shouted.

"What are they saying?" asked Beth.

Mr. Graham did not answer. Maybe he hadn't heard her ask the question.

For a while, Beth was nervous that they would have to stay overnight in those slums in some shabby hostel filled with backpackers. She was too old for such things. She longed for a cool shower and a bed to stretch out in so she could sleep. Much to her relief, the jeep swung into a gated driveway guarded by two men holding weapons.

Inside the gate, everything was different. The hotel was everything she'd longed for.

The next morning they sat in the garden for breakfast. Mr. Graham strolled up to the table. He looked a little haggard, his round cheeks droopy.

"I hope you are well and had a restful night," he greeted them.

"Yes, we have," replied Ulf. "This is an excellent hotel."

Ulf was wearing his dark blue shorts and a T-shirt. His thick hair was still damp after his shower. Beth looked at his bony knees. She wanted to hold them, stroke them, kiss the soft skin behind them; but it had nothing to do with sexual desire. Rather it was a flowing sense of tenderness. She carefully placed her hand on his, but he drew his away.

Mr. Graham sat down in the empty chair next to Juni.

"I'm sorry," he said. "We've run into some difficulties."

Mr. Graham had a way of hunching his shoulders so that he looked sick and defeated. According to their original plans, they were to go and meet the Maasai the first day. For some reason, that had been postponed. They didn't really understand why. "We'll have to wait for a while," said Mr. Graham without explaining. He bent down and pulled at the laces of his shiny black shoes. "Meanwhile, please enjoy life here in Arusha."

Mr. Graham took them to the center of town where they could change money. Arusha was a shabby town worn down by poverty. Next Mr. Graham brought them to his office and asked them to wait for a while on an old leather sofa while he made a few calls.

Beth had to go to the bathroom. She asked a woman behind the desk for directions. She appeared to be Mr. Graham's secretary. J Croeze was engraved on a small metal plate next to her computer. These two were the only people in the office.

The woman took a key from her desk drawer and silently pointed toward the hallway, and showed she had no intention of coming with Beth to show her the way.

Beth walked into the hall and tried a few doors. The key did not fit any of them. Suddenly one door gave, and she found herself outside in the blinding sunshine. She was surrounded at once by a gang of boys who almost seemed to have been waiting for her exit. They wanted to sell her necklaces and batik cloth.

"No," she said. "I don't want to buy anything."

They pretended not to hear her. They tugged at her sleeves, almost aggressively. She tried to go back inside, but realized that the door had locked automatically. One of the boys, perhaps fourteen years old, pretended to knock on the door and then shook his head. The others laughed. Beth could smell dirt and rancid oil.

Again she said that she didn't want anything.

"Very cheap!" said the tallest boy. He wore a shirt that was ripped all over the back. "Look at this necklace!"

He dangled the necklace right in front of her eyes.

"Tell me a price! Tell me what you will pay!"

In order to get rid of them, Beth pointed to a piece of batik, which had the pattern of a trumpeting elephant.

"Beautiful!" the boy said, his voice hard. "Very beautiful and cheap, too!"

"Okay," said Beth. The sun shimmered off the road and the heat was unbearable. Why didn't Ulf or Juni come to help her? They must have known by now that something had happened to her. She did not want to pull out her pocketbook where the boys could see where she kept it. She stuck her hand into her backpack and finally found a dollar bill at the bottom. She had no idea how much it was worth. The boy grabbed the bill, stuffed it in his pocket, and handed her the batik cloth. She found herself motionless, clutching it in her hand.

The other boys looked angry that she had chosen to buy from that boy and not them. One of them pulled at her blouse and she tried to pull herself away but he did not let go. Their faces came right into hers. She could feel their breath.

"Look at this necklace!" they yelled. "Tell us a price! What you want to pay! Very, very cheap!"

"Go away!" she yelled in English. "Leave me be!"

At that moment, the door flew open. Mr. Graham stepped out onto the street.

"*Ondokeni!*" he roared.

The boys immediately let Beth go and ran away down the alley.

Beth sniffed. "*Jävlar!*" she swore in Swedish. She spoke English to Mr. Graham. "Where is my husband? Where are Ulf and Juni?"

"They're coming," Mr. Graham said. "I see you've been . . . shopping. Be careful. Next time make sure I am there to help you."

After this incident, Beth no longer wanted anything to do with the town. She wanted only to stay in the hotel. She tried to relax in the garden with a Swedish paperback she'd bought at the Arlanda Airport, but she couldn't follow the story, she couldn't concentrate.

Ulf and Juni made some sorties, a kind of reconnaissance, and a few days later, they made some decisions.

"Our friend, Mr. Graham, seems to have goofed," Ulf said one evening at dinner. "He admits his mistake and is ready to make amends. He's offered to let us stay at his brother's newly opened hotel in Zanzibar at a very reduced rate. We can stay there until Mr. Graham has fixed things with the Maasai."

"Zanzibar!" Beth exclaimed. "God, that sounds so exotic!"

"Zanzibar: the city of Spices and Slaves," Juni said. "What a history! A real slave trader there had the name of Tippu Tip. I know . . . it sounds like someone in a nursery rhyme, but he was a real person. I read about him before we came out here. You can still see his house. Stanley . . . you know the guy who was hunting for Livingstone . . . he was really impressed by this Tippu Tip guy. I could get an article out of this. The story of Tippu Tip. I can imagine the title already: *He sold Black Gold.*"

"Can we extend our trip just like that?" asked Beth. "What about our plane tickets and visas and stuff?"

Ulf gave Beth a friendly shove.

"Not to worry, Beth," he said. "We can have a little bit of a beach vacation, too. Meanwhile, all our friends back in Sweden are shivering from the cold!"

2

THE HOTEL HAD A DREAM LOCATION. It was directly on the beach with the shimmering green Indian Ocean playing out right in front. As they sat on the veranda for lunch, they heard the thunder of the tide on its way back in.

The main building, with the reception desk and restaurant, was in the middle of the complex. It had a high vaulted ceiling which gave it an almost religious, cathedral-like atmosphere. The floor was made of shining stone and there seemed always some employee down on hands and knees polishing it. About fifty white bungalows were set around the area, each with large rooms and verandas, where visitors could sit and listen to the cicadas during the evening. Stone paths wound between the buildings and the center, and all kinds of grasses and decorative bushes were planted along the edges. Every morning, when Beth woke up, she could see women working, bent over in the plantings, gardening with ancient tools.

Beth recognized a few of the plants because in the teacher's lounge a few of them were in pots near the southern window. Hibiscus and one with gold-flecked leaves. Görel was the one who had taken on their care as her personal duty. The week after mid-winter break, Görel would remove everything from the coffee table and spread out newspapers. Then she'd change the soil in every pot. Her movements were oddly stiff and deliberate as if someone had forced her to take on the job.

Beth felt her body become heavy and slow at the thought of the school and her coworkers. She tried to feel happy that she was no longer there, but she couldn't relax. This vacation was nothing more than playing 'let's pretend.' The beaches, the sun, the waves. She walked around this pretend paradise but did not feel as if she were actually present.

Down by the beach there was a large, rectangular pool with a bar beside it. She would find a deck chair and stretch out to read a book and immediately a lifeguard would come up to her and hand her a plush towel. This made her feel a little trapped even though she felt more restless by the minute. She would flip through her book but have no idea what it was about. Finally, she felt she had to get up and walk to the edge of the pool. The lifeguard would watch her and sometimes he would even come up to her and ask, with a slight bow, if there was anything she needed. This made her embarrassed. She would wrap the towel closer around herself and shake her head no.

"Thank you, I'm fine," she said.

The lifeguard must have noticed the fib.

"Would you like to take a swim in our fine pool, Ma'am?" He tried to use English to make her more comfortable. He was very young. He never let her out of his sight. "The water is clean. No germs, no illnesses."

Beth felt herself turn red.

"Maybe later," she said. She always said 'maybe later.'

Ulf and Juni were busy with their work. Every morning they would take the overloaded local dalla–dalla buses from the bus stop next to the hotel. Beth did not dare ask to come with, nor did they invite her. She would go with them to the bus stop and watch them climb onboard and find a seat on one of the side benches. They'd push past the other passengers, who would giggle as they made room for them.

Juni had learned a few words of Swahili.

"*Kwaheri,*" she'd call from the bus and wave exaggeratedly as the bus started to move. Beth waved back. She noticed that the roof of the bus was always full with sacks, bundles, and packages. Sometimes people would stand on the stairs and hold onto the doors.

There was not a single thing in this country which reminded her of Sweden.

Beth would get homesick once the bus had gone in its cloud of dust and she would be on her own. The area was protected by a huge cement wall with barbed wire on top. Armed guards were always at the gate. Local people were never allowed inside, except for those who had work in the complex, and there were many of those.

Beth would smile slightly at the armed guards, dressed in their khaki uniforms. They would stare at her but would not move. Did she read something of disgust in their eyes? She tried to mentally transmit, *I'm a rich white woman. Don't you dare look at me like that, you assholes!* Above her eyes, her head would start to ache.

The entire hotel seemed deserted. When they'd arrived, there were other guests, at least three. A fat German and his two daughters. The daughters had gotten diving lessons in the pool from a white man wearing a ponytail. But they'd left and taken their baggage with them. So Beth was entirely on her own. She guessed that the complex was so new no one had heard of it yet. Things would get better soon. There'll be new guests, she thought. Every time she walked back from the bus stop, she would think the same thought.

Once evening came, however, it would always be just the three of them: Beth, Ulf, and Juni.

She walked to her bungalow. She ached as if she were getting her period. The door was open. A woman in a blue uniform was busy cleaning. Beth delayed going inside. Shyness overtook her and she knew that she would not be able to answer if the woman asked her anything.

Beth walked to the beach. The tide was ebbing and she could see local women from the village working on their plots of seaweed, cutting it to export to Japan. One of their waiters had told them that the Japanese thought seaweed raised potency. His wife had a seaweed plot.

Beth sat in the sand for a while. She watched some almost see-through crabs scurry over the hard-packed sand. They moved in a funny way by running sideways. Beth got up and tried to catch one. It immediately disappeared down its hole formed in a perfect circle.

The heat waves undulated over the sand. Beth remembered that she should have put on some suntan lotion. Her skin was much too light to tolerate this burning sunshine. She waded into the marshy water and watched the far-off women in their brightly colored clothes. She wondered how they worked. She saw rows of sticks pointing up above the surface of the water. When the tide came in, seaweed wrapped around, fully covering the sticks. The women lifted the bundles of seaweed onto their heads and struggled back to land.

Their toes and fingers have to be all wrinkled from the water, Beth thought. It must be strange to have to work underwater to scavenge the seaweed. Beth never saw men do the work. It must be a typical job for women.

The heat made her thirsty. Beth went to the bar, which was just a countertop beneath a round, palm branch roof. A man in black pants and a white long-sleeved shirt was drying glasses. Beth was thinking of ordering a Coke, but she changed her mind once she reached the bar.

"A glass of white wine, please," she requested.

The man nodded. His black hands were leathery and he had a thin ring on one of his fingers.

Beth hoisted herself onto one of the bar chairs and sipped her wine. It was calming.

The man looked out over the Indian Ocean.

"It's beautiful here," Beth said.

The man nodded slowly.

"But . . . it looks like there aren't many guests."

"Not yet," he answered. "It's a new place."

"It's very nice here."

"Yes, indeed it is."

"Are you from one of the villages around here?"

"Yes. Many of us have employment here. The hotel is important for us. It allows us to make a living."

"Make a living?"

"Yes, buy food and clothes and books for the children."

"I understand."

"Are you from Europe?" the man asked.

"Yes. Do you know the country of Sweden? It's in Scandinavia, far up in the north. It's almost at the North Pole."

The man laughed. "It must be very cold and dark by the North Pole!"

"It is indeed!" Beth finished her wine. She sat for a minute, picking at her cuticles with a toothpick. Then she asked, "What's your name?"

The man did not answer, but he turned to her and poured her another glass of wine.

"It's hot today," he said, his mouth turning up slightly at the corners.

"Yes, it's very hot."

"Where are your friends?"

"They're working. They're journalists."

"And what about you?"

"I just am."

That evening, the three of them sat in the restaurant.

"We went to the Stone Town," said Juni. Her conversation sounded stilted. "I'm going to write an article about an Arabic princess who lived here in the seventeenth century. Her name was Salme. She kept a diary. I want to track it down. She was the daughter of a sultan and was a member of a harem . . . a concubine, I guess they called it. Maybe being a concubine was higher status than just being a harem girl. Anyway, she ran away with a German guy she fell in love with. He was living next door and I imagine they looked at each other from the balconies. Salme's family was furious. They sent her away from the palace. What a story, right? I'd like to write an entire book about her. She was a modern woman, even though this happened so long ago."

Ulf laughed. "You have to curb your enthusiasm, Juni! You have to make a living, too. You can't earn enough to eat if you spend all your time writing a book!"

"But I'm sure this book would be a best-seller, just you wait! And besides, in the meantime I can write articles about her."

Beth had taken a shower before dinner. She was wearing her wide, light pants. The skin on her shoulders burned and she felt as if she had a slight fever.

The wine she'd drunk that morning had just made her tired. She'd gone back to her room to rest and fallen asleep on her bed. That was not good. She would not be able to sleep at night.

"You two were gone a long time," she said.

"We kept getting lost in all those tiny alleyways," Juni said. "It's totally crazy, like a labyrinth. And my sense of direction is pretty bad most of the time anyway. Finally we had to ask a few boys who were playing with a kind of ball made from rags. We gave them some money, and then we couldn't get rid of them."

Juni appeared happier today. Her moods could swing from crying jags to manic excitement.

"How did you make out, Ulf?" Beth asked. "Did you find a princess to write about?"

"I'm still trying to make some connections," Ulf said evasively. "All of this waiting is getting on my nerves. I'm really disappointed in Mr. Graham. I'm losing patience with him."

"What's he waiting for?"

"He has to get permission from the Maasai village. We were supposed to be with the Maasai a few days. I guess they need to check up on us."

"Well, we're living cheaply enough here," Juni said. "I guess we shouldn't complain."

They'd chosen a table right in the middle of the huge dining hall. The servers ran about, nervously bringing napkins and trays. Ulf ordered a bottle of wine but it took awhile to come.

"Every time I call Graham, he says 'soon, soon.' I'm beginning to suspect that they want to keep us here as hostages." Ulf laughed darkly. "Maybe we're decoys to lure more guests to this place!"

"Why would they . . . ?" Beth started.

"It was just a joke!" Ulf snapped.

"What about you, Beth?" Juni asked, changing the subject. "Did you do anything fun?"

"I tried to read. There's not much to do around here, really."

"Is it a good book?"

"Not really."

"You can borrow a book from me if you want to. It's a thriller. I'm almost done with it. It's a gruesome one about a female psychopath."

Juni had stopped putting on her usual make-up. Now her hair hung limp. She lit a cigarette.

"I wish Werner were here," Juni said suddenly. "He would have liked being here with us."

Ulf draped an arm around Juni's shoulder.

"He really would have," Ulf agreed.

Juni blew out a cloud of smoke. She emptied her wine glass.

"Is the bottle empty already? They have small bottles in this country. Have you noticed that?"

"Let's order beer instead. Otherwise we might have to wait all night for another bottle. Wine is not one of their specialties."

Chicken and rice was served. The chicken was dry and sinewy.

I'm not all that hungry, Beth thought.

They each received a bottle of Kiru, the good local beer.

"Asante sana," said Juni and the server's face lit up.

"That means 'thank you,'" Juni said with satisfaction. They sat in silence for a moment and then Juni said, "By the way, I should say hi from Pappa. I called him to see how Kaiser was doing."

Juni had handed over Kaiser to her father, though her father was not especially happy about the arrangement. "They were doing just fine. They were just about to go for a walk. I think it's great that our dad can have some company now that Mamma's in the nursing home. He'll become attached to Kaiser soon enough. He always liked animals."

Beth looked out into the darkness distractedly. There were small points of light in the tall, thick grass: fireflies. Ulf had captured some the night before and put them in the veranda, but the next day they were gone.

"I wonder if there is a lot of snow back home," Beth said quietly. "I hope that there's a great deal of snow. Then we can enjoy being here all the more."

Juni burst out in laughter.

"We can sure hope so! But Pappa said that all the snow had melted. It's above freezing and pretty windy. The lawns have turned into mud puddles. You can just imagine what Kaiser looks like!"

Beth could not sleep, as she had expected. Ulf was on his side, his back to her. He was breathing heavily as if each breath was torture.

As soon as she shut her eyes, the old images were back. She'd hoped that they might fade in the new sensations of this strange country.

Not at all.

His cold dead face. The heap of hair and blood.

The thump, that thump of the body falling into the hole.

The clay sliding down the sides.

The arms that would not stay down, even though they pressed on them.

The smell of earth and roots.

She kept trying to keep it all away, but the sights returned.

The tracks of boots. The pine cones.

Someone back there knew. Someone had turned a flattened hole into a real grave.

A place where someone went to mourn.

The thought made her incredibly afraid.

3

BETH WALKED OUTSIDE AND THE DARKNESS EMBRACED HER. The air was thick and warm. It was not quiet at all. Sounds of cicadas and frogs came from every direction. Beth stood on the veranda and smoked a cigarette. All around her were the other small bungalows with their pointed clay tile roofs and no one inside them. Somehow the place seemed haunted. The large gray prison fence loomed.

What if she were already in prison?

No. This was not a prison. This was supposed to be paradise.

Still, prison was where she would end up. That is, if it all came out. She'd be stuck with whores and drug addicts. Vulgar, uneducated women with whom she had nothing in common. They would notice her at once and go on the attack. They'd ridicule her; they'd hurt her.

Beth swallowed hard.

This must not happen!

Never!

Juni's bungalow was right next to theirs. Beth noticed a weak light and heard a door open. Juni came out on the steps. She was wearing a short nightgown. Juni lit a cigarette and, for a second, her whole face was illuminated. Then she saw Beth and she waved.

Maybe she still has some sleeping pills, Beth thought. *I should go ask.*

"Come sit down for a minute, Sis," Juni said. "Do you want a cigarette?"

"Sure."

Juni pulled her hair behind her ears and sat down in a chair.

"What a night," she said. "Like velvet. What a night to be all alone in."

"I can't sleep," said Beth. "I'm not active enough so I'm not getting tired."

Juni grabbed Beth's arm. Her hands were dry and bony.

"You can't know how much I miss him!" Juni exclaimed. "I'm so heartbroken! You don't know how happy you are . . . try to take good care of each other . . . try to appreciate each other, while you are still . . . ."

Juni had started to cry quietly.

"I can only imagine how empty it must feel," Beth said helplessly.

Juni wiped her nose with an irritated gesture. "And I can be pretty fucking angry with him, too! How can he just leave me here like this!"

"I see . . ."

"Just not be here any longer! Just up and die! That whole shit! Just leave me standing here all by myself. All alone. It's so terrible . . . there's no chance to prepare . . . no time to arrange anything . . . to say . . . goodbye."

Beth nodded, waited a little while, then, "May I have another cigarette?" she asked.

"Sure, go ahead. Take as many as you want. You know, Kaiser . . . he can't understand it. Every evening he'd go to the outer door and wait. He'd stand there, all tensed up, and listen and listen. His whole doggy body . . . . How can you make an animal understand that his master is not coming home ever again, Beth? How can you do that?"

There was a slithering sound on the porch. A lizard stopped to look at them. It was motionless for a minute and then slid away.

"You get so many strange thoughts," Juni said. "How things are. How things will be. Once you're dead, I mean. What if you come back as an animal? What if that little gecko was Werner . . . . I want to know. I can't believe that everything just ends."

"Of course, that's it. When you're dead, that's the end. How else should . . ."

Juni turned her face to Beth. She appeared tired and older. She now had deep creases from her nostrils to the edges of her mouth. In the weak light, it appeared as if her chin had been cut off. She looked like a marionette. Juni stood up.

"I have a bottle of whiskey. Would you like some?"

Beth stayed where she was. She heard the toilet flush. Then she felt as if someone were standing right behind her. Something cool against her burnt shoulder. She breathed hard, and whirled around. No one was there. Maybe it was an insect, a moth. Or maybe even a bat. Beth heard her heart pound.

Juni came back out with a bottle and two glasses.

"Here! Drink up! And I'm going to tell you something."

Beth poured a finger of the light golden drink. She took a sip and it burned as it went down her throat.

"Don't think that I'm going crazy now," Juni said. "Promise me!"

"I promise."

"When I was in bed . . . just a moment ago . . . you know, there's these large mirrors. Our rooms are alike, so you know what I mean. I was lying in bed and reading . . . and it seemed to me . . . as if someone was there watching me . . . it was such a strong feeling . . . it felt real . . . I can't describe it . . . and when I put down the book and looked . . . it seemed as if someone moved in the mirror. I promise you, it's true."

Beth's fingertips felt cold.

"I wasn't afraid. Strange, isn't it? But I wasn't afraid. I felt a bit weak, a bit delicate . . . . I tried to sit up and see if someone else was really in the room. But of course, I didn't see anyone."

Juni became silent and stubbed out her cigarette.

Below them on the beach came the sound of the surf pounding the shore.

"I believe it was him," Juni finally said. "I believe it was Werner. I think that the dead are still with us and they follow us and watch over us. I'm convinced of it. And do you know, Beth, it feels very comforting. Very safe. I know that he is always near me and he will never leave me . . . as long as I live."

4

A NOTHER DAY. Ulf and Beth fought. She'd begged to come with
them to Stone Town. Beth said she could not handle being on
her own for another day.

"No, that won't work," Ulf said shortly.

Beth started to scream and wail even though she felt she was
demeaning herself.

Ulf said, "You chose to come and promised not to make a nuisance of yourself."

Make a nuisance of herself.

As if she were a troublesome child.

She'd awoken with a headache that pressed around her entire head
like a vice. *Just like a crown of thorns*, Beth thought.

She was also filled with desire: a swollen weight between her
thighs.

Her period had not yet started, and often her desire was strongest
right before it came.

She turned toward Ulf and began to stroke him: his long, wide
back, his buttocks. She placed her fingers beneath his scrotum until
the palm of her hand was full. She began to kiss him with short,
quick movements, and covered him with her kisses.

He groaned and woke up. He stretched out and turned away
from her.

"What is it?" she whispered.

"What time is it?"

"Don't worry about that . . . I want you . . . I've been lying here thinking of you . . . and I'm . . ."

Ulf swung his legs over the edge of the bed and got up.

"What's wrong, Ulf?" Her voice broke just like her insides felt. Nothing about her was whole.

Ulf said nothing.

Beth crept out of the sheets and clung to him.

"Is it Juni?" she asked, shrilly.

"What in the hell are you talking about?"

"Are the two of you up to something? Something besides your so-called work together?"

Ulf pulled away from her and stumbled over to the wall. He turned on the light, but he still stood there, his hand on the wall. He spoke over his shoulder to her, never turning his head as he talked.

"You want the truth? This is the way it is, Beth: I've become impotent. Maybe I'll never be able to get it up again. Never! Neither with you nor with anyone else. I've lost my ability to make love."

"What?" Beth said emptily.

"Doesn't it torture you? What happened last summer? Yes, I know that we said we'd never mention it again, but we just can't . . . a thing like that . . . we should have gone to the police. We ought to have gone to the police! He . . . that man . . . he's going to be with us no matter what we do. Nothing will ever be the same again. We will never be normal again!"

"Have you told anyone?" she demanded. "Have you said anything to anyone?"

Ulf shook his head.

"No," he said, tiredly. "I haven't told anyone. But there are times I feel so bad I wish I were no longer alive."

Beth strode along the beach and thought about music. She wondered why she did not miss music. Classical music used to fill her soul, strengthen her.

Her brain was nothing but air. Complete emptiness.

She ought to have been wearing a hat. The sun beat down on her head and made her ill. She could see the women far out in the half-meter-deep water. Their backs were bent. Every morning they were there working on their seaweed plots. They had work to do.

She had nothing.

She was barefoot and the sand burned.

"Don't go too far away from the hotel," Mr. Graham had warned her. "It's a new place and people aren't used to it yet."

Some boats were pulled up onto shore. She'd watched them go out to sea during high tide. The boats were simple hollowed-out tree trunks with side carriers and sails sewn from old rice bags. 'White Rice' could still be read in faded black or red letters.

Beth sank down to her knees in the wet sand. It bubbled and popped. Small creatures ran about: some kind of tiny centipedes. Beth dug into the sand and some of it, along with tiny, broken shells, got under her nails. She sat for a while, letting her palms fall heavy and open. She marveled at the strange form of the sand.

She felt the prickling sensation of stress. She pressed her wet hands to her forehead, and then got up clumsily. Her feet flapped in the mud as she started to walk.

In the distance, she saw a small collection of gray mud houses. She'd never walked this far away from the hotel before. On the grass in front of the houses, she saw drying racks filled with harvested seaweed. To her, the heaps appeared to have the shape of dead animals. The wind brought a sour, damp stench to her nose. She did not see a single human being.

I'll just keep walking, she thought.

From far away, dimly and fleetingly, she saw a dot appear. It started to grow and come alive. She sighted on the dot, fixed it in her gaze with wide open eyes. As she got closer, she saw that it was a man. He was walking along the beach in front of her, slowly, as if he were waiting for her to catch up. He wore cut-off jeans and a shirt with rolled-up, unbuttoned sleeves. He'd wound a turban around his head.

Beth saw his footprints in the packed sand, and followed them. When she was just a few yards behind him, he turned. She saw his eyes and some hair that had fallen over his forehead. His hair was blonde.

Sand was harsh against her arms and filled her mouth. She moved the tip of her tongue over her lips. She tasted salty dryness. There was a shred of skin where her lip had split.

A nail scraped against her throat and she heard a voice:

"Oh, you're coming to. I'm so happy to see you're coming to!"

The voice spoke in hesitating, formal Swedish.

She lay on the beach with her face toward the sun. She saw the man as a dark shadow bent over her, without color or light.

Then she remembered.

He'd turned to look at her and she'd stared right into his blue eyes and shaggy blonde bangs. Fear hit her like a violent, powerful wave and she'd run away as fast as she could in that soft sand which resisted every step.

"You slipped and fell down," he said. His voice was hoarse and somewhat wheezy, and he had to keep clearing his throat. "I think you've had too much of the strong sun."

She shuddered and pulled her arms over her body. He handed her a bottle of tepid water and helped her to sit up.

The water was lukewarm and soothing.

"I've seen you around," he said. "You're staying at the new hotel."

"Yes." The word came out like a hiss.

"I've seen you walking about over there. It's not a good idea to leave that safe area, though."

"Why not?"

He shook his head.

"What about you, then?"

"It's different for me. I've lived here most of my life."

Beth slowly got to her feet. The man kept close in case she got dizzy.

Beth took a deep, shaky breath.

"All right, I'll head back to the hotel," she said. "Thanks for helping me."

From where he was standing, the light shone right into his eyes. She thought that it had been a long time since she'd seen eyes other than brown.

"I'll walk you back," he said. "I have some people waiting for me at the hotel. I'm giving them diving lessons."

She realized that she'd seen him before: a diving instructor.

Beth began to walk and he walked ahead of her as if to show her the way.

There was something about the way he held his body, the way he let one shoulder lead, even his lightly tanned hands. In her mind she heard the dampened scream and the crash afterwards, the scrape . . . of iron against skin and bone.

How he'd lifted his arm to defend himself . . .

How he was not able to deflect the blow.

Was hit right in the middle of the forehead

Right into the brain

And she also remembered the weight of the ax.

In her own hands.

She fell forward again, face first into the sand, this time without losing consciousness. With a snort of frustration, she rolled over onto her back and blew the sand out of her mouth. She tried to lift her arms to wipe the sand from her eyes, but they had gone limp.

The man had stopped. He'd not tried to stop her fall, just watched.

Beth tried to say something with her sunburned, ruined lips.

He raised a finger to his mouth.

"Shh. I know how to solve this."

She watched him from her prone position as he went to his knees. Slowly, he unwound his turban. She wanted to close her eyes. Her eyelashes were rubbed raw like shredded paper. She lay there.

He got up and she idly observed the fringed edge of his shorts, which were stained from salt and water. He held the turban in one hand. It had transformed into one long piece of patterned cotton. He turned his back to her and walked into the water. He bent over to soak the cotton. The tide was on its way in.

He lifted the cloth and wrung it out once, twice.

Then he returned to her.

She sat up now and let her right hand touch his forehead. While he wound the wet cloth around her head, she stroked him. His hair was straight and rather long, rough and as hard as clay.

His forehead was smooth. Whole.

A wild sound bubbled up from her throat, almost like a laugh. She pressed her hands to her mouth and bit them. Snot and saliva ran down her chin.

She tasted blood and fear. She whined like a tiny, hurt animal, but the strange sound disappeared.

He stood there: blonde hair, face in the shadows.

"The sun can make people crazy," he said. He pointed at her head. "You must protect yourself or the heat will fry your brain."

He was right next to her. His forehead was clean and sunburned. She reached up and tugged his hair, then brushed aside the hanging bangs.

"You look like someone . . . ," she said softly. "Please forgive me. I'm not feeling all that well."

5

HIS NAME WAS JÓHANN AND HE WAS THE SON OF ICELANDIC FARMERS. He'd left his home in northern Iceland more than ten years ago.

"My hometown is Varmahlíð," he said. "It sounds beautiful but reality is something else again."

"What do you mean?"

"People freeze in a climate like that. They harden. They are only good for one thing: surviving."

"But don't you ever get homesick?"

"Homesick? No, this is my home. I'm not made for living in darkness and ice. It's not natural."

He told her that he had a new family now. He'd been adopted by a woman from Zanzibar.

"Seriously? Adopted?"

"Her name is Maja She takes good care of me and makes sure I have enough to eat." He began to laugh. "Now, however, I'm able to contribute more and more to the family income."

Beth experienced an uncertain feeling, astonishingly, of jealousy.

"The tourists," he continued. "The tourists have money. Otherwise, they'd never be able to come here. I teach them the basics of diving, you know, scuba diving."

He handed her the bottle of water and she drank some more. Her nausea was receding.

"Come to my house some evening. Bring your friends, too. Maja makes better food than they do at the hotel. All kinds of food, and not too expensive, either. We can set the price in advance."

Beth shrugged her shoulders.

"I'll let them know, but they're really busy with their jobs."

Slight disappointment came over her. He was walking so close to her and her head was wrapped in his turban. She wanted him to ask her questions about who she was and why she was so alone. She wanted him to know her name and to say it out loud.

They got back to the hotel compound. He shook her hand.

"I have to meet a group of people here."

Beth reached for her head and then stopped herself.

"Let me clean the turban before I give it back."

"That's not necessary."

"I want to!"

A large black man came out from behind some lounge chairs. He waved at Jóhann and yelled something Beth did not understand.

"*Kwaheri*," Jóhann said. "I have to run."

There was a tiny boutique across from the reception desk. Beth had been there a number of times and had gone through the assortment on the half-empty shelves. The young woman at the counter looked embarrassed every time. There was not much to buy at all. Some pieces of jewelry, some clay pots, and some bottles of shampoo made for black hair. Also a few boring postcards.

As Beth came into the shop, she saw that the girl was slipping some new pieces of clothing onto hangers. They were simple dresses with batik patterns. The girl appeared triumphant.

There were no changing rooms. Beth held a light-blue dress in front of her. It was sewn in two parts and was tied at the shoulders. Beth noticed that she'd lost weight, a great deal of weight actually. She felt flat and dried out. She bought the dress and did not bother to do the usual haggling ceremony.

When she left, she thought that the girl wore a superior smile.

The bungalow was made up and ready. The cleaning woman had put a vase with a single flower, of a kind that Beth had never seen before. Its shiny, fleshy petals made it appear artificial, and it gave off a strong, almost sleepy aroma. She had the impulse to put it outside on the porch, but she did not dare to; she didn't want to insult anyone.

She lay down on the bed and fell asleep at once. She slept for quite some time without dreams and, when she woke up, she no longer had a headache. She got out of bed and went to take a shower. She stood for a long time underneath its weak stream.

The new dress was a bit large, but Beth could use a belt to pull it in at the waist. She looked at herself critically in the blotchy mirror.

"Wo-man!" she said out loud in English. She pouted her lips. Then that laugh came again and she could not stop.

She bit the inside of her cheeks and tasted metal.

She pulled out a whiskey bottle from her suitcase. There was not much left. They should have bought more bottles duty-free at the airport. Ulf had protested, though. *We're not going there to drink ourselves silly. I have a job to do and I want to form clear impressions, not half-buzzed ones.*

"I'll show you some impressions!" she whispered to the mirror.

She poured a finger and drank it all at once.

She'd washed the turban and hung it over the veranda fence to dry. The sun dried it almost at once. Now she pulled it down and folded it into a proper square.

She did not know where Jóhann lived, so she walked back toward the beach. The pool was abandoned and if anyone had been there practicing scuba diving, they must have done so while she was sleeping.

Beth wore a sunhat. Her neck was already starting to sweat. This time she went in the other direction toward the caves. When the tide was out, you could creep into the damp holes and come out the other side, but now the tide was in. She realized she'd have to climb over them to get past.

As she stood there wondering what to do, she heard a voice.

"Jambo!"

Beth saw a girl sitting higher up on the cliff. She must have been around seven years old. The girl sullenly picked at her bare feet. Her dress had once been a pink little princess-style dress, but now it was dirty, too small, and the flounces hung in tatters.

"Jambo!" Beth repeated.

The girl kept staring at her toes.

"Habari," she said.

Jambo and *habari* seemed to be the common greeting phrases in this country. *Jambo* was used for the tourists. She thought that the phrase had a sense of distance to it and was a threat not to come too close.

Stop thinking that you're somebody just because you're white, Beth thought.

Carefully, Beth smiled at the girl.

"Jóhann," she tried. "Do you know where Jóhann is?"

The girl grimaced.

Beth tried again: "Jóhann? Do you know Jóhann?"

The girl got up, turned around and began to climb the stones like a quick, lively mountain goat. Beth followed her. She tied the turban cloth loosely around her neck so she could grab onto the rocks. The girl waited for her. The girl's arms were covered in bug bites. She'd ripped the skin off some of them and others had already scabbed over.

"Come," the girl said, and the way she pronounced the word made it almost sound Swedish.

There was a thin, well-trodden path between the cliffs. The girl gave Beth a sly look and then started to walk along it.

Behind the mountain there were a few run-down houses. There were some cackling hens pecking and a thin cow tied to a rope.

The girl had gone ahead and was now standing in front of one of the houses. She turned her face away from Beth and giggled. Beth approached the house doubtfully.

"Jóhann?" she said.

The girl nodded and scratched her arm vehemently.

"Jóhann. *Ndiyo*," she called.

Then Beth saw him step out from behind the curtain, yawning. He did not see her at first. Beth said his name again, louder.

"What do you want?" he said, shortly.

Beth felt the sweat itch under her hair.

"I just wanted to return your . . ."

She'd unwound the turban from her neck and had folded it, holding it out to him.

"Oh, it's you."

It seemed as if he had not recognized her.

"Thanks," she said, confused. "I don't need it now. I've turned into a smart tourist who wears a hat."

He watched her for a minute without saying anything.

"Come on in," he said at last with no hurry. "I'm alone."

A sound hit her ears. It seemed to from the earth: a wonderful, high sound, like music.

"Sure," she said.

She walked toward him as he talked to the girl. He dug into his shorts pocket and pulled out a bill. The girl nodded and ran away. Beth realized the girl resembled the man, especially in the way she moved her shoulders. He might be the girl's father.

They were all alone. Jóhann walked between the houses until he seemed to choose one of the entrances.

"Step inside," he said. "*Karibu nyumbani!*"

There was not much furniture in the room. The floor was covered with bast-mat covers. Some plastic cushions were heaped against the wall. In one corner there was an ashtray and a bowl with a bunch of tiny bananas.

Jóhann sat down cross-legged. He patted the bast-mat as a sign that she should sit down. The room was hot and suffocating. The walls had once been painted green, but the paint was peeling and even the stucco was flaking off in places.

Beth sat down on her knees.

"That's a beautiful dress you're wearing," he said. "Maja made it. She's a good worker. If you want, I bet she can paint you in henna."

"Do the two of you live here?"

"Yes, this is my home."

"Where are all the other people? It seems so empty."

"They're all working."

"Maja, too?"

"Every day she gets on the bus and goes to town to sew."

"So now it's just you and . . . the little girl?"

"Yes," he said, and closed the drapery to cover the door.

He did it without much finesse, but Beth did not mind. She'd kept her dress on. She just kicked off her panties as she lay down on the lumpy floor.

He was tanned and well-shaped. He stood over her naked and his penis rose from his reddish-yellow, thick pubic hair. He squatted, balanced on his knuckles, and came inside her.

She lay there with her eyes open as he thrust and pushed. He found his rhythm finally and she stared at the ceiling. She saw a spider in one corner. It was huge and furry everywhere. She felt no fear.

Afterward, he lay on her, panting and heavy. She stroked his back. He lifted his face and her neck was cold without his breath.

"Are you hungry?" he asked.

"A little."

He slid down to the floor and reached for a banana.

"Here."

She ate the banana with her sticky fingers. Then she put on her underwear and stood up. She looked out the small window at the dusty, empty yard.

"Are you leaving?" he asked.

Beth nodded.

He got up and put on his jeans.

"Don't you ever think of going home?" she asked him.

"I told you. This is my home."

"Don't you ever miss the clear air of Iceland? Or the snow as it blows over the fields?"

He stood quietly, thinking. "There's one thing I miss. I miss our Icelandic ponies. How strong they are. How they run down the mountainside by the hundreds when fall comes. I might long to see that sight once more, perhaps."

He started to laugh. "A horse like that could not survive in Africa! But horses and people are not the same thing."

"True."

Beth held out her hand to shake his. "I've really got to go, now."

He grabbed her fingers and did not let go.

"Well, there's something you might have noticed . . . we're not exactly rich. And my Matilda is going to start school. She'll need a school uniform."

"I understand." Beth took a number of large bills from her backpack. He took them without a word.

"Isn't it difficult," she asked roughly. "Doing . . . this . . . for the tourists?"

"Not really," he said. "With you it wasn't hard at all. Though some of those large German women . . . and they're so old that they look like elephants. Have you ever seen an elephant close up? They are covered in deep wrinkles."

When they stepped outside into the light, the girl who was named Matilda was there holding a cat. The cat struggled against being held and was clawing the girl. She held it tightly with both hands.

"Can you find your way back?" Jóhann asked. He was cleaning his ear with his pinky finger. Beth wanted to scream at him to stop. She found it insulting that he would dig at his ear with herself, a lady, present.

"I'll find the way," she said.

"Otherwise, Matilda can go with you."

"I'll be fine," she said, shortly.

The cat still squirmed in Matilda's arms.

Matilda shrieked and dropped the cat. It hissed as it disappeared underneath a tin-plate door. The girl held up her arm and there was a deep, long scratch.

Jóhann told her something and she sniffed and walked into the house.

"I've warned her dozens of times," he muttered. "You can't be too careful around animals. A boy in a neighboring village was bitten by a cat and he died of blood poisoning."

6

WHEN BETH GOT BACK TO THE BUNGALOW, ULF AND JUNI HAD RETURNED. Ulf was busy packing. His suitcase was open on the bed.

"Tomorrow morning early, we're on our way," he said exultantly. He put a few rolls of film into a plastic bag.

"Where?" Beth asked lamely.

"To the Maasai. They've sent us a message that they're ready to have us."

"What about me?"

Ulf looked at her with surprise.

"You're coming with us, of course."

"Well, thank you so much."

Beth went into the bathroom, pulled off the dress and shut her eyes.

This was the first time since she'd met Ulf that she'd been with another man.

A harsh phrase swirled around her head: *Turned to stone.*

She stroked her flat stomach. Her skin was soft with faint traces of stretch marks left from the unsuccessful pregnancy.

Her unsuccessful pregnancy.

She returned to the bedroom completely nude.

Ulf was standing in the middle of the room with a notebook in his hand. He was flipping though it with a scowl.

"Ulf," she said, tension in her voice.

He did not answer.

"Ulf!" she said again, much louder.

Ulf looked up at her, but his mind was elsewhere. He was thinking about the lines he'd written, revisions, better formulations.

"I'm totally different from you!" she said straight out.

Ulf looked doubtful.

"What are you talking about?"

"Even if you can never sleep with anyone again, I'm different! I had to go and try it for myself!"

"Huh?"

"I met a man today and he wanted me and we made love!"

Ulf threw his notebook toward the bed. It landed on the floor. The pages had bent and she could see his handwriting: tiny, crooked letters. Ulf had turned very pale.

"Have you lost your mind?" he growled.

"You mean you would have forbidden me? Is that what you would have wanted?"

"Beth!"

"He wanted my body and he came into me and he was young and strong!"

"You disgust me!"

"I know. I already figured that out this morning. But don't think for one second that your disgust will keep me from living! And that man, the one who died, he won't keep me from living anymore, either! I'm going to drive out every memory just by living as hard as I can!"

Ulf sank down on the bed. He drew in his shoulders and sat absolutely still. This made Beth's rage lose steam. She ran across the room, knelt down, took his arm. She wanted him to hold her, to curse her. Something. With a gurgle, he pushed her away.

"You killed someone back there, an absolute stranger. You hit him in the head with an ax and now he's buried on our land . . . and the worst thing of all is that you don't seem to regret it. Can't you see how you frighten me? I can't keep going on like this . . . I don't want to hurt you . . . but when we get home . . . we must go to the police."

There was a noise at the door. Juni was there, her mouth open and her body ready to run.

Ulf spoke first, took control of the situation.

"Come on inside and make yourself at home in our humble bungalow!"

Juni's face seemed misshapen and her breath came in short gasps.

Beth found a towel and wrapped herself in it.

Juni shrank away. She stared at them, her mouth twitching.

"Did I . . . hear you correctly? Tell me it's not true. Tell me that I must have misunderstood you . . . that I'm just tired . . ."

"Your sister has a number of problems," said Ulf. He walked over to the table and picked up a cigarette from the pack there. He lit it. "We can't do anything about her problems now. We have to wait until we return to Sweden."

Juni saw a shoe on the floor. She picked it up and began to finger it absentmindedly.

"So, last summer," she said, "when we arrived at Skogslyckan . . . everything seemed so sick and wrong . . . but now it's starting to make sense to me."

"So what do you think is now making sense?" Beth sneered.

Juni stared at her sister. She lifted the shoe in her hand and then slung it straight into Beth's face. It hit Beth on the chin. Beth yelped from the pain.

Juni panted as if she'd been running.

"That's why! That's why you were kicking Kaiser! You can't fool a dog! You know you can't fool a dog! He knew that there was something buried there . . . a body . . . a dead person . . . oh, God, please tell me it's not true!"

"Juni, do you have any whiskey left? Lord in Heaven, do I need some whiskey!" Ulf pushed past Beth on his way to the door.

"In my room . . . on the desk," said Juni.

Ulf left.

"Juni, you were always so quick to judge," Beth said.

She could hear Juni's quiet snuffling.

"Oh yes, you know what I'm talking about. You always wanted to believe the worst about me. Like that time with Markus, when we were little. You terrorized me for years and threatened to tell on me so you could get whatever you wanted . . . . It was sheer blackmail!"

Juni went over to a chair by the desk and sank down into it.

"We were just kids, then," she said in a thin voice.

"It was an unfortunate accident!" Beth suddenly screamed. She took hold of Juni's arms and began to shake her. "It was self-defense! He was dangerous . . . . He was grabbing me by the neck! I had to defend myself, can't you understand? He would've killed me otherwise! You have to understand that! I was acting in self-defense!"

Slowly, Juni began to sway from side to side. She whimpered a small soft sound.

"We were going to go to the police," Beth continued more quietly. "I thought that it was one of the prisoners who'd escaped from Tidaholm jail. Then we saw . . . that the police had captured them . . . and so we went home . . . and . . . we realized there were no witnesses . . . so why should we get involved with all those interrogations and investigations . . . to try to prove . . . . I've never had anything to do with the police before, Juni."

"You're not in your right mind!"

"But that's what happened. We buried him right outside the fence. No one need ever know. People disappear all the time and no one ever knows what happens to them."

"But what kind of a person . . . ? Who was he? Old? Young?" Juni sniffed loudly, tears streaming down her cheeks.

"I don't know," Beth answered irritably. "Some homeless guy. He *looked* homeless."

"He has to have a family somewhere. Somebody must miss him. You know you can't keep this hidden . . . . People have to know so they . . . can mourn."

"I don't think he had a family or we would have read about it in the newspaper."

"So Ulf was . . . in on this the whole time?"

"It was the only way we could think of, Juni. It really was the only way."

Beth IV

1

THEY TOOK A BOAT FROM STONE TOWN TO DAR ES-SALAAM. The wind was strong, and seasick people huddled with bags to their mouths. Beth had managed to find a place in the salon but the stench and sound drove her back out onto the deck again. She felt as if she were in the middle of the churning water and she held fast to the small pipe railing which crept along the edge of the boat's deck. Many times she felt close to vomiting. When they finally made their way into the harbor, she was soaking wet and exhausted.

Both Ulf and Juni had vomited during the voyage. Beth was now the strong one who had to find their luggage and get them down the gangway. She was also the first one to catch sight of Mr. Graham. He was standing by the road, waving eagerly.

As he greeted them, he looked alarmed.

"You're so thin and pale. Did you enjoy the hotel?"

"The hotel was fine," said Ulf. "It was just this damned boat."

"Yes, the seas are rough today. Maybe you're not used to heavy seas?"

"Can people ever get used to all that heaving water?" Ulf muttered to himself in Swedish.

Mr. Graham said he would like to take them on a little sightseeing tour through the town. They were too exhausted to say no, so they all got into the jeep. Beth sat in front and Juni and Ulf crept into the back seats.

None of them had said much to each other since last night. Beth had had a sleep filled with nightmares. She dreamed that she'd returned to Skogslyckan and it had snowed and she'd had to work through the snow and she fell deep inside its icy wet cold. In the dream, she arrived at the grave and knew that she had to hurry to remove any traces before it revealed itself as a grave. But when she got there, it was gone. Just an empty, dug-out hole. In the dream, she clearly saw how the dirt was in heaps around the hole on top of the snow. She heard a movement and she whirled around and saw him standing there and she saw the wound in his forehead, the gaping sides of it. At that moment, she woke up. She felt something loose in her mouth. She had lost a tooth. She had been clenching her jaws so tightly that the tooth had broken from the gum. It was gray and the enamel was ugly. She had put it in her toilet bag.

Her body was covered in small red bites. She couldn't help scratching herself and once she started, she could not stop. The itch was incessant. She clenched her hands together and tried to concentrate on the sights outside the jeep.

"What do you know about Dar es-Salaam?" Mr. Graham asked with expectation in his voice.

"Not much," Beth admitted.

"Let me tell you then. I was born here. This is the city of my forefathers."

Beth turned to the two in the back seats. "Pay attention!" she ordered in Swedish. "You're embarrassing me!"

They didn't answer. She felt just as she had long ago, when she was young, maybe eight years old. She'd wanted to play with Juni and Juni's friend Camilla. They didn't want her with them. They'd stopped talking to her and acted as if she did not exist.

The jeep turned into a street jammed with traffic. The sidewalks were covered with people who were walking around or standing in groups chatting.

"Dar es-Salaam is Arabic for Place of Peace," Mr. Graham explained. "Don't be lured into a false sense of security, however. I must ask you to keep the doors locked and the windows properly shut. I'm very sorry, but that is the way it is. White people are uncommon here and you must realize that this is an extremely poor country. Temptation can be difficult to withstand for our country-men."

He smiled expectantly at Beth. "But it is surely beautiful, is it not?"

Beth nodded nervously.

"Right now we are driving down Samora Machel Avenue and over there you can see one of our most famous monuments: the Askari Monument. Maybe you have heard of the Ice Cream War, which happened during the First World War. You see the soldier, he is an *Askari*; he is a symbol. Just think of all these African soldiers who have died in conflicts which had nothing to do with Africa. The Ice Cream War was between the British and the Germans."

"Why was it called the Ice Cream War?" asked Beth. She turned to look at the two in the back seat again. Juni was sitting straight, her sunglasses on.

"That's what the English called it. They said that the Germans were going to melt like ice cream in the sun. And that's exactly what they did, so to speak. Look over there, now. You can see the Botanic Gardens on the one side and the National Museum on the other. Juni, weren't you the one who was interested in Lucy and all our other earliest ancestors? Inside that museum you can find the skull of the so-called Nutcracker Man. He's also called Dear Boy, but he's not so young anymore. He's almost two million years old. Shall we stop and go inside?"

"I really don't think I'm up to seeing a bunch of bones," muttered Juni. "But thanks, I'll remember that when I write my article."

"How are you doing, really?" asked Mr. Graham.

"The boat trip took a lot out of them," Beth said quickly. "They were extremely seasick."

"Was it really that bad? I didn't understand they'd been so ill. Well, let's go and find something that is easy to digest. And after that, we'll go on to the Maasai village. That's a long drive, and it's a terrible road."

2

THEY ARRIVED AT THE MAASAI VILLAGE LATE THAT AFTERNOON. Mr. Graham had not exaggerated the terrible condition of the road. Some stretches were not a road at all but worn clay with deep furrows and potholes. At times, the jeep got stuck and the three of them had to get out and push. There was constant kicked-up dust the entire time they were driving. Sand lodged in their skin, eyes and ears. Beth longed for a hot shower though she guessed it would be a long time before she could have one. Water was scarce in this region, especially for herders.

The personal tension among the three of them was still bad. Ulf and Juni kept silent. Juni kept her sunglasses on. One time when they were out pushing the jeep, Beth noticed Juni was crying. Beth felt only anger. What did she have to cry about! If only Ulf had kept his mouth shut! Now it was as if the dead man had followed them here, and Juni had heard his story and everything had gone wrong. The only reason they'd come so far was to escape all that death!

I'm *the victim here,* Beth thought. *Why can't the two of them realize what really happened? They almost lost me, a sister, a life partner . . . . I was close to being killed! He held my throat so tight I almost strangled. They don't care about me one bit. They don't care whether I'm alive or not.*

The itching had increased. Beth could not stop scratching. Ulf noticed her scratching and it only made him irritated.

The soft, caring part of her was beginning to drain away.

307

I don't need you! She thought. *I'll be just fine without you!*

Beth sat in the front seat and talked to Mr. Graham. He was a clever man, able to spot wild animals and point them out to her. He taught her the difference between a Thompson gazelle and a Grant gazelle, and he told her that the tiniest gazelle of them all was called a *dikdik.*

Mr. Graham pointed to a long-billed bird taking flight from a tree.

"I understand that the Marabou stork is used to market your Swedish chocolate." Mr. Graham's voice became as soft as a woman's. "I find that a bit strange, since the Marabou stork is a scavenger and eats dead carcasses."

"You're kidding!"

"It's true." Mr. Graham chuckled. "Look over there! Oh, it's gone. Well, we'll see more of them later. I thought that we should spend one day on a true safari. You can't be in Tanzania and not see an elephant. What do you say—how about the day after tomorrow?"

Late that afternoon, they arrived at the *enkangen,* the Maasai word for their settlements. Along the road, they'd met individual Maasai clothed in their traditional red-checked robes. In the distance, they could see boys watching goats and cattle. Their faces were painted white and they were wearing feathers. Some were wearing entire birds. Mr. Graham told them that the boys had recently completed their circumcision ceremony, and after some time wandering in the wilderness, they would return to the village as *ilmurran,* warriors.

The village itself was a wide circle of huts in the center of an enclosure. The fence was made of branches stuck deep down into the ground. The branches had been there so long that some of them had taken root and were turning green.

Mr. Graham drove carefully through the entrance of the palisade. He turned off the engine. Everything seemed quiet.

"Here we are. You may get out of the jeep, now," he said. "They're certainly waiting for us."

They climbed out and stood beside the jeep, not really knowing what to do. From the jouncing ride, Beth felt as tender as pounded meat. The sand in her mouth crunched. In the space left by the missing tooth, the sand particles had built up. Beth constantly had to poke the gap with her tongue. The space was slippery and warm and had a sweet taste.

At first the settlement seemed deserted, but then two puppies appeared. They didn't bark, but they wagged their tales and jumped up and down in the dust. Men and women followed them. They were wearing robes and some were wrapped in lengths of cloth. Mr. Graham motioned to them to come closer to the jeep. They walked over shyly and began to shake Mr. Graham's hand with their cool fingers.

Mr. Graham asked them a question. One of the men pointed at a hut and then began to walk toward it. He went inside and came out again almost immediately with a tall thin man, who was much older than all the others. He had a sparse, white mustache, yet his steps were sprightly as he came toward them.

"Welcome to our village!" the old man said in English. The blue-and-red-checked robe he wore was fraying at the edges, but he also wore a modern wristwatch.

"May I introduce Kinaru, the leader of the clan," Mr. Graham said. "Kinaru is a friend of mine. We once were hunting together and we killed a speckled one . . . I mean a leopard . . . that almost got us first!"

Kinaru laughed and they could see he was missing two lower teeth. Later Beth noticed the same thing about everyone there. Mr. Graham explained: "They take out the teeth as soon as the children get them in. That's so they can still eat if they are struck by lockjaw, that is, tetanus, and can't open their mouths. Diseases like that are still common here."

"Speaking of the speckled one," said Kinaru and Beth noticed that his English really was excellent, "I would like you to keep a few things in mind. You are here as our guests. We will protect you from all possible dangers. But a few things depend on you. Do not ever go outside the compound on your own. You must always have a warrior with you. Otherwise things can go very wrong. The other night, a leopard broke into the compound and took a goat. The speckled one is afraid of us and our spears, but great hunger will overcome his fear."

"And when it comes to toilets," Mr. Graham explained. "You must use the bushes over here, as there is no running water."

3

A LL OF A SUDDEN THUDDING NOISE FILLED THE AIR ALONG WITH A STRONG STENCH OF MANURE AND ANIMAL. A stream of cows, goats, and donkeys, braying and mooing, flowed into the compound until their little party was surrounded by the herd which quickly filled all the space. The animals shied away from the jeep on their way straight for the middle. There was a smaller enclosure there, also formed as a circle and built with tight, thorny branches. A few boys, not much more than children, were herding the animals, and they cracked the air with long whips.

The compound was full of activity now. Beth saw that a few of the goats must have had kids during the day. A few dried streams of blood ran under their tails and toward their shapeless udders. At least ten tiny kids ran about bleating for their mothers. Some women came out. They wore colorful clothing, pearls, and bracelets. They lifted the kids, eyed them, and then helped them find their mothers. Their movements were soft and appeared loving.

"The animals are our gold," Kinaru said contentedly.

One of the tiny newborn kids had something wrong with one of its legs. It could not stand properly and kept falling over on its side. A woman tried to get it to stand on its own but it could not.

"Oh, look at that little one," Juni exclaimed. "What's wrong with it? Does it have a birth defect?"

The woman looked at Juni from under her brows. She pulled a goat over, stuck her hand in its mouth and held it tight by its lower jaw. Another woman brought the kid to its udder so it could nurse.

"Oh, the sweet little thing," Juni said.

Juni squatted next to it. She petted its dusty coat. The woman was holding the kid by its stomach, from which a dried string of umbilical cord was dangling. The kid butted its nose against the goat until it had one of the teats and then began to drink milk greedily.

"He sure was hungry," Juni said. "Is there a bottle for it? But, wait, that still wouldn't fix its leg."

Mr. Graham laughed. "That's the way it is in nature. Sometimes things go wrong and there's nothing you can do about it."

He shrugged his shoulders.

One of the puppies came up to Beth and started to sniff her. She bent down to pet it but jerked her hand away when she saw its fur was full of crawling, creeping tiny bugs. At the same time, two men walked into the herd of goats, looking them over, and then finally pointed to a big, well-rounded one with a black, shaggy coat. By now the sun was going down and the shadows had lengthened. The sun glittered in the goat's yellow eye and it was standing completely still, as if basking in the mild warmth.

The younger of the two men caught the goat and slung it over his shoulders. It bleated and jerked. Then it calmed down. Beth looked straight into its honey-yellow iris. She thought that it was hard to tell by an animal's expression if it was afraid or in pain. It seemed to her that they were born with just one expression. She wondered if that made it easier for people who abused animals.

The herd was now driven into the smaller compound to spend the night. It was amazing that the leopard had managed to get at one of the goats in spite of the warriors with their spears. Beth's throat went dry at the thought.

Branches were brought to close the space and, inside, the women set to milking the goats. Beth watched them work through little gaps in the branches.

Only the crippled white kid was left in the sun. No one seemed to care about it.

"I've put up a tent for you," Mr. Graham said. "It's over there. It's quite simple but it ought to be fine for a few nights. Strangers have trouble sleeping in Maasai huts. There's always a large fire inside so you begin to feel poisoned by smoke."

Beth and Ulf carried their luggage to the tent. A few children watched them. A half-naked boy was spinning a plastic container on a stick.

"Jambo," Beth called to him.

The boy stopped playing.

"Children are taught to respect their elders," Mr. Graham said. He placed his hand on the boy's head. The boy looked afraid.

"Ask him his name!" Beth exclaimed.

But the boy had already turned around and run away.

Mr. Graham unzipped the tent and opened the flap.

"I hope you'll find it satisfactory," he said.

"Maybe we could get a peek inside one of the huts," Ulf asked.

Kinaru had come with them. He asked Mr. Graham a question and gestured toward Ulf. Mr. Graham nodded.

"What were you saying?" asked Ulf.

"I told him that you were a man, of course," said Mr. Graham.

"Well, hmm . . . I should hope so."

"You can come with us, and we'll head over there right away. But not the two women. This is something that women are not allowed to watch. It's just for men."

"What's going to happen?" asked Juni uncomfortably.

"We're going to slaughter the goat."

Juni and Beth stayed in the tent. Beth had laid out the mattresses and arranged the luggage to take up as little space as possible. The two of them sat and listened to the noises from the compound. Cows mooed. Bells tinkled.

"You'd think we were in a Swedish herder's hut up in the mountains," Beth said.

Juni lay on her stomach. "I'm so exhausted."

Beth took out a pack of cigarettes. "Do you think I can smoke in here?"

Then she noticed that Juni was crying.

"Juni," she whispered.

Juni didn't answer.

Then tears welled up in Beth's eyes as well. The tears felt hot, and her forehead hurt.

"Juni . . . were we ever happy together?" she asked.

Juni rolled over on her back. Her face was streaked with dirt and seemed misshapen. Juni crawled over to Beth and pressed her forehead to Beth's shoulder.

"Oh, Juni," Beth said. "My sweet, sweet sister."

"I'm so unhappy. Right to my heart," Juni said. "That little baby goat lying out there. It was so soft to the touch. Why couldn't it have been born with strong legs? What's the purpose of being born if you're just going to die again right away? What a grim, wrong world we live in. And the goat . . . the proud, black goat . . . it had no idea what was going to happen . . . and now . . ."

"They're only animals, Juni," Beth said. "They don't think the same way we do. They don't feel the same things, either."

Beth slowly lifted her hand to stroke Juni's back softly.

"Do you remember . . . ," Beth said quietly, "do you remember when I was four years old and had to go to the hospital for an operation? They were going to take out some polyps."

Juni swallowed.

"I didn't want to go," Beth continued. "I understood that it was going to hurt. I can still remember how I yelled and fought. But children have no rights, just as animals have no rights. When I came home, you'd cut out lots of funny pictures from old magazines. Pigs and small children sitting on the potty, I really don't remember all of them . . . and you'd pasted them all over the railing of my bed."

"I remember that."

"You wanted to comfort me. You wanted to make me happy."

Beth stroked her sister's head.

"And another time . . . we went to a small market . . . it was with Grandma and Grandpa . . . do you remember that? We went to a booth and bought Surprise Bags . . . and in mine there was a hairpin, and I still remember what it looked like. It had tiny blue flowers. When we went home . . . we were on the backs of Grandma and Grandpa's bicycles . . . I dropped the hair pin. We went back and forth looking for it, but we never found it. And then you gave me your surprise . . . it was a tiny comb with the same blue flowers."

Beth's blouse was turning wet and warm from Juni's tears.

"We're sisters, Juni. We're the same flesh and blood. Whatever happens . . . and whatever has happened . . . we must never stop loving each other."

Ulf returned looking pale and upset.

"Get me some whiskey," he said.

"So what happened?" Beth asked.

"It was something else again, but it'll be a good article."

"So what did they do?" Juni asked. She sat up, pulled her knees to her chest and lit a cigarette.

"They suffocated the damn thing. They put it on its side and wrestled its head backwards and one of them stuffed his fingers in its nose and the others held its mouth shut."

"Suffocated?"

"It took quite awhile to die."

Ulf drank some whiskey and handed the bottle around.

"Then they butchered it. They cut it open and began to eat its organs. They had a ranking of some kind as to who could eat what. The insides were still warm. Heart, kidneys . . ."

"Stop! I can't hear anymore," said Juni.

"What? That's real. That's life. Too bad I didn't have the camera with me."

"I wonder if you could have taken pictures, if they'd allow it," Juni said. "It's so primitive here, isn't it. Yet some of them have these modern watches . . ."

Juni had calmed herself down and stopped crying. She rummaged through her luggage and found a sweater and some thick socks.

"I'm freezing," she said. "Plus, I have to go to the bathroom."

"Let's go together," Beth said.

A warrior fell in beside them. He was a tall, muscular man and they could see his calf muscles beneath the robe. He wore shoes made of old car tires and one wrist wore a wide, pearl-encrusted wristwatch.

He carried a spear.

Mr. Graham was by the jeep, unloading some boxes.

"He's a good escort," he said. "He's killed two lions."

They left the compound and the warrior pointed to some bushes. He showed them, somewhat embarrassed, how to stamp on the ground to scare away snakes. As they squatted, he hovered like a shadow in the setting sun.

"What's your name?" Beth asked him as they walked back.

"My name is Manketi," he replied without hesitation.

He had clean, well-shaped features. On one cheek was a scar, burned in, in the shape of an eye. Juni and Beth told him their names and he repeated them, stumbling over the sound.

Mr. Graham was making dinner. He was boiling rice and cutting strips of meat and vegetables. Beth sat down next to him.

"Can I help?" she asked.

"No, I'm almost done. Right now we just have to wait for the rice to cook."

Beth scratched her arms. Mr. Graham saw that and told her to be careful.

"These things can easily get infected."

"I thought we were going to eat with the Maasai."

"That wouldn't work. They don't have enough food. The harvest wasn't that good plus they've just been through an epidemic of malaria on top of influenza. Some people died from it."

"Oh," Beth said.

"That's why we couldn't come here as we'd planned. They had to finish recovering."

"Do they have any medicine?"

"They have their own herbal concoctions. But sometimes sickness is just stronger."

Juni joined them. She was now wearing a jacket over her sweater. She looked pale.

"Come sit by the fire," said Mr. Graham. "It gets very cold in the evening."

"Are we eating the goat?"

"You can taste some if you want. They're grilling it over there."

It was now completely dark. The man named Manketi walked past them carrying a small child.

"His wife died from influenza," said Mr. Graham.

"Is that his baby?"

"I believe so. They had several children. That must be their youngest."

"So he's raising them by himself?"

"The other women help him."

"He's really good-looking," Juni said. "I bet the other women would fight to get him."

"He's well-liked," said Mr. Graham, "but he's also unlucky. His mother died fetching water a few months back. Because of the drought, women had to go to a water hole farther away. As she bent over to fill her water bucket, a hyena attacked her from behind. The hyena had rabies."

"Rabies?" asked Juni.

"Mad dog disease. Hyenas often get it. As it happened, she died from her wounds before she could get sick, which was just as well. But it was a big loss to the community. Her name was Koko and she was a respected woman."

"What do they do when . . . I mean, do they have a cemetery?"

"Well, let's just say they have a different attitude about death than we do. Once you are dead, you are gone. People don't mourn and bury the dead in graves. Instead, they want as little as possible to do with the corpse. One time I was helping a young mother. She had given birth to twin girls and one of the girls was very sick. I was going to drive to Arusha anyway, so I offered to take them with me to find a doctor. The woman agreed, but the baby died before we arrived."

Beth felt Juni watching her. She pulled her jacket tighter around herself.

"She took off the necklace the daughter wore and asked me to stop the jeep so she could throw the body into the bushes. I asked her to at least let me dig a hole for it. She sat in the jeep the whole time, impatient to get away."

"So strange," Beth said. "Her own tiny daughter . . ."

317

"It's better when a child dies as a baby. If it is weak and sickly, it can't survive these harsh conditions. They'll die in a few years anyway."

"Like the baby goat," Juni whispered.

"Yes. You have to be strong to live here. This is an unbelievably hard environment, especially for women."

"And . . .," Juni continued, "they have to be circumcised?"

"Of course," said Mr. Graham, but he was uncomfortable with the question.

"But women as well as men?"

"It's an important ceremony for both men and women. There's a great feast, since they are entering the adult world."

"And no one talks about breaking with tradition? I've read that circumcised women have so many health problems later. All their natural functions become painful."

"It's their culture," Mr. Graham shrugged.

"The pain must be extraordinary," Beth added.

Mr. Graham's eyes twinkled. "The Maasai can endure pain. No one is supposed to show any signs of weakness. Otherwise they are ridiculed for the rest of their lives. The ability to endure pain is part of the cost of living here."

They sat quietly for a while.

"Would you like some beer?" asked Mr. Graham.

"Yes, please," said Beth.

Mr. Graham went to the jeep and came back with two bottles of Kilimanjaro beer. Beth and Juni drank directly from the bottles.

"Well, I guess I'll need to pee again soon," Juni said. "What do people do in the middle of the night?"

Beth laughed. "That's a big problem, isn't it? I plan to pee behind the tent."

Mr. Graham lifted the lid of the pot. The aroma of meat and spices wafted out. Beth realized that it had been a long time since they'd eaten.

Juni was pulling her fingers through her hair.

"If you don't mind me asking," she said doubtfully, "we were just talking about death and I was wondering . . . what do they do with their dead? You see, I just lost my husband not so long ago . . . and I'd like to know . . ."

"Oh, I see," Mr. Graham said. "I was wondering because you always seemed to be a little sad. There seemed to be a shadow over all three of you, maybe even, may I say, a destructive shadow. I had been wondering, but this must be the explanation."

"If I hadn't had a grave . . . a memorial stone to go to . . . I don't know how I would have coped," Juni said.

"Here things are very different. You must understand this. Maybe a very wealthy person here can afford a stone monument. Otherwise . . . well, they bring the corpse to the wilderness and cover it with some leaves. The next morning they return to see if the hyenas have done their job. And if they haven't, then the people slaughter a goat and drag the meat in three different directions from the body. That's usually enough."

That evening, after everyone had eaten, the Maasai held a dance in the compound. They stood in a circle and began to sing. The voices were deep and slowly rising in tone. One by one, a dancer jumped into the middle of the ring and danced, leaping higher and higher, egged on by the song.

The women wore flat necklaces made of colored rings in two shades. As they danced, they moved their bodies so that the necklaces rattled.

Beth, Ulf, and Juni stayed in the background. Overhead, swiftly passing clouds gave an occasional glimpse of the moon or the clear stars.

The entrance to the *enkagen* was now closed by branches both large and small. They heard noises like a dog fight on the other side. But the two dogs were curled up by the fire.

"It's probably a lion," said Mr. Graham. "But there's no danger. We're all awake and alert."

Beth stood, with her hands deep in her pockets. She was cold, stiff, and aching. All she wanted to do was go to sleep. The dance grew more and more frenetic.

Suddenly, Beth heard frightened squeals and shouts. One of the men had jumped through the dance ring and was running toward her, his spear held out, his eyes rolled back. It looked like he wanted to stab her. She screamed. Someone pushed her aside. The man kept running a few more meters and others ran after him. They knocked him to the ground and held him fast. His throat gurgled.

Beth shook all over. She dug her nails into her palms so that it hurt. She stared at her feet and did not dare raise her head.

The look in the dancer's eyes—she'd seen that look before. Fear but also something else. Hatred. The murdered man had looked at her that way.

The dancer had wanted to kill her.

Mr. Graham leaned protectively close, took her chin and raised it up.

In the glow of the fire, Beth saw his friendly round face.

"He wanted to kill me . . . ," she whispered. "I saw it in his eyes . . . he came right for me."

"Don't think like that."

"I saw it in his eyes!"

"It really had nothing to do with you. Really. Sometimes when they've been dancing too long, someone gets . . . how can I explain it? Psychotic. They dance so hard that they drive themselves over the edge."

They'd gone to bed. Ulf lay between Juni and Beth. Beth had seen the look on his face while Mr. Graham comforted her. She knew what Ulf was thinking.

They avoided all discussion of the incident.

She couldn't sleep. She could not forget the look in the crazed man's eyes. That man was still somewhere in the compound. She sensed how near he was. It made her freeze.

Ulf and Juni were fast asleep. She heard the little whistles of their breath. It had been a long day.

Beth turned onto her side. She felt the cloth of the tent against her face.

She curled into a fetal position and let the tears come.

4

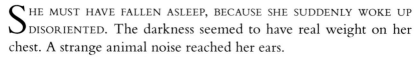

S HE MUST HAVE FALLEN ASLEEP, BECAUSE SHE SUDDENLY WOKE UP DISORIENTED. The darkness seemed to have real weight on her chest. A strange animal noise reached her ears.

She remembered where she was.

A predator! Maybe the leopard!

They were out there somewhere. Maybe they could smell newborn goat kids.

Oh, dear Lord, she thought. *I hope the warriors are awake.*

Just then she felt something move beside her. She was on her back and one of her arms was outside the sleeping bag. A heavy, slithering movement on her exposed arm. She lay completely still. She could smell her own sweat as it came out of her pores.

A snake. There was a snake in the tent.

Her first impulse was to flee. She wanted to throw everything aside, tear open the tent and run away.

Of course, the leopard could be outside.

She forced herself to breathe. She had to hold her body still so that her movements would not provoke an attack. She knew enough not to scare it or appear as a threat.

She felt the snake clearly now. Its warm, smooth body which was nothing more than one single long muscle. She started to shake and could not stop herself. The snake felt it, too, and started to crawl toward her collarbone.

Her teeth were chattering.

"Uuuuuulf," her voice was small. She swallowed and tried again. "Uuuuulf!"

A low, whining complaint: "Uuuuulf!"

He slept so hard he did not hear her.

What could she do? If she screamed, she might scare the snake . . . or were snakes deaf? Maybe it would bite the soft skin of her neck. Wasn't there a major artery in the neck, bringing blood right to the heart?

Beth held her upper body completely still. She tried to raise one of her legs without alarming anything to kick Ulf, trying to make him react.

"Uuuulf," she said again, and her voice box shook. "Uuuulf."

Ulf coughed and raised his head.

"Ulf," she said, and now she had more strength to speak. Cold, hard fear changed her voice. She pressed her tongue to the back of her mouth. Her breathing was raspy and dry.

"What is it?" Ulf asked.

"Stay . . . very . . . still. Don't move. We have a snake in the tent."

Too late. He sat up and there was lots of rustling and she could not stand it any longer, so she leapt up, too. Their hands fumbled, searched, and finally found the zipper and unzipped the tent.

Beth stood barefoot in the dust. She'd scraped her knee and blood ran down her leg. Ulf was right behind her, followed by Juni, who looked like a ghost in her white gym outfit.

"There was a snake! I felt it creeping along my arm! It woke me up!"

"Damn it, I'll have to go back in there and get the flashlight," said Ulf.

The moon was out, shining on the huts and casting strange shadows. Ulf crawled on his hands and knees and felt inside the tent for the flashlight.

"Please be careful, Ulf," Beth whispered. "Please, please, be careful!"

"Here's the flashlight," Ulf grumbled and the tent lit up from the inside.

That moment the grunting animal sound that Beth had first heard was back. It was on the other side of the compound.

"What the fuck is going on?" complained Juni. She wrapped her arms around her body.

"That's the leopard," said Beth. "Thank God it's on the other side of the fence." Beth was shaking from an inward chill.

Two shadow-like figures appeared suddenly next to them.

Two warriors, carrying spears, their expressions closed and stern.

Behind the barricade, they heard more grunting and then a loud roar.

Beth grabbed one of the warrior's spears and held on for dear life.

"A lion," the warrior said shortly.

Beth nodded. "In the tent . . . there's a snake!"

Ulf got up and turned his flashlight toward the fence. Silence.

"The lion has gone," said the warrior. Beth let go of his spear. She pointed toward the tent.

"But the snake . . ."

"I didn't see any snake," said Ulf.

"I know there was a snake! I felt it!"

"All right, then. We have to take everything out and go through all our luggage!"

The two warriors watched as they emptied the tent of their belongings. One of the men took the flashlight and examined every inch of the tent. He shined the light into their luggage as they took out each item and examined every seam.

A tiny smile appeared. "No snake," the warrior said.

"It must have gotten out in all the commotion," Beth said. "I know there was a snake! I felt it."

The warrior silently handed her the flashlight, and the two men disappeared into the night.

Beth pulled at her hair. It was damp from dew. Everything around her was damp and dirty. The three of them carried their things back inside.

"You must have been dreaming," Ulf said.

"I swear, it wasn't a dream!"

"Then it was a product of your sick imagination."

"No one wants me here. They don't want me here. I saw it in that man's eyes last night. He wanted to kill me . . . . And now . . . I know it was a snake. I felt it. It was real!"

"Why don't the two of you just shut up!" exclaimed Juni. "We should just go back to sleep. Things will be better in the morning."

They crawled back into their sleeping bags. Juni said that she was reminded of a movie set in India. The camera showed a sleeping family and suddenly a snake appeared in the darkness. The camera followed the snake as it slithered over the children's bodies.

"You have a sick mind, telling me that story now," Beth hissed.

Juni didn't stop. "It was a scary thriller . . . and this will be a great story for the article, don't you think so, Ulf?"

Juni appeared so calm. Beth suddenly understood that Juni did not believe her. Neither of them believed her. They thought she'd just had a bad dream.

Nevertheless she could still feel the snake's body as it slithered across her skin. It was warm. Dry.

5

AT THE FIRST LIGHT OF DAWN, A GOAT BEGAN TO BLEAT. A moment later, a cow mooed. The bells began to jingle and clang.

Beth had stayed awake with the flashlight right next to her hand, but the rest of the night had been peaceful.

With the pale light of dawn, Beth unzipped the tent opening a bit to look out. It was cold and she was freezing. Beth watched some of the women, who were carrying gourds. They moved aside some of the branches of the entrance to the small enclosure so they could slip in. The mooing increased.

Beth had to pee. She put on her sneakers and slipped out of the tent. Behind it, she was somewhat hidden from sight. She looked up at the gray sky.

"Thank you, God," she said. "Thank you that morning has come."

Mr. Graham made them breakfast. He was boiling eggs in the bent pot and cutting bananas to put on slices of bread. He talked as he prepared the meal.

"Did you notice the eyes marked on their cheeks? They make the scars with red-hot steel wire. They're considered to be eyes in reserve, just in case a real eye is lost."

Beth watched her sister as Juni wrote down everything Mr. Graham said into her notebook. *She has a little monkey face,* Beth thought. *She has a pointy little monkey face.*

An impulsive thought crossed Beth's mind. *What if someone stuck their fingers in her mouth and twisted her neck? Her face would slough off and she'd just be a smiling cranium . . . yet her smile would be unchanged, just like now . . . grinning teeth don't change . . . they stay the same when everything else has turned to dust.*

I really have lost my mind, Beth thought. *I've gone fucking crazy.*

Her skin itched from head to toe. She noticed that her scratching bothered Ulf, even as he sat there writing down Mr. Graham's stories.

I'm working, Beth.

No, he hadn't said that out loud, but she could see it by the tense way he held his pen while she scratched her calves.

Can't you sit still, woman. What the fuck is wrong with you?

Some boys were taking away the rest of the brush to open the animal enclosure all the way. The cows started to walk out. They were brown and white and tan and every shade in between.

"Aren't the children too small to be watching the animals?" asked Juni. "What could they do if a lion or leopard attacks the herd? They have only tiny spears and they're barefoot."

"Oh, there's always a warrior somewhere close by."

Mr. Graham handed each of them a cup of coffee. Beth felt the hot drink slide down into her stomach. She cupped it in her hands.

I just want to go home, she thought.

Mr. Graham looked worried.

"It looks like bad dreams have left a new wrinkle in your forehead," said Mr. Graham.

"Oh, Beth had a snake in her sleeping bag," said Ulf sarcastically.

Was this the same Ulf that she'd loved? His gray hair hanging down. He is ugly, he wants to hurt me, he's making fun of me.

"I . . . ," she began.

"You were frightened by the dance last night," Mr. Graham soothed. "That's what I believe, Beth. So I think today's a good day to go on our safari. It will calm everyone down. We'll enjoy seeing the wild animals and then we'll spend the night in a hotel. We will avoid unpleasant surprises. Plus we will be able to take a shower. What do you think?"

"I came here to meet the Maasai," Ulf said as he reached for another slice of bread. "How can I write about them if I don't spend time with them? We've been waiting so long. Every idiot Swedish tourist has gone on a safari. I can't write about that."

"We'll come back. But I'm thinking of your wife. She needs to recover. You must be more patient. We'll find some cream for her rash, too, so she won't have to suffer any more."

The Maasai stood in a group and watched them leave. On the other side of the palisade, Beth saw the man who'd run at her during the dance. He had drawn a flap of his robe over his face, but she still recognized him. He was standing absolutely still holding his spear which pointed straight toward the sky. She met his glance for a second.

Mr. Graham had made lunches for them. He seemed to have endless resources stowed away in his jeep. This morning, Ulf sat up front so that he could ask Mr. Graham questions. Beth sat directly behind him and stared at the cloth of Ulf's shirt. Her eyes followed the stitching in the rough seams. Everything about him was so strange, every smallest detail: the crease in his neck, the sour smell from his body, the way he cleared his throat. She wanted to touch his skin. She wanted to caress him so he would turn around . . . .

And everything would be normal again.

Normal Ulf, the way he used to be.

I don't remember the way he was. I don't have any of the old feelings.

He was changing the film in his camera. She looked at his short fingernails.

"He almost killed me," she said in Swedish. Her voice was loud but expressionless. "I felt his hands and his power. I am the only one who knows. That scares me."

"What the hell are you talking about?" Ulf snapped back.

"I feel totally alone . . . that's all."

Ulf pulled out his cap and shoved it on his head. He said nothing.

"You know very well what I'm talking about, and right now you're avoiding the subject. That hurts me and makes me feel even more alone."

"Can't you let me be for a change? Just don't bother me! I realize I was wrong to bring you with us. It was one huge mistake from beginning to end. Evil shadows, or however our friendly guide put it. You spread evil shadows everywhere you go—do you realize that? It's your fault that we had to leave the village."

"How can you say such a thing!"

"Well, he's the one who said it would be best for *you*, not us, if we took the safari today."

"And you think it's all my fault!"

"Just shut the fuck up! You're stressing me out! You know I've been paid a hell of a lot of money to get here. I want to do a great job! I've got to interview and research and use my time wisely. I'll be damned if I let you ruin it for me!" Beth's mouth suddenly went completely dry.

The jeep shook. They'd reached the pot-holed road.

Juni, in her black reflective sunglasses and sun hat, sat beside her. Beth turned to her sister.

"Would you have cried if I had died?" she asked. She found she used the same whiny tones she used to use when they were playing on the floor and she wanted one of Juni's toys.

Juni frowned.

"You do know there've been two times . . . where I'd been close to getting killed. You saw that yourself. First that crazy Maasai warrior . . . what if *he* was the one who stuck the snake into our tent? I know he wanted to harm me. And last summer . . . I know that man wanted to hurt me . . . how he attacked me. He was waiting. He'd invaded our home. He'd been in the house and taken things for himself. Do you remember those pillows Mamma sewed? A totally strange guy taking our things . . . he was frightened when he saw me coming toward the shed . . . the shit was scared right out of him . . . but I can take care of myself! Juni, I can take care of myself because I am a strong person!"

Mr. Graham said in English, "Do you see the vultures over there? I imagine game is out there."

A few drops of rain had spattered down while they'd been load-
ing the jeep but now the weather was dry again. A hot wind stirred
up the sandy dust on the road.

"We're almost at Serengeti National Park. I promise you'll see
not only the Big Five, but also the Big Nine."

Mr. Graham looked at them. Beth noticed for the first time that a
corner was missing from one of his front teeth. Odd that she hadn't
seen that before.

"Not that I want to boast," he said, "but I *am* good at locating
wild animals. Are you thirsty? I put bottles of beer and water in the
seat pockets."

Apes were the first animals they caught sight of. There was a whole
herd of them grooming each other's fur. The air shimmered in the
heat. They had no fear at all. They stared sourly at the jeep. Beth saw
how close together their eyes were. A tiny child clung to its mother.

"Look how cute they are!" Juni exclaimed.

Animals. All she thinks about are animals.

"Yes, but they can be quite fierce," said Mr. Graham. "They can
wreck an entire village if they feel the urge. They are usually led by
an old male. I think he's sitting over there. To the left. Can you see
him?"

*But when it comes to human beings . . . like her own sister. . . . I need
the two of them more than ever . . . they have to protect me and take care of
me when we get home . . . .No one is going to force me to go to prison . . .
no one is going to put me in a tiny cell . . . they'll be witnesses for my defense
. . . they'll tell the court that he was attacking me . . . he raised his spear
. . . his hands . . .*

"Cut it out!" Beth heard herself muttering. "What is wrong with
you?" But no one could hear her.

The jeep had a retractable cloth roof so its passengers could stand
up to watch the wild game without leaving the safety of the jeep.
And the open roof protected them from the heat. Beth stood up to
look over the wide savanna

She raised the binoculars from where they hung down around
her neck and looked through them. Far in the distance, she could

see a herd of large water buffaloes. She had to say something and she burst out in Swedish: "Oh! Look at the buffalo over there! Their horns look like Pippi Longstocking braids!"

"Are you asking about the buffalo?" Mr. Graham asked in English.

"Yes, they look like . . ."

"They are extremely dangerous, some of the most dangerous animals out here. They are unbelievably aggressive. Imagine a bull in a Spanish bull ring. They have that kind of temperament."

"Will they attack us?"

Mr. Graham chuckled with professional pride.

"Not while we're in the jeep."

"Maybe they'll get angry at the jeep?"

Mr. Graham smiled at her and his nose wrinkled. "As I told you, I'm used to wild animals. You have to trust me. I can tell when things start to get dangerous."

They began to drive on slowly. A herd of zebras was their next find. The animals grazed with their striped backsides all lined up in the same direction. A few gnus were grazing beside them.

"Listen to them!" Juni said. "This is the first time I've ever heard what a gnu sounds like!"

"They got their name from the sound they make," Mr. Graham explained. "It's that *gnuh, gnuh, gnuh* they make."

After that they saw lions. The lions lay sprawled out. It was a large pride, and Mr. Graham drove right up to them. Their jaws and paws were bloody—a leg from their prey stuck straight up in the air.

"They've caught a gnu," said Mr. Graham. "If we'd gotten here a bit earlier, we would have seen the hunt and the kill."

"I'm extraordinarily grateful that we did not," mumbled Juni. "Should we really drive so close to them? Don't they want to defend their meal?"

"They're used to vehicles," said Mr. Graham. "On the other hand, don't get out of the jeep."

A few feet away, there was a lonely gnu calf. It was looking at the lions and every once in a while it made a small attempt to rush at them. Mr. Graham pointed out the calf.

"They're eating his mother for lunch. He'll probably be the dessert."

Mr. Graham had turned off the engine. Loud crunching and munching sounds, including low growls, came from the large cats. The stench of fresh blood and dung swirled into the jeep through the open roof.

Beth took out a bottle of water and drank. Her hands were shaking. The lack of sleep had exhausted her and made her irritable. Ulf was braced in front of her, hanging from the jeep with his camera. The backs of his knees were at the level of her eyes. The thin, light skin . . . she remembered how she used to tickle him with her tongue and how he'd taken her gently by the neck and pulled her to him.

All that is over now.

Beth felt violently ill, almost as she'd felt when she'd been pregnant and just the sight and smell of an orange would make her vomit.

We had our entire future in front of us . . . you'd hold me with your thin, strong hands and we joked about the child we were going to have, and the grandchildren and the great-grandchildren . . . and we'd sit in the grass by the blue house in the countryside . . . we'd sit in the swing while the babies slept in our arms . . . lulled to sleep by their feelings of security with us . . . and everything was still ahead of us . . . and now . . . now it's all over . . . everything went so fast and when we go home, it's not going to be you and me because you're driving me away, Ulf, away from you, and I'll never again lie in bed and look at you . . . watch you as you take off your pants and hang your shirt over the back of the chair . . . you'd give me that look . . . . Do you want to play a little while . . . ?

Mr. Graham started the jeep. Beth sat down and held tight to the seat. She heard the guide's reassuring voice talking about the lions:

". . . the females think the male is very sexy with his mane, and he is useful for fighting off other male lions, but the male is not helpful when they have to hunt. Young males will hunt with their mothers, but when they're older and have manes, they'll stop. It's the females . . ."

Mr. Graham drove on. His hands waved and pointed. His voice went on and on. Beth leaned her head against the window and began to doze. She knew she was falling asleep in that rocking, jerking, uncomfortable jeep, and even in her sleep she knew that the others knew she was going to sleep and would let her be. Perhaps they thought it was easier to let her sleep.

More peaceful.

She woke up as she drew in a deep breath. The engine was off. She had a crick in her neck. She saw the other three standing up through the roof. She felt extremely thirsty.

The sun was lower in the sky. She must have been sleeping for some time. She heard the low click of Ulf's camera. Then something entirely different. Snorting. A hard crashing sound.

She slowly turned her head.

An elephant stood only a few feet away from the jeep.

Beth saw its wrinkled skin and its extremely tiny eyes. The eyes seemed crusted in mud. The animal snorted again and flapped its ears wildly. When its ears hit its body, the sound was thunderous.

Beth felt great sudden fear.

She heard Mr. Graham's strident voice. He sat down and frantically turned the key in the lock. Time sped up. A gray, looming wall. A deep roar. Then the enormous beast threw itself at the jeep and knocked it over on its side.

Beth fell forward and hit her head on the instrument panel. The last thing she saw was a huge leg coming right down through the jeep's cloth roof and then she heard the tearing sound as it ripped free.

6

THE SILENCE WOKE HER.

Her tongue was a swollen mash of flesh in her mouth. She must have bitten it many times. For the first few seconds she was awake, her tongue was the only thing she could think about. She coughed and tried to breathe. She noticed she was curled up in suffocating darkness.

"Help," she said weakly, but her voice was inaudible. She could not speak. She felt terrified.

She felt warm, wet liquid dripping onto her chin. She could not tell what it was, and her arms were immobile. As she tried to move them, a burst of pain from her shoulder rolled over her.

She gradually began to remember.

She did not want to remember.

Pictures jarred into her mind and came into focus.

The jeep.

Mr. Graham's hand as it turned the key. She remembered the click, click, click very well. She remembered the ring on his finger . . . then the coughing sound of the engine starting, Mr. Graham's high, frightened voice, the motor roaring and then dying.

It seemed so long ago.

Yet, here she was, still in the jeep.

She could feel one of the pedals pressing into her side, hindering her breathing. She had to take short breaths. She could not take deep ones. Everything hurt. Something was lying on top of her. It weighed her down and did not allow her lungs to expand. She heard whistling sounds inside her chest.

She simply lay still and waited.

The earth shook. A huge snort and a great trumpeting.

The jeep swayed and creaked.

A violent bump made her body slide further down.

The elephant was still there. He was trying to kill the jeep. She whimpered. She'd heard that elephants sometimes ran amok.

That Maasai warrior ran amok, too! Everything's crazy in this country. I want to go home!

Things pounded and thundered as if a whirlwind was trying to smash the vehicle to bits. She thought that she heard screaming. She wanted to scream. A red wave of pain threw her into unconsciousness.

She could move only the fingers of one hand. The rest of her body was pressed down.

Ulf and Juni.

They've left me here. I'm trapped in the jeep and they've gone off and left me here.

She felt as if she were going to cry, but forced herself to be calm. She would not be able to breathe if she cried. She had to try to think clearly.

Juni and Ulf. Glimpses. Ulf's irritated voice: *It was stupid to bring you here, Beth; the whole thing was stupid from the start.* Juni's black reflective sunglasses. So black, so shiny. So you could not see what she thought. Juni's fingernails bitten down to the quick. Juni lighting one cigarette after another.

The little gnu and the lions.

That's right: we went on a safari.

Maybe they'll eat it for dessert.

Where was Mr. Graham? He should have stayed to help her if Juni and Ulf had run away. She licked her lips and tried to say his name, but she could not. Her tongue was swollen and her throat was blocked.

She was gone. Or she was at home.

She was in the cool green summer garden: Skogslyckan. Forest happiness. The trees were old and moss-covered. They'd often talked about cutting them down and planting apple trees: Cox Pomona and Gravenstein and Phlox.

Phlox? That's not a fruit. What's over there? Oh, the pillows Mamma sewed and the cat, the gray cat, she's there between them with her two little ones . . . and there's the man. Maybe it was his cat all along, yes, go ahead and take them. I'm allergic to cats anyway, and I can hardly breathe. Sometimes I think I have asthma. No, I don't want to hurt you, I really do not want to hurt you, please don't touch me, it hurts.

7

PEOPLE WERE LIFTING HER UP. It was dark. A cool wind blew over her eyelashes, and her head was heavy and hard to hold up. She did not know these people. She tried to look through swollen eyelids: young, black hands.

Even though they'd freed her from the jeep, the pressure on her chest was still there, and every shaky breath made her feel like her chest was breaking up. She was being placed on a stretcher. She had a glimpse of the night sky. Around her, there were flashes of light. Her brain felt as if it were mush.

Later on, in a hospital room full of echoes, they told her that Mr. Graham and Juni were both dead. They had died instantly. Beth noticed a bucket beside her bed. It was probably there for her use.

"Instantly?" she tried to say. Her speech was muddled.

"Mr. Eugene Graham should not have driven so close. There were warnings. He should have been more careful."

Eugene, she thought. *I didn't know his first name was Eugene.*

A man, a doctor, stood next to her bed. His skin was light, but he was not a white man. He was wearing a name plate, but she could not make out his name.

"The fourth passenger . . . ," he was saying.

That sounds like a movie title, she thought.

"He is your husband, isn't he?"

How do they know?

"He is alive and you should go to him."

"Later," she said. "Not now. Later."

The doctor gave her a sad look. "No, you should go to him now."

They helped her into a wheelchair. Beth was surprised that she was able to sit. She looked at her body and her legs.

Look how they've dressed me, she thought, and then, *What a ridiculous thought.*

One leg was wrapped in a bandage and the other one was naked. It was blue, covered in cuts and bruises.

They pushed her chair along a short corridor. The floor was made of cement. People were standing alongside the walls and waiting. They avoided looking at her as she passed by. Beth could hear a newborn wail.

Ulf was lying on a bed hidden behind a dirty curtain. A fly crept along his forehead. His face was clean and pale, but she saw a cut along the length of his throat. He had been connected to an IV. Beth noticed the bandage over the spot where it entered his arm. A woman wearing white and holding a chart was sitting beside him.

The doctor touched Beth's shoulder. She gasped. Every touch hurt.

"So Mr. Graham is dead?" she asked.

"Yes. Very unfortunate."

"Mr. Eugene Graham?"

"Yes, he's dead."

"He knew so much. He liked me."

"The woman who was with you is also dead."

"She was my sister."

"My condolences."

The doctor rolled her right up to Ulf's bed.

"That is my husband," she said. "His name is Ulf Nordin. There are times when he's happy and laughing."

"We found his passport."

"He no longer loves me."

"Oh, no, don't say that. He loves you."

The man in the bed moved. His eyelashes quivered. The nurse leaned forward and wet his lips with a damp gauze. "Mr. Nordin? Your wife is here."

"You may call him Ulf," Beth said.

Ulf opened his eyes with great difficulty.

Ulf looked at her and blood was running from his nose.

"It's just you and me!" she said shrilly. "Juni and Mr. Graham are dead! We have to go home and start over—from the beginning!"

Ulf closed his eyes and a groan rose out of his body.

"Listen! Let me tell you! You really have something to write about now. A real scoop! Elephants running amok."

Ulf opened his eyes, looked at her, and tears welled from under his eyelids. He tried to lift his hand. Beth was too far away in the wheelchair and could not reach him. She did not like the restraint.

Ulf moved his lips slowly. "Go home, Beth, go home."

She yelled: "I'm not leaving here without you! We'll go home together!"

A smile froze on his lips, but there were no more words.

Beth turned her face up to the doctor.

"Be sure, you will go home together," he soothed.

Ulf's life ended in that room. She was sitting in a wheelchair beside him, but could not reach him. She was too broken.

It did not matter.

Death was a fleeting instant and hardly unpleasant.

But you should not have anything to do with the dead.

So it did not matter that she did not see Juni afterwards. They had asked her if she wished to see the body, but they did not meet her eyes as they spoke.

Juni had been flung from the jeep and was trampled by the elephant.

Once she was dead, the elephant turned his rage back on the jeep.

Another jeep filled with tourists had seen the entire thing. They'd called for help. Their guide managed to telephone the rangers.

The elephant was shot, a volley of bullets to the heart.

It had gone mad. Perhaps there was poison in the environment. This had happened before. A few years ago, a German couple had been killed by a rogue elephant. That elephant, a female, had been shot as well.

"They can go crazy sometimes," the doctor said. "You were extremely lucky. Mr. Graham protected you with his body."

"I told you he liked me," Beth whispered.

She waited for grief.

She sat in the iron bed and noticed how the white paint had been scratched away after many years of use.

People have died in this bed, she thought. *In this very bed they gave up the ghost.*

She felt her insides had hardened as if into wood, a tree, unyielding, in which her heart and head were twisted.

What had happened to her?

She thought she heard Juni's voice.

Come back so I can see you again, she thought. *I want to look into your eyes. Surely you don't blame me for my life when you had to die.*

Everything was shut down tight inside her.

Mr. Graham's light chuckle.

She knew they blamed him.

A representative from the park met with her, and they brought along some policemen.

"We regret this incident."

They did not want to meet her eyes. She realized they feared she might sue.

"Mr. Graham was a wonderful guide," she said, to provoke them.

"A very good guide, indeed!"

They nodded and agreed with her.

She had to describe for the officers everything that led up to the attack. How they'd been in the jeep. How the elephant threw itself right at them. Something had annoyed it.

It had been a rogue male.

Now he, too, was dead.

340

She waited for grief, but it did not arrive.

She felt relief.

No guilt.

The day came when she was stable enough to be sent home.

Something has changed me, she thought. *I'm not grieving. Maybe the spirit of the Maasai has entered into me, too. I am a tree, straight and tall.*

No one will ever put me in jail.

8

HER NEIGHBOR, BIRGITTA, SAW WHEN SHE CAME HOME. She was looking out her window, peering through her Advent candelabra, when the taxi arrived. As the driver lifted Beth's luggage out of the trunk, Birgitta came through her front door.

"My dear, dear, dear Beth," she said, as Beth paid the driver. Birgitta hurried down the front steps to Beth. She'd wrapped her fur hurriedly around her shoulders without buttoning the buttons. "If I'd known you were coming, I would have bought some food and turned on your heat. I can do it now, though. Just hand me a list of what you need and I'll dash away and get it for you."

"I'm fine," Beth said.

Beth still had trouble with one of her legs. She couldn't balance on it properly. They'd given her a wooden crutch, and the leather of the handle was worn smooth.

Her house looked different. The color seemed so dark it almost hurt her eyes. A layer of hard-packed snow covered the lawn.

I don't want to see the crocus come up, she thought. *I'm tired of this house. I'm going to move.*

Birgitta fluttered around next to her. She helped support Beth and she carried the luggage.

"My dear, sweet girl," Birgitta said. "I've been thinking of you so much! I've read everything they wrote in the newspapers. And do you know that it was all over TV, too? They showed an elephant . . .

it wasn't *the* elephant, of course . . . but, my goodness, those beasts are huge and how strong they are!"

"I really don't want to talk about it," Beth said.

"Oh, I'm sorry, of course. Forgive me."

Birgitta came into the house with her.

Beth saw the gray cat next to Birgitta's place. It was licking itself between its toe pads.

"So you still have the cat?" Beth asked.

"Oh yes, that sweet little pussy-wussy. No one ever came to claim it, you see, and the cat feels at home in my house. She's a good kitty. Now let me set the coffeepot on. You must have some coffee left in the tin."

Beth could not bring herself to protest. In a way, it was nice to hear Swedish again. It felt comforting, like returning to a routine.

"I think I'll sell the house," Beth said as she sat down at the kitchen table.

Her neighbor paused in the middle of her preparations.

"Well, perhaps that's something you need time to think about," Birgitta said slowly. "I mean, I'm a widow, too. It does work out. And I imagine that the insurance is going to pay you a great deal of money to let you keep the house. I mean, financially, if that's the problem. You'll be able to afford it. And we can help each other. We've always helped each other."

Beth had not imagined herself as a widow.

"Yes, let me think about it," she said.

There was a great heap of newspapers and magazines on the kitchen table. Birgitta looked through them to find a copy of *Dagens Nyheter*, the major Stockholm morning daily.

"Here it is," Birgitta said carefully as she unwrapped the edition.

It had been front-page news.

Swedes killed by enraged elephant!

Inside the paper was a smaller headline:

Swedish woman miracle survivor!

They'd published Ulf's and Juni's passport photos.

"What a terrible tragedy," said Birgitta. "You poor, poor thing. I can't imagine what you've been through."

Beth nodded. Her mind was elsewhere.

She had not cried.

The people at the hospital had helped her place a call to her father. His voice was hoarse and raw. It seemed to come from far away.

"I'm the only one left, Pappa," she said. "I was the only one to survive. Juni, Ulf, and Mr. Eugene Graham, our guide . . . the elephant trampled them to death. All three of them."

Her father said nothing about being glad she was alive. He sighed and moaned and wondered what to do about Juni's dog.

Beth could not bear to listen, so she hung up.

They finished drinking coffee and Beth had to urge Birgitta to leave.

"I have to rest," Beth said. "Thank you so much for watching over my house."

"Don't you think I should stay overnight and make sure you're all right?"

Beth swallowed. Then she made herself clear: "You're very kind, Birgitta. I know where you are, and if I need you, I'll call. But for now, I'm fine. Thank you for everything you've done."

Beth barely managed to shut the door behind Birgitta when the phone rang.

It was Ulf's ex-wife, Ylva. Ylva burst into tears the minute she heard Beth's voice.

"Why did you have to go there near those dangerous beasts?" howled Ylva. "Why didn't you all just stay home?"

"How did you know I'd gotten home?"

"What? I've been calling every single day since I heard about the accident! To your home, to your cell phone . . ."

"We didn't take our cell phones with us," Beth said.

"This is so awful, so terrible! I have to know everything!"

"I really can't talk about it right now," Beth said.

"What about the funeral? Have you thought about that? Has he been sent home?"

"Ylva, I . . ."

"And Albin. He's lost his father! My poor son . . . how will he ever recover from the shock?"

Beth hung up the phone.

Immediately, it rang again.

It was Micke Larsson, one of Ulf's journalist friends. Beth had never really liked him. He was loud and obnoxious and usually ignored her. Now he welcomed her home with an unusually friendly voice.

"How are you?"

"That's a strange question," Beth replied.

"Oh, yes, of course. Of course. Under the circumstances, you can't be doing fine, can you? Everything you've gone through. It just slipped out, the standard question . . ."

Beth said nothing.

"I was thinking . . . for Ulf's sake . . . could you answer a few questions? Maybe a full interview? You know which paper I work for . . . if I could just swing by your place . . . well, maybe not today since you sound tired . . . tomorrow? It doesn't have to take too long. You can just tell me . . . how it happened and how you felt . . . some details."

"For Ulf's sake," she repeated his phrase.

"It'll be a good piece of reporting, just as he would have wanted. That was the whole point of the trip, wasn't it? This would honor his memory . . . ."

"No," she said and hung up abruptly.

She hobbled over to the jack and pulled out the phone plug. Her knee ached. The flight home had not been easy. She had an aisle seat so she could stretch out her hurt leg, but the flight attendants seemed to trip over it, so she finally had to bend it.

The flight noise still echoed in her head. She decided to go lie down, but when she came into the bedroom the breath left her body.

She understood fully now that she would never again wake up with Ulf beside her. He was gone. He no longer existed. They were sending him back as a piece of freight . . . so they could sink him into the ground and forget all about him. In the face of this understanding, something broke inside and the floodgates opened. She collapsed onto the white rug and sobbed bitterly for the first time.

She wept for about five minutes. No longer. It was enough to give her a headache.

She knew she ought to put the telephone plug back into the jack so that people wouldn't start streaming to her house. They would worry and imagine she needed help. She did not want them to come. She did not want to see a single human being.

She had to become strong.

She decided to brew another pot of coffee.

She wasn't hungry, but she knew there was food in the freezer so she would not have to go out.

Her arms began to itch. They'd given her a cream at the hospital which had helped, but now the itch was back.

She got her pile of mail and the letter opener which had been a gift from her father. She dragged the letter opener across her arm. It helped the itch for a moment, but not for long.

She tried to ignore this small torment by turning her attention to the mail. Birgitta had already sorted the mail and placed like with like. There were a number of bills and bank statements. She realized that she now had to open Ulf's mail, too. She did not have the courage to cope with that yet. One of his colleagues had written a postcard: *Greetings from Paris! There's still some summer weather and we've heard about your winter weather! See you soon! Sara.*

She set the postcard on top of Ulf's stack of mail. Sara. She'll be another person calling in the next few days. She'll want details and answers. Not to mention all of Juni's friends. Beth's headache increased.

A small envelope was addressed to her. *Beth Svärd.* Her name was written with a fountain pen and the person who wrote it had pressed down hard. Who was this from?

Beth held the letter up to the lamp but could not see through it to any of the words. Somehow she felt a rising worry as she hastily slit open the envelope.

The letter was written on a piece of paper ripped out of an old-fashioned school exercise book. She eyed the text without reading it at first. The ink had clumped and there were splotches everywhere. She put the piece of paper aside and finished her coffee.

Then she picked it up again and forced herself to read it. Her back stiffened as she read, and she slid forward to the edge of the sofa. She read it over and over again.

To Beth Svärd who lives in the Red House during the Summers. I have reason to believe that You know Something about a certain Man's disappearance. Because I have found his Grave and I know he had been at Your Place and now I want to know for Certain. Because this man was close to me. So I have to Know. My name is Kaarina Jussila and call me at This Number.

Kaarina II

1

The woman called Beth Svärd telephoned. Her voice sounded old and grumpy. Not at all what Kaarina had expected. She'd just fed the hens and was walking inside when she heard the phone ring. She raced to grab it before Holger could .

Every time the phone rang, she'd run for it. Usually it was someone they knew. Someone who wanted to chew the fat with Holger.

It had already been many weeks since she'd written the letter. She had fantasized about what would happen when it reached the woman, but it was taking so long, she began to doubt anything would come of it.

She'd also called once or twice, before she decided to write the letter. She'd gotten the number from directory assistance.

She didn't dare say anything. She just started crying and she hung up. That was stupid.

If you don't answer, I'm going to the police, she had thought.

She had her old school friend, Lars-Göran. He'd become a policeman with the Tidaholm police department. They'd been in the same class. She would be able to talk to him. He was someone she could place her confidence in.

The worst thing about all this would be the uproar.

She wouldn't have his grave to herself any more.

She would have to tell what she knew.

And Holger would be angry. He thought he knew everything there was to know about her.

"I'd like to speak with Kaarina Jussila," the woman's voice on the other end of the line said.

Kaarina was still wearing her boots, and mud had been tracked into the house. She'd run so fast, she'd forgotten to take them off.

"That's me," Kaarina said tensely.

"My name is Beth Svärd. You wrote me a letter."

"That's right." Kaarina stalled for time. She had to find the proper words.

"I'm at the house. I drove up here, and if you come to my place, we can meet. There is something you should know."

Kaarina looked at herself in the mirror. She saw herself nod. Her old knitted hat slid off, down the back of her neck.

"So you are there right now?" Kaarina repeated.

"Yes, I'm here waiting for you."

"I'll be there, soon."

The woman hung up. Her voice seemed odd, as if it were about to disappear. She was probably using a cell phone.

Kaarina kicked off her boots and cleaned up the muddy tracks. A brown feather had floated there. Kaarina knew it was from Ida, the littlest hen. Ida seemed droopy lately. Kaarina hoped she wasn't coming down with something.

Kaarina climbed the stairs to her room and changed into a clean blouse and a sweater. She combed her hair. She should have washed it yesterday, as she'd planned. Whenever she came in from the barnyard, she smelled. The smell stuck in her hair: the smell of hens and chicken feed. Here at home it wasn't a problem, but when she had to leave the house . . . she decided to wipe some cologne on her skin. The cologne had come in a magazine: a tiny, thin bottle which had been taped to the cover. She'd bought the magazine at the grocery store.

When she came down, she heard Holger in the bathroom.

"Kaarina, is that you?" he yelled through the door.

"Of course it's me."

"What have you sprayed on yourself? It stinks all the way to here!"

"Nothing much, just some perfume for a change."

"Why?"

"Why not?"

She heard the toilet flush. He walked into the kitchen. His eyes were red and bloodshot.

"I was on my way into the woods," he said. "Then I just had to come back and take a shit."

"Yes."

"What's going on with you, Kaarina? You stink like a whore house!"

"I just put on some perfume. I got tired of smelling like chickens!"

"If you say so." Holger lumbered into the hallway and put on his winter jacket. "Well, I better get going. What are you going to make for dinner? Have you thought about that yet?"

She felt forced to wait awhile. Maybe that woman would get tired and go away. But there was nothing Kaarina could do about that. She had to wait until she heard the tractor start and head down the hill.

Then she started to walk. The snow had been on the ground for days, but today it had melted away. What a strange winter it was turning out to be. She pulled on her fingerless gloves as she walked. She made sure to avoid the patches of ice. Last winter, she'd slipped on a patch of ice near the gate and whacked her head. She didn't want to do that again.

She did not dare take Holger's bicycle. She kept to the forest. She did not want to be seen. The air was still, and that morning the fog had been so thick that they'd hardly been able to see the gable on the barn. Water droplets fell from the fir tree branches. She heard a mild, soft twitter. Some tiny birds were flicking among the branches.

She found herself running over the last stretch of road. She feared that the woman had gotten tired of waiting and had driven off. Her heart pounded. Finally she saw the house and her heart came up into her throat. A car was parked in the driveway. She did not know what to do. What was she supposed to say to that woman? How could she explain how she'd gotten that woman's name and address?

Kaarina saw no one. The door to the house was closed. Kaarina followed the fence. She knew the way by heart now as she often walked to his grave. She went when she needed to talk to him and when a familiar pain hit her midsection. The pain of loneliness. Then she'd come here to take care of the grave. She'd make sure the dirt was smooth and she'd decorate it with pine cones and twigs. At times, she felt as if he were with her, as if he were swaying above her, unseen but present.

There were times when she felt angry. She was angry because he'd disappeared. It was not right. She knew it wasn't his choice, but that didn't help. She was still angry. There was no longer anyone she could look forward to. Expectation was such a big part of life. He'd taken her expectations with him when he disappeared.

She got to the grave. The last time she'd been there, she'd found a really pretty stone and had set it in place on the right side of the mound. Somehow it had slid down, so she bent to straighten it.

Then she heard the voice.

"Good afternoon. You must be Kaarina. Am I right?"

Kaarina drew a deep breath and turned around.

The strange woman was standing a few yards away. She wore a dark green down jacket with a fur collar on the hood and black pants. She'd mispronounced Kaarina's name with an accent on the second syllable.

"KAA-ri-na." She felt forced to correct that woman.

They stood still and stared at each other.

"Well, I'm Beth, as you probably know," the woman said. She shook a cigarette out of a pack. "Do you smoke?"

"No."

The woman's lips were strangely swollen and her face a bright brown. The woman blew a few rings of smoke. They hung in the air and then dissipated.

"Do you live nearby?" this strange woman named Beth asked.

Kaarina took another deep breath. "Yes."

"I had no idea that there was another house in the vicinity."

"Well, it's a bit of a distance when you walk. Do you know who Holger is? Holger Karlsson?"

Beth turned her head away for a second. Then she looked directly into Kaarina's eyes. "Is he the one . . . resting here?"

"Here? Oh no. Holger's at home. He's my brother, you could say."

"Your brother. I see."

Kaarina's feet were freezing. She stamped them. The ground was muddy and slippery. Beth watched her and took deep drags on her cigarette.

"You wrote me a letter," said Beth. Her voice was now shrill and hard.

"Yes, I needed to know . . ."

"You wrote that he had been close to you. Were you engaged or what?"

Kaarina reddened and she felt a tingle near her privates.

"Yes," she said at last. "You could say that."

"So I see! You were engaged! So what makes you think that I know anything about him?"

"He's buried on your property. I found him here."

"How could you? What made you think there was anything buried here?"

"His arm stuck up." Kaarina whispered.

Beth threw the cigarette stub away and it landed in a pool of water, sizzling as it went out.

"Have you told anyone?"

"No."

"Why not?"

Kaarina shrugged her shoulders.

"I haven't told anyone, either."

"You haven't?"

"You should be happy. Otherwise, the whole district would know what kind of man he was."

Kaarina's face went deep red and she saw black spots in front of her eyes.

"He was trying to kill me, you see, trying to strangle me. I found him as he was stealing our stuff . . . . He was nothing more than a thief and a killer . . . . But maybe you knew that already, since you are so fond of him?"

"No, that's not true!" Kaarina screamed. "He was not like that at all!"

That strange woman from Stockholm—her face turned so ugly. She pushed her hair out of her eyes and came closer to Kaarina. She was holding herself up with a crutch.

"You must forget the dead," hissed that woman. Her breath smelled terrible—smoke and old straw. "Once they're dead, you should forget all about them . . . I should know . . . I myself . . . Ulf, the man who came here with me . . . don't you think I know?"

Kaarina wanted to leave. She turned around but that woman took hold of her arm. Her tiny hand clenched so hard it hurt.

"I have to go," Kaarina said.

"Listen to me first! You wanted to know everything! You said so in your letter. Let me tell you, your man has tormented me, too. Your heart's love! His hands grabbed my neck to strangle me and the marks lasted for days. He was here in our shed and he was going to kill me. I could see it in his eyes. He would have killed me if I . . ."

She quieted down and let go of Kaarina's wrists.

"If you hadn't killed him first," Kaarina said.

"Let the dead stay dead, I tell you. They're never coming back. And as for this memorial you've made, get rid of it! At once. While I'm standing here. I want to see every trace disappear. He must disappear. He is gone, and there is nothing left of those who die . . ."

"I don't believe a word you say! He was not that kind of person!"

Kaarina decided to run for it, but she slipped in the mud and fell face first in the soaking wet, flattened grass. She felt someone hit the back of her head. Beth Svärd was standing over her, and her teeth were grinning like those in a skull. She was hitting Kaarina with her crutch. She slammed down hard on her neck and head.

Kaarina curled herself into a ball—like a hedgehog.

A slam to the side of her face. Her lip split and she could taste the blood. She tried to get up on her knees so she could find some way to run. That woman from Stockholm was insane, completely insane. But Kaarina's boots slipped and she fell again—her stomach hit the mud.

All of a sudden, the beating stopped. She heard muffled screaming and then the sound of a man's voice. *Stop moving, you whore!* Kaarina peeked out between her fingers.

That woman was now on the ground herself, just like Kaarina. Holger sat on her and he was forcing her face into the mud. She saw dirt and blood on Beth's hands.

"Get her cell phone and call the police!" yelled Holger. "It fell out of her pocket on the ground over there! Get it and hurry up!"

As Beth heard this, she wriggled like an eel and kicked as hard as she could. Holger had to use all his strength to keep her still.

Holger hit Beth hard in the neck.

"You have to call the police, Kaarina! Don't be such an idiot, pick up the phone!"

"How . . . how do I use it?" Kaarina asked.

"What the hell! You dial one-two-two. That's not hard! Then you hit the green button!"

Kaarina crawled over to the cell phone. Her knees in her thin stockings felt cold against the ground. She was crying so hard that she couldn't speak.

Holger yelled at her. "Throw it over here!"

Holger kept sitting on Beth, using his weight to hold her down. He caught the telephone.

Beth had stopped moving. Her ear was to the ground.

Kaarina managed to stagger to her feet. She turned away from the grave and leaned on the closest tree. It was an old apple tree with silver moss growing on its trunk. She felt its support, the old tree, as she was hit by wave after wave of shaking.

She heard Holger talking behind her. He was using the tone of voice he used for the authorities.

Holger had followed her here and soon he would know everything.

"Get me the police!" he was yelling. "As fast as you can!"

Kaarina watched, unmoving, as several police cars drove up. The first one to get out of a car was Lars-Göran. He greeted Holger and then he passed beyond her point of vision. She heard them surround the woman on the ground. She heard the snap of handcuffs.

She was freezing. She felt dirty. Holger was now leaning on the fence. Even his large hands were shaking.

Lars-Göran appeared in the focus of her eyes.

"Well, hello there, Kaarina. I didn't expect to see you here!"

"What are you going to do to her?"

"We'll take her to the station and figure it all out. What was going on?"

"It was a mistake. A misunderstanding," Kaarina said. "Nothing much."

"I see. We'll talk some more later."

At that moment, one of the other policemen yelled: "What the fuck! Look what Rocko found! Come over here and check this out!"

Kaarina watched them surround the grave. She saw that they'd taken a police dog with them. A large, powerful German Shepherd. It was starting to dig in the dirt.

Kaarina turned to look at the police cars. Beth Svärd was sitting in the backseat of one car. Beth's face seemed to waver. Kaarina swallowed hard and tears ran down her cheeks and dripped from her chin.

The two of them stared at each other. Kaarina saw that she was crying, too.

Then everything came to light.

About the Author

Inger Frimansson, author and journalist, is considered by critics to be Sweden's premier author of psychological thrillers. They place her novels in the same class as the best English and American novels in the genre. Inger Frimansson's writing is characterized by the way she sees the dark and morbid reality behind what seems to be an idyll. Her style is concise and suggestive and she has established herself as one of Sweden's bestselling thriller writers. Frimansson is the only  female writer to be awarded **twice** with the Swedish Academy of Crime Writers' Award (for *Good Night, My Darling* in 1998 and for *The Shadow in the Water* in 2005, both of which have been published by Caravel Books).

Caravel Books, a mystery imprint of Pleasure Boat Studio:
A Literary Press.

The Other Romanian ~ Anne Argula ~ $16

Deadly Negatives ~ Russell Hill ~ $16

The Dog Sox ~ Russell Hill ~ $16 ~ Nominated for an Edgar Award

Music of the Spheres ~ Michael Burke ~ $16

Swan Dive ~ Michael Burke ~ $15

The Lord God Bird ~ Russell Hill ~ $15 ~ Nominated for an Edgar Award

Island of the Naked Women ~ Inger Frimansson, trans. by Laura Wideburg ~ $18

The Shadow in the Water ~ Inger Frimansson, trans. by Laura Wideburg ~ $18 ~ Winner of Best Swedish Mystery 2005

Good Night, My Darling ~ Inger Frimansson, trans. by Laura Wideburg ~ $16 ~ Winner of Best Swedish Mystery 1998 ~ Winner of Best Translation Prize from ForeWord Magazine 2007

The Case of Emily V. ~ Keith Oatley ~ $18 ~ Commonwealth Writers Prize for Best First Novel

Homicide My Own ~ Anne Argula ~ $16 ~ Nominated for an Edgar Award

Orders: Pleasure Boat Studio books are available by order from your bookstore, directly from our website, or through the following:

SPD (Small Press Distribution) Tel. 800-869-7553, Fax 510-524-0852
Partners/West Tel. 425-227-8486, Fax 425-204-2448
Baker & Taylor Tel. 800-775-1100, Fax 800-775-7480
Ingram Tel. 615-793-5000, Fax 615-287-5429
Amazon.com or **Barnesandnoble.com**

Pleasure Boat Studio: A Literary Press
201 West 89th Street
New York, NY 10024
Tel / Fax: 888-810-5308
www.pleasureboatstudio.com / pleasboat@nyc.rr.com

CPSIA information can be obtained at www.ICGtesting.com
Printed in the USA
LVOW080520050413

327751LV00004B/189/P